The Dinosaur's Descendants

The Dinosaur's Descendants

Mark Ellsberry

iUniverse, Inc.
Bloomington

THE DINOSAUR'S DESCENDANTS

iUniverse books may be ordered through booksellers or by contacting:

iUniverse
1663 Liberty Drive
Bloomington, IN 47403
www.iuniverse.com
1-800-Authors (1-800-288-4677)

ISBN: 978-1-4759-9016-4 (sc)
ISBN: 978-1-4759-9017-1 (hc)
ISBN: 978-1-4759-9018-8 (e)

Library of Congress Control Number: 2013908276

Printed in the United States of America

iUniverse rev. date: 5/24/2013

prologue

The tall man wearing a shabby gray robe with a hood that obscured his entire head looked like he was homeless even though he had just paid al-Qaeda fifty million US dollars to blow up the Rose Bowl in California. This terror attack was to occur on New Year's Day in front of a worldwide television audience. He had also promised an additional fifty million US dollars upon successful completion of the task.

As he disappeared into the shadows of an alley in downtown Kabul, Afghanistan, he reflected upon how well his plan had progressed. It created a feeling of intense gratification for him to learn the details of a person's destiny and then use the knowledge to bend that destiny to his own will. That was why he had been a spy his whole life. Now he would return to his superior to find out his next assignment to advance this, the biggest, most important mission he had ever been given. The very survival of his country and possibly his civilization was at stake.

chapter 1

MISSION 1 FROM WHITE SANDS

"Open the hatch for precisely two minutes to perform observation," announced the vessel's computer. "Then close the hatch and secure your seat belt for the return trip."

Ellie Johnston quickly climbed a ladder leading to the hatch. Opening it was fast, requiring only the push of a button. Outside the vessel she saw a peaceful plain with small shrub-like pine trees intermixed with flowering shrubs. The sky was a vivid blue and the sun burned hotter than normal. The landscape looked the same in all directions except for a pile of rocks about forty feet to Ellie's left.

The scene was beautiful but did not provide a single clue as to its identity. The purpose of this brief trip was to determine if the passenger could survive a round-trip. The observation period was to try to gather evidence if the system had accurately placed the vessel at the desired target.

Looking out the open hatch Ellie could see nothing that would help verify her current location. After the two-minute interval, three beeps announced that the hatch would automatically close. As it began to move there was a loud roaring sound that startled Ellie. Out of the corner of her eye she saw the pile of rocks appear to move. The hatch closing meant she could not investigate the cause of the noise or the movement. For this test only, the vessel was programmed to return to its origin with no option for control by the passenger in case the passenger was somehow incapacitated during the trip.

CARCASSONNE, FRANCE

In Southern France, tourists swarmed over the beautiful medieval town of Carcassonne, frantically trying to fit in their holidays before the fall storms visited the area. Today had been spectacular, a brilliant day with an azure sky until the sun started to approach the western end of its daily route. And then dark clouds began to gather about the mountaintops to the south. On the east side of a narrow cobblestone street, within the medieval walls of the old city, the owner of a small souvenir shop, Wasim Darzi, had locked the door so he could retire to his living quarters above the shop. It had been a good sales day, and now it would be nice to relax. The phone rang and startled him. Living a highly secretive life, Wasim received few phone calls. He stared at the receiver, wondering who it could be. When he answered, he heard words spoken in almost undistinguishable, accented French, if you could even call it an accent because it sounded so strange. He had never heard such a hissing, garbled attempt at speech before. From the other end of the connection, someone had said, "Allahu Akbar, you don't know me, but I call as a friend and sympathizer to your holy cause."

Wasim replied, "I have no idea what you're talking about. Is there some way I may help you in a matter pertaining to my shop?"

"You have it wrong. I want to help you," the caller had responded. "I realize you don't know who I am or if you can trust me, but you have nothing to lose so just listen a minute. Tomorrow at ten o'clock in the morning, the police will conduct a massive citywide raid. Your place of business and those of eleven other members of al-Qaeda will be hit, wiping out all three cells in Carcassonne. They have information from a mole that infiltrated your organization giving them the identity of the persons to raid. If arrested, your usefulness is at an end. Evacuate your store during the early hours of the night to avoid arrest. You can warn the other members of your organization if you choose, but I would not bother to warn Muhammad Nadir since he is the one working with the infidels."

Wasim felt that he should have denied the implication that he was a terrorist, but as he began to protest, the line went dead. Who was that person? How could some stranger have even known that he was a member of al-Qaeda? What few details the caller had mentioned were actually correct. There were three cells working within the city to raise money and to plan an as-yet-undetermined attack on the Church of Saint-Nazairo at the height of next year's tourist season. The leadership of al-Qaeda had decided that Europe should be the focus of their activity for the next few years.

Muhammad Nadir had been assigned about a month ago as a courier to carry messages between Wasim's cell, the other cells in Carcassonne, and al-Qaeda leadership. Nadir had been in the ideal position to collect information. Wasim and the other cell members knew only the members of their own cell. But why had this stranger gone to the effort to warn him? Was this some twisted plot to get him to expose himself? Before the sun came up tomorrow Wasim needed to decide what to do about this unusual warning.

BOZEMAN, MONTANA

Eight thousand miles away the scarlet orb of the setting sun slid behind the distant mountains to the west of Bozeman, Montana.

Steven Andrews, PhD, jogged along a residential street near the end of his daily five-mile run. Steven was of average height at five foot eleven and a solid two hundred pounds. His dark hair had begun to recede, so he decided to keep it cut close to his head. He had struggled with the effort of running today because the weather was unseasonably hot and humid for September. Steven did not particularly like to run, he would rather study a fossil of a dinosaur bone, but it was the only way to keep off the extra pounds.

Steven did love this time of day. It had been true ever since his very first paleontology dig. He had been a sixteen-year-old high school junior who volunteered for the dig to get extra credit in a biology course. He found far more than a grade during that summer. Each day he and his companions had spent grueling hours in the sun on their knees digging for nuggets of information in the form of fossils. Sunset was the time when everyone returned to camp and shared the items they had found that day. Steven was so caught up in the excitement of discovering previously unknown information about prehistoric creatures that he made it his life's work.

His mind and body relaxed from the tensions of the day as he soaked in the beautiful mountains outlined along the horizon. The quiet residential street he ran on could have been Anytown, USA, on a typical end of summer day. There had been a few diligent people out working in their yards, preparing them for winter, while others lounged in whatever shade they could find. It was a simple environment that had always been the setting of Steven's life.

He liked to use the time when he was jogging to contemplate whatever problems he was addressing in his current research. As an assistant professor of paleontology at Montana State University, he was continually in the middle of writing a new article for one scientific journal or another. He was obsessed with learning everything there was to know about dinosaurs.

It seemed that his teenage fascination with those magnificent creatures from the distant past had never diminished.

"Publish or perish" was alive and well in the institution where he hoped to achieve tenure in a few years. But the truth was that if he did not start a new paper before the current one was complete, he felt lost. As if his life had no firm direction However, the events of today had presented him with a completely different issue to think over.

CARCASSONNE, FRANCE

At ten o'clock the next morning, Wasim stood two short blocks from his shop, he shivered under a large umbrella as he listened to the rain pour down and watched a SWAT team of local police crash through the door of his comfortable little shop. He had called the three members of his cell to warn them, but he did not know the other eight people who were involved. He had no way to warn them so they could also evade the raid. He had taken all incriminating evidence from his store along with a stash of cash and an alternate identity given to him by al-Qaeda for just this kind of emergency. He needed to move to another city and make contact with another al-Qaeda group to continue his life. With the loss of his wife and daughter, collateral damage in the struggle between Israel and the Palestinian refugees, he had nothing else to cling to, nothing else that gave him a reason to live. Wasim was a timid man by nature with no real place in an organization like al-Qaeda but now the only emotion he ever truly felt was rage. Joining the terrorist organization was the only outlet he could find to express that rage.

Still he wondered how the anonymous caller had known about the police raid and what his motive for warning him was.

BOZEMAN, MONTANA

Steven walked into his apartment after he had taught his last class of the day. He heard the phone ringing in his study, and he hurried to answer it before it went to voice mail. "Hello, Andrews here," he announced. *This had better not be one of my students asking about the next quiz,* he thought.

"Mr. Andrews, this is Marsha Dixon with the National Security Agency. I'm in the human resources department of the NSA. One of our senior-level people is interested in your research published in the *Scientific American* and *The Journal of Vertebrate Paleontology*. He would like to invite you to come to Washington, DC, to discuss a position we are trying to fill."

Steven replied, "I'm very happy in my present job and have no particular desire to make a change. But I'm intrigued by your phone call, and I'd like to think I have an open mind. So what exactly is your agency proposing? What would this job entail?"

"The specifics of the position are highly confidential and can only be discussed in person. I realize this is an unsatisfactory answer and makes it difficult for you to even decide to make the trip. I'm authorized to tell you that unlike most government jobs, this is a high-paying position, over twice your current salary. It will also allow you, in a way, to continue working at the leading edge of your current studies in paleontology. At the end of a five-year stint with our organization, you would be in an improved position financially and could return to your current field of study if you chose to. Please come to DC and give us a chance to discuss this further with you."

"You do understand that I'll need a little time to think about this?" said Steven. *Some extra cash would come in handy to finance the field trip I've been thinking about,* he thought.

"Could I give you an answer tomorrow? Say about this same time? I'll give you my cell number to be sure we connect."

Sounding somewhat disappointed, Marsha said, "Please give this opportunity a chance. You won't be sorry you came to visit once we discuss the position in more detail. Off the record, I just want to say that you owe it to yourself to come to DC for this interview. It's the chance of a lifetime for someone in your line of work."

MADRID, SPAIN

After three months, Wasim had established a completely new identity as a waiter in a small coffee shop in Madrid. He was unhappy with the loss of his wonderful little shop, but he knew that sacrifices must be made to achieve his revenge. During his first meeting with the leader of his new cell, the leader had asked how a small almost timid person like Wasim had ever joined al-Qaeda. He answered that rage and desire for revenge was all he had after his wife and son were killed by an Israeli bomb in Gaza City ten years ago.

Wasim had been lucky to quickly make contact with this new cell. They were actively pursuing a plan to blow up a train in the city's main station at Christmas. They had been very interested in his knowledge of bomb-making but less enthusiastic about his trouble in Carcassonne. He was only now beginning to feel that the new organization trusted him, and that he could breathe a little easier after his near disaster in France.

Today was a Monday, Wasim's day off. He did not have any specific duties to perform for the cell so he decided to attend a prayer session at the Abu-Bakr Mosque. Wasim was proud that he could pray in this noteworthy mosque. It had opened in 1988, and it had been the first mosque built in Madrid since the Spanish drove the Moors out of the city. As he kneeled in prayer in the shadows near the back, a tall man in a large gray robe with a very deep hood over his head came to kneel beside him. In the same hard-to-understand French that Wasim had only heard once before over the phone, the man said, "Allahu Akbar, I see you were able to escape the little trap the French police set for you. No! Please don't turn around or call attention to us."

Wasim felt as if the ground had dropped out from under him. *Who is this person?* "How can you continue to find me so easily? What do you want with me?"

"My name is SuHa. I have searched for you because this time I request your help. I will not be able to answer most of your questions, but as I said once before, I am a friend and sympathizer in your work. I cannot reveal my sources of information, and you would not believe me if I could tell you. As you have seen, I can be of use on occasion, but now I have a request for you. My associates and I would like to make a monetary contribution to the organization that you work for. I want to meet with someone with authority in Kabul on December 25, Christmas Day, to discuss the terms of a very beneficial transaction for your organization."

Great, this guy is going to get me killed, thought Wasim as he revisited that feeling with the ground again. *What am I getting myself into?* The organization would tolerate no more failures that involved him. "I know nothing about you," he growled. "Why should I trust you so far as to put a senior member of our organization at risk by making them known to you?"

"I realize my request is unorthodox; however, my time is limited, and I am not permitted the luxury of an extended dance to set up this meeting," said SuHa. "All I need is for you to pass on my satellite phone number and the information that my associates are prepared to give your organization a hundred million US dollars to finance your ongoing operations, including one operation that we will designate. If your leaders are interested, they may call me and set up a meeting in Kabul at a place and time of their choice. I have done everything I can to make this situation palatable for your side, considering our mutual lack of information about each other. The next move is up to you."

chapter 2

Bozeman, Montana

Steven found himself jogging along, wondering if he should take time away from the work he loved at Montana State University to fly to Washington, DC, with no real data to help in the decision. *What was this chance of a lifetime? Why would the NSA be interested in him?* It would be easy to relocate from the standpoint of roots, even though he had spent his whole life in Montana. He was an only child, and his parents were both dead. His father had died from a stroke four years ago, just after Steven had completed his PhD. His mother had passed away a year later, probably from missing his father. At the age of thirty-six, he had dated several women for extended periods but he still had met no one that he wanted to settle down and raise a family with.

His current relationship with Melissa had become more and more uncomfortable. A year and a half ago, they were hiking on a mountain trail when a group of three crude men attacked them. Steven was beaten senseless and Melissa would have been raped. Luckily, a pair of armed park rangers came along the trail as part of their routine patrol. Now, every time Steven saw Melissa he relived the consuming humiliation of what almost happened, remembering the three men throwing her down and tearing off her clothes. She was not saved as a result of anything Steven did. He had tried to stop them but two of them held him while the third punched him in the face and ribs repeatedly until he was unconscious. There was nothing he could have done but he felt so inadequate every time he remembered the scene in his mind. Both he and Melissa tried to go on as if the incident had not happened, but it wasn't working for Steven. He had been thinking of ending their two year relationship but felt terrible about doing it since it was not Melissa's fault. Taking a job out of town seemed like a cowardly way out of this, but it would be the easiest way to get out of the strained situation.

So right after the sun slipped behind the mountains and the temperature began to ease, Steven's indecision also eased as he vowed to agree to a trip tomorrow when Ms. Dixon called. *Why not! Making more money is always appealing, and what could it hurt to get a free trip to the nation's capital?*

KABUL, AFGHANISTAN

Since the overthrow of the Taliban, Kabul, Afghanistan, had been struggling to bring itself into the modern world. Terrorist attacks had diminished to the point where people felt that they could go out on the streets to conduct their business and even occasionally go out for fun. However, the usually bustling streets were dark and deserted this late at night.

At exactly midnight, a tall figure stepped from the shadows of a shabby alley. All his clothes were the same dark gray and consisted of baggy pants that seemed to be filled out more than one would expect and a waist-length coat that seemed almost too empty on top. The figure just seemed out of proportion. He walked rapidly through the empty streets and slipped down a short flight of stairs. He made his way to a dark employee entrance into the Safi Landmark Hotel near the center of Kabul.

The gray coat had a hood that was so deep that no part of the traveler was visible, not even as he stepped into the dimly lit hotel basement. The tall mystery man walked with long, powerful strides like an athletic youth. However, his robust image was tarnished by how he stooped forward somewhat like an old man.

KABUL, AFGHANISTAN

Khaliq Abujamal sat on the bed in a room on the third floor of the Safi Landmark Hotel, chain-smoking to try to calm his nerves. He was not a man who was used to feeling nervous, but this assignment was out of the ordinary. His gun rested beside him on the bed within easy reach. He hadn't lived to be fifty-six years old by taking outrageous risks. Khaliq was a slightly overweight man of average height with sun-darkened skin. He had short black hair, and many would probably consider him handsome in a movie-star kind of a way, except for the deep red scar running from the right side of his mouth to his ear. It made him look like he was smiling on one side of his face. But he never smiled. It had been several years since he had been in a training camp to harden his body for the holy battle taking place around the world. However, his discipline and resolve for revenge on the infidels was as hard as granite.

As a middle-level member of al-Qaeda, Khaliq was the handler of about a third of the terror cells in Afghanistan. In the past, this had been a very important position with occasional access to the very top of the al-Qaeda organization. Recently, because of the Great Satan's stepped-up involvement in Afghanistan, the focus of al-Qaeda had moved to other countries. At present, Khaliq was assigned to meet with a self-proclaimed supporter of the jihad, a man who was apparently willing to donate one hundred million US dollars to fund terror activities, the only provision being that one of the terror acts had to take place within the continental United States. The information known about this potential donor was far from sufficient to be sure this meeting was not a trap, but the organization had learned of the man through a member of a Spanish al-Qaeda cell, a member who claimed this man had saved him and three other al-Qaeda members from arrest by the French police. The possibility of gaining access to the stated amount of money meant someone would have to meet with the mystery man to find out if his offer was real. One hundred million dollars was a lot of money, and it could finance a lot of infidel-cleansing. Even though the supporter insisted that he would meet with only one al-Qaeda member, Khaliq had three handpicked associates salted throughout the hotel in case of a trap.

At the knock on the door, Khaliq got off the bed and cautiously approached it from the side ensuring that he would not be in the line of fire for someone shooting through the door. "Come," said Khaliq, he had already disabled the automatic lock on the hotel room's door so he would not need to open it himself. The door opened slowly, and a hooded figure emerged from the shadows in the hall. In barely understandable English, the visitor said, "Please turn off the lights in this room. It is imperative that my identity remain unknown. If you like, you may use the light in the bathroom. I need little light myself."

"Please sit," Khaliq said, gesturing to the only chair in the room. He turned on the bathroom light and then edged away into the shadows of the main room. His hand hovered near his gun, which he had slipped into his belt at his back. "I understand you have a proposal to make. This meeting is very unusual for someone in my circumstances, so please excuse my being abrupt. I like to be much more prepared with information before I meet someone. Could I know your name and who you represent?"

The visitor sat with his head turned slightly to the side so that Khaliq could not see any part of his face. Again in almost undistinguishable English, he replied, "You may call me SuHa, but I'm not at liberty to discuss who I represent. However, my proposal is simple. I will give one hundred million US dollars to your organization putting only the slightest of demands on you and your associates. First, I'll hand to you fifty million dollars in cash. You will use whatever portion of it that is required to accomplish a specific terrorist act in the state of California in the United States. We expect this initial amount to be more than sufficient to allow you to assemble a team to blow up the stadium in California, where the Rose Bowl is played. This should be accomplished while the game is in progress, and we expect all or the vast majority of the attendees to be killed in front of a worldwide television audience. Upon the successful completion of this task, I will return to pay you the remaining fifty million dollars.

"If you agree to take on this task, I will provide the money in cash immediately. You will know nothing about me or the people I work with. In turn, I will need to know nothing about your organization or how you intend to accomplish your task. This becomes an act of faith on both of our parts. You must trust me to provide the second payment, and I must wait until New Year's Day of next year to see if you have successfully spent the initial money. However, I must add that if there is no televised explosion, then I will return for full repayment or your life. This may seem harsh, but if you can't agree to the terms in advance, don't take the money. I know your organization specializes in remaining hidden, but I have no doubt of my ability to carry out this threat, should it become necessary.

"Do you have any questions that I can answer? I will return to this room at six a.m., five and a half hours from now, with the money. If you agree to my proposal, I will hand it over with no additional strings attached."

Khaliq was both shocked and offended by this offer; things

just weren't done like this in his way of thinking. This offer represented too much arrogance and too much trust on the part of this stranger and his backers. The problem was, the deal just considering the initial fifty million dollars represented a huge amount of money and was too good to pass up. It was a good deal, even if the stranger did not ultimately complete the bargain by paying the second fifty million dollars. "But I know nothing about you. How do I know that I can trust you?" asked Khaliq, suspicion in his voice.

In his difficult-to-understand English, SuHa responded, "With the proposal I have just made to you, why do you need to know anything about me or my reasons for wanting to do this. I am asking you to engage in activities that I believe are clearly the reason for the existence of your organization and I am providing the money to finance it. To sweeten the deal, I will pay you an additional fifty million dollars to fund further acts of terror of your own choosing when the job is done."

chapter 3

WASHINGTON, DC

As he sat in the backseat of a limo on the way from his hotel to his meeting with the NSA, Steven Andrews was beginning to wonder if the trip to Washington, DC, had been a good idea after all. The trip from Bozeman to Reagan International was as exhausting as only a trip from west to east over multiple time zones could be. After he flew to Chicago, his connecting flight was three hours late. The silver lining to the situation was a chance to indulge in the famous Chicago pizza at O'Hare Airport. When he finally exited the security area at Reagan International, Steven saw a driver with his name printed on a card, waiting to take him to his hotel. The hotel was comfortable, but because of the jet lag, Steven tossed and turned in his bed until three o'clock in the morning, so the 7:30 wake-up call was difficult to live with. But now he was pulling up to a building that looked like an expensive warehouse in a suburban area outside of Washington, DC, which was not what he would have expected from such an important government agency.

Ms. Dixon was waiting for Steven when the elevator doors opened on the floor the driver had relayed to him. "Welcome to Washington, DC, and to the National Security Agency. We really appreciate your taking the time to come to visit since the amount of information I was able to give you was so limited. Please follow me to the conference room we've set up for you.

We can get the preliminaries out of the way in there." The empty conference room looked like it could accommodate about fifteen people. It was decorated in the standard style of corporate America—long, polished wood conference table and padded chairs that one could rock back and swivel.

"As you may know, the National Security Agency is responsible for the collection and analysis of the com-munications of foreign countries and is administered by the Department of Defense," said Ms. Dixon. "Virtually all of the information we collect and the methods we use to obtain it are classified at the highest levels of confidentiality. We have already done extensive background checks on you to be sure you will be able to receive the required security clearances. Now I just need you to sign this nondisclosure agreement that I e-mailed to you last week for your review. I will witness it, and then we can discuss the details of the position you have traveled so far to hear. You'll see this is the opportunity of a lifetime for someone in your field."

With the formalities taken care of, Jonas McCormick, a tall, skinny, redheaded man with a doctorate in quantum physics, replaced Ms. Dixon in the conference room. He looked the part of a PhD in physics, dressed in a wrinkled suit with a white shirt that looked like it had never seen an iron. A tie had been carefully knotted around his neck. His hands were constantly moving as he talked, and when he wasn't gesturing, he fussed with an old-fashioned wooden pipe (unlit because of federal regulations). After he introduced himself, he started in with virtually no small talk. "Sorry for all of the cloak-and-dagger stuff, but even after I tell you what we have in mind for you, you probably won't believe it. I am the head of a project that is so covert that only the agency director, Gen. Kenneth Attwood, and the national security advisor really know what we are doing. The project started off fifteen years ago as a small study group of three physicists, myself included, analyzing the feasibility of practical time travel. Quantum mechanics has told us for over seventy years that time travel is theoretically possible in the forward direction. But virtually all physicists feel that any practical form of time travel in the backward direction is not possible. They are wrong!"

KABUL, AFGHANISTAN

Precisely at six a.m. the next morning, SuHa knocked on the same door he had been to earlier. Khaliq answered the door as he had before, only this time there was a more relaxed air about him. He said, "My associates and I agree to your proposal as you have presented it."

SuHa laid a large black suitcase with fifty million dollars in cash on the bed and turned to leave as he said, "Allahu Akbar."

WASHINGTON, DC

Theoretically speaking, Steven was very interested in the NSA project but could not think how he could possibly fit into the picture.

"Thirteen years ago, our little group made a slight adjustment to the modeling equations that are the basis of quantum mechanics," explained Jonas. "We assumed that one did not move abruptly from the conditions modeled by classical physics into the conditions modeled by quantum physics but that there was a transition condition that must be modeled differently from either the classical physics or the quantum physics models. Once we had made the adjustment to account for this transition realm and began to work out various possible solutions to the modified equations, we found a solution that not only allowed backward time travel but predicted that this could be accomplished under practical conditions. In other words, we did not need to find a way to fly through a black hole or to cram matter through an infinitely small wormhole in the fabric of the universe. The theoretical solutions showed that an object under the influence of the transition conditions could be moved in space as well as time. But as I said, this was all theoretical, predicted by a computer solution to an untried variation of the equations that are the basis of quantum mechanics."

"Wow, this is fascinating," Steven commented. "But why is this project under the control of the NSA?"

"If you think about the basic charter of the NSA, you may see how the concept of time travel could be as much of a breakthrough tool for us as the discovery of radio waves," answered Jonas. "If we could go back in time days, weeks, or months, we could position an agent to accomplish surveillance of meetings and decisions we did not even know about at the time they were taking place. After the agent obtains the information, he can be whisked away to a safe place in the present time when no one is even concerned about protecting the secret. With this tool, we could find out what decisions our enemies or even our friends have made that affect us and make the correct, fully informed responses."

"Have you found a way to prove or disprove the equations predictions?" Steven wondered out loud.

"We have accomplished amazing results. As the only two people who, for all practical purposes, oversee this project began to see that the theoretical was actually reality, the funding became virtually unlimited. At this time, we have a fully functional system. It was first tested by sending an object back in time by one week. The object was transported into a locked vault with a security camera that utilized a time/date recorder. The camera was focused on the place where the bar was to arrive. After the bar was sent, the camera recorded the exact time when the bar just appeared out of nowhere. The accuracy of the system in sending this object a small amount of time was not particularly good. It missed the target time by two days further back in time. That is about a 29 percent error. At this point, we still must answer two big questions about the concept."

"I suppose problems should be expected while achieving such an amazing potential advancement in science. What do you see as the remaining questions?" Steven queried.

Jonas continued, "The hardest question to wrap our minds around relates to the various time paradoxes that scientists and philosophers postulate. Obviously, we have the grandfather paradox wherein a time traveler goes back in time and kills his grandfather or father, whether on purpose or by accident, before he is conceived. This is a very simplistic way to come at the real problem, which is this: What happens if a time traveler does something to significantly or even insignificantly change the past. Can the future or the present be changed by actions in the past? If so what level of action is required to make such changes? We have spent an incredible amount of time talking about these issues."

"Have you come to any conclusions?" asked Steven.

"We have no direct experience to allow us to be sure what will happen. Our discussion focused on how we should conduct manned trial runs through time to minimize potential problems. From our understanding of time, as seen through our physical model, the time space continuum is made up of an infinite number of individual existence threads that cluster and entangle with each other when the events the threads represent come together. If events diverge then the threads become separated again. At some point threads end, such as with the death of a creature or the destruction of a tool. Only the threads directly touched by an action are changed and the amount of change is proportional to the strength of the action and its distance from any given thread.

"When we move an object in time it replaces a like amount of matter for as long as it remains in the new time, but it does not permanently change the threads it touches unless it creates an actual perturbation to the threads.

"The initial thought was that we should try going back only a few days. The number of events or threads that could potentially be changed by a time traveler's actions would be minimal to the present, at least as long as he or she did nothing significant. However, we quickly figured out this thinking was defective once we realized that there could and probably would be negative effects in our future that would not be apparent when the time travelers returned to the present."

"Can you explain this problem more clearly?" asked Steven.

"As an example, if a time traveler had some disease when he traveled two days into the past and he transmitted this disease to someone that was vital to some future event, no one would recognize that a change had occurred since the disease would not present itself that soon. However, later, this important person could die and significantly change the future possibly for the worst.

"The other option in this debate was that we should travel very far back in time. Far enough into the past that the effect of any changes to threads in the past should be strongly diluted by the time they reach threads of the present. Then we revisited this thinking based on the concept of the butterfly effect, as defined in chaos theory. The butterfly effect postulates that small differences in the initial condition of a dynamic system, such as ongoing time, may produce large variations in the long-term behavior of the system. In other words, there would possibly be no dilution but an actual increase in the effect of the change. That was when we had the idea to go back over sixty-five million years with the hope that the Cretaceous-Paleogene extinction (C-Pg) event could block or greatly reduce ongoing perturbations in space-time. It represents a distinct ending to most event threads that occurred before it. The effect of changes moving forward in time should be blocked by the natural disaster that occurred on the Earth during one of the largest mass extinctions ever."

"Wait! You're telling me that you are worried about theoretical time paradoxes because you have a working system and you are planning to send a human being back in time!" Steven exclaimed.

"Yes, just to close off the previous discussion, we decided on the far distant past as our target time," Jonas answered. It turns out that the energy and effort required to go back sixty-five million years or to go back two days is nearly the same. As a result, we have done some preliminary tests with a target time transit of exactly sixty-six million years."

"By tests, you mean you have actually sent something that far back in time?" queried Steven.

"We think so," said Jonas. "See, I told you that you would not believe what I am telling you. We started with sending an inanimate object, the metal bar. It disappeared and then reappeared as expected, but we had no way to verify how much time it traversed. The target was sixty-six million years, but there was no way to verify the actual result. Remember our accuracy problem when we went back only a single week?

"Then to test for traveler safety, we sent living organisms back. With these tests, we started to use an enclosed vessel to protect the organism from whatever unknown physical forces it might encounter. Another reason was so we could be sure not to send back unintended organisms. Since the vessel was never opened during these initial, non-human tests we eliminated that potential problem. First we sent a mouse with a collar around its neck to be sure we knew it was our mouse when it returned. The mouse survived, disappearing and reappearing, but again, we had no way to verify how far back in time it had traveled. The transit did not alter the physiology of the mouse. It may have gone in time and space exactly where we intended, or it could have missed by 30 percent. To be cautious, we then sent a higher-level creature, a chimpanzee back. He also survived the trip in good condition. After five trips with the chimp, we sent a human volunteer back to the target date. There was a slight hope that the volunteer would see something that would give us an idea of what general era the vessel, our time travel device, landed in. For the initial test, we decided the volunteer should spend just two minutes at the target site and be automatically returned for the traveler's safety. We had no idea of what stresses the transit would put on the time traveler. The volunteer reported that the landing site had a flat plains type of landscape. The climate was hot and damp with scrub brush but no visible trees. No other plants or animals were visible during the brief time."

"So you have really sent a person back in time. How will you finally test if the system is working to your expectations?" asked Steven. "I mean, how in the world could you ever verify a specific time that far in the past?"

"That, Mr. Andrews, is where you come into the picture. We intend to send back a four-man team designated Team T-REX to spend twenty-four hours on site with the tools and knowledge to begin to determine what time we are reaching. We would like you to lead the team."

TEL AVIV, ISRAEL

SuHa sat in a barely lit bar near the Mossad headquarters building in Tel Aviv, drinking water with ice. He had tried a kosher brandy, but it had seriously burned his mouth. He would never understand the human desire to drink such stuff. With his deep hood and gray garments, he looked more like an Arab than an Israeli.

He was randomly chatting with patrons of the bar. He would walk up and offer to buy them a drink, saying that he was celebrating the death of a rich relative who had no other heirs. Actually, he was trying to gather data on the operation and practices of Mossad. If he thought the conversation might prove useful, he bought another drink. If not, he moved on to the next patron.

Just now he was talking to a man who said he was a clerk in Mossad headquarters. "I can't believe it," the new acquaintance complained. "Someone is convinced that the Palestinians are going to launch an anthrax biological attack. They have no data except an intercepted cell phone conversation picked up from the Gaza Strip saying that a bioterrorist attack is being planned. So some putz decided to give everyone in the entire organization a vaccination against anthrax. My arm hurts, and I have a temperature just to satisfy someone's paranoia."

"I am sorry you are feeling badly. Let me buy you another drink," said SuHa. "It's a shame that they have put you through all this trouble for no reason. I heard a rumor from a friend who says he is in Hamas that they are planning a biological attack but not using anthrax. He says they have developed fleas that carry the bacterium *Yersinia pestis*, better known as the Black Death. They have bred millions of these fleas and intend to turn them loose in Jerusalem and Tel Aviv. The fleas will attach themselves to rats and other vermin and spread the plague. They hope to weaken the infrastructure of Jerusalem to the point that they can invade it and take over the city permanently. Since most of the government is there, the attack will also slow down any response by the Israeli military. Since Tel Aviv is the commercial center of the country, the plague there will devastate the economy. Apparently, they argued whether or not to try to infect other places but decided to concentrate on those two cities and hope that the disease will spread beyond the two cities."

"How do you know all this?" asked the astonished Mossad clerk.

"Oops! I think I must have had too much to drink. My mouth is working overtime. It is probably just rumors anyway," SuHa said and laughed as he quickly left the bar.

chapter 4

WASHINGTON, DC

Steven found himself laughing until he was almost out of breath from Jonas' suggestion that he could lead an expedition back in time. Then he realized Jonas had not meant the comment to be humorous. "Wow, that's quite a leap of faith on your part. I basically see myself as a small-town schoolteacher lecturing on a somewhat obscure subject. What the hell would qualify me to lead a team of people on an expedition through a time machine?" Steven exclaimed. "By the way, what's the significance of the name T-REX?"

McCormick stood up and began to pace as he warmed to his topic of conversation, "Government agencies love acronyms and this part of the NSA is the Department of Time Research and Exploration, therefore T-REX.

"It is exactly your academic field of study that caught our attention. You're a well-respected researcher studying the basic time period in which we're interested. Also, you're young and physically fit to withstand the rigors of the mission, which unfortunately eliminates most of your peers as candidates for this position. These are important attributes for the leader of this team. Your lack of close family ties should make it possible for you to disappear for an extended period without raising undue questions. Finally we hope to discuss and offer this position to a minimum number of people for securities sake.

"We don't really know what the team will find when they step onto the ground that far in the past. We are looking for a person who has a broad knowledge of the time to help him interpret what he will observe and to determine if the team has arrived in the world of sixty-five million years ago.

"While you're trying to wrap your mind around this idea, just think of the possibilities for your field of research this experience would provide. Unfortunately, you can't publish any of your direct discoveries. This project is not only a secret now. There is a very strong possibility that we may never release the knowledge that we have developed this capability. It will remain secret as long as the secrecy gives us a strategic advantage. If the subjects of our surveillance don't have any idea of what capability we have that they need to protect against, think of the strategic advantage. However, for your future career, if you have actually traveled back in time and seen things for yourself, you will have untold additional insight when trying to interpret fossils and other data from that time. A big advantage if you decide to go back to your current profession in the future."

"I'd be lying if I told you I am not intrigued by this. However, I'm still trying to see how well I fit in," Steven said.

"We're creating a team of four people with you potentially acting as the leader," answered Jonas. "We don't want to send too many people back until we can study the consequences both to the team and to the overall time environment. You will report to me for the present time. Your ability to identify the living things you encounter will give us a fast ballpark time estimate. Also you should have a better understanding of the overall environment and how to interact responsibly with it. We have found a geologist for the team who has worked for two oil companies over the last ten years looking for new potential oil fields. His name is Fred Watkins, and he has a PhD in geology. The underground formations he was looking for as an oil man are the lands Team T-REX will be walking on during the missions. We expect him to analyze the geology around your landing site and to collect rock samples to bring home for radio chronology analysis. The team will also carry equipment to measure the magnetic field of the earth at the arrival site as another aid in making a more accurate determination of the time traveled. As you know, the position, strength, and polarity of the magnetic pole has varied greatly over time.

"The member we have not yet found is specified to be an astronomer. This person will photograph and study the position of the stars at the site. We expect this will be another useful tool in determining the general era of the landing site.

"The final member of the team is Colonel Eleanor Johnston. As the security Officer, she will be responsible for the weapons and protection of the team. For various reasons, she is absolutely the most qualified for the job."

Steven stared vacantly into space as he replied, "So this first mission will be to go back over sixty-five million years, do quick exploration of the arrival site to determine its exact time, take star position readings and magnetic field measurements, and bring back geological samples for further analysis."

"That sums up the objectives for the first twenty-four-hour mission which is officially designated Mission 2. Once that is accomplished, then we can plan other missions to determine the ongoing accuracy of the placement of our system and create experiments to determine the effects of time travel on the passengers and on the space-time continuum itself. By the way, the system is the name people around here have begun to use. It just seems too weird to be talking about a time machine."

After he took a deep breath and slowly let it out, Steven said, "Okay... wow, this is actually very cool. When would I start?"

"As soon as we complete the team, we will spend a week of training for the mission and go. We are most anxious to begin, how about starting work in three days. That should give you enough time to notify your employer and make any excuses for your absence."

GAZA CITY, GAZA STRIP

In Gaza City at 10:00 a.m., the mayor's personal phone rang in his office in the Palestinian Legislative Council building. His assistant was out getting him a pot of Arabic coffee, so Ajam al-Shawa was forced to answer his phone himself. "Salaam," al-Shawa answered.

"Do you speak English?" asked the caller in terribly mangled English.

"A little, though I detest using the crude language," answered al-Shawa. "What do you want?"

"I have a little story to tell you about the Israelis and what they are currently up to," replied the caller.

"Who are you, and what is your interest in this?" asked al-Shawa.

"I am just a concerned party that wants to help," said the caller. "Mossad is currently planning an attack on your city with a very deadly biological weapon within the week. I do not know the exact date, but they are nearly ready. As part of their preparation for this terrible act, they have given anthrax vaccine to every member of their organization to protect them. The intent is to have this disease spread to all of the Gaza Strip and to end the stalemate between their government and the PNA. They have developed a mass transmission method for the Ames strain of the anthrax bacterium. If you do not find a way to stop this attack, eight hundred to nine hundred thousand of the people in the Gaza Strip will die."

"How do I know that this is not a trick? Why should I trust you?" shouted al-Shawa.

"Surely, you have sources of information within Mossad. Now that you are alerted, you can check for yourself. However,

I suggest that you begin whatever preparation for the attack you can. I am informed that it will come very soon."

White Sands, New Mexico

As soon as Steven returned home, he spent a minimal amount of time putting his affairs in order. He was excited to arrive in New Mexico because he wanted to see this amazing project with his own eyes. The only difficult task was to tell his girlfriend Melissa that he was moving to New Mexico.

The training facility was housed within the White Sands Missile Range. With an area of 3,200 square miles, it was the largest military instillation in the United States.

During Steven's brief time at home, the NSA found the last member of the team. David Spencer recently received a PhD in astrophysics from UC Berkley, specializing in the study of both axial and orbital precession of the Earth.

Steven was looking forward to meeting the whole team, and the kickoff meeting of Team T-REX took place first thing Monday morning within the secure military area of the White Sands complex. As Steven walked into the conference room, he recognized Jonas McCormick and Marsha Dixon but not the other two men and woman. The woman, Eleanor Johnston, was very attractive in a sun baked, outdoor kind of way. She had lustrous black hair that she had put up in a bun. Her military fatigues were pressed to perfection. She was slender at five foot eight and 125 pounds, and she moved with the grace of a dancer. Her handshake was very firm and confident. Steven had to admit that his pulse jumped a bit just from meeting her.

Fred Watkins and David Spencer were both stereotypes of high academic achievers with longish brown hair and wire-rimmed glasses. Spencer was the taller at six foot two and 190 pounds. He looked like he could take care of himself easily enough. At five foot nine and slim, Fred was in good physical shape as well. At forty, Fred was the older of the two by seven years.

Jonas opened the meeting with an overview of the mission and how the equipment worked in theory. "We decided early in the concept stage that for such a huge jump in time, the travelers should be enclosed within a protective skin because we really have no idea of what they will find at any new target site. After the physics were folded into our thinking, we decided that we would use one vessel to enclose the whole team instead of single vessels for each member. The landing site could be significantly higher or lower than the launch site because of earthquakes or other phenomenon. The target site could even be underwater, considering the length of time we plan to traverse.

Physics theory tells us that the matter we send back in time temporarily replaces the matter that was there. For example, if the vessel appeared where a tree was growing, it would probably topple the tree by replacing a portion of the trunk. When the vessel returned to the present, the tree trunk would still be there, but the tree would have fallen because the trunk was replaced in time and not there for support while the vessel was. If the vessel appeared underground, it would be trapped until the system caused it to retrace its path in time."

"The vessel you will travel in is a sphere made with half-inch-thick titanium walls, and it is fifteen feet in diameter. We have isolated the inner passenger area from the outer wall to absorb shocks from falls of up to twenty feet. It floats so if it appears underwater, it will float up to the surface. There is air for about two hours if there is a full complement of four passengers."

"What happens if the drop is more than twenty feet?" asked Fred.

"We are not too worried about that because we send a sophisticated monitoring device to the site before the manned transit. This would warn us if there is some risk that would warrant reconfiguring or calling off the mission. From an operational point of view, the White Sands team operating the system would not send the vessel unless the drop is ten feet or less. This eliminates complications for the return trip. This is all planning for contingences anyway since we expect missions for the foreseeable future to go to only one site plus or minus a few years due to the placement accuracy of the system."

Steven asked, "Can you give us any idea of how the transit feels to the traveler? Are there any sensory issues during or after we arrive? How do we get back?"

"You are certainly full of good questions," Jonas said and laughed. "But let's have the only person who has ever made the trip tell you about that, Ellie?"

"Wow, so we have a real, live time travel veteran with us today," said Dave Spencer. "How was it?"

GAZA CITY, GAZA STRIP

Early in the morning of the day after the mayor of Gaza City received his anonymous warning, a small old-fashioned biplane began circling over Gaza City, advertising the grand opening of a new department store. The flight pattern was cleverly designed to give the maximum number of people the chance to see the banner towed by the plane. Circling the city many times and covering the suburbs as well as the center of the city, the biplane spent about eight hours flying over the city. The flight was approved by the Gaza City Police and Hamas. Everyone was happy to think the new store might give a good boost to the city's and the country's economies. Maybe the owners of the store had found a way to smuggle goods past the Israeli blockade. However, while it was displaying the advertisement, the plane was also covertly distributing anthrax spores across the city. This was a proven method developed and used experimentally by the infamous Unit 731 of the Japanese Imperial Army in China in the 1940s. It had been proven effective when the spores were distributed over several towns in Northern China. The death rate reached over 50 percent then.

White Sands, New Mexico

Colonel Johnston seemed uncomfortable with all of the eyes in the room focused on her, waiting to hear about her trip back in time, but she persevered, "When I made the jump back, it was only for a short time, so I'm not really sure it should count as an actual trip. After I got into the vessel, I strapped in and pushed the control signifying I was ready. I waited to feel something. Suddenly, an unbelievable spectacle of light and sound engulfed the capsule. It built to an intense crescendo, and abruptly, everything went black. I heard the double beep sound in the vessel, telling me that I had arrived but I really wondered if the system had worked properly. I'm not sure what I expected, but what I felt was not it. I opened the hatch and found myself looking out on a flat plain with sparsely spaced, shrub like plants growing as far as I could see. The sun was very bright and high in the sky. The air smelled different, pleasant and fresh. I barely had time to absorb the scene before the vessel was telling me that it was time to go back. The hatch closed, and the return trip initiated itself to the accompaniment of the light and sound show. This is not the normal procedure, but since we did not know if I would be conscious after I arrived, the return initiated automatically. At the double beep, I just opened the hatch when told to do so and found ten excited people huddled around the vessel, asking me questions."

Jonas stepped in at this point and said, "The mechanism for returning is simple. The act of going back in time is like pushing a car up a hill. You push it up twenty feet and gravity pulls on it to make it roll back down. The vessel is drawn to return constantly throughout the whole trip but is held at the target time by a special type of electromagnetic field. Using the car analogy, it is like putting blocks under the wheels. The car cannot roll back until the blocks are removed. In the case of the vessel, we have a complex radio transmitter sending a radio beam consisting of two critical frequencies, which are modulated to actually travel through the electromagnetic connection and back to the system. As long as the radio beams are received in the present time, the system keeps the vessel at the target site. When the signal is turned off, the system lets the vessel return to the present. For safety consideration, we have put a keypad with a combination to be entered before the signal can be turned off. This subsystem of the vessel is powered by a long-lasting battery. This is actually one of the few items used to control the vessel that requires power from within. Most of the other control components are powered from the present time side of the system."

"When you say the vessel returns to the present, does that mean the time when it left or to a present that was moving forward during the mission?" asked Steven.

"The vessel returns to the system that sent it," answered Jonas. "The system is moving forward at the time rate of the universe which is a fixed constant; therefore the vessel returns to a present that has moved forward the period of time the vessel was gone.

"Someone, in one of our ongoing discussions, proposed that we should just bring the vessel back to the time when it left. However this would actually involve a second operation requiring twice the power. One operation would be the initial transition, for example, going back to the past. The vessel would return, without additional power consumption, to the moving present. Then an additional transition would be required to go back to the original time the vessel left."

JERUSALEM, ISRAEL

As if in response to the Israeli bio-attack on Gaza City, on the third day after the mayor of Gaza City received an anonymous phone call warning of a pending Israeli biological attack, a tall, shadowy figure in a long gray robe with a hood crept through the alleys of Jerusalem. He wore a large bulky backpack over his hooded coat. Periodically, the figure would remove a square object from his backpack and stoop over a pile of garbage to hide the object. The object had a numerical display on top and appeared to be a bomb. However, the object was not a bomb. It actually contained thousands of fleas with a timer to release them after a five-hour delay. The stranger wandered the alleys of Jerusalem for six hours until dawn, leaving his packages around the city. At six o'clock the next morning, the stranger stepped into a deep shadow near the end of an abandoned alley and disappeared.

WHITE SANDS, NEW MEXICO

The next five days for Team T-REX were a blur of instruction on the details of the vessel and its compliment of equipment. A team of technicians also gave them instruction on the setup and the use of the different pieces of equipment needed to determine the exact time at the site. Finally, they discussed possible scenarios that they could encounter during the mission and how they should react. The team made it a point to eat dinner together each evening in order to get to know each other better. Luckily, everyone seemed to get along well, probably because they were all so completely focused on the task at hand.

On the second evening after dinner, Steven invited Ellie to take a walk in the cactus garden outside the cafeteria. She accepted, but so did Fred and Dave. The same thing happened the next evening. Finally, on the third try to get Ellie alone, Steven suggested that Fred and Dave should go practice taking magnetic field measurements with the new equipment an instructor had introduced them to just before dinner.

"So, how did you ever land in this project?" asked Steven.

"I grew up as the only daughter of a two-star general who really wanted a son," said Ellie. "I guess I've been trying my whole life to show him that I was as good as a son. I entered the military and found that I excelled in most aspects of military life. When I made colonel at thirty-five years of age, I think Dad finally realized he could be proud of a daughter. His West Point classmate and close friend Kenneth Attwood is the director of the NSA. Dad was bragging about my promotion to General Attwood at dinner one night, and they somehow decided I would be perfect for this posting. And here I am. I think Dad would have a stroke if he knew that I volunteered to be the time travel guinea pig."

"I'm sure he will be proud when he finds out," said Steven. *That's if we're ever able to tell anyone about what we do.*

"As I said, I do well with the military style of life, but it has not been without challenges," said Ellie with a mildly defiant look on her face. "You are our leader based on your academic work, and I'm really good with that. When we get into a threat situation that requires knowledge of weapons and tactics, I hope you will listen to my suggestions. As you could probably guess I have been in many situations where colleagues let their male hormones override my suggestions. I may be a woman, but I'm highly trained in the arts of war. I just bring this up to help us get off to a good start."

I wonder what brought this on, Steven thought to himself. "As an academic, I don't feel I pay attention to my male hormones as much as a military man might," said Steven. *She must have fought hard to get where she is.* "If you feel strongly about this we can go to talk to Jonas together about changing the team structure. A strong team should have only one leader, but it does not need to be me. I think Jonas is trying to build our team as a scientific group with military protection, not a military group with some scientists along."

"Oh, how embarrassing, I guess I totally misread you." said Ellie. "I owe you an apology."

On Sunday, everyone gathered in the same conference room where they had first met. They discussed their state of readiness. The team members were all hyped and ready to go immediately. After three hours of going through a checklist Jonas had prepared, he declared the team ready. Technicians would work through the night on the few minor unfinished items. The mission would commence at 10:00 a.m. tomorrow.

chapter 5

At 9:30 the next morning the team lined up in desert fatigue uniforms. A patch that spelled out T-Rex over a picture of a dinosaur on each person's shoulder was the only identifying mark. They each were outfitted with Sig Sauer P220 Pistols, an M9 multipurpose bayonet and top secret ear inserted communication devices developed by the NSA. These com units allowed the team to be in constant communication to a distance of two miles. In fact, the technicians on the project predicted that the com units might carry over a much longer distance since there would be none of the background electrical noise and other communication noise associated with modern civilization.

The vessel was painted a flat black and did not return the glare of the overhead lights. It stood on four legs in the center of an equipment-filled room that was about the size of a basketball court. There were four rings made of a newly created material that was superconductive at room temperature. The rings were suspended surrounding the vessel at various angles, creating a magnetic field the vessel floats in just before it launches through time and space. The rings did not move in time with the vessel.

The entry hatch was placed on the top of the vessel, not the most convenient place for the passengers to enter, but a position

38

assuring better access to the vessel in emergency situations, such as a transit into water or a transit that left the vessel partially embedded in the ground. The outside ladder consisted of insets in the skin of the vessel so the passengers had toe and handholds.

Jonas gave the order for the team to board along with a wish for a successful journey. As the team climbed up the outside and then down into the passenger compartment, they talked sparingly. When he looked around the small space, Steven saw four seats, each facing the center of the cramped passenger compartment. The ladder was centered in the square area formed by the seats. Even though the vessel was fifteen feet in diameter, the passenger compartment was only large enough for the passengers to slip in and buckle up. Fred closed the hatch as the team buckled themselves into seats that were heavily padded in case of a rough landing. The area between the passenger compartment and the outer skin was storage space filled with equipment along with food and water for five days. Doors on the outside skin of the vessel allowed access to the equipment. Dave quipped, "I never expected to be traveling in a more cramped space than a commercial airline seat. I thought that was the maximum in discomfort." Fred and Steven laughed and shook their heads while Ellie smiled. Steven pushed the ready button, and the vessel communication device announced transit in one minute.

Mission 2 from White Sands

The transition began with a simultaneous mechanical vibration induced within all the structural components of the vessel along with the application of an electromagnetic field surrounding and permeating the vessel, this field created by the rings around the outside. The vibration frequency of the structure increased until it was a high-pitched screech, and then it finally went beyond the range of human hearing. The frequency of the electromechanical field increased until the waves finally became visible as they passed through all the colors of the rainbow starting with red and progressing toward blue. The vibration and changing light inside of the vessel was quite chaotic. The inside of the vessel was immersed in these colors until the blue finally faded as the electromagnetic waves progressed beyond the visible spectrum. At this point, the passengers were suddenly dropped into an inky blackness. There was a sense of the vessel spinning on its vertical axis but no visual clues to confirm this. Next, there came a loud cracking sound, which was a sonic boom. A short time later, a brilliant burst of white light flashed through the vessel. Scientists postulated these events were the result of moving faster than the speed of sound and then breaking through the speed of light, though they currently have no idea exactly what caused this phenomenon within the vessel. Shortly after the bang and flash of light, the structure of the vessel popped abruptly back into visible space, and the transition was complete.

The next sound in the cabin was the double beep announcing that they were on site and it was time to open the hatch. Steven climbed up to release it and then climbed higher to see out.

The area around the vessel looked like they had traveled to another planet, one covered by a riot of color and movement. There were no trees or grass anywhere to be seen. There were shrubs that looked like they had pine needles on them, and others that were covered with beautiful flowers like it was springtime. They were predominantly reds and oranges with a few blues and purples mixed in. And then there were the butterflies, four or five different types, all with about a two- to three-inch wingspan and with brilliant colors of blue, yellow, orange, black, and white. They flew in profusion around the vessel. Steven was stunned by the sight and lingered on the ladder inside the vessel for too long to suit the others. Their grumbles got him moving out of the vessel. As everyone filed out, they understood Steven's hesitation. The sky was a brilliant shade of blue that none of them had ever seen before, and it was completely devoid of clouds. The sun was so bright that it hurt their eyes. The only movement they could see was the butterflies, no other animals.

"The first order of business is to check communications," said Steven. "Everyone walk ten steps in a different direction and count off." After they checked the com units, they began to get the equipment for magnetic field testing out of the vessel and set up. Steven said, "Ellie, set up the observation balloon. Fred and Dave, get the magnetic testing started. We only have twenty-four hours here, so let's maximize the results. I'll unpack the two electric dirt bikes and do a bit of exploration. Let's get back together in three hours to see what we have found and what we should do next."

The observation balloon was a two-foot-diameter helium balloon that was designed to float to as high as 1,500 feet. There was a remote-controlled camera hanging from it. The idea was to get video data of an extended area in a short time. As soon as Ellie got the balloon to maximum height, she attached the small video monitor/recorder unit to the camera wires that were embedded within the balloon's tether line. She began to pan the camera in a 360 degree arc. The initial camera sweep started pointing to the north and rotated counter clockwise. As it came around to point northwesterly from their position, she began to see a change in the landscape around 150 miles away. First, she saw a large body of water that extended north and south as far as the camera could resolve. The shoreline was about one hundred miles from the site at its closest point. The water extended west all the way to the horizon. As Ellie panned the camera along the shoreline, she saw an image of something low and flat consisting of many straight lines intersecting at right angles that did not fit with the rest of the landscape. There appeared to be some type of living creatures moving around this area, but they were too small to see well in the display screen, even at the camera's highest magnification.

Steven was just finishing with unpacking the electric dirt bikes when he heard a burst of sound from his com device. It sounded more structured than just electromagnetic noise but only consisted of guttural bursts of hisses. "Did anyone else hear that noise?" Steven said through the com link.

"We did," said Fred, who was working with Dave to calibrate the magnetic monitoring equipment. "Was it EM noise? It didn't sound like anything I've heard on these com devices while we were training."

"I have hundreds of hours of experience with these devices and I've never heard a sound like that," said Ellie. "What do you make of it? What kind of natural phenomenon could cause this type of interference?"

"Not any natural phenomenon I've ever heard of," said Steven. "Well, we'll just have to wait and see if it happens again. We don't know enough about this place to figure it out. Just stay alert to see if we hear anything else. I guess we should have brought a recorder to capture com link conversations for future study."

Steven got on one of the dirt bikes. After he took an emergency backpack, he rode in a rough circle around the site about a mile out. The bikes were capable of a top speed of forty miles per hour, but twenty to thirty was a more reasonable speed expectation in this rough, shrub-infested area. He wove around between the shrubs until he was roughly due east of the site. There, he came to the top of a drop-off of about forty feet. He got off the bike, and went up to the edge to look down. There was a canyon running north and south that was about fifty feet wide. It ran south as far as Steven could see but turned sharply east about one hundred yards to the north. He was just standing quietly, trying to see if he could hear any sounds of animal life when two creatures walking upright came around the bend of the gully. *What the hell are they?* Steven dropped to his stomach to observe the creatures without scaring them off. They looked vaguely human at first glance walking upright on two long, powerful legs that were very muscular in the thigh. Their knees did not become completely straight as they strolled through the gully. They had no tails and no scales but as they came closer to Steven, he could make out more details and they also looked vaguely reptilian.

They both appeared to be about six feet tall with almost featureless heads that were generally oval-shaped and swiveled on slender necks. They had two large black eyes and openings in the skin on the side of their heads that appeared to be ears. A large mouth contained many sharp-looking teeth, and there were two nose openings above it. *They look like the aliens those conspiracy nuts say kidnapped them.* Their forelegs were shorter than their hind legs, which gave the impression that they were not used for walking. In fact, they looked like human arms ending in four slender, flexible fingers and an opposable thumb. Both creatures were built the same but had different color markings on their bodies. One was a light shade of gray with a leathery skin; no scales were visible on their skin. The other one had the same overall coloring except for areas smudged with red and orange on its chest and belly area. As he watched them, Steven fumbled for his small digital camera and frantically took pictures of these unusual creatures. They were completely unlike anything Steven had ever seen in the fossil records. That was when he noticed something very odd about their behavior. They seemed to be walking side by side and talking like humans, not like two reptiles hunting together.

When Team T-REX assembled three hours later, the members found they had much to talk about. The magnetic field measurements were well underway. Ellie replayed parts of the balloon video showing the structure she saw near the body of water. Steven showed everyone the pictures he had taken of the strange reptiles.

"Wow! Do you realize those things could be the same as the ones I saw moving around the structure by the sea," Ellie said as she stared at Steven's camera. "I take it that you do not recognize the species to help us set the current time. We should try to find out more about them before we return. Also, we should try to find other creatures that may help date the site."

Steven summed up their work plan, "We still need to stay focused on the main mission and tasks. Fred can explore around the site to find rock samples for us to take back for radio chronology testing while Dave finishes the magnetic field readings and starts his star mapping as soon as it gets dark enough. In the meantime, Ellie and I will take the bikes and see if we can find out more about this structure by the sea. We also need to find some other living creatures that can help us determine the current era. Okay, let's get to it."

Steven and Ellie set out on the dirt bikes a half hour later. They rode to the west toward the structures Ellie had seen. Mounted in quick-release brackets, each bike had a Browning BAR MkII Safari rifle chambered to take Winchester Magnum .338-caliber cartridges. They had a lightweight backpack with some food, water, and miscellaneous items in case of emergency.

After they rode for about an hour, they saw something that surprised and delighted them. It was a nineteen-member herd group of *Maiasauras*, according to Steven. These were plant-eating, duck-billed dinosaurs with a flat skull and small crests in front of the eyes. The snout tapered down to a flattened, toothless beak, somewhat like a duck's beak. The largest one was about thirty feet long, eight feet of which was tail that stuck straight out behind them as they walked. Most walked on their two strong hind legs and they also had front legs that were shorter than their rear ones but long and strong enough to help them walk over rough terrain.

There were fifteen adult animals in the group and four smaller juveniles that were about twelve feet in length. Their heads bobbed back and forth as they walked. Steven could hardly contain his excitement, "Look how the *Maiasauras* are moving in a herd just as we thought. The fact that these dinosaurs are alive confirms that we have come at least seventy to sixty-five million years into the past."

"How can you be so sure what kind of dinosaur they are?" asked Ellie. "Don't they all look similar?" They had gotten off their bikes for a better look.

"Oh, no, each different species has very specific identifying features," said Steven. "We studied these creatures at Montana State and they look almost exactly as we projected, except we never dreamed they would be that shade of blue-green with a tan frill down their vertebrae. Wow! Look at the red markings some have on their neck and stomach. There is no camouflage value to that. The color must be entirely related to attraction between the sexes."

The *Maiasauras* were so calm in the presence of the two humans that when one of the smaller ones came over to satisfy its curiosity about the strange mammals, Ellie felt comfortable moving toward it for a better look. Steven was caught up in the scene until he noticed a movement from his right. "Look out," he yelled. A much larger dinosaur, one with the red markings, was heading in Ellie's direction, apparently poised to protect the young, more inquisitive one. Steven pushed Ellie out of the path of the oncoming brute. It thundered past and missed them both, but they had now moved in the opposite direction from where they had parked the bikes. The charging dinosaur turned back for them. "Get to the bikes," yelled Steven. "I don't think we can outrun this big guy on foot." They had to dart past the young dinosaur to get back to the bikes, which seemed to enrage their attacker even more. The *Maiasaura* did not seem capable of accelerating quickly, but it flicked out a foreleg and knocked Ellie to the ground. Before she could move to get away, it opened its mouth, bent down, and tried to bite her but only got her backpack because she was still lying flat on her stomach. It raised its head, and Ellie was pulled upright by her backpack.

She seemed dazed because she just hung there limply. Then the *Maiasaura* gave a tentative shake of its head. By now, Steven realized Ellie's plight and pulled his bayonet out of the sheath at his side. When he stepped closer, he grabbed one shoulder strap of Ellie's backpack and cut through it. He then grabbed Ellie, pulled her other arm out of its shoulder strap, and dragged her toward the bikes. The *Maiasaura* noticed the change of weight and gave the backpack a couple more shakes before it realized that the source of its irritation was getting away. Ellie quickly regained her wits, and she and Steven both ran back to the bikes. It was good that the bikes were electric because it took only the flip of a switch to get them moving and away from the enraged *Maiasaura*.

"Thanks, Steven," said Ellie after she had a few seconds to clear her head. "That was a really close call. I need to be more careful around those things. They look gentle and peaceful around their own kind, but everything changes if they think one of their young is threatened."

After another hour of travel, they began to see a change in the landscape. Up until now, the shrubs had been scattered, and the reddish dirt had been sandy and dry. Now the dirt was a richer black and damp. The shrubs had given way to ferns that grew profusely and were beginning to make it difficult to find a riding path. The sun had moved about halfway down from its zenith toward the western horizon. It would be dark in three or four more hours. All this conspired to make their travel on the bikes more difficult. To make things worse, the sun now shone directly in their eyes. Suddenly, they heard that noise again in their com units. This time, it lasted longer giving them a better chance to carefully listen to it and attempt to figure out what it was. Steven looked at Ellie with total surprise in his expression. "That sounds like a spoken message to me. What do you think?" asked Steven.

"It doesn't sound even remotely like any language I've ever heard, but the cadence and feel is like someone speaking," replied Ellie. "Where do you think it's coming from?"

"I have no idea, but hopefully, we will hear it again. For the next trip here, we should bring some radio direction-finding equipment so we can locate the source of these transmissions. Who would have thought we would find electromagnetic wave transmissions of any kind sixty-five million years in the past?"

Just as they were thinking about giving up on their exploration because of the damp, slippery ground and the dense foliage, they came to a ribbon of ground where the shrubs were gone. It was about eight to ten feet wide. "What the hell is that?" asked Ellie. "It looks like a road. Do you think another country has gotten here before us and has set up a permanent base? If so, what country would have the technical prowess to do it? I suppose it could just as likely be a friend as an enemy."

"I guess anything is possible, but the probability of us coming to the same place and time as another group from our world is exponentially approaching zero," said Steven. "Let's try to follow this path and see where it leads."

"We'd better watch for any sign of someone coming along the path," said Ellie. "I just feel it will be to our benefit if we don't alert whoever built the road until we know more about them."

The path they followed curved slowly to the left, and too soon, the sun was back in their eyes. Steven said, "We're going west again toward the structure you saw from the observation balloon, but I think it's too far away to be the source of the radio transmissions."

They had traveled on the path for about another fifteen minutes when they heard the noise in their com units again. This time, it was even longer than the previous two. Steven pulled his bike over to the side of the path so that he could listen better. Ellie was slightly behind him. Suddenly, she saw the glint of light reflecting off of some metal on the road ahead. "Off the trail and into the bushes," whispered Ellie. "It sounds like we have company coming." It was easy to conceal the bikes in the dense ferns. Steven and Ellie peered through the brush. They heard a dim noise that sounded like the hum of an electric motor, and it was getting louder. Both of them craned their necks to get a view of what was coming.

"Look at that," hissed Ellie as they saw a strange vehicle come down the path. It had three wheels, two in the back and one in the front for steering. It was about nine or ten feet long and about five feet wide. There was an open-air compartment for four passengers, but the space was occupied by only two figures sitting in the front. One was driving the vehicle.

"Oh my God!" breathed Steven. "Those two are just like the creatures I saw walking along the gully back by our arrival site. How can this be? They seem to be intelligent beings, but where could they have come from?"

"From a security point of view, this changes our mission completely," whispered Ellie. "We need to reevaluate what to do next. Should we continue on with our exploration or get back to camp and return to White Sands with this news?"

Thinking out loud, Steven said, "We really don't know what we have here to report so far. We only have time for this one reconnaissance mission before we have to return to our time. Let's continue on to see if we can learn anything else to help future mission planning after we return. But we should be extra careful not to be discovered."

"Okay, then let's go a little farther along this path," agreed Ellie. "We estimated that the strange object I saw with the observation balloon was about one hundred miles from the site. "We have probably covered about sixty miles of that. In that case, I doubt that we could expect to find anything of interest within walking distance. So I guess we need to risk using the bikes."

The sun was even closer to the horizon now, so it was even

harder to look directly down the road when they resumed their trip. As well as they could, they kept their eyes focused ahead for any hint of more activity on the path. They traveled another hour at reduced speed without incident when they suddenly heard noises indicating something was happening just ahead. Now they decided to hide their bikes and explore on foot. The ground to the side of the path was becoming mushy and slippery underfoot. However, the ferns were very thick and provided good cover.

As they crept through the brush, they saw a structure ahead that was only two feet above the ground but covered a large area of the ground. There were six of the tri-wheelers stopped by the building, and many of the reptile people were walking around, some carrying objects that appeared to be weapons. "This seems to be some kind of a guard station to me," said Ellie.

"By their coloration, I think we can guess these reptiles are all males," suggested Steven. They all seem to be moving with a purpose, and most have weapons. Let's try to get around to the left and check out that side of the building. That seems to be where most of the activity is happening."

As they crept to within two hundred feet of the busy side of the building, they could see that there was a ramp leading inside the structure and that there were several reptiles walking down the ramp. Ellie whispered, "Since the reptile people appear to be about six feet tall and there is not enough room in the part of the building we can see, most of that building must be underground."

"I agree," said Steven.

Again, they heard noise in their com units. They decided it must be radio communication between the creatures. "I think we have learned as much as we are going to be able to without being discovered," said Steven. "Let's take some photos and get out of here."

"Great idea," said Ellie, nodding in agreement

Creeping back to the bikes took about thirty minutes. The creatures had not discovered the bikes, so Ellie and Steven pulled them out of the brush and headed back to the arrival site. They stayed on the road until it began to curve to the right. Here, they left the road, turned on the bikes' headlights, and began a slow journey over land toward the east.

As Steven and Ellie got within range of the com devices in the camp, they heard conversation between Fred and Dave. Dave shouted, "Hang in there, Fred. I'll get the first-aid kit as soon as I find something to tie up this thing."

"I can't feel my hands and feet," hissed Fred. "I think that dart it shot into my shoulder must have had some kind of neurotoxin on it. I pulled it out, but maybe you need to suck out the poison like with snakebites."

"Hey, guys, this is Steven. What's happening there?"

"Get back here as soon as you can," shouted Dave. "We were attacked by one of those things you took pictures of. It came right into the site, making all kinds of hisses and grunts just like we heard on the com unit. Fred turned toward it to see what the commotion was all about, and it shot him in the shoulder with a projectile weapon. Apparently, it didn't see me because I was sitting on the ground by a rock to steady my hands for a few seconds while I took some manual star shots. I jumped up and smacked it in the head with a shovel. I'm tying it up so I can look after Fred."

"Keep an eye out in case it came with friends," said Ellie. "We're almost there."

As they rolled up to the vessel, they saw Dave giving Fred a shot of broad spectrum antivenin from the first-aid kit. Fred appeared to be unconscious. "We need to get him back to White Sands so a doctor can see to him," said Dave. "I don't know if this stuff from the first-aid kit will help or not, but he is still breathing."

"Okay, let's get everything into the vessel so we don't leave any trace of our being here," said Steven. "What should we do with this thing?"

Ellie was kneeling by the reptile. "It seems to still be alive. We should take it with us so we don't alert the local population to our presence."

"Agreed," said Steven. "We may make some change in the timeline by doing it, but I think a change was inevitable from the instant this creature saw Fred."

Ten minutes later, they had hastily thrown everything into the vessel. Dave strapped Fred into his seat while Steven and Ellie draped the reptile across their laps. Steven initiated the protocol to allow them to return.

chapter 6

As the sound and light show for the return trip started, Steven had an uncomfortable thought. *We have to alert the system's crew to initiate quarantine provisions for the returning vessel. That probably should have been standard operating procedure for every mission.*

When they arrived at White Sands, Ellie opened the hatch. Dave and Steven began lifting Fred out of the vessel. As Steven's head cleared the hatch, he yelled, "We have a medical emergency. Fred has been wounded, and we suspect he has been injected with a neurotoxin. Get medical personnel in here now! We also have a prisoner. Yes, I said prisoner. We need a way to hold it until we can study it. Also, institute quarantine around it as a precaution. It is currently restrained and unconscious in the vessel. It is not human but does not weigh much more than an average man. Let's get it out of the vessel before it wakes up."

Jonas came through the door on the run. "What the hell happened? Do you realize that you may have caused a huge glitch in the space-time continuum? Let's get to the conference room to debrief and see if there is anything we can do to fix this mess."

The group that sat down in the conference room was somber and quiet. Jonas started the meeting, "Fred is still alive, but the doctors are not sure what type of chemical compound he was subjected to. He is unconscious but breathing on his own. The doctors will interrupt the meeting if his condition changes. Your prisoner is locked in the brig of the army base. It's awake and making noise that clearly sounds like a drill instructor yelling at a new recruit. It seems you have stumbled on an unknown group of intelligent creatures with speech and a level of technology that we never anticipated. The projectile weapon the prisoner used on Fred seems to be highly sophisticated. How could a seemingly advanced civilization have existed without our knowledge?"

"I've been thinking about that question since we stumbled onto this discovery," said Steven. "Sixty-five million years is a long time to wear away any traces of a civilization. Especially since this civilization appears to live underground. Any of their construction that has not been destroyed by the natural forces would be mistaken for natural cave formations. Their tools and other implements would have long since corroded to nothing. The everyday aspects of the Egyptian civilization like common homes and palaces are completely wiped away after less than five thousand years. The only things that survived there are the huge stone monuments they built and some of the things they put inside those monuments. After millions of years even those will probably be gone,"

"I understand what you're saying, let's move on," said Jonas. "The tentative information your team gathered indicates that the site was in the general ballpark of where we intended to send you plus or minus a couple of years. We'll get more accurate information after further study."

"Let's put the photos we took with my camera on the projection screen," said Steven. "The pictures Ellie and I took of the guard building and the surrounding area show about twenty of these creatures and six of their tri-wheelers. By the way, all these creatures are like the one we brought back. I tend to think of them as male because of the markings on their stomach. We seem to have only captured one female on video.

She is one of the pair walking in the gully. The videos from the observation balloon show an even larger complex of buildings by the body of water Ellie discovered. These two places are around forty miles apart. I think we can assume that there is a significant population of these creatures in the area around the arrival site.

"As you mentioned before Jonas, this civilization seems to be highly advanced in some respects based upon what we've seen so far," said Steven. "This is especially true considering the resources they have to work with. In that geologic age there was no oil in the world yet. It will not be created by nature for many million years. This means they would probably have no way to manufacture plastics. Also rubber made from plants had not evolved yet.

"From what we've seen, their technology is a curious mixture of capabilities. Some are as advanced as ours or even a little better. On the other hand some of their capabilities seem primitive compared to ours. I am guessing that has something to do with the way their minds work and with the scientific directions they chose to pursue based on their needs.

"I'd like to go back to the site as soon as possible to continue learning about these creatures. Where did they come from? Are they from this world but a different evolutionary direction?"

McCormick looked uneasy. "We never really staffed your team for this type of situation. This has become more like a covert infiltration than a mission to collect scientific data. That makes it more like a military operation than a scientific expedition."

"But we don't even know if these reptile creatures are dangerous," argued Steven. "I think we should gather more evidence about the situation before we send in troops."

"This thing you brought back attacked Fred with no provocation," retorted McCormick.

"It could have easily been a mistake," interjected Dave. "The reptile man could have been telling Fred to put up his hands or the equivalent for them. Fred was startled by its appearance in our site. He jumped up and whirled toward the creature, and maybe that was taken as a threatening gesture. I'm betting that the reptile was just as startled to see a human as we were to see him."

"I also feel we should keep this mission scientific in nature a little longer," said Ellie. "We don't have enough data to determine if there is any real threat from the creatures we just discovered. A pure military presence would jeopardize our chance to learn about this civilization. Let's just add a few members to the team to guard our site so we don't get surprised again. Dave could continue with the time and paradox verification experiments. We could equip ourselves to record and determine where the sources of the apparent radio communications are coming from. Then Steven and I could try to get near a couple of the sources to get a much better idea of what we're dealing with. We could bring back recordings for further analysis and a translation attempt. I think we may need to do a lot of our surveillance on foot, so we would need to stay on site for a longer time. Can we work out a way to communicate from the site without bringing the vessel back to the present?"

"Okay, Okay! I can see that you really want to do this. I guess I could go along with this plan for another trip," said McCormick. "It was my own thought that it was important to very gradually increase the number of personnel we send back until we get a sense if there will be any time paradox problems. We add two soldiers for guard duty, and I'm sure Fred will not be ready to go back for a while. We have a net increase in personnel of one. That last part about communication is easy. We can modulate the signal that controls the return field to enable two-way communications."

"Next, we should decide what to do with the prisoner," said Dave. "We should try to find some way to communicate with it. It would greatly simplify the discovery process about this civilization if we could talk to it and ask questions. We should get a couple of experts to see if it is really speaking a language we can learn."

"That's a good idea, Dave," said Ellie. "We should try to find out more about the stuff Fred was injected with. Finding an antidote would be even better. There should be a sample of the neurotoxin in the projectiles we brought back with the reptile's weapon."

A group of three linguists entered the area outside the reptile's cell. Jonas sent them in to try to discover a way of communicating with the life form. William Thomas, the head of the team, stepped up to the bars. He pointed to himself and said, "William." Then he gestured to the reptile to see if it would understand to tell them its name. Apparently, the reptile understood at once because it pointed its hand toward itself and said, "YaSi." Then it pointed to Dr. Thomas and said, "William."

"Wow," said Dr. Thomas. "This creature has a very high intelligence level." Then he pulled out a power bar that he unwrapped and took a bite. He said, "Eat." The reptile made a whole string of utterances that sounded different than the ones it had been yelling earlier. All of a sudden, one of Dr. Thomas's teammates said, "Oh my god! This creature speaks really bad Russian."

chapter 7

LAURASIA, 65 MILLION YEARS BCE

The sun was exactly at its peak in the sky when Exalted Lord
YaKo entered the council chambers deep beneath the city of
SoMu. The other members of the High Council of SuHuRa, which
translates into English as Laurasia, were already in their seats
as dictated by protocol. YaKo sat down on the right side of the
circular lounge next to the opening that allowed entry into the
sitting circle. To his immediate right sat Laurasia's chancellor,
FaPa, second in command within the dictatorship government
of the country. Next in the circle sat SaSu, the director of the
compliance force, and WaTu, the sacred scientist. The meeting
convened to discuss progress of the most important and most
secret program under the purview of the government—how
to deal with the disastrous shortage of energy resources that
threatened to end their ancient civilization. *If the workers of
Laurasia were told of this problem before we have a solution,
it would cause widespread panic and great risk for the
leadership of the country,* thought YaKo.

"As everyone knows, the gigantic landmass of Laurasia has
little in the way of resources required to generate our form of
transportable energy called MaKe," said YaKo. "In the whole
continental landmass, real trees have become extinct. There are
a number of taller fern species because they grow very rapidly
and many types of shrubs but nowhere near enough mass of

combustible plant life to fuel the needs of our civilization. We are currently burning the combustibles from shrubs and the thicker branches of ferns to generate the contained electromagnetic plasma we call MaKe that powers all of our modern devices."

For hundreds of years, this combustible plant life had been harvested on a five-year rotational basis. Each year, 20 percent of the existing plant life was cut to the ground all over Laurasia. The area was immediately replanted, but it wasn't enough. When this plan had been originally developed, the rotation cycle was twenty years, but as demand for energy became greater, the cycle was shortened to keep up. Five years was not enough time for conifer and other large treelike plants to gain sufficient size. Over the centuries, trees became completely extinct in Laurasia, and they had been for over eight hundred years. They were all but forgotten by the present citizens of Laurasia.

Due to the warm, stable climate over millions of years, there was no need to burn wood for fires, and the reptiles did not prefer to eat cooked food. The people were herbivores, and they only heated certain exotic foods. So plant combustibles were only burned to generate MaKe.

The rapid advances in Laurasian science capabilities had created a rapidly growing demand for MaKe to power this advanced civilization. The demand for energy was growing exponentially, but the sources of power were actually decreasing because of the cooler climate and five-year rotational harvesting. The backbone technologies Laurasia depended upon were at risk.

The country had become quite dependent on audio-video communication for disbursing information from the government, disseminating propaganda to keep the people happy with their current government, and directing confer units to keep the people under strict control. All of their communication equipment depended upon MaKe.

Laurasian cities were virtually all below ground with as many as twenty-five underground levels. This required huge amounts of artificial lighting, which again used MaKe. MaKe battery powered vehicles had become indispensable to distribute food and other goods over a country that was about seven thousand miles across. MaKe battery vehicles had also become necessary to move military units around the country to quell any disturbances. The growth of the MaKe battery powered vehicles had probably been the final straw for the energy situation. The scientists predicted twenty years ago that Laurasia's demand would surpass its supply of combustibles within twenty-five years. Something had to be done immediately.

The government began a program to save their civilization as soon as officials fully comprehended the problem. An ever-increasing demand for energy actually accelerated the twenty-five year deadline by three years during the course of the program. The piece of technology that gave birth to the program was created by the current sacred scientist when he discovered the secret to time travel. WaTu worked on the invention in secret, on his own time, and somehow completed it just when it was needed. This was the very reason he received the promotion to the top spot within the powerful science community.

As the Laurasians explored the future, they were shocked to discover that the Earth would be dominated by furless, two-legged descendants of mice. They also discovered the existence of oil and gas that would have been the answer to their energy problems if it existed in their world. But it didn't. This oil, they found out, was composed of plant and animal material from their own and later periods of the earth's life. After millions of years of heat and pressure the organic material was transformed into this wonderful source of energy. The Laurasian government decided it should be theirs. It seemed unfair that the mice men had inherited the fruits of their forests. They decided that they could solve their energy crisis by bringing back oil from the future.

The council had divided the effort into three parts. Chancellor FaPa controlled the first part to launch an all-out effort to study the future civilization of mammals in great detail, looking particularly for their strengths and weaknesses. The goal was to find ways they could plant seeds of strife and discontent. They wanted to cause a global war between the mammals that would severely impair the ability of the future civilization to stop Laurasia from harvesting energy at their convenience. This part of the plan had been underway for over eighteen years. The huge amount of information amassed about life in the future was made public knowledge and taught at all levels of education in Laurasia. This broad education program included four selected languages used by the mammals. "Chancellor FaPa, you will now proceed with your formal annual report on the effort to subvert the mammal civilization," ordered Lord YaKo.

"Exalted Lord and my fellow members of the High Council of Laurasia, we have had many annual reports on this topic over the last eighteen years. I will try to keep the historical part of the report as brief as possible. As you know, once this project was initiated, we began kidnapping a few selected mammals from the future starting in the year 1980 as measured by the calendar system their civilization created.

"When WaTu finished his design of the time machine, we decided to explore in the future direction because we know of the past. We went ahead 10 years and found that things had not changed much. We decided to go significantly farther, so we jumped 250 thousand years. This jump caused surprise and concern because there was no trace of our civilization. We assume this was because of our energy shortage and the future will be rewritten once we solve the problem. This 250 thousand year jump felt as if we had gone to a completely different planet populated by creatures we had never seen before. They were predominately mammals. We began jumping ahead by larger and larger time periods until we jumped into the 1900s per their calendar. About this time in Laurasia we discovered the energy shortage and we discovered the material called oil in the future. From then on we assigned all time machine effort to be spent on solving our current problems.

"We visited earlier times in the life of the mammal civilization when they were not so militarily strong, but they had not developed practical methods of finding and harvesting their oil and gas until after their late 1900s. We decided to concentrate on 2000 plus or minus a twenty-year period so we did not need to look for the oil ourselves. We only needed to take it from the mammal's storage facilities.

"This time period seemed to be particularly unstable from a political point of view. Using great care to conduct this study without alerting the mammals, we started by taking a few random specimens from various parts of their world. As you know, the two continents of our current world have moved about on the surface of the planet and divided into seven continents in their time frame. As we interrogated the specimens, we learned that major centers of innovation are on the continents known as Europe, Asia, and North America during the period under our study. Note that those three areas are all currently part of Laurasia.

"As a result, we concentrated our harvesting of specimens in those three areas. We sent collection teams, with two members each, to randomly kidnap specimens from the future and bring them immediately back to Laurasia for interrogation concerning any and all aspects of their lives. We focused on learning how to speak popular languages called English, French, Russian, and Chinese. Once we learned the basics of the languages, we had teams of scholars spread the knowledge by teaching one or two languages to each of our border guards and foreign agents.

"Academics were taught the languages so they could carry out the massive amount of work involved in our study of the future civilization. This was all done under the holy Laurasian doctrine that makes gaining knowledge the highest calling for a citizen. However, nothing about the effort to destroy the future civilization and steal their energy supplies has ever been mentioned outside the High Council. The number of languages the students learned depended upon their abilities. As with other areas of learning, the more a student learned, the higher his status in our society. We distributed the language education so that roughly an equal number of our citizens speak each language."

"I would hope this learning of languages is complete by now," said the Exalted Lord.

"Yes, within the physical capabilities of our race, we have mastered the languages," said Chancellor FaPa. His chest and stomach area lost the red and orange hues it had before the Exalted Lord asked his question. FaPa also began to fidget with his writing implement. "When we dissected some of the early specimens taken from the future, we found that these mammals have a very peculiar structure connecting their nose, mouth, and lungs that they call a pharynx. This allows them to form sounds that we are not able to make easily. I cannot understand why natural selection created this anomaly, but as a result, we have a difficult time making ourselves understood to the specimens.

"As previously mentioned, at the beginning of the program, we dissected a broad sample of the specimens, some of each gender, to learn more about them. After we had learned their physiology, we stopped dissecting and simply interrogated them under mind control about their lives and beliefs. When we finished with our questioning and we had no further use for them, we released them back to their time. We erased their memories of our questioning by using our standard mind control process and returned them where we found them. We thought this would create less chance of their leaders learning that they were being studied. This didn't work out so well. It seems some of them were able to break the mind control bond over time. They started remembering and telling others about their experiences while they were abducted. As soon as we discovered this problem, we stopped releasing them after study and just disposed of them."

"Yes, Chancellor FaPa, we almost lost our element of surprise as a result of that mistake," said the Exalted Lord.

"We have built up through hundreds of interrogations an accurate picture of their civilization and their thought processes," said FaPa. "A vast number of them believe in various super beings that are supposed to help them in times of trouble. The interesting thing about these strange beliefs is the depth to which they cling to them. Many of these different belief groups are completely willing to fight and kill anyone who does not agree with them.

"In addition to their groupings by super being, they have divided themselves into various other groupings called countries. This is somewhat like the division we have in our civilization between Laurasia and Gondwana, our mortal enemies. They seem to try very hard to find excuses to oppress or kill members of other divisions. We have focused on this aspect of their nature as the weakness to exploit in order to destroy their civilization. Director SaSu and I have created a plan for sowing dissention between members of several major groups that believe in different super beings. We are sure that with enough encouragement, we can get the mammals to destroy themselves by the millions with their own weapons of mass destruction that they continue to prolifically invent."

"This concept seems to have become the keystone of our project," said the Exalted Lord. "You had better be correct. Now we would hear from Director SaSu."

"As Chancellor FaPa has recited into the record, we intend to exploit a significant weakness in the mammals of the future," said SaSu. "These are their arbitrary belief structures that they call religions and to which they are dedicated. Those within a given religion seem happy, or in some cases, they are compelled to kill anyone who disagrees with its teachings. We decided to build on an existing war between Muslims and Jews. These two religions are frequently at war without any outside help. We have begun to fan the flames of their conflict, and through covert operations, we are working to draw the more powerful Christian countries into the conflict. Some Christian countries will join the Jews, and different Christian countries will join the Muslims to promote their own agendas. We have sent an agent to the future, around 2010 in their time scale. This agent is our best English speaker, and he has learned two other languages in case he needs them. It seems that there are hundreds of these languages in use. I do not know how they can carry on any commerce with everyone jabbering in a different language."

"What actions have been taken to push the mammals into open warfare?" asked the Exalted Lord. "Why have they not destroyed themselves by now?"

"Our agent, SuHa by name, has infiltrated an organization called al-Qaeda, which is the military arm of the Muslim religion. Al-Qaeda is famous for hit-and-run tactics against any enemy they choose, whether there is a declared war or not between the Muslims and the people they attack. First, SuHa went forward in time to a country called France. He traveled back and forth in time to learn certain details about a particular member of this al-Qaeda organization in France. He used this information to gain the trust of this individual. Unfortunately we then learned that he didn't have much standing in the organization but, using this trust, SuHa set up a higher-level meeting where he gave al-Qaeda a very large sum of legal tender that they call money. We exactly reproduced some of this money to give to them in exchange for an increase in their attacks on the Christian people. These attacks will have very high visibility and will inflame the Christians to retaliate against the Muslims directly. We believe this will push the mammals into an intense local war that will inflame other sectors of the populace to join in. Finally, as the conflict escalates, they will be forced to use weapons that they consider to be weapons of last resort. These weapons not only achieve immediate devastation but will probably render vast amounts of the planet unfit for mammal life for thousands of years. This would make it very easy for us to go to the devastated areas and bring back the resources we need."

"What do you think the probability of success is for your operation?" asked the Exalted Lord.

"These mammals are very unpredictable in stress situations, but we estimate 70 percent probability of success," replied SaSu. "I realize this is not as high as you require, so I personally have tasked SuHa to begin another operation that will almost certainly bring the Muslims into an open conflict with their Jewish neighbors. We will initiate attacks using biological weapons, which the humans particularly despise. This will further inflame the entire civilization of mammals. This operation should raise the probability of success to over 90 percent. We plan to continue along the current path and look for additional triggers to use while the mammals' tension is high. We will add more fuel to the flames at a strategic time, and then our probability of success will be assured."

"Just remember all of our lives depend on your success," pronounced the Exalted Lord. "Why have you not already identified these trigger points you speak of? Increase the urgency of your efforts from their current level. Now we will hear from our sacred scientist, WaTu."

"My role in this project is to determine and implement a practical method to transport oil back from the future," said WaTu. This has been somewhat hampered by the fact that we must keep any knowledge of the reason for the project a complete secret from our people. Some members of my team think that it would be optimal if we could build a pipeline directly from oil storage facilities in the mammal world back to our Laurasian storage facilities. This would require that we open and maintain a permanent hole in the time-space continuum. To date, we do not have the technology to do this, and frankly, if we achieve a breakthrough on this front, I expect it would require more energy to keep a portal open than we could bring back. The next best method is to transmit large oil containers back and forth in time. This is clearly feasible but we have no idea if such a mass transport of material from one time to another will create any negative effects to our time period. We are not concerned if there is damage to the mammal's future time period."

"We are now calculating the optimum size for these containers. We want to get the maximum oil with the least energy expenditure. From hearing the previous two reports, it sounds like this war creation effort in the mammal world will be concluded within the next year. We can have a fully functional transport capability in half of that time, six months."

"Why is this capability not already complete?" asked the Exalted Lord. "We should be able to direct our time portal to the conclusion of the mammal's war and begin harvesting oil right away. The timing for us to begin harvesting oil must be sooner than a year so that we can ensure a smooth transition to actually using the new energy source. What can we do to accomplish this? The current timing is too close to the time we are projected to run out of combustibles."

"Exalted Lord," said WaTu, "we have already begun making the equipment that will convert from using plant material to using oil to generate MaKe. The conversion from burning plant combustibles to burning oil will be simple and quick once we are assured of the success of causing war between the mammal nations. Then we can begin training workers to make the changes.

"Because of our time travel capability, we could move the harvesting point further into the future after the mammals destroy their civilization as you say. But this requires that events in the future reflect our efforts to actually create a war. Currently, a visit to this future time period does not reflect our efforts to disrupt the mammal civilization. To change this, we need to do something that will make our desired war the firm result. After the point when this happens, moving into the future will reveal the war-torn reality. I would suggest that my esteemed colleagues determine an event, a trigger point using their words, in their plan that must occur to ensure that the future reflects war. Once this trigger point is accomplished, then we can begin harvesting oil."

chapter 8

A search of personnel records showed the White Sands facility had two soldiers stationed there that spoke fluent Russian. These men were quickly interviewed for a position on Team T-REX. One was a sixty-three-year-old army major who was due for retirement. He was not considered for the team. The second Russian speaker was a thirty-year-old army captain. Juan Garcia sat completely still, staring at Jonas for a full twenty seconds after Jonas had told him about the job and that his first duty as a member of Team T-REX would be to interview a reptile from the distant past who spoke Russian. "Are you kidding me?" he asked once he got over the initial shock. "Where would you even get a talking reptile?"

You should get ready for several surprises as I fill you in on the function of Team T-REX," said Jonas.

After hearing the full story, Juan was fascinated about what he would be doing as a member of the team. "We will be on the forefront, seeing history being made with everything we do," he said. "It's a great honor, thank for putting me on the team."

Steven met Juan the day after the debriefing on Team T-REX's trip to the past. Juan was short with a dark complexion and black hair that was cut short. They met outside the cell block where the reptile was being held. "Fred Watkins woke up last night," said Steven. "He's able to move slowly, but it may be a long time before he is 100 percent. At least our prisoner is not a killer. We need to find out what toxin it used and if there is an antidote. This is one of our priority questions to ask the prisoner. Then we need to work our way around to outlining the reptile civilization, getting as many details as we can."

Juan said, "Do you think the prisoner and its people know about us? Could you tell me its name again?"

"Its name is YaSi, according to the linguistics team," said Steven. "At this point, we don't understand how they could know so much about us. However, it cannot be a coincidence that the prisoner knows how to speak modern Russian. So that is another priority—to find out how they learned Russian. Let's go in, and you can try to get it to cooperate."

"I brought some water for it," said Juan. "By trying to find out what it needs to eat and drink, we may be able to get started in a cooperative direction."

Juan and Steven entered the cell block of the holding area for the prisoner. To break the ice and generate conversation, Juan offered the creature a drink of water. Juan poured a small amount of water into a glass and offered it to the reptile through the bars. "This is water for you to drink," he said in Russian.

The reptile took the glass in both hands very carefully. "What am I supposed to do with this tiny thing?" asked YaSi.

"What kind of vessel do you require?" asked Juan. "Can you describe it?"

YaSi used his hands to simulate a shape like a small flat bowl.

"I will have something brought in," said Juan.

"Where is my identification medallion?" asked YaSi in a nervous, almost childish manner.

"What are you talking about?" replied Juan.

"It is a black medallion that is about three inches in diameter," explained YaSi. It has all of my personal information encoded on it. It was put around my neck by my father when I was three years old and updated every year. It was the only time I ever met my mother and father."

"I don't know where it is. It must have come off your neck during your capture," said Juan. "I will personally look for it and return it if I find it."

"Thank you," said YaSi. "Also, I was wondering if you intended to execute me through starvation."

Juan held back a laugh, not sure if YaSi was making a joke, "No, the problem is we don't know what to feed you. Can you describe what we should bring you to eat?"

"Our agents, when they spend an extended time in your era, say they eat something called corn and also greens," said YaSi. "However, I can try whatever you bring to me to see if it is suitable."

"What do you mean by your agents?" asked Juan.

YaSi explained, "We Laurasians have been studying your civilization for many years. People of your time have been brought to Laurasia to be studied, and we have learned four of your languages over the time, though I was only able to learn one."

"Why have you been doing this?" asked Juan. "More importantly, how have you been doing this?"

"It is a Laurasian's highest duty to study and learn everything we can. Our sacred scientist learned the secret of moving through time about twenty years ago. We have been studying the mammal civilization ever since we accidently discovered it."

Steven asked through Juan, "Why have your agents not made contact with us in all this time?"

"I do not know," answered YaSi. "I guess the Exalted Lord YaKo does not allow it. Maybe he does not want to change your civilization by intruding."

"Why did you attack our man back in your time?" asked Juan.

"Humans are not allowed to run loose in Laurasia. I assumed

that the creature was a specimen brought back for study that had wandered off and was lost. I intended to take it back to its habitat so it would not starve or be attacked by a large dinosaur. Also, I didn't understand the purpose of all the equipment there. I was afraid the human would break it. It was the first time I ever actually saw a human, but this one looked different because it had something covering its body like the things you are using now to cover your body. I had only seen videos of humans with no body covering before that. I only stunned it with my projectile gun so that I could find out where it was supposed to be."

"Your stun dart almost killed him," said Juan. "He only woke up last night, and he still is very weak."

"That is because someone knocked me senseless, and I was not able to give him the reviving medicine. It is also possible that the dart was too strong. It was designed for use with antisocials in our society. I have read that humans are very fragile in some respects."

"Do you have some of the reviving medicine with you?" asked Juan. "Can I try to give it to him now?"

"Yes, there is a container of small white pellets in the stock of the projectile gun that was taken from me. It is too late to be of use to the mammal I shot."

"How do you use it?" asked Juan.

"Just put one of the small pellets under your tongue. It will dissolve fairly quickly and help the target's body eliminate the dart toxin. At least that is how it works on Laurasians."

"Thank you. We will analyze it to be sure it is safe for humans," said Juan. "Please tell us about your civilization."

"Our glorious government of Laurasia rules the entire northern continent of the planet. We have the best and most efficient government possible. We are ruled by one man, the Exalted Lord YaKo. The High Council of Laurasia administers his rule through its three members, the chancellor, the director of the conformance force, also known as confors, and the sacred scientist. Our mortal enemies that live in Gondwana in the southern hemisphere are ruled by a ridiculously weak group of old women called the Council of Mothers."

Juan could see from his posture and way of speaking that YaSi felt strong nationalistic pride in his country.

"Our race has evolved over a period of three hundred thousand years from our ancestors, which you call dinosaurs. About one hundred and fifty thousand years ago, our ancestors left the overcrowded swamps near the great waters, moving inland to seek a better, healthier food supply and environment. It is a fact that in this flat, open, shrub-infested land, it was easier to survive, walking fully upright to see around better so our body configuration changed."

"This is similar to the evolution of humans and why we walk on two legs," said Steven.

At this point, the conversation was interrupted by a soldier arriving with the bowl, a bottle of water and a salad in a plastic container. Finally, YaSi was able to drink water and eat.

"Let us start where we left off before," said Steven when YaSi finished eating. "Do you know when your species diverged from dinosaurs?"

"We have traced our family tree back to the genus you call *Hadrosaurus*," said YaSi. "The first identified branch away from *Hadrosaurus* was a creature you know as a *Parksosaurus*. It walked on two legs and was a warm-blooded herbivore of vastly improved intelligence. As our ancestors progressed, they began to use their front limbs to hold things they wanted to take along with them. First, this was food to take back to their nests, and later, it became tools to accomplish certain tasks like cutting branches off of shrubs to eat."

"When did your species evolve into its present form?" asked Steven.

"About 100 thousand years ago we began gradually using simple tools, such as flat, oval stones with rough edges used to cut off twigs and other greens. Then our ancestors began to use more complicated tools, such as rounded stones for hammers and crushers," said YaSi. "As they progressed further, our ancestors developed tools to cultivate the land, which created the need to settle in one place. The benefit was they could grow the specific kinds of food they liked the best. Nice tender green leaves, nuts, and berries are our preferred food. Our ancestors domesticated other species of dinosaurs to help them in their work. They used some to help plow new planting grounds and others to drag heavy loads. We have even bred a species that is just the correct size to ride on. As our ancestors began using more complex tools, their brain size increased and along with it, their manual dexterity. The concept of the wheel was developed, allowing us to make land vehicles that allowed us to move even more cargo when pulled by larger domesticated dinosaurs."

Steven suggested to Juan that they move the discussion to an interrogation room where they could easily record what YaSi was saying. The guards assigned to escort YaSi to the new room stood far back, their guns pointed directly at the creature. Unfortunately, handcuffs did not work on YaSi because they slipped off his small hands. The guards had to be satisfied with manacles on his feet.

"Is the race living in Gondwana the same as your race?" asked Steven through Juan.

"We spread out more and more over Laurasia as our population grew," answered YaSi. "Our land has many places where the sea extends inland, creating bays that make traveling between certain cities difficult. The area where you captured me is one such area. The water known in your language as the Bear Paw Sea almost completely separates the western mountains of our land from the main body of land to the east. Boats were built to carry food and cargo across the sea to facilitate trade. Laurasia is a huge country, so the use of boats became quite common to carry large loads. Occasionally, these boats were caught up in the large storms that periodically sweep over the water, and in this way, we accidently populated Gondwana. After several generations of castaways had lived and prospered in Gondwana, an adventurous person decided to try to find the land of his origins. Laurasia was rediscovered, and over time, some limited commerce developed between the two large continents.

"Our race multiplies rapidly when conditions are favorable. Females lay as many as ten eggs at a time. They all hatch into either males or females, depending on the incubation temperature chosen by the potential parents. Within a thousand years, our race was scattered over the entire planet."

"So at this point in your history, Laurasia was made up of small, scattered farming communities?" asked Steven.

"Yes, and it seems that the most successful ones were those controlled by a single overlord who made the important decisions. As the size of the farming settlements grew, the lords of the villages began to arm their male subjects with weapons, such as clubs and pointed sticks, to protect their land. Warfare began when one village lord took over another village lord's land by force. Our technology increased rapidly thanks to the efforts of our holy scientists and the competition between the village lords who financed them."

"You are saying the settlements became bigger and therefore generated more wealth for the lords to use to educate and hire more scientists," said Juan.

"Yes. The additional amounts of wealth that became available due to the larger land holdings enabled the lords to hire more and better scientists," replied YaSi. "They rapidly discovered new technology, such as methods of forming metal into useful tools, and then more deadly weapons. The process went on for several thousand years."

"How did your civilization transition to the type of city life we saw in the city by the Bear Paw Sea?" asked Steven through Juan.

"Since the Lords held the majority of the wealth, people

wanted to live near them to sell their goods and services," explained YaSi. "Our habitats have always been underground and for more people to live around the lord, the habitats began to be dug deeper and deeper below the ground. These clusters of habitats became our cities. A long time later, scientists discovered how to generate and use MaKe power to light our underground homes and commercial offices. MaKe led to mechanical digging machines, enabling us to dig our living spaces even deeper. Some cities are as deep as twenty-five levels underground. In addition, the capabilities of MaKe power led to communication over long distances. With improved communication, a few lords were able to take over vast areas of land. The lords were constantly fighting for larger holdings and more power. The people were constantly being killed or enslaved to the point that everyone became dissatisfied and desperate."

"Did your civilization find a way to solve this problem?" asked Juan.

"In a way," answered YaSi. "We currently have two different types of government, one in Laurasia and one in Gondwana. The Laurasian government is clearly better."

"Why do you say that?" asked Juan.

"In Gondwana, a lord became so powerful that he took over the whole southern continent," YaSi continued. "Unfortunately, he died when his designated heir was still only two years old. His mate became the effective power over Gondwana, aided by the grand marshal of the deceased lord's army. Through subterfuge and female wiles, she convinced the grand marshal to support her concept for the government. They divided their country into eight provinces, and each province chose an elderly woman for their ruling council. She had to have at least one litter of children to be eligible, and together, these women try to rule their land."

MIAMI, FLORIDA

Khaliq Abujamal stood in the line, nervously shifting his weight from one foot to the other. He reflected on the events of the last few months that had led him to stand in line in Miami, Florida, and go through immigration to enter the country of the Great Satan, the United States of America. Khaliq had left the hotel room that fateful night in Kabul with more money than he had ever dreamed of. He would be lying if he didn't admit to a brief moment of temptation to take the large black suitcase and disappear as a rich man. However, within moments, he was joined by the three al-Qaeda agents that had been his backup for the mission and were practically the only friends he had.

Khaliq was not a typical al-Qaeda recruit in the sense that he had no horror tales in his past that had turned him into a bitter terrorist. He actually just had the luck of being born into a terrorist family in Egypt. As a result, all of his family members were dead before he reached twelve years of age. He never knew his father and could only vaguely remember his mother. He grew up in terrorist training camps in Pakistan and later Afghanistan. He received the standard religious training of extremist Muslims and a solid education in terrorist fighting tactics.

In 1979, the director of the camp where Khaliq was living at the time decided to set up several secret terrorist cells in Kabul to resist what he called the Russian intrusion into Afghanistan. Khaliq was assigned by this training camp director to form one of these cells by picking four other trainees from the camp to work in his cell. All five cell members went individually into Kabul and found jobs and lodgings before any of them made contact. Now forty years later, Khaliq was the only one of them still alive.

Over time, Khaliq married and had a son and a daughter to reinforce his cover as a bellman at the Safi Landmark Hotel, a simple but quite stable job. Khaliq thought he loved his family, but he never clearly understood the concept based on his own history. His cell had kept its identity secret even during the rule of the Taliban. This remained true even after al-Qaeda was formed by the same people who had been financing the training camp, and Khaliq found himself a member with seniority of al-Qaeda. He always thought it funny that al-Qaeda and the Taliban, both dedicated Muslim organizations, did not trust each other. In fact, he was not even sure if he was really a Muslim, but his life as a terrorist seemed preordained. It was all he knew, and he was determined to succeed in his given profession.

Khaliq was somewhat surprised when he was chosen to lead the mission to destroy the Rose Bowl on worldwide television. He supposed that returning from a questionable meeting in a hotel room with fifty million US dollars may have helped. Originally, he assumed al-Qaeda would activate sleeper agents that were already in the United States. However, leadership finally decided to use a special team that was secret even from the existing organization in America. Khaliq had a single contact in this organization if he needed any unexpected assistance. The contact knew nothing about Khaliq except a fictitious name, a general description, and the fact that the contact was there to provide anything Khaliq requested.

Khaliq hated to give up his job at the hotel. He had worked there for thirty years. However, he was a soldier, and al-Qaeda had given him enough money for his family to live well for approximately one year, the time he would be gone. His wife knew nothing of his mission, only that he would be out of the country on a job that provided the money she would receive each month.

Each member of the five-man team arrived in the United States through a different city. They had been picked partially because they had a reasonable ability to speak English, and thus, they were expected to arrive on their own at a house in a residential neighborhood of Santa Monica, California. This single house, rented in the name of the Compton Construction Company, would be their living and staging area. Everyone in the group was picked to look somewhat alike. They would dress similarly in work clothes and wear the same cut of short beard and haircut. They would come and go from the house in random groups in an attempt to confuse anyone watching the house about the number of people living there.

Again, following instructions from Khaliq's sleeper contact, an al-Qaeda agent in the Los Angeles area arranged for the Compton Construction Company, known as 3C, to win the bid for a scheduled summer renovation of the Rose Bowl facility. 3C was a six-year-old construction company run by a sleeper agent with its offices on Hawthorne Boulevard in Compton, California. However, the owner of 3C had no idea who would actually perform the work at the Rose Bowl even though he had won the bid. This owner was told never to go back to the Rose Bowl or to contact anyone about the work to be done there after winning the bid.

As Khaliq reached the front of the line, he took out a Saudi Arabian passport with the name Ikram Kader. "Mr. Kader, what is your reason for traveling to the United States?" asked the immigration officer.

WHITE SANDS, NEW MEXICO

"What do you mean the Gondwanians try to rule their land?" Juan asked YaSi.

"The Laurasian government is superior because the Exalted Lord tells us very clearly what to do. There is no confusion, and no one questions him," answered YaSi. "I do not see how the Gondwanians can be ruled with so many people in control. It must be chaos."

"How did the government of Laurasia come to its present form?" asked Juan.

"After Gondwana became ruled by the Council of Mothers, there was virtually no more fighting in their land. For some unexplained reason, they suddenly went through a period of great prosperity and prolific invention. Their scientists invented flying machines of several kinds. Some fly in the air, and some even fly above the atmosphere. The Lords in Laurasia feared that with their new technologies, Gondwana would try to invade Laurasia. By this time in our history, there were four very strong lords ruling most of Laurasia. They created a treaty of cooperation. The strongest lord was declared the Exalted Lord, and the others became the prototype of the high council. When the existing Exalted Lord dies, the high council picks one from their group to become the new Exalted Lord, and his position is permanently replaced in the high council by a member from the class the recently promoted leader came from. Our race has a long life span, so this affords great stability in the government."

"Does this form of government meet the needs of the Laurasian people?" asked Juan as he rose from his chair and began to pace around the interrogation room.

"It provides clear direction of how we should live our lives," answered YaSi. "The Exalted Lord dispenses direction to everyone in the country. Through this direction, he also provides the opportunity to join ourselves with the universal knowledge base when we die."

"So you have religions like Christianity or Buddhism as we do?" commented Steven.

"Yes, but I think not as violent and dogmatic as your religions," said YaSi. "Over time, we put all of our faith in science as it has been instrumental in improving our standard of life.

We attend mandatory classes every seventh day to learn about how we evolved from our ancestors, how to prepare our spirit to join the scientific knowledge base, and what science is currently doing to make our lives better in the future. Custom teaches us that if we live obediently when we die, our personal knowledge merges with the great scientific knowledge base. There is no further use for our bodies. In fact, our physical bodies are the concentration of all of the sins and mistakes we made during our lifetimes. The ritual we observe to mark death is designed to dispose of this corruption as quickly and simply as possible. The closest living male relative takes the body of the deceased to a sacred scavenging pit. This holds fifty to one hundred devil mammals called *Alphadon* in your science books. They are kept near the point of starvation. They are an omnivorous, marsupial species that is only about a foot long with sharp claws and teeth. The dead body is dropped into the pit of devil mammals. They strip the soft tissue and all trace of corruption from the body. A day later, the relative returns to collect the purified bones from the pit after the mammals are temporarily driven from it. The last step in our funeral ritual is for the male relative to deliver the cleaned and purified bones to science during one of the seventh-day meetings to be burned as fuel to assist in the generation of MaKe. The corrupt part of a person's body is consumed by mammals, and all of this corruption is concentrated within the bodies of the devil mammals.

"The only mammals in our world are the devil mammals, which literally live off of the sins and corruption of our people. Since evil is concentrated within their bodies, they are the embodiment of everything bad to our world. We were very surprised to see a world ruled by mammals that was not in chaos."

"Thanks for the information," said Juan. "You've been most helpful."

"It is the sacred duty of Laurasians to acquire and share

knowledge. It has been a righteous experience to talk to you. Will you share with me about your culture?"

"We must go now to talk to our superiors, and two of our doctors will come to give you a physical examination," said Juan. "Maybe we can share information after that."

"Will you go back in time again and contact my people?" asked YaSi. "I would be happy to introduce you to an intermediate-level official in the Laurasian government."

Jonas McCormick was completely shocked when Steven and Juan reported to the group everything that they had learned from the reptile. "I wonder if they are all so forthcoming with information about their people," said Jonas.

"I came away with the impression that it is a genetic characteristic or some religious tenet of their race to openly answer whatever questions someone in authority asks them," answered Juan. "This creature seems so open and friendly; I wonder why they have never contacted one of our governments directly."

"So do you think it was telling us the truth?" asked Jonas.

"It will take some time for me to learn how to read these creatures' inadvertent actions to determine if they are telling the truth or lies," said Juan. "YaSi's grasp of our language is limited enough that he may not always be saying exactly what he intends to say. In interrogation, we learn to look for certain tells that a person may have unconsciously. I am sure YaSi's tells are completely different from those of a human. On the videos of the initial interviews with YaSi, I saw that when he was first put in the cell and was frustrated, his stomach coloring showed a broad range of reds and oranges. Also, the calmer he got, the dimmer the stomach color was. During our interview, I also think I picked up a hint of pheromones that seem to change with his moods. However, at this point, I would guess he gave us true, open answers to our questions. I would have to say I believe him."

"So it looks like the original objectives we set in the debrief meeting yesterday still stand," said Jonas. "I guess we should look for someone to speak French or Chinese for the last security member of Team T-REX. That should maximize the probability that you can communicate with any reptile you come across."

"I can hold my own with Mandarin," said Ellie. "I spent most of my army career in intelligence. The army sent me to several advanced schools, and I learned to speak and read Mandarin fluently. If the reptiles went to the trouble to learn a Chinese language, it surely would be Mandarin. I suggest we only need to look for a French speaker."

Jonas responded, "From an equipment modification point of view, we are ready to send you back. So you can go as soon as we find the last new security member of the team."

chapter 9

MISSION 3 FROM WHITE SANDS

The vessel was really crowded when they all climbed aboard. It had been built to only hold four people. Until the team could make more permanent arrangements, they secured Juan with rope to the ladder while he sat on thick padding on the floor. He had been a true gentleman to let George Deveraux have the spare seat. George was an alpha-male type and a gunnery sergeant in the US Marines. He spoke perfect French because his mother had been born and raised in France. She met George's father when he was stationed in the consulate in Marseille. George was six feet tall and 220 pounds of bullheadedness that had gotten stronger over his forty-nine years.

As the inside of the vessel reentered the visible spectrum, George said, "Now that was definitely an E-ticket ride."

"Yeah, I'm glad I didn't do that on a full stomach," murmured Juan.

After they completed the transition to the past, they got busy setting up a more formal camp than they had the last time. The site was surrounded by a ten-foot metal fence made of light titanium. The fence was connected to a portable electrical generator to ensure nothing could sneak into their camp. There was only one gate in the fence, making the site easy to defend. Juan and George planned to build a fifteen-foot-high wooden watchtower in the middle of the camp as soon as George quit complaining about the heat. Dave also got started on the experiments Jonas had asked him to complete.

Steven and Ellie set up a very high-gain antenna on a twenty-foot pole as part of their job to record and find the locations of the radio transmissions. The antenna activated a digital recorder and direction-finding equipment each time a signal was detected. It recorded the message as well as the direction it came from. They both had smaller antennas attached to their bikes. In this way, they could triangulate where the transmissions originated.

They rode out as soon as the initial work to set up the camp was complete. Their clothes were wet from perspiration from the work, so the breeze from their motion felt good. The sun was high, and there were no clouds in the sky. The landscape was mostly miniature pine shrubs and several other versions of beautiful flowering shrubs. The butterflies seen on the last trip were gone.

The electric bikes made so little noise that Steven had to keep looking back to see if Ellie was still there. They had agreed to set their ear communicators to mute so they did not announce their presence prematurely. If they heard someone broadcast on their frequency, then they knew that others could also hear them. Standard military hand signals seemed a better way to communicate as long as they could see each other. They had decided to retrace their previous route so they could find the reptile people's road again. This made traveling faster, especially as they got closer to the damper areas near the coast. As they approached the place that they thought of as a guard post, everything seemed the same. There were a few more tri-wheelers and a few less reptile people visible. All seemed quiet and orderly as before.

Now they needed to figure out how to get around this guard station that blocked them from going farther on the path with their bikes. They dismounted and set up the portable recorder and frequency scanner to monitor transmissions. Ellie stayed to monitor the equipment and protect their bikes. Steven went ahead on foot to try to find a passage through the dense foliage that was out of sight of the guard post.

As he wandered through the shrubs and ferns in roughly the correct direction, Steven realized that he was going to have to cut brush out of the way in some places. He started quietly clearing a path when he encountered blockage. He worked his way around so that he was about a quarter of a mile beyond the guardhouse when he heard quiet hissing sounds nearby. Wiping away the sweat in his eyes, he stopped his hacking and concentrated on finding the sound again. Just as he was about to give up and go back to work, he heard it. Steven decided to creep in the direction of the noise to find the source. As he slipped through the foliage, he saw some movement. He stopped abruptly, surprised at what he saw.

His face went flush with a bit of embarrassment when he realized he was looking at the private procreation activities of these two reptile people. The pair, one with and one without the orange and red markings on the stomach had set a shallow, three foot diameter container on the ground. The container looked like plastic but probably was a form of processed dinosaur hide. The female was sitting on the container. The male was crouched by her, rubbing her back and stomach as if trying to help her produce the eggs. Apparently, he had already taken care of his fertilization duties, and he was now providing moral support. There were already nine eggs in the container, and it looked like she was having trouble with the one she was working on.

After about ten more minutes, the pair seemed satisfied that they had completed their task. The two reptiles stood, put a lid over the eggs in the container, grabbed the container on opposite sides, and picked it up. They headed in the direction of the building Team T-REX had been calling a guard station. From what YaSi had told Juan, the eggs would now need to be held at a stable warm temperature for about one week.

Apparently, the guard station held more than soldiers. It also seemed to house their families and medical facilities as well.

Steven completed his task and went back to find Ellie. "Did you hear anything?" he asked.

"I recorded two messages while you were gone," said Ellie. "What took you so long? I was getting worried. Did you have to make a path?"

"Actually, I did for all practical purposes," Steven said and laughed. "But I also came upon a happy couple making babies out in the woods. The female laid her eggs in a natural setting but into a special container, and then they carried the container into the guard station to be incubated."

"I guess everything gets more complicated as the level of civilization increases," said Ellie. "No more simple nests and using body heat to incubate the eggs."

"At least they sought out natural surroundings to begin the process," said Steven. "We should be on the move. I cut away some shrubs so we can pass, but I don't think it will give away our presence to the reptiles."

The pair resumed their exploration on the path after they went around the guard building. They had been moving in a westerly direction for over an hour when Ellie saw movement off to the right of the path. There were several large creatures moving toward them. "Look ... another type of dinosaur. Can you tell what it is from here?" asked Ellie.

Steven replied, "No, let's get a closer look, and there is plenty of light to get some good pictures. Look how big they are!" Steven recognized the dinosaurs as *Edmontosaurus*, a large plant-eating, duck-billed dinosaur dated by paleontologists to have lived in the late Cretaceous period. They had short arms and long, pointed tails, three-toed, hoofed feet, and webbed fingers on their hands. Their heads were flat and sloping down to a wide toothless beak. But their cheek pouches were lined with hundreds of closely packed teeth to grind food. They walked on two legs, but they could use their front legs to support themselves when they were eating low foliage. Their most astonishing feature was their forty-two-foot length.

Soon after they left the dinosaurs, they caught their first glimpse of the city by the Bear Paw Sea that Ellie had seen using the observation balloon. It was not very impressive to see from the outside. The buildings looked like unfinished foundations with people walking between them. When they were still about a mile from the city, they left the path and worked their way through the dense foliage in a southwesterly direction on foot. As they neared the sea, they came upon another road that more or less followed the coastline. This one was paved with large flat stones and had frequent traffic moving both north and south. There were some really big tri-wheelers and some tri-wheelers that looked like the ones they were accustomed to seeing on the other path, except these were painted in bright colors. Some had only one passenger while others were filled with five or sometimes six people. "This must be their equivalent of a freeway," said Steven. "Let's leave the bikes hidden here and follow this road, hiding in the foliage along the way. We'll go toward the city as long as we can stay hidden."

As they approached the city, they were surprised that there were no outlying buildings, and the brush was still thick enough to hide them. They walked over a bit of a rise, and there lay the city only two hundred yards away. Each individual building was separated by wide avenues that were full of reptiles walking or riding in the tri-wheelers. During this walk toward the city, they began to hear more frequent radio transmissions. They could not understand anything that was said, but they carefully recorded as much as they could. At one point when they were both focused on the recorder, they heard a rustle in the brush. "Down," hissed Ellie. "I think someone is coming." As they lay on the damp ground, they heard the sound of footsteps more clearly. Something was coming toward them.

Suddenly, two reptiles, a male and a female walking close together, stepped past some shrubs and looked down directly at Steven and Ellie. The female and Ellie cried out in surprise at the same time. Steven stayed down on the ground and tried to look nonthreatening. In Chinese, Ellie said, "Do you speak Chinese?"

Both of the reptiles looked stunned and uncomprehending, so she tried in English, "Do you speak English?"

The male reptile hissed something that sounded like yes. Then the female said with a terrible accent, "PuFo, how brilliant that one of them can speak two languages. Do you know any more? PuFo and I are learning Russian."

"No, I only know two languages," said Ellie. "I would really like to learn to speak your language."

In the manner that Steven and Ellie were beginning to realize was a basic, genetic characteristic of the reptile people the female began to blast out her thoughts in a rapid-fire stream of words. "My name is MeMo, and my life mate is called PuFo," said the female reptile. What are you called? How did you get here? How exciting it is to actually meet humans."

Ellie said, "This is Steven, and I'm called Ellie. It's very nice to meet you. We came directly from the future."

"Of course you came from the future. All talking mammals come from the future," said PuFo. "Who brought you here and was careless enough to let you travel alone?"

"You don't understand," explained Steven in a patient tone of voice. "We came from the future by ourselves to meet with representatives of your government. We came to share information about our respective civilizations. Isn't that a primary goal of your culture?"

"Yes, it is," said MeMo. "But I don't know what we should do with you right now. I guess we should start by taking you to our habitat. Please walk close together and follow me. PuFo will follow behind as if he is guarding you. Mammals are not allowed to walk around freely in Laurasia."

As they walked into the city, they drew the stares of most of the reptiles, but no one stopped them or bothered them.

The buildings began at the same place in both directions as if someone had drawn a straight line in the dirt and said the city began here. The streets were laid out in a regular grid pattern and extended as far as they could see on the right, left, and straight ahead. It was a strange view because none of the buildings blocked the view of people and vehicles using the streets.

A reptile with a black medallion hanging from a chain around its neck stood at each intersection to direct traffic. They seemed to have absolute control of the mass of people and vehicles moving through their intersections. There were no sidewalks; however, the people generally moved in a single direction on each side of the street, and the vehicles moved in lanes in the center of the street. The overall effect was very organized and efficient.

After about twenty minutes of walking into the city, they had passed sixteen intersections when MeMo turned left.

"How do you know where you are? Do the streets have names?" Ellie asked.

"Of course," said MeMo. "See that symbol on the poles on each corner of the intersection? It says we are on Eighty-Fourth Avenue. The street we just left was Mu Street. We have fifty syllables in our language arranged in a specific order like your alphabet. The symbol *Mu* is close to the middle of the order. Combinations of these fifty symbols in pairs, threes, or fours make up all of the words in our language. Also, the streets are numbered zero to ninety-nine going east and west. The avenues are called *Fa* through *Yu*. It is a very simple system, and we know where we are all the time. All of the cities in Laurasia are designated like this, though larger cities have more numbered streets. And for the lettered streets, we start over with the alphabet, using two syllables together, still in the proper order."

After they passed two more intersections, MeMo turned onto a ramp leading down into a building. "The first five levels are commercial stores and workshops," said MeMo. "Our habitat is eleven levels below the ground level. In our society, we consider the deepest habitats to be the most desirable. I am sorry, but PuFo and I have been mated and working for only two years, so our habitat is not on such a desirable level."

"Do you have elevators in your buildings?" asked Steven.

"What is an elevator?" asked MeMo.

"A mechanical device to take a person vertically up or down in buildings with many levels," answered Steven.

"Why would you want to do that?" asked MeMo. "Ah, I think I understand. Your legs are smaller than and not as strong as ours. It is no different for us to walk on flat ground or on sloped ground due to the strength and structure of our legs. At least that is true as long as the slope is not too steep. I guess we have no need for an elevator. This is so exciting. We both have studied mammals and the future civilization for over seven years. I never believed we would be lucky enough to actually meet two mammals in person."

When they reached the eleventh level, MeMo turned right and went down a long hall about one hundred feet. They came to a door with a number symbol on it, but Steven and Ellie could not read it. MeMo opened the door without the apparent use of a key. Ellie asked, "Do you leave your door unlocked when you are away?"

"Oh, no," said MeMo. "The door automatically detects my hand or PuFo's hand and opens to let us in." The habitat was spacious and open with nine-foot-high ceilings. The walls were a light brown. There were mosaic designs inlaid into the wall made up of colored stones. An area was divided from the main room by a four-foot-high wall. Many pillows and blankets that looked like they were made of some kind of soft leather were lying around. The top of the wall was decorated with potted ferns growing prolifically. The furniture displayed wonderful craftsmanship in contoured, polished stone with a beautiful reddish grain pattern. The chairs were slightly different shapes than Steven and Ellie were used to seeing, but they matched the different shape of the reptiles' bodies. There were several tables of various sizes also made of polished stone. The largest table had a single circular shape for the tabletop with beautiful, carved stone attached for legs. The light was dim, and the air was cool and a little damp. "Your living space is beautiful," said Ellie. "I see you don't have anything made of wood."

"What is wood?" asked MeMo.

"A building material we use quite extensively," answered Ellie. "It comes from trees."

"What are trees?" asked MeMo. "Ah, there is so much to learn about your world."

"Very large plants," said Ellie. "Some can grow over one hundred feet tall, and some are over thirty feet around. Like a fern but the trunk and branches are thicker and stronger. Does that mean you do not have trees in your world?"

"Actually, I have heard of such things because I am a teacher of biology at the advanced level," said MeMo. "We are not to talk of them because they no longer exist. They were burned as fuel to generate MaKe along with all the other shrubs and other combustibles.

"What is MaKe?" asked Steven.

"It is contained electromagnetic plasma that we use to power virtually everything in our world," said MeMo. "Our scientists figured out how to generate the contained plasma, how to transport it where needed, and how to store it in special batteries several hundred years ago. We generate the MaKe with special generators that use heat and catalysts."

"PuFo and I were born into the holy science class. See our white medallions. We are researchers and teachers of biology. We possibly could use the main branches of some species of ferns in place of trees, but the material is in extremely short supply. Whatever we have must be reserved for burning to generate MaKe. The government has not mentioned it publically, but PuFo and I think, based on our own informal observations, we may be running out of combustibles, which would be a disaster for our civilization."

OAXACA, MEXICO

The little group of Mexicans sat huddled in the back of a midsized commercial truck. There were twenty-two people ranging in age from eighteen to forty-six. About fifteen were men, and the rest were women. No children were present. The back of the truck was sweltering hot and the entire group had been locked in there for thirty-seven hours with only the food and water some had thought to bring with them. They were given three flashlights and three empty pails as they entered the truck in Oaxaca, Mexico, on a hot April evening. They were told to conserve the batteries of the flashlights because once the trip had begun; the back of the truck would stay locked.

The truck drove as fast as the poorly maintained back roads would allow. It was quite a miserable trip for the people in the back, but the coyote had told them that it was too easy for the Federales to spot them if they traveled on the main highway. If Federales discovered them, they would be expected to pay several hundred US dollars in bribe money to continue their journey, or else they would be taken back to their home village. They had paid the coyote 1,500 dollars each for the complete trip from Oaxaca to Ojinaga, Mexico, across the border to Presidio, Texas, and then on to Denver, Colorado.

None of refugees could afford to come up with any more cash until they found work in the United States. Also, the coyote did not want to share any money the passengers still had with the Federales because he expected to extort the rest from them when they arrived at the border. As many of the passengers became motion sick, the three buckets were not large enough to hold the required volume. Two of the men had pocket knives, which they used to gouge a hole in the wooden floor of the truck near the back door. Only the solid waste remained in the buckets, the rest was poured through the hole. The real problem for the ragged group was the lack of drinking water. Most of them were severely dehydrated by the end of the first day.

Eventually, the truck's journey came to an end just at the outskirts of Ojinaga. Those who were still strong enough to walk helped the others out of the truck. The coyote gave the passengers some drinking water, bread, and cheese. The truck was parked beside an abandoned farmhouse in which the little group was allowed to sleep until it was time to walk to Presidio. At about 11:00 p.m., a different coyote awakened them and gave each of them a backpack that weighed about forty pounds. The coyote told them that instead of his usual two-hundred-dollar tip to lead them across the Rio Grande River, they would need to carry the backpack. The coyote told them delivering the backpacks to a man on the other side should be considered the most important thing they had ever done in their lives. If they lost any backpacks, there would be severe consequences for the whole group.

The new coyote introduced himself as Jose. "There are men in Texas who do not want to allow foreigners to come to their country," said Jose. "Since the US government has not been able to stop the flow of people, those men decided to take matters into their own hands. At night, they roam the border areas in small groups, looking for people trying to cross the river and shoot them. While we are on route to Presidio, here are the rules. We must walk nine miles to get to the rest site on the other side of the river. Everyone will follow me single file with no talking unless there is an emergency.

"We will be walking on a fairly concealed path most of the time, so we should not run into any vigilantes, but if we do, run for your lives when I tell you and stay close to me. If anyone is wounded, someone else must pick up their backpack.

"If anyone finds us along the route and they identify themselves as INS or Border Patrol, hide your backpack and surrender to them. Do not under any circumstances tell them I am the guide. Just say that you are trying to sneak into the United States by yourselves. The worst that will happen in this situation is that they will return all of us to Mexico. If you have not told them who I am, they will also take me back to Mexico as one of you, and I will be able to lead you across the river at another time. If anyone becomes so tired they cannot go on, give your backpack to someone else to carry. The group will not stop to wait for you, so do not become too tired or you are on your own.

"When we get to the rest place in the United States, someone will collect the backpacks. If there is the correct number of backpacks when we arrive, your group will make the connection with your ride to Denver. Before you ask what is in the backpacks, I am too smart to have asked. I suggest you do the same. Now let's go."

The path wound through very rough badlands for about four miles and then sloped down toward the Rio Grande River. The river's gentle current was cool and only knee-deep. The little group was beginning to relax as they walked out of the river toward the woodland on the north side. Just as the last person, a forty-nine-year-old man who was struggling to keep up stepped out of the water, a shot rang out, and he fell to the ground and did not move again. The coyote pulled out a handgun and shot several bullets in the direction that the shot had come from. Then he yelled for the group to run as fast as they could into the woods until he told them they could stop.

About ten minutes later, Jose stopped and called to the group to gather around him and be quiet. As luck would have it, there were only two people missing, the old man who was shot and a young woman they apparently lost during the dash through the trees. "Okay, let's get going before the people who shot at us at the river come looking for us," said Jose. An hour and a half later, the tired group gathered in a farmhouse just outside Presidio, Texas. An overweight Latino named Antonio came to the house to pick up the backpacks. "We were lucky this time. The vigilantes found us and shot one of the people, but the rest did well getting away from them," said Jose. "We only lost one girl in the woods, so you get twenty more backpacks, and that means you owe me four thousand dollars. How many more of these backpacks will you need carried across?"

"I need at least one hundred more before I can take off for home in Los Angeles," said Antonio. "Then I get my payday, and I can afford to buy my family a little house in Riverside. My wife will be so happy I might get laid."

Mission 3 from White Sands

"How can your civilization run out of combustible material? There is so much foliage outside the city," said Steven. "If it extends over most of Laurasia, there should be plenty of this plant life to burn."

"I am afraid you don't understand the extent of the problem," said PuFo. "There are over six hundred thousand people in SoMu. This is the capital city of Laurasia, but it is small compared to most of the other cities. There are twenty-six major cities in Laurasia bigger than SoMu. All of Laurasia has a population of just fewer than fifty-six million people. The amount of electricity we consume every year is astronomical. On a rotation of five years, work details clear 20 percent of the combustibles from all lands in Laurasia. They take more than can grow in five years to replace what was taken according to our estimates. We told the head of our department last year but have not heard a response."

"Why don't you ask your department head when you will hear something?" asked Ellie. "A year without a response doesn't seem reasonable."

"Oh, no," hissed MeMo. "That would be totally inappropriate. Our superiors have infinite wisdom and should never be questioned or hurried to answer. We must wait until those above us in the governing structure decide what response is acceptable."

"Do you mean you can never question superiors no matter how wrong they may be?" asked Steven, somewhat shocked.

"Absolutely not," said MeMo. "About a year ago, I pointed out a small grammar error in a report prepared by my department head. The next day, we were notified that the conformance force had gone to our nest in the hospital and destroyed all of the eggs we had prepared for hatching. PuFo was most distressed with me. I must be very careful to control my overactive mind and mouth. If I am guilty of another transgression, we may not be allowed to ever have any young."

"What a cruel punishment," gasped Ellie.

"Oh, no," said MeMo. "The teachings of the first Exalted Lord, PaKo, say there can be no civilization if the people question their leaders."

"Can you have young now?" asked Ellie.

"Not now, but in a few months, we can prepare another nest," said MeMo.

"PuFo, are all of the Laurasian cities along the coast?" asked Steven.

"No, actually the largest cities are in the central drier parts of our continent," said PuFo. "Pardon me if I don't talk as much as MeMo. Her English is much better than mine. Too much speaking in English gives me a headache. Our people prefer the drier parts of our land because most of the coastline of Laurasia is swampland and populated by large dinosaurs. The large herbivores attract the large dangerous predators. Also, with our habitats underground, we would prefer to not come home to find our habitats filled with water. That is what would likely happen in most coastal land. The type of ground this city is built on is very rare this near to the coast. It is solid rock that was carved out so none of the water in the high water table can seep in. SoMu was chosen as the capital city by the first Exalted Lord, PaKo, for this reason."

"What is the largest city in Laurasia?" asked Ellie.

"That would be PuRo to the northeast of here on the great plains," answered MeMo. "There are over two million people there. It is famous as a source for the stone with beautiful red patterns like the chairs you are sitting on. A majority of the people there are born without a class. They are stone workers."

"What do you mean born without a class?" asked Steven.

"Our society is made up of three classes," answered MeMo. "The holy science class, which we belong to, is considered the highest class. Our class is headed by the sacred scientist. Then we have the bureaucrat class, which is comprised of government administrators and all bureaucrats, clerks, and accountants. This class is headed by the chancellor. They are recognized by the red medallion around their neck. Finally, we have the conformance force class, also called confors, made up of police and military personnel. This class is headed by the director. These three consuls make up the high council and report directly to the Exalted Lord. The word of the Exalted Lord is the final law of the land. We become members of the same class as our parents, and if we are deemed worthy, we will progress up in the ranks of our own class. Anyone who is not born in one of these three classes is classless. They can work hard, earn great wealth, and live very well but can never participate in the governing of Laurasia."

"Now, PuFo, we must decide what to do with our guests for tonight," said MeMo. "I think we have enough covers and pads for them to sleep, but what can we feed them? We have none of the nasty flesh that most mammals prefer to eat. Let's try PuFo's favorite, red fern leaves with pine needles."

MeMo went to a shelf near the biggest table in the room and took down a package of leaves wrapped in a translucent, flexible material. There was a circular stone bench made up of four curved sections around the table. She put four thick stone disks around on the table, placed greens on each stone disk, and invited everyone to sit down and eat.

"We can help with the problem of what to feed us," said Ellie. "We have some food in our backpacks. We have some MREs, which means "meals ready to eat." Do you have a way to heat them up?"

"You mean you heat your food?" asked MeMo mystified. What is in your MRE?"

"Scrambled eggs and chicken," answered Ellie.

"Oh, no!" howled MeMo. "How can you eat eggs? That was to be someone's child! What is chicken?"

"Chicken is a kind of bird," said Steven. "You have no birds yet, but they are evolving even now. That is the source of the eggs. I think we should give up on the MREs, Ellie. Maybe we can just eat some bread with our salad."

"Is bread another terrible mammal food?" asked MeMo tentatively.

"No, I think you may even like to try bread," said Ellie. "It is made from the seeds of a plant called wheat. The seeds are broken up to become a powder and then heated to solidify it. But it does not need to be hot to eat. Will you try some?"

"Oh, this is pleasant, but I think I could only eat a tiny bit before I would have enough," said MeMo. "It is so heavy in my mouth and sticks to my teeth."

Miami, Florida

"I'm going to visit my brother, who has suffered a brain aneurism," Khaliq answered the immigration agent. "I need to run his small grocery store near San Jose, California, until he has recovered enough to do it himself. How long can I remain here before I must leave and reenter the country?"

"Six months, Mr. Kader," answered the officer. "I suggest you begin applying for an extension of your visit at your earliest opportunity. This may involve a significant amount of paperwork."

Khaliq took a connecting flight to San Jose through Dallas. In San Jose, he briefly met Hashim Kader, his al-Qaeda contact living in America. "You will need to apply for an extended medical emergency visit for me using this passport," said Khaliq as he gave Hashim a specially prepared Saudi passport. This new counterfeit passport had a picture of Hashim but all of the other data was from the passport that Khaliq had just used to enter the United States as Ikram. Khaliq then gave Hashim the cash to purchase a secondhand car in Hashim's name to provide transportation for Khaliq. Once Khaliq received the car, he left San Jose without giving Hashim any further information about his mission or even telling him that he was the one who would use the Santa Monica house. All Hashim's instructions had come from his handler. He had no idea there was a connection between this Ikram Kader and the things he had been told to do in Southern California. Within the next five days, all of the members of the cell arrived at their destination in Santa Monica.

MISSION 3 FROM WHITE SANDS

The next morning, MeMo and PuFo left their habitat early and went to the local government administration office to explain that they had found two humans walking outside the city. They should have reported them immediately but MeMo had been so involved in their conversation that she had simply forgot to do it before the government office closed. PuFo often allowed MeMo to follow her own path. He would be held as responsible for any violations she committed, but she was just so much fun to be around he followed her lead.

MeMo explained to the government official, "the humans claim to have come directly from the future and want to talk to representatives of Laurasia. They want to start a mutual study program. It seemed that the mammals knew almost nothing about Laurasia and were surprised that the Laurasians knew so much about them."

The local official had no idea what to do about the situation. He had never heard of mammals coming to Laurasia by themselves. Also, it was against the law for humans to walk freely in Laurasia. In typical middle management noncommittal style, he decided he would have to talk to his superior to find out what to do. In the meantime, MeMo and PuFo should keep the mammals in their habitat and come back tomorrow at the same time to find out what to do with them.

The mated pair went back to their habitat after they informed the head of their department that they would not be in to work for a day until the government told them what to do with the humans they had found.

Everyone had another meal of red fern leaves with pine needles. Ellie asked, "What is the material you use to wrap the food?"

"It is the dried and stretched intestines of a type of large dinosaur," answered MeMo. "It protects the flavor of the leaves that are wrapped in it very well."

At that moment, there was a loud knocking on the door. PuFo opened the door, and four confors burst into the room, projectile weapons drawn. "You cannot have unapproved humans in your habitat," the leader said. "These humans are under arrest. Please surrender your weapons and come with us."

When one of the reptiles spun Steven around and secured his hands, Ellie drew her sidearm and pointed it at the one holding Steven. "We came here in peace and don't expect to be treated in such a manner," she said. As she spoke, the leader of the group shot Ellie with his projectile gun. When he saw her fall to the floor, Steven went a little crazy. The situation felt too much like the incident he had been through with his girlfriend. Without thinking he kicked the reptile that was holding him in the knee. The confor hissed as he dropped to the floor like he had been shot. Steven pushed another confor out the entrance with his shoulder and slammed the door closed with his foot. While the reptiles were stunned, Steven rushed at the leader and pushed him backwards over one of the stone chairs. At that moment, the last reptile slammed the butt of his weapon into the side of Steven's face, and the leader shot him with a projectile dart. As he was falling to the floor, he heard MeMo and PuFo talking at a high speed in their language. He never found out what they were saying.

Steven was not sure how much time had passed since he had been tranquilized, but every muscle in his body ached, so it must have been awhile. When he turned his head, a sharp pain stabbed through it. He realized his right eye was swollen shut. He saw Ellie sitting against a wall, with her head in her hands, looking as groggy as Steven felt. "Where are we?" he asked in a hoarse voice.

"I don't know where we are, but we seem to be in some sort

of holding cell for prisoners," groaned Ellie. "We must have been given the wake-up medicine. I think we survived better than Fred, but I really don't know how much time has gone by. There are no windows, and a solid-looking door appears to be the only way out. Our weapons and equipment are gone. I guess we didn't do too well in our clandestine surveillance. By the way, what happened to you? A projectile wasn't enough to put you down?"

A little while later Ellie and Steven felt somewhat better, but not good enough to get up off the floor to explore their surroundings. The door rattled and began to open. Three reptiles walked into the crowded cell. The first one asked in English, "What language do you speak?"

Steven answered, "English is just fine. Where are we, and why did you attack us?"

The speaker countered, "Mammals are not allowed to run free in Laurasia. Where did you escape from? We have no alerts for any escapes in the last two weeks?"

This conversation did not go well. Steven and Ellie tried to explain their purpose for coming to Laurasia, but in the end, the three reptiles claimed that they did not know what to do with them but would inform their superiors.

About a day later, Steven and Ellie were led from their cell. They walked down ramps that took them two more levels down in the structure. They were pushed into what looked like an interrogation room. A table sat in the middle of the room. There were two empty stools on their side of the table. Two reptiles occupied the two chairs on the opposite side. In the shadows of a corner lurked a wrinkled, older reptile with a band around his neck. From the band hung a very large black medallion centered in the middle of his chest.

"Please sit down," said one of the reptiles seated across the table. "We would like to understand which one of our facilities you escaped from."

"My name is Steven Andrews, and this is Eleanor Johnston,"

said Steven. "We came directly from the future to learn more about the culture of Laurasia. No one brought us here. We came to establish an exchange between our two cultures."

The reptile on the other side of the table said, "When did you come here?"

"We have only been here a little more than a day," said Steven.

"Did you use SuHa's portal in France?" asked the reptile.

"I don't know who SuHa is," said Steven. "Is he one of your agents studying our civilization?"

"I'll ask the questions here," snarled the reptile in a very human manner. "Where did you arrive in Laurasia?"

"About ten miles out of the city on the road that leads south." Steven decided that inaccurate information might be appropriate in this particular situation.

"How do you plan to return to the future?" asked the reptile.

"We must return to our arrival point within twelve hours. That is when the return window will open," replied Steven.

Suddenly, the older reptile in the corner said, "Clear the room. This proceeding is going nowhere. I want to talk to these two mammals alone for a moment." After the other reptiles reluctantly left the room, the old one walked over to the far side of the table and stared at them for a full minute. Then he said, "I grow bored with the lying going on in this room. I am SaSu, director of the compliance force of Laurasia. I know exactly why you are here, and I want to tell you that you are too late. Our plan to create war within your world is too far along for you to do anything about it. We have planned the terrorist attacks and the deceptions in such a way that your world will erupt in nuclear war by the end of the year. Your kind will be your own exterminators to cleanse the world of evil mammals."

Steven and Ellie were shocked at these words. "But why?" asked Ellie. "What would you possibly hope to gain with such an act?"

"I see you do not know as much of our plan as I thought," said SaSu.

"What I do know is that you will never get the human race to destroy itself," said Ellie. "Our self preservation instincts will come into play before we get that far. What do you think you will accomplish?"

"I guess I can tell you of the fate of your race since you will not live to see it. We in Laurasia are in dire need of combustibles to fuel our glorious civilization. It seems like fate has given your race access to untold resources to generate mobile power while giving us virtually nothing. All the plant and animal life of the world dies and is reduced by eons of time to coal and oil for your era to use. We will begin extracting oil resources from your world for our own use within the year. We decided we wanted to eliminate the evil presence of mammals to ensure an uninterrupted supply."

"This is insane," said Steven. "You are going to kill billions of humans just to take our oil?"

"I did not ask your opinion of our project," said SaSu. "Now I will send you back to your cell to await your execution."

Once they were alone back in their cell, Ellie said, "We have to find a way to escape so we can warn our world about what is happening."

"I know, but how do we get out of here?" asked Steven. "We are locked in a cell several levels below the surface, and we don't even know where we are."

"I don't think we can rely on them to come to feed us," said Ellie. "We need a plan to lure them here, and then we need to overpower the guards and find some weapons."

"The rank and file here seems so open and trusting," said Ellie. "Maybe we can get them to come in here by appearing to be sick. You lie on the floor and look like you're having a fit. I'll get behind the door and take out the guard that comes in last. If two come in, you need to take out the one closest to you. If more than two come in, I guess we'll need a new plan."

Steven lay down on the floor and began howling like a wolf and rolling around. A guard looked in the cell, and when he saw Steven, he opened the door and came toward him to see what was happening. At this point, Ellie jumped on his back and grabbed his head in both hands and twisted violently. The guard fell to the floor, dead with a broken neck. Steven was up and ready in case another guard was waiting outside the door. No one else came in. They exited their cell and ran into a short hallway with doors on both sides. They found the exit from the cell block they had been through earlier. From this exit, they could see the ramps that led both up and down. Still, they saw no sign of another guard. Staying close to the wall, they hurried up the ramp. As they approached the next higher level, Steven and Ellie could hear guards hurrying toward the ramp on that level. After ducking back, they watched a pair of guards hurry up the ramp above as if they were late for something. As soon as the guards were out of sight, Ellie led the way up the ramp. Steven asked, "Did either of those guards have a weapon?"

"I don't think so. The jailer didn't either," said Ellie. "I guess they keep weapons out of the cell blocks to keep them out of the hands of prisoners."

"Bad luck," said Steven. "We should really try to get our hands on some weapons before we get out of this building." They walked up three more levels, and then the décor of the hall changed. "I'll bet this means we are out of the cell block area," said Steven. "We should see if we can find weapons on this level."

"Maybe a quick look around," said Ellie. "Then we'd better concentrate on getting out of this building." They walked halfway down the hall and then quietly opened a door to the right. This was clearly an office with no weapons. Ellie went over to the other side of the hall and opened another door a crack and then quickly eased it closed again. "Someone is in there," she whispered. They tried a few more doors near the end of the hall before they hit the jackpot. They found a room that was used as an armory. Not only did they find projectile weapons on a shelf, a cable running through their stocks, but they also found their own pistols and bayonets lying on a table. Ellie picked up her bayonet and walked over to the shelf. A fixture on each end of the shelf secured the cable. She began gouging at the rock to loosen the cable on one end. After some frantic work, she removed the cable and picked out two projectile weapons. When she looked down on another shelf, she saw projectiles and several little vials of the reviving medicine, which she picked up. "Okay, let's get out of here," she said.

"I'm glad you made us take the time to learn how to use these weapons before we left on this mission," said Steven. They went up three more levels before they saw the sun shining on the wall beside the ramp. "Do you think we should wait for dark before we try to sneak out of this building?" he whispered.

"I don't think we have the time to spare," Ellie whispered back. "We really need to get back and warn our world about what's happening." When she looked out from the entrance, Ellie saw one of those large tri-wheelers coming slowly down their side of the street. "Let's see if we can slip into the back of that vehicle and catch a ride out of town."

As they stepped out of the building, they saw why there were no reptiles blocking their escape. They were all standing and looking at communication devices similar to televisions that were mounted along the sides of the street. The reptiles were totally absorbed in listening to a broadcast by some government official making an announcement. All the reptiles were intent on whatever was being said. Steven and Ellie jumped into the back of the tri-wheeler and pulled a covering over themselves.

"So far we have had a serious run of good luck," said Steven. "I hope it holds a little longer. That was some move you put on that guard in the cell."

"I hate that we went off on this trip without finding out anything about the reptiles physiology," said Ellie. "I guessed the neck would be a vulnerable spot, and it luckily worked."

They rode along for about fifteen minutes then they felt the speed of the tri-wheeler pick up. "We're out of town, going in the right direction. Now we need to work on getting out of this vehicle," she said. From under the cover, Ellie could see that there were several other vehicles driving along behind them. "We can't jump out now, even if we weren't going too fast because of the traffic behind us."

They rode on for about forty-five minutes before the tri-wheeler slowed down and turned off the road. Ellie slipped out of the vehicle and peered around the side as the driver exited his vehicle. She put a projectile in his back, and he fell to the ground without a noise. "I hope we can figure out how to drive this thing," she said. "It's much too far to simply walk back to the place where we left the bikes. It would take too much time. I'm also worried that if that director of the compliance force finds out that we've escaped after he shot off his big mouth, we may have the whole confor group looking for us. Let's drag the driver around to the back and hide him in his cargo area."

Steven found that driving the tri-wheeler was fairly intuitive as soon as he sat behind the controls. After they made a U-turn, they drove for about thirty minutes before Ellie said, "I think this is the place where we first intersected the road. Let's drive the tri-wheeler into the brush to delay the reptiles finding where we left it."

The electric bikes were still where they had hidden them, and the trip back to the vessel was tense but uneventful.

chapter 10

Team T-REX had returned to the present after less than two days, much to the surprise of everyone at the White Sands site. Jonas came trotting into the reception area, shouting, "Is everyone okay? Has there been an accident?"

Steven was the first out of the vessel. "Everyone is healthy, but we have some momentous news. Ellie and I did not take the time to brief the rest of the team. We just packed up and came back to the present."

Jonas said, "Let's go to the conference room. We can get your team something to eat while you fill us all in."

Steven told the abbreviated version of their trip to the Laurasian capital city and their subsequent capture. "Since we were discovered, we decided to act like we had come to start a dialogue with their government," said Steven. "I suppose you can guess our complete shock when one of the top guys in their whole government is sitting in the interrogation room. Then after they ask us a few questions, he stops the discussion, runs everyone else out of the room, and then accuses us of being spies supposedly trying to stop an operation being executed by their government in complete secrecy. We didn't have a clue what he was talking about at first. It got really tense when he mentioned that we would not live long enough to inform anyone about what was happening."

Jonas had a thoughtful look on his face as he said, "You realize what a serious credibility problem we have to overcome before we can even mobilize our world to address this situation. There are only two people outside this building that even know about our capabilities. We really have no proof of what we are claiming."

"We have pictures and data to prove time travel and the existence of the reptile people," said Steven. "We can use some video of our prisoner to help prove the validity of our story. The real problem is that at this moment, we don't really know what the reptiles are doing in our world to stir up a war. Where do we start looking for proof in our world and what do we do to stop them?"

"For now, Team T-REX should put together the most impressive evidence we have from the two trips to the past to start proving our story," said Jonas. "I'll push the information up my chain of command to see how we are going to be received."

WASHINGTON, DC

The next day, Jonas called Steven and Ellie early to tell them they had forty-five minutes to be on an air force flight to Washington DC. They were to bring the presentation they had prepared discussing the existence and intentions of the Laurasians. The national security advisor, Jason Sanders would have them picked up upon their arrival at Andrews Air Force Base and meet with them at his office in the white house.

Steven and Ellie were seated in a large conference room facing Jason Sanders preparing to discuss the situation in Laurasia. They heard the door behind them open, and Sanders quickly stood looking at something behind them. Both Steven and Ellie casually turned to see what was happening. There stood the President of the United States, wearing an open-neck white shirt and black slacks. "So this is the team that went back sixty-five million years to find us a completely new enemy," he said with a smile on his face. "I'm told the directors of the CIA and the FBI along with the chairman of the Joint Chiefs of Staff will be here in about five minutes. Possibly the secretary of homeland security will be here as well. The urgency of this meeting has caught us all by surprise. As you probably know, I was informed last night by the national security advisor that our country has succeeded in developing the capability for time travel. After I got past the disbelief and thinking he was joking, I decided to hear about this for myself." As the president stepped forward to shake Ellie's hand, Steven nearly fell over his chair when he tried to stand and turn around at the same time.

"I fully realize it's an issue for a later time," said the president of the United States as the briefing began. "But I want to go on record saying that this country has developed the capability of traveling through time without my knowledge. How could this happen? Where did the money come from?"

"Mr. President, this is a very long story that I'll be happy to share with you at another time," said Sanders. "But I would suggest that you hear these people out on a really urgent issue before we get into the development details."

Steven then stood before some of the most powerful people in the country and related the recent events that had occurred in Laurasia and White Sands, New Mexico. When he finished, the room was quiet for about thirty seconds.

Finally, the president said, "This is the most preposterous story I have ever heard. I feel like I just stepped into a science-fiction novel. If Mr. Sanders, whom I have known for more years than I care to admit, was not telling me it is true, I would have stayed in my office and gone on with my busy day. Let's just assume for the moment that I have actually assimilated this information correctly. Does anyone have a recommendation as to what we should do?"

Jason Sanders took the floor and said, "The first problem I see is we currently don't have a single piece of evidence to share that would justify our enlisting the aid of our political allies. I further believe that it would be a major tactical error to reveal our time travel capabilities to anyone unless it becomes absolutely necessary. That leaves us with the need to develop some current world evidence to try to prove our case."

"Then I want the CIA, as a first priority, to begin looking for evidence of third-party involvement in the current hotspots of the world," said the president. Also, the FBI and Homeland Security should ratchet up their efforts for discovering any potential terrorist threats being developed within the country. I want the NSA to assign some senior-level strategic thinkers to develop a list of scenarios they predict a third party would take to start a global conflict. Using the scenarios they develop, have the NSA compile a comprehensive list of key words and put all of the communication-monitoring resources that we can make available into finding what these alleged Laurasians are up to."

"Each department will create a daily report," said the president. "Send them to the national security advisor by close of business each day. He will coordinate disseminating this information."

At the close of the meeting, the president stayed behind as most of the attendees filed out of the room to get back to their busy schedules. He came over to where Steven and Ellie were sitting alone and said, "I just want to say to you two, and the rest of your team, thanks from all the American people for the work you have done over the last few days. I guess what you have found was a perfect justification of why the NSA funded this project, though no one could have foreseen the threat it has uncovered. Last night Mr. Sanders convinced me to allow your White Sands team, it's called Team T-REX I think, to continue handling the part of our effort that happens back in time, since you are the only people with any practical experience. If there is anything I can do to help you thwart this new enemy, feel free to call me directly."

The very next day, the presidential morning briefing contained the news reported by Al Jazeera and the Syrian Arab News Agency, known as SANA, that Israel had launched a biological attack on Gaza City using anthrax spores. No one was exactly sure how they distributed the spores, but there were cases of infection being reported over the whole of Gaza City. The death rate was expected to reach one hundred thousand people, about 25 percent of the city population. Hamas was calling for the support of all other Muslim countries to punish the Israelis for this heinous crime. Syria and Iran already declared war on Israel and asked the United Nations to support their effort to punish this crime against humanity. Al Jazeera reports that Egypt and Saudi Arabia condemned Israel for this underhanded and illegal type of attack.

First in the briefing to speak, the secretary of state said, "We can't allow this ridiculously dangerous move on Israel's part to occur without a very strong form of censor against the Israeli government."

The president looked directly at the national security advisor and said, "If we had not had the briefing we had yesterday, I would take a very dim view of this incident. However, I suppose we will need to widen the circle of people who know the real situation. I expect that it makes our response quite a bit different than it would have been." The president said to the secretary of state, "I want you to talk directly to the prime minister of Israel and find out what he has to say about this. At noon today, we will have a briefing right here to update the members of this group on a very interesting and unbelievable data point we picked up yesterday. Mr. Sanders, please provide us with the update this afternoon."

chapter 11

The US ambassador to Israel had no trouble setting up the phone call between the prime minister of Israel and the secretary of state. "Mr. Secretary how is it that your country is the only major country that has not publically blasted Israel as a result of the bio-attack on Gaza?" asked the Prime Minister. "While we greatly appreciate your restraint, I cannot help asking why this is true."

"I admit my own first impulse was to do just that," said the secretary. "However, my boss, the president, has apparently received information within the last day or so that led him to have me make this call before we make any public statements. He ordered me to ask you to give us the true answer to the following question, not the political answer. Did Israel launch or in any way encourage a third party to make this attack?"

"First, let me give you the simple answer to your question," answered the prime minster. "No, we had nothing to do with this heinous attack. We have never even discussed such an option. If the other so-called world leaders spent even one moment thinking about this scenario, they would realize that we would not do such a thing for perfectly selfish reasons. We might use missiles or bombs to discourage enemies from attacking our homeland but not this type of weapon. The capability for this kind of attack is easily obtained and costs relatively little. This is why the world is so fearful of terrorist attacks using these methods. Now that the idea is in the public mind, I fully expect that our country will be the victim of some similar attacks. Because Israel exists in some respects at the benevolence of the major world powers, we cannot afford to indulge in this kind of senseless act. Now please tell me what information your president has that lead him to possibly question if we were involved in the attack on Gaza City? The rest of the world seems to have no doubt as to our guilt."

"I wish I could, but I was not involved in the initial briefing that he received," replied the secretary. "A few more of us with a need to know, including myself, will be updated later today. If the president will allow me to share the information with you, I will make another call. The question now becomes this: If Israel or some Jewish extremist group is not responsible for the attack, what group is? Your country's prowess in gathering covert information is legendary. You must have at least an educated guess."

"I'm reluctant to report that this attack has caught us completely by surprise," said the prime minister. "There wasn't even the hint of a rumor before we heard about this through the Arab news agencies. From those sources, we have heard that thousands of people are sick and dying. Their medical facilities are completely overwhelmed. All of our offers to help with the problem have been rebuffed by Hamas without explanation. We offered vaccines and medical teams to help care for the afflicted, but they completely refuse to respond. It's like they don't want us to show the world that we had nothing to do with this. I guess they intend to milk the world media for every ounce of sympathy."

"What will you do about the countries that have declared war on Israel?" asked the secretary.

"We do not plan any offensive moves at this time," said the prime minister. "However, if we receive intelligence that either Iran or Syria is planning a direct attack, we may act to preempt it."

White Sands, New Mexico

Jonas McCormick paced across the front of the conference room where Team T-REX was meeting for its daily update. "How do we put a stop to the plans of the Laurasians? As I understand it from your own reports, the Laurasians' need for energy is desperate, and short of providing them with some form of energy, I doubt that they will voluntarily halt their plans."

"We could go back to Laurasia and try to find out where they originate their trips into the future," said Ellie. "Maybe we could destroy their time machine."

"What if they have more than one?" asked Jonas, playing devil's advocate. "They undoubtedly have the capability to build another one, so that move would only delay them for some unspecified time."

"I hear the army and marine high commands, consulting with our operations people, have decided that we could not transfer enough resources into the past to support a viable attack on Laurasia," said Steven thoughtfully. Anyway, a mass move of resources like that may cause time paradox consequences that could be felt beyond the C-Pg extinction event, "Also, an attack launched with our limited information about their ability to fight back could easily be suicide. However, maybe we should follow that old adage that says the enemy of my enemy is my friend. Why don't we open a dialogue with Gondwana and see if we can find some common interests that would convince them to help us against Laurasia."

"Great idea," shouted Jonas, his eyes flashing. "And I just received information that will make this possible. The three-man team tasked to learn to speak Laurasian has basically accomplished their task. We now have a couple of humans who can speak the Laurasian language. I realize we don't know if the Gondwanians speak the same language, but surely, they have people who can speak Laurasian. I can't imagine that they're so isolated from each other that they don't know the language."

"How should we staff this mission?" asked Steven. "We should probably take more personnel for defense, and we need the language expert that speaks the best Laurasian. The problem is the size of the vessel."

"I suggest taking eight people," said Jonas. "We could make two trips. You, Ellie, Juan, and George can go first. While you set up a secure perimeter, we can pull the vessel back and send it with another group of four. This would be a huge expenditure of energy, but I think the situation justifies doing it. Fred is ready for another trip, and he has been studying the Laurasian language while he has been recuperating. Dave, Bill Thomas, and another soldier from here would complete the group. Hopefully, the group is small enough not to threaten the Gondwanians but large enough to keep you safe long enough to get back here in the vessel in case the Gondwanians are unfriendly. We'll put some serious thinking into what type of weapons to equip the group with."

"The next problem is where to send us," said Steven. "I wonder if YaSi could tell us where the Gondwanian capital city is located. It would sure save a lot of time if we could arrive near the city."

WASHINGTON, DC

Exactly five days after the bio-attack on Gaza City was reported, the Arab news agencies were announcing that thirty-six thousand people had either died or been afflicted by the anthrax spores. The rate of new cases being reported was still increasing with no end of the increase in sight. New cases were now being reported in the Gaza Strip outside Gaza City. People who feared for their lives were hard to contain within the city limits, thus putting the entire Palestinian population at risk.

During the US president's morning briefing, reports suggested that six cases of infection by the bacterium *Yersinia pestis*, otherwise known as the Black Death, had been found in Jerusalem. Doctors and government agents were desperately trying to figure out where the outbreak had originated because the six patients lived and worked in widely scattered parts of the city.

"Mr. Secretary of State, please place another call to the prime minister of Israel," said the president. "You may tell him that we believe a third, as-yet-unidentified party is responsible for the anthrax attack on Gaza City. Also, explain to him that these new cases of plague are probably the beginning of a horrible epidemic caused by another bio-attack. The world will believe the Arab Alliance is responsible, but tell him that this is not true. We must find a way to keep a lid on flaring tempers, or we will find ourselves in a global war. Under no circumstances are you to tell him how we know this information, but assure him the source is totally reliable. Now I would like to hear from Mr. Sanders what progress, if any is being made to find out how these acts were accomplished."

"The CIA has been very active in the Middle East but have only found scraps of information," said the national security advisor. "Surprisingly, no group is claiming responsibility for the Gaza City attack. One strange data point is that the mayor of Gaza City allegedly received an anonymous phone call warning of a bio-attack by Israel using anthrax. The caller, who spoke with a horrible accent in English, claimed that Mossad was vaccinating their entire organization in preparation for launching the attack. The vaccination information is the only data from that phone call that Hamas operatives were able to verify as true, but as a result, the Arab world convinced itself that Israel did this thing. The delivery method for the anthrax attack was a biplane that was hired by phone to fly over the city and advertise a new department store that was set to open in Gaza City. I find it unbelievable that the Gaza authorities would allow such a thing with all of their current tensions, but I guess they were trying to be optimistic about the store's effect on the economy of the Gaza Strip. At the last minute, the pilot was bribed to install a dispersal device in his plane by a hooded man who talked strangely and paid in cash. The pilot has been subjected to the Middle East's version of rigorous interrogation and knows nothing else. Other than that, there has been no other lead about who planned and executed the attack on Gaza City.

"On the other side, a lower-level clerk at Mossad's headquarters reported a conversation in a bar with a hooded man who claimed to have heard that Hamas would launch a bio-attack on Jerusalem and Tel Aviv using plague bacteria transmitted by fleas. Based on that, I would say that you are 100 percent correct in telling Israel that they are currently under attack, and I would add that they should expect the source of the disease to be fleas released over a broad area of the city.

"Based on the tiny amount of information about the attacks available in the whole of the Middle East, it would be plausible that they were accomplished by a single person who hides his identity by wearing a hood that completely covers his face. Nothing about this description rules out the possibility that the suspect could be a reptile from the past. Unfortunately, this is not the kind of evidence that we need to present to our friends or foes to prove our story. This hooded guy is really good and seems to have unlimited resources. The only time we even glimpse his existence is when he is planting false information about the responsibility for the attacks. If we had not heard about this possibility from White Sands, we would have no idea there was a subplot working here.

"The worst thing I have to report is that we have no information from homeland security or the FBI hinting of a terrorist attack being planned within the United States. The best they can do is mounting an all-out effort to cut off any potential financing for terrorists in the United States until they find some concrete information to help track down the actual group."

chapter 12

MISSION 4 FROM WHITE SANDS

The first half of the team climbed into the vessel in preparation for the trip to Gondwana. YaSi had in fact been able to tell them where the capital of Gondwana was located. According to the Laurasians, the location was just another example of their incompetence in government. In an attempt to satisfy everyone, they located the city near the middle of the landmass. This was meant to allow the seat of government to be as readily accessible to everyone as possible. In fact, after a thousand years, the land that the capitol was built on had become highly unstable and subject to frequent and serious earthquakes. According to mammal science, it appears the Gondwanians situated their capital right where the modern continents of Africa and South America were separating from each other.

Upon arrival, the first half of Team T-REX pitched in enthusiastically to get the area cleared and the perimeter fence built. Once the vessel returned to White Sands, Steven and Ellie spent some time looking out through the fence before they went to work raising the observation balloon.

The landscape was very different from the Laurasian site. The weather was noticeably hotter and more humid. The Gondwanian site was only a few degrees south of the equator. The landscape included rolling hills instead of flat plains, and they had arrived at a spot that was near the top of one of those hills. They saw a mountain range about one hundred miles to the south with some form of living creatures flying nearby. They had arrived around sunrise and could see several isolated groups of dinosaurs to the north and east. The biggest difference from Laurasia seemed to be the foliage covering the ground. There were huge, deciduous trees growing to a height of forty to fifty feet. Below the trees the undergrowth appeared to be the same flowering varieties of shrubs with no sign of the short pine variety they had seen in Laurasia. In places that received a moderate amount of sunlight, the flowers covered the bushes with bright reds and yellows, and in other places, there was no sign of any color except bright, beautiful green. The air shimmered above the bushes because of the heat, which gave the place the quality of a dream world. The undergrowth plants covered the ground completely to a height of three to four feet. Steven and Ellie worked hard to clear a circular area about fifty feet in diameter with machetes while Juan and George put up the perimeter fence.

As they were gazing to the east, they saw a large creature eating the shrubs about one hundred yards away. It was only about two feet taller than the shrubs, but it appeared to be about thirty feet long and six feet wide. It moved slowly, leaving a path cleared of shrubs as it went like a lawnmower. While Steven was trying to figure out what it was, a medium-sized *Tyrannosaurus* came charging from the east directly toward the creature. As it dashed to within ten feet of its prey, Steven and Ellie watched the creature swing a tail that had heavy, bony spikes on each side at the very end like a hammerhead. It hit the *Tyrannosaurus* about halfway up its leg, which caused the T. rex to let out a loud roar and jump back out of range. As the adversaries stood glaring at each other, another larger *Tyrannosaurus* came from the north and pounced on the creature's back. The strange creature crouched down near the ground. After giving a loud roar of its own, the new *Tyrannosaurus* bent down and fastened its incredibly long and sharp teeth onto the neck of the creature. The creature continued to hunker down, apparently taking little notice of the huge dinosaur on its back.

"I saw one of those when I arrived in Laurasia on the test trip," said Ellie. "It looked like a pile of rocks. What is it?"

The large T. rex could find no way to pierce the thick armor of the creature. Finally, the large *Tyrannosaurus* leaped off of the creature and ducked aside just as the brutal tail came whooshing by for a near miss. The pair of aggressors circled the creature until the larger one darted in. It used its powerful mouth and neck muscles to lift the creature on one side and flip it over onto its back. In this position, the creature was helpless. Its four small legs could get no purchase, and even its tail swing was ineffective. The smaller T. rex jumped on the creature's stomach, and with its viciously sharp teeth, it ripped out a large chunk of flesh.

"Of course," said Steven. "That thing is called an *Ankylosaurus*. It is a huge, armored herbivore. Fossil bones discovered in Bolivia show they grew up to thirty-five feet long and six feet wide. Even though they grew to only six or seven feet tall, they were estimated to weigh between three and four tons. That T. rex must be incredibly strong to flip it over. As we saw, its entire top was heavily protected by thick oval plates embedded in its skin. With the spikes all over its body, the small triangular horns coming out of the back of its head, and that club like tail, it is virtually untouchable by large predators when it's standing upright. I think we have just seen a demonstration of the only way a predator could kill an *Ankylosaurus*. You can see that it has four very short legs, so it cannot right itself once it has been flipped over. It has a broad skull, but its brain is tiny, so it would never be able to outthink an attacker. However, did you notice how quickly the large T. rex figured out what to do? I wonder if this was some kind of a hunting lesson for the smaller one. It sure won't forget that *Ankylosaurus's* tail anytime soon."

"Let's put up the observation balloon and see if we can find RoHo, the capital city," said Ellie. They ran the balloon up to 1,500 feet and connected the monitoring equipment. With the camera pointed toward the south to start, they intended to pan the camera toward the east and then around the rest of a circle. "What are those things flying over by that mountain range?" asked Ellie as she operated the zoom feature of the camera for a closer look. "They look like birds," she said after she examined the magnified image.

"They are some type of pterosaur, a descendant of the pterodactyl," said Steven. "I think it's from the genus *Pteranodon*, which means 'winged without teeth.' It is a carnivore, but it has no teeth. At Montana State, we postulated that it ate like a modern-day pelican, catching fish at the surface of the water and swallowing them whole. I would love to get a chance to see how they actually eat. We thought its diet consisted of fish, crabs, mollusks, and insects, but it was also a scavenger. This dinosaur was capable of flying long distances using air currents to assist it. Its wingspan was huge, much larger than any known bird's. The wings were covered by a leathery membrane that stretched between the body, the top of its legs, and the hugely elongated fourth finger on the end of each arm. Its other fingers ended in sharp claws. I wonder how the Gondwanians deal with all the large and dangerous creatures that inhabit their neighborhood."

As they panned the camera around to the southwest, they saw the capital city of Gondwana gleaming in the sun. It was only about ten miles away, so they had a very good view. There were no buildings above the ground just as in Laurasia; however, there were artworks and decorative plants throughout the city and on top of most buildings. There were statues of metal that shined in the sunlight. Many portrayed reptiles, and others had abstract forms. In the center of the city, there was a grouping of eight statues, each about thirty feet tall, each made of gray stone that made the figures look lifelike except for the size.

There were many vehicles with four wheels and virtually all of them were sleek and painted in bright colors. In a magnificent arch over much of the city, there was a rainbow made of a polished metal. The rainbow was about three hundred feet tall at the peak of its arch. A gold-colored sphere hung from the middle of the arch.

There were two main streets that crossed in the middle of the city, and these were wider than the other streets. They had eight lanes for each direction, and just where they entered the city, there were one hundred feet tall obelisks with beautiful written characters on them. Nearly everything Steve and Ellie saw appeared to have been carefully created for beauty.

"How will we approach them?" asked Ellie. "Maybe we should have brought a gift to formally present to them."

"We'll have to wait for another visit when we can bring an appropriate piece of artwork," said Steven. "From the look of their city, I think that might be appreciated. Can you see a road or path we can use to get there? If we have to walk through this brush the whole way, getting there will be very difficult."

"Yes," said Ellie. "There's one coming from the northeast that appears to go directly toward RoHo about a mile from here."

"Let's just try walking into the city with Bill, who can do the talking," said Steven. "From a ten-mile-distant first impression, I feel that these people are more peace-loving than the Laurasians, so we probably should only take our pistols as protection. We want to appear as friendly as possible."

The first mile of the trip was difficult as they battled through the ground cover, but once they got to the road, the walk was much easier. They had been on the road for only about ten minutes when the first vehicle, one that looked like a miniature delivery truck with four wheels, came by. Steven, Ellie, and Bill did not know how the Gondwanians would receive them, but they were pleasantly surprised when the vehicle stopped and two male reptiles climbed out. "Hello, my name is Bill," he said in the Laurasian language. "Could you take us to meet with one of your leaders?"

"Hello, I am called SiPa, and this is my helper FuMe. You are very strange-looking. I have never seen anyone that looks like you," said FuMe the shorter of the two reptiles. "Please excuse me for saying so, but something very bad must have happened to your eggs before you were hatched."

"We are of a different species than you," said Steven, talking through Bill. We are evolved from mammals just as you are evolved from dinosaurs. We want to explain everything in detail once we meet one of your leaders."

"The Council of Mothers is very busy," said SiPa. "We will take you to the City Hall of RoHo. I am sure the mayor of the city can help you?"

"Well, I guess they speak the same language as the Laurasians," said Bill with a great sigh of relief.

"Where are you from?" asked SiPa. "I heard you say Laurasia when you were speaking in your strange language. You have very different skin, but I guess it makes it easier to conceal yourselves in the desert."

"We come from the very distant future, not Laurasia," answered Bill. "This is not our skin. It is a covering to protect our bodies. Would you like to feel it? We call the covering clothes."

"Please tell us how your government works so we will know what to expect when we meet with your leaders?" asked Steven with Bill's help.

As the team had come to expect, the reptiles began to freely answer questions put to them. This openness appeared to be a genetic characteristic of the race. "Our government is basically elected by the people of Gondwana," said FuMe with an air of pride. "Every five years, we elect the members of a provincial forum in each of our eight provinces. The people elect twenty-five members to each provincial forum. These forum members set policy and make laws for their province. The provincial forum in each province then chooses three of their members to be part of the national forum. These twenty-four delegates set policy and make laws for the nation.

"Overall, we are guided by the Council of Mothers, which consists of eight females who have borne children and are known for their benevolent wisdom. One female is picked by the local provincial forum from among the most worthy of the province that needs a representative. The members of the Council of Mothers are chosen for life, so not all provincial forums have the opportunity to choose during their tenure. The council reviews new laws and pronounces them valid or invalid after they are passed by the national forum. The Council of Mothers also may recommend laws that need to be created for the national good. This does not happen often, but their suggestions are never refused. The Council of Mothers acts as the conscience of our nation. Their job is to see that the nation runs smoothly and according to what is morally right.

"Each city also has a government department to ensure the city's residents are following the laws of the land. The city government looks after maintenance and helps residents during emergencies. The government is very simple, but it works because it is the duty of every member of society to work together in harmony with each other. This universal good behavior ensures we do not go back to the behavior of the early times when many warlords ruled our country and fought constantly among themselves. Now please sit in the back of our electric wagon, and we will take you to the City Hall of RoHo."

The little diplomatic delegation consisting of Steven, Ellie, and Bill did not get to see the city as they rode into it because the back of the vehicle was enclosed and lacked windows. SiPa sat in the back with them as they rode. "Do you have a conformance force as they do in Laurasia?" asked Bill.

"We have people in each city called the Emergency Corp who are in charge of enforcing the laws of the province and nation," said SiPa. "But we do not have vast forces of soldiers to keep order and suppress rebellion as in Laurasia. Nearly 25 percent of their population is in the conformance force. Our emergency services personnel look upon their service as a job, not as a privilege of their class."

"Our emergency services also helps citizens in case of emergencies, such as fires, or in the case of RoHo, they help during the aftermath of earthquakes. We have had a lot of them lately."

"Is there anything you can do about these earthquakes?" asked Ellie. "Have you thought about moving your capital city?"

"Well we have no idea how to stop the earth's crust from moving but we do have early warning capabilities," said SiPa. Since the level of the problem increased in the last one to two hundred years we have increased the strength of our newer habitats so we have much fewer injuries and less repair costs now.

"In Laurasia, they virtually all think of Gondwanians as mortal enemies," said Bill. "Do you feel the same way?"

"Not really," answered SiPa. "We have no desire to fight with them or try to invade their country as they wish to invade ours. We have developed strong military technologies that we hope keep us safe from their attack. As long as they leave us alone, there will be peace."

When they arrived at city hall, the two truckers courteously showed the strange group into the building. Like the Laurasian buildings, this one was underground, but the top was decorated with statues and flowering shrubs. The result was that the roof of the building looked like a garden.

After a brief wait, the assistant to RoHo's mayor met with them. "Hello, my name is KoMu. I was told that one of you speak our language. Is that true?"

"I can speak your language but please speak slowly so I will understand," said Bill.

"Please explain the purpose of your visit so that I can properly brief the mayor," said KoMu. "Please follow me to a meeting habitat so we can sit and talk. We have never seen your kind of people before. Where do you come from?"

Steven answered through Bill's translation, "We come from the future. This may be hard to believe, but sixty-five million years in the future. We have come to try to enlist the help of Gondwana. When we first arrived in your time, we came to the central part of Laurasia. We transitioned there because in our time, we live in a part of the earth that is now Laurasia. I'm surprised that you know so little about us. The people in Laurasia know very much because they have been studying us for nearly twenty years."

"Wait a minute," said KoMu. "How are they able to study your people?"

"Because they developed a method of their own to travel through time about twenty years ago and have been kidnapping people from our world to question and study ever since. We think these people are put under some kind of mind control while they are being held by the Laurasians."

"Oh yes, I remember hearing something about that from our spy master about fifteen years ago. At the time I didn't think it was significant." said KoMu. "Over a thousand years ago, our two countries cut off all but the most negligible official contact. Since then, we believe the direction taken by their science and our own to be very different. I can see that I should get the mayor to come here to listen to your story. This must be escalated to the very highest levels of the national government, and the mayor will know how this should be done."

Soon, a fairly short, slightly less than six feet but somehow distinguished-looking reptile entered the meeting chamber. "Hello, my name is TaSu, the mayor of this great city. KoMu has told me of your prior discussion with him. You say you seek the help of Gondwana. In what way may we help you?"

Again, Steven talked, and Bill translated his words. "As we

said to KoMu, the Laurasians have been studying our civilization for nearly twenty years. Now they have decided to covertly instigate a global war between our various political groups. The intent is to cause us to destroy our own civilization."

"This is an almost unbelievable idea, even for the Laurasians," said TaSu. "Why would they even think to carry out such an outlandish plot?"

"I forgot to give you one very important part of the puzzle," said Steven. "Apparently, Laurasia has determined that their country will run out of the combustible material they require to generate their form of portable energy within the next two years. They view this as a national emergency of such devastating proportion that they have kept the information a secret from virtually all of their population."

"I do understand their problem, said TaSu thoughtfully. "We project a similar problem coming for our country, but we project it to be much further in the future than two years, more like two hundred years, and we have already begun to look for alternative energy sources. We do burn plant combustibles to generate a portion of our energy requirements, but we have also developed alternate energy sources so our dependence is much less. We, too, have a program within our country to help solve our long-term energy needs. But tell me... why does Laurasia think destroying your civilization will help them with their problem?"

"By our time, the world has gone through many physical changes," said Steven. "As time moves forward, plant and animal life continues to evolve. The types of plants you have today have evolved from single-cell algae into the trees and shrubs that you are familiar with. In the future, they will further evolve into very large trees that can grow as tall as one hundred feet and as big in diameter as thirty feet. Huge, dense stands of trees will grow and then die over the coming millions of years. With time, the material from these dead forests is covered by hundreds of feet of dirt, and it is crushed and concentrated into a thick liquid material we call oil. This is a compact source of vast energy. Usually, to find it, we must look thousands of feet underground. We have developed efficient ways to find and recover this oil, and so we use it as our primary source of energy. The Laurasians plan to destroy our civilization so that they can transport the oil back to Laurasia to solve their energy problem with no interference from us."

"If they expect to run out of energy within two years, they must be very desperate," said TaSu. "No wonder they hatched such a dangerous and immoral plan. I see that Gondwana should worry about the outcome of this situation. If the Laurasians acquire a source of plentiful energy, it may tip the balance of power in their favor."

chapter 13

The secretary of state led the daily presidential update by saying, "The prime minister of Israel called to thank me for the information I passed on to him last month about the source of the plague that infected Jerusalem. Because they launched an immediate, all-out campaign to eradicate both fleas and rats in Jerusalem, the death toll was only a few hundred versus the tens of thousands it could have been. As a result, panic was averted. By the way, there has been no attack on Tel Aviv as we feared. I think his call was also to see if we had any further information about who launched these attacks."

"The mess in Gaza City is a completely different story," said the national security advisor. "They have refused any help with their fight against the anthrax epidemic unless it comes from a country that has declared war on Israel. The death toll has soared to about three hundred thousand people and is threatening everyone in the whole Gaza Strip. I don't really believe they would do such a barbaric thing, but it seems as if they want the maximum death count so they can get more support for their new publicly stated plan to drive all of the Jews completely out of Israel and the Middle East."

"Since you are already making your report, we should have an update about the investigation into the worldwide terrorism situation," said the president to Jason Sanders.

"The CIA has absolutely zero additional information that we can use about the perpetrators of the bio-attacks on Gaza City and Jerusalem," said Jason Sanders. "I'm afraid that we will get no additional information on the subject, so I have tasked the CIA to try to find any suspicious activity involved with setting up an attack on an undefined target within the United States scheduled around the end of the year. I am hoping this outside-in view of the problem will give better results than the FBI and Homeland Security have had to date."

"The NSA has completed their updated list of key words to listen for in the mass of worldwide communication. They started to monitor both international and US communication traffic about three weeks ago. To date, they have uncovered no leads to help find the expected terrorist activity. Unfortunately, this activity is generating hundreds of false leads, which are consuming thousands of man hours to follow up."

"Homeland security has found no persons of interest to our particular situation entering the country. The FBI reported something at the last minute just before I came to this meeting. I am not sure why they reported it for this venue, so I will need to do some further checking. The incident they reported was something about a murder down around the border with Mexico."

LAURASIA, 65 MILLION YEARS BCE

SuHa was meeting with SaSu, the director of the conformance force of Laurasia, his direct superior. "I don't understand what happened in Jerusalem," said SuHa. "I released millions of the fleas provided by the Laurasian Central Weapons Laboratory all over the city, but currently, the Jewish information media is reporting 237 cases of plague with about 65 percent mortality rate. I cannot imagine how their health workers could contain the spread so effectively. It's almost like they knew what to expect—that is unless there was something wrong with the bacterial strain I received."

"There was nothing wrong with the bacteria. It was tested on eighty-one mammals in our detention cells," said SaSu. "There was an 87 percent death rate among the prisoners. Of course, they received no medical treatment to try to save them. What about the other attack. Has it achieved your expectation?"

"Wildly better than we could have hoped for," said SuHa. "Almost 25 percent of the entire population of the political entity called Gaza Strip has died. The mammals in the Muslim cult are furious with the Jews and are trying to get any and all countries to agree to declare war on the Jewish political division. Several of the countries that strictly adhere to the Muslim cult have joined in condemning the Jews and done everything they could to hurt Israel, short of an actual attack. We were hoping the radical elements of the Jewish group would be so inflamed by the plague attack on Jerusalem that they would be the ones to start an active war with the Muslims. Since the Jerusalem attack was so ineffective, this has not happened. We have created tremendous tension between the two groups but unfortunately no conflict.

"Another problem is that the country with the strongest military force, the so-called United States, has not reacted as predicted. In fact, they have remained very calm and silent about the two bio-attacks that we thought would be so repugnant to them. It's a good thing we have an alternate plan in motion to inflame tempers in that country."

"The Exalted Lord is uncomfortable with our results so far," said SaSu. "I fear we have not pushed the mammals enough to guarantee a worldwide conflict. See if you can find out why our first two moves with anthrax and plague did not have the intended result. Also, I think you should get with your planning group and find another high-leverage activity to really set off these mammals."

As SuHa was leaving the office, SaSu sat and stared at the wall of awards he had received during his years of service to Laurasia. *I made a mistake talking about Laurasia's plans with those prisoner mammals that escaped. Could that possibly have anything to do with the poor results being achieved by SuHa? Oh, well, no one really knows what was said in that cell, and my subordinates would never dare to question me. It should not come home to haunt me if SuHa's mission fails.*

chapter 14

MISSION 4 FROM WHITE SANDS

Steven, Ellie, and Bill were shown into the office of the senior delegate to the national forum from RoHo's province. His skin was wrinkled, and he was stooped with age. The red and orange splotches on his stomach had faded to a dull pink color. However, when he greeted them, he did so with a very powerful voice. "My name is RaKe," he said. "Mayor TaSu has told me of your strange tale. In a few minutes, we will be joined by WeKu, our national information chief. He is very interested in your story."

WeKu arrived, and everyone introduced themselves. As they settled in for the discussion, WeKu said, "I assume you have come to us for our help with the Laurasians. To save time, I should tell you a little about Gondwanian philosophy. The history of our race began in what is now known as Laurasia. Our civilization was born amidst constant fighting. Over a thousand years ago in Gondwana, we got the chance to change all that. We created a democratic government that protects its citizens and works diligently to maintain peace but with a minimum number of people involved with government.

"The Laurasians did manage to put a halt to their constant fighting, but they did it by creating a perpetual dictatorship. Their so-called Exalted Lord is merely the strongest and most ruthless person in their government. They care little for the people they govern, and no one questions even the next level above them without dire consequences. However, in the name of maintaining peace, we do not make any effort to intervene in their affairs."

"Since the Laurasians are so aggressive and warlike, why haven't they already invaded your country?" asked Ellie through Bill.

"They would invade Gondwana tomorrow if they thought they had a reasonable chance to win," said WeKu. "However, we have consistently maintained stronger technologies in a broad range of weapons categories. As a result, the Laurasian leaders are convinced that we could beat them in an outright war and so have not attacked us. A result of this rather delicate situation is that we must continue to invest heavily in the development of war-related technologies. A second and possibly more burdensome result is that we must spend large amounts of money spying on the Laurasians to be sure we can evaluate the balance of strength between the two countries."

"If you think you would win a war with Laurasia, why don't you invade them?" asked Steven. "You could end this weapons race once and for all."

"We have many citizens that believe such an action would be the right thing to do," said WeKu. "We would probably lose many people in such an attempt, but think of the benefits if we could secure world peace. However, our society is guided by the Council of Mothers, which does not believe in starting a war of aggression for any reason."

"I understand your council's position. War is never really a good thing, even when it is for the right reasons," said Steven. "It should always be considered the last resort after all other options have been eliminated. We would try to thwart the Laurasians' actions in our own world, but we are convinced that they will just keep trying different plans to destroy our civilization because they are so desperate. That is why we have come to ask for your help. We are convinced that the Laurasians must be stopped somehow in this era. You say that you expend large resources in spying on them. Maybe together we could devise a plan to stop them without starting a war."

"I think we could get the support of the Council of Mothers to do this," said WeKu. "Do you have anything in mind?"

"We have the ability to move in time and to possibly change the historical events that have created the Laurasian government in its current form," said Steven. "For example, what if we went back in time about twenty years and stopped the Laurasians from inventing their capability for time travel. Also, you could look for a moment in time that, if altered, would change the Laurasian approach to governing their people."

Steven thought, *The C-Pg extinction should isolate this action from our time but we don't know what effect an action like this will have on the Gondwanians future. I wonder if the Laurasian's even know about the C-Pg extinction event.*

"These ideas have some good potential," said WeKu. "What would you need from us to do something along these lines?"

"The first very serious thing we lack is good intelligence information on the Laurasians," said Steven. "My guess is that the only really good information must be learned from the very highest levels of their government. I think the lower-level people are not given significant data as evidenced by the fact that the high council thinks they are going to run out of energy within two years and have virtually told no one outside the high council."

"You are absolutely correct about that," said WeKu. "We must plant ten operatives just to get one person promoted to levels where they can help us so our information on some topics is incomplete."

"The second thing we lack is the ability to move among the Laurasians without being obvious," said Steven. "They have many of our people in detention centers around their country, but they do not allow any of them to move about unguarded.

We were arrested and sentenced to death the one time we tried to peacefully contact them."

"So you would need help in the form of operatives to help implement any plan we could come up with," stated WeKu. "These requirements are within my ability to approve. I would like to flesh out a plan and then present it to the council for their blessing, which I feel sure they will give."

"Is your current intelligence aware of the Laurasian time machine?" asked Steven. "We should try to find out where it is located and how many of them they have. We know their current sacred scientist, WaTu, invented the capability about twenty years ago. If we could learn more exact information on when and where he did his work, maybe we could go back into the past to stop him."

"Our information about Laurasian time travel capability is embarrassingly weak," said WeKu. "It is general knowledge throughout the whole Laurasian population about you creatures from the future. They are even teaching a large portion of their population to speak the languages of you future people. We think this is mostly being done as a distraction from the real issues within Laurasia. As for where their time travel device is located, I don't know for sure. There are only two places where creatures from the future have ever been reported. One is in SoMu on the Bear Paw Sea, and the other is a city called PuRo to the northeast of SoMu. Its major industry is rock harvesting and carving. They make beautiful furniture. There is also a small scientific campus in PuRo. If I remember correctly, I think WaTu was born and educated there. I will request our information network to see if there are any other reported sightings of creatures from the future in other cities in Laurasia. By the way, what do you prefer to be called besides creatures from the future?"

"The Laurasians usually refer to us as mammals," said Steven. "We would prefer to be called humans."

"So the rumors are true, and your species are really not

born from eggs outside your mother but actually spend the beginning of your lives inside your mothers' bodies. How curious," said RaKe. "In my entire life of 143 years, I have never heard a stranger tale."

"I will also get our network to see if we can pinpoint the exact location of these time machines as you call them," said WeKu. "I think we can guess from the location of humans that they probably have two machines—one in SoMu and the other in PuRo. We can set our operatives to the task of pinpointing exactly where these machines are currently located. I will search our historical archive to see what we know about the life of WaTu. This other idea you mentioned intrigues me very much. If we could find a particular moment or even several moments that could be changed to make Laurasian society less warlike, we could have peace all over the world."

"I would urge the utmost caution with respect to that course of action," said Steven. "We are new to time travel, and as yet, we have not tried to intentionally alter the space-time continuum. If we change the direction of Laurasia, we could inadvertently change Gondwanian history at the same time. The pivotal moments should be carefully chosen to not have a secondary effect on Gondwana."

I understand," said WeKu. "I will get our historians to begin a study of the true history of Laurasia, not the propaganda they peddle to their masses."

VESSEL SITE, GONDWANA 65 MILLION YEARS BCE

Life at the vessel site in Gondwana was quiet for the first few days. Then a group of Gondwanian botanists on a field trip chanced to walk right up to the gate, and things got more interesting. "Hello is there anyone around?" yelled one of the reptiles named ToSe. The Team T-REX members left to guard the site were unsure how to proceed. They had set up a tent to keep themselves out of the direct sun so that they were not visible to the reptiles when they walked up to the gate. They were unsure if they should talk to the visitors or stay hidden?

Finally, Fred stepped out of the tent over George's protests and walked up to the gate. "Hello, what do you want?" he asked.

"Oh, my, what manner of creature are you?" asked ToSe. "Wait... please excuse my rudeness my ancestors would disown me for calling attention to a person's physical defects. I am most embarrassed. We are teachers from the RoHo Academy out on a field trip to study the smaller non-Saurian species of creatures living within the shrubs. We left our vehicle at the side of the road back about a mile. I just realized I brought food for lunch out in the wild, but I forgot to bring water. Could you spare a small amount of water? We would gladly pay you for it."

"Please stay here, and I will get you some water," said Fred. "How many of you are out there?"

"Just the four you see. It is a very informal outing to find samples of the wildlife to show to our students," said ToSe. "We are about to sit down over in that bare spot to eat. Would you care to join us? We have plenty of food, just no water."

As Fred stepped into the tent, he said, "We're here on a peace mission. It won't hurt to give them some water and chat a little. You four stay out of sight so they don't know our strength. I'll go eat with them."

"I think you are making a big mistake," said George. "There is nothing in our orders about chatting up the locals. You could be putting the site at risk. Those creatures may just be trying to infiltrate our camp."

Despite George's objections, Fred took some bread and cheese with him along with plastic bottles of water. He remembered hearing the story of Steven and Ellie's experience when they shared a meal with their reptile acquaintances. After he stepped through the gate, it slid closed automatically. The four reptiles had settled down in a comfortable place only thirty feet away. They were passing around packets of food as Fred approached and offered everyone a bottle of water. Fred had to quickly stop ToSe, who was about to bite off the bottle cap and neck. After Fred showed them how to open the bottles, he took a packet of food from ToSe. "What is this?" he asked.

"This is the newest fad for outdoor eating," answered ToSe. "It is several types of tasty greens ground up with the flowers from three different shrubs. Then it is compressed into a convenient square. It is called a mobile meal and was invented for our moon travelers to make eating easy while traveling, and it is very nutritious."

"Excuse me?" blurted Fred, his outburst startled the visitors. They could not understand his intense interest. "Did you say moon travelers?"

"Of course," answered ToSe startled. "Where have you been the last ten years? Everyone knows about the explorations of the moon and Planet 4. Those are practically ancient history, but please tell us your story. Where did you come from, and why are you here out in the wilderness?"

"I'll tell you my whole story," said Fred. "But please first tell me about moon travelers. I have heard nothing about your civilization and its accomplishments."

"Okay, we have projected that we will run out of certain natural resources that are very vital to industry and the growth of our civilization within the next two hundred years or so," explained ToSe. This includes metals and radioactive materials that we use to generate energy. Our government decided to sponsor a project to adapt electrogliders to fly outside the atmosphere. We learned how to neutralize gravity for these special electrogliders to allow them to fly outside of the atmosphere but propulsion was still a problem. Later we learned how to actually reverse the force of gravity to propel the electrogliders. This project was complete about fifteen years ago, and then using these vehicles, we flew people to the moon to prospect for the materials we need. Unfortunately, the moon is surprisingly devoid of useful materials. We had originally thought that it would be of similar composition to this planet, but that was wrong. It is made up almost entirely of basalt rock with no metallic minerals or radioactive minerals."

"So then we decided to send prospectors to the red planet that orbits the sun outside of this planet's orbit. We call it Planet 4. We also explored the planet that orbits inside this planet. We call it Planet 2. But the atmosphere there is mostly carbon dioxide, and the temperature is very hot. It was judged to be an impossible place to work and therefore useless as a mining planet. The atmosphere of the red planet had a little less oxygen than this planet, but it was breathable. The prospectors had good success finding the minerals we need, so we began designing cargo vessels to bring back the refined materials. Just after we began full-scale operations, a natural disaster of gigantic proportions occurred."

"So you are telling me that Gondwana has sent people to Mars and back?" asked Fred.

"What is Mars?" asked ToSe. "Oh, you mean the red planet. Yes, that was over ten years ago."

"What was the disaster?" asked Fred.

"There was a small planet, smaller than Planet 4, that orbited just slightly further out from the sun than Planet 4 therefore it was called Planet 5," said ToSe. "The orbit of this planet was tilted about ten degrees from the plane of the other planets in the solar system. Planet 5 had been in that orbit for millions of years. Five years after we began to prospect and map the red planet these two planets approached each other in their natural orbits, but coming closer to each other than they had ever been. Both planets simultaneously approached the point where the two orbits were at a minimum distance apart, and Planet 5 was also crossing the plane of the red planet's orbit at exactly the same time. Our scientists tell us the two planets had probably never been that close together before. As they approached minimum distance, Planet 5 suddenly exploded because of the increased forces of gravity. The body of the red planet was not seriously damaged. It just suffered massive earthquakes. However, much of its atmosphere was pulled away to dissipate in the vacuum of space. The prospectors that were working there died in the disaster."

"So has this stopped your plans to find additional resources?" asked Fred.

"At first, we were afraid that was true," answered ToSe. "The air of Planet 4 became too poor in oxygen, and the temperature on the planet's surface dropped too low for us because of the lack of atmosphere. This lack of oxygen is what killed the prospectors because they were not prepared for the abrupt change.

"Then after a few months, we found out that this disaster may have been a stroke of luck. The vast majority of pieces of the exploded planet stayed near their original orbit, just spread out over a vast distance. However, there were some fragments that were blown out of the orbit. Two of the pieces of Planet 5 have actually gone into orbit around Planet 4 as moons. Also, chunks of Planet 5 were captured by the strong gravity of Planet 6 and became moons. One fairly large chunk dipped inside the orbit of Planet 4 and is approaching the orbit of this planet."

"Have you carefully plotted the flight path of this piece of Planet 5?" asked Fred. "Could it be on a path to hit this planet?"

"Oh, no, the rock will not hit this planet. In fact, it migrated to its closest approach last month, and it is gradually moving away from us now," said ToSe. "But we sent prospectors to visit the rock and found it to be rich in the materials we need, especially the radioactive minerals needed to generate electricity. Right now, our government is initiating a project to try to change its trajectory to bring it into orbit around this planet. Just think. We will be able to mine this piece of the destroyed planet from a position closer than our moon. The cost of acquiring these materials will be only a fraction of what we thought it would be if we brought them from Planet 4."

"You must be very proud of the accomplishments of your space program," said Fred.

"Yes, we are all excited to hear whether the project to move the rock into orbit is successful," said ToSe. "But now please tell us your story."

"As I said, I will tell you about myself and where I come from," answered Fred. "My story may be as hard to believe for you as the one you have just told is for me." Fred explained his origin and the fact that the rest of his party was currently in RoHo to meet with government officials. The Gondwanian botanists were very interested in him and the future world. Fred was so intent on answering questions that he forgot about his lunch until ToSe reminded him.

"Hey, this is pretty good," said Fred. "May I have more?"

"Here, take the last two. We thank you for the water and your very interesting tale," said ToSe. "I know we have all learned much from you. It is really hard to believe the little creatures we were out here studying will someday evolve into intelligent beings. By the way, I have recently learned how to fly an electroglider. If you would like to go for a flight and see more of Gondwana, just come look me up at the academy. When you get to the school, ask anyone, and they can tell you how to find me."

chapter 15

Khaliq was already sick of being in America. It seemed to him that someone was constantly trying to sell him something or get him to fill out a survey. The safe house did not have a phone, so they did not have to put up with the dinnertime sales calls, but they still had to go out for food and other items where sales people bothered them. The people coming to his door at night unannounced to sell things were particularly worrisome because he was afraid they might learn too much about the inhabitants of the house which meant they would need to be killed. However, his plan was coming together very well, and so far, no one in authority had detected any trace of his little group. The electronics expert, Masud, had finished building the remote detonation transmitter. He had tested it out using a receiver that he had brought from Kabul when he first entered the United States. The receiver was small enough not to raise suspicion when he went through US customs, and by bringing it, he knew he had an exact copy of the ones he would be working with later. They were currently testing its range. The plan called for it to work at a distance of one mile. Then they would use it from a distance of half a mile. It paid high dividends to build a margin for error into a plan like theirs. The balance of the two hundred-plus receivers would be coming later.

One morning about two weeks before the Rose Bowl

renovation was scheduled to start, Khaliq called the five members of his crew to the dining room of their little house. "Here is five hundred dollars in cash for each of you to go out and get the things we will need for the job at the Rose Bowl," said Khaliq. "Huda, you and Nadir will go to different rental agencies where you will each rent a truck-mounted cherry picker that can allow us to work up to ninety feet above the ground. Find a fairly busy place where you will not be unduly noticed to make your rental. Use the Internet from the coffee shop in the next block south to find your rental agency. Pay with the cash I just gave you and give the fake addresses printed on the cards I am handing you now. Do not give the cards to anyone. Only tell them verbally the address from the card. Have the cherry pickers delivered to the Rose Bowl at the location spelled out on this separate card. We have permission to store our equipment there starting the beginning of July."

"Can we use the car?" asked Huda.

"No, it is too dangerous," said Khaliq. "We need to try to minimize any situations where there is a trail that could lead back to us. Take the bus using directions you get from the Internet. Masud, Rafiq, and Kamil, go separately to the Inglewood area to different hardware stores and buy all the things on these lists. Buy large backpacks to help you carry your items on the bus. I don't want to sound like your mothers, but this is the most important operation al-Qaeda has ever undertaken. I don't want you to do anything that will call attention to yourselves. Be sure to constantly check to see if you are being followed. Get going and proceed carefully."

INGLEWOOD, CALIFORNIA

Rafiq had no trouble buying the tools and supplies on his list, and he still had over 150 dollars left when he was finished. He walked out of the hardware store and strolled down the busy street, enjoying the sunshine and pleasant temperature. The neighborhood seemed shabby, and there were many people just lounging around, doing nothing. It reminded him of Kabul and the friends he had left there. He was the youngest member of the terror cell and homesick.

"Hey baby," called out a woman who was leaning against the wall of a Goodwill store. "Would you like a date?" The woman was not particularly pretty, but she was dressed very provocatively.

"What do you mean?" asked Rafiq. "What would we do?"

"Anything you want to do if you have the cash," she replied. "Let's get off the street and talk about it. What's your name, honey?" They walked around the corner of a building into a small alley.

"How much money do you want?" asked Rafiq, thinking this might be good practice for when he met up with his forty virgins.

"If you have seventy-five dollars, I will make your dreams come true," said the woman. "I need the money in advance please."

Rafiq pulled out the cash in his front pocket, counted out seventy-five dollars, and handed it to the woman. The next thing he knew, he had a handcuff around the wrist he had extended and quickly found his arms locked behind him. "Sorry, buddy, but you're busted. I'm a LAPD vice cop, and I'm arresting you for solicitation of a prostitute. The patrol car will be here in just a minute, and we'll take you to the precinct station."

SANTA MONICA, CALIFORNIA

"I can't believe it," screamed Khaliq. "I send Rafiq on a simple assignment to buy tools, and he gets arrested for paying a whore. I must find a lawyer and give this lawyer enough cash to get Rafiq bailed out. We must pay the whole bail, not get a bail bondsman involved to avoid questions. This will not help our cash situation. Huda, you go to the lawyer's office to drop off the bail money and then go back when you can pick Rafiq up. At least he had enough sense to give the fake address I gave him. Park the car several blocks away from the lawyer's office when you go back to get him so no one can associate Rafiq with the car and its license plate number. I want you to tell Rafiq that I have another job for the two of you. You are to pick up some explosives that another operative left buried in the desert. After you both have dug the hole to find the explosive, shoot Rafiq, make sure he is dead, put him in the hole, and cover up the entire mess. Drive around for several hours to be sure you are not being followed before you come back here. Do you think you can handle the job?"

"Of course," mumbled Huda.

"Well, that's good because if this job does not go off smoothly, dig another hole out there in the desert for yourself," Khaliq said calmly with no emotion. Huda felt a chill run down his spine.

LAURASIA, 65 MILLION YEARS BCE

"So you need yet another dirty trick to play on the mammals," said FiRu, the chief of SuHa's planning group. "I would have thought that their world would be in ruins after the things we have already done. Hear me, my leader. Something went very wrong with the plague attack on Jerusalem, and the mammals' reaction to our intervention has been wrong ever since. It is as if they knew there was an outside hand responsible."

"I don't see how that is possible," said SuHa. "I am the only one of our people that travels to the future now that our mammal research is complete. Our mortal enemies, the Gondwanians, do not have time travel. Our spies have recently verified this once again. So even if someone highly placed in the Laurasian government told the Gondwanians of our project, they would still have no way to communicate the information to the mammals."

"My leader," said FiRu. "There is a story I have heard from the warden of prisons in SoMu, a sibling of mine. A while ago, there were two mammals captured in the city. A husband-and-wife from the scientist class reported finding them at the edge of the city. The warden could never verify what facility the mammals escaped from. He was one of the members of an interrogation team to question them. They claimed to be from the future and wanted to initiate communication between our two civilizations. No one believed this, and at one point in the questioning, your superior, SaSu, stopped the meeting and made everyone except the mammals leave the room. After only a few minutes, SaSu also left the room. He told the prison guards to execute the prisoners the next morning. But the really interesting part of the story is that they escaped, killing a guard in the process, and they have not been found yet. With the few mammals we still have imprisoned in Laurasia, I cannot understand how two of them could run free for four or five weeks and not leave a trace that would have been reported."

"I know, FiRu, you don't believe in coincidences," said SuHa. "But I don't see how two mammals in Laurasia would know about our project. Even if they did somehow know our plan, how would this information get to the mammals sixty-five million years in the future?"

"I see no possibility my leader," said FiRu. "However, I see no possibility that the mammals of Jerusalem could have been able to contain our little plague attack under normal circumstances, and I see no possibility that the US government would not condemn Israel for a bio-attack on the Gaza Strip."

"I need your staff to come up with another attack to rile up our evil mammal adversaries," said SuHa. "I need it by tomorrow. I would also suggest we try to push a completely different button this time. If for some reason the mammals involved with the Middle East really know about our involvement, we should strike in another area where they will not expect."

AMERICAN SOUTHWEST

Antonio Garza was sitting comfortably in the cab of his truck, singing along with the radio, and tapping his feet. He had finally collected 210 backpacks from illegals crossing from Mexico. He still did not know what was in them, but he did not really care. When he met up with his contact in the Los Angeles area, the contact would give him one hundred and fifty thousand dollars. He could not earn that much money in two years in his normal trucking job. All he had been asked to do was to collect the backpacks from the illegal Mexican nationals and hide the backpacks until he collected over two hundred. He could go about his regular business while he waited for the groups of illegals to cross from Mexico. Now he was taking the backpacks, which were concealed within his normal cargo, from Presidio, Texas, to LA. When he was near LA, he would call the cell number of his contact and set up a meeting place and time.

He had left Presidio the day before at about 8:00 p.m. It was 10:00 p.m. a day later when Antonio stopped for fuel at a truck stop just outside of the Los Angeles county line on Interstate 10. Antonio dialed the number that he had been given and waited as it rang three times. "Yes?" was the response from the other end.

"I hear you are going to take a group for a hike in the mountains and need some extra backpacks," said Antonio. "Where should I deliver them?"

They set the meet at a rest stop about one hour's drive east of the truck stop where Antonio had made the call. Once there, Antonio was to look for a silver Toyota Camry to arrive and then follow the car to the place where he could drop off the backpacks. Once he found the car, he followed it for another hour into the desert. At last, they stopped in front of an abandoned barn. The two men who had met him looked Middle Eastern with dark hair and short dark beards. The three unloaded the backpacks without much conversation and hid them in the barn, all except for two. Once everything was put in order, it was time for Antonio's payment. As one of the Middle-Eastern men showed Antonio a large briefcase full of one-hundred-dollar bills, the other man walked up behind Antonio and shot him in the back of the head.

"Put the body in the sleeping compartment behind the cab of the truck after you clean out his pockets of any identification," said Huda. "You drive the truck along this road about twenty-five miles farther north deeper into the desert. I'll just put these two backpacks in the Toyota's trunk so that we can come back here tomorrow, when Khaliq will check out the detonation transmitter one last time. I'll come behind you to pick you up and take you back to the safe house. Just leave the keys in the truck and leave the cargo doors unlocked. We can hope some greedy infidel comes along and muddles the evidence surrounding the death of the driver by making it look like part of a theft."

Laurasia, 65 Million years BCE

"My leader," said FiRu when SuHa returned the next day. "We stayed up all night plotting, and I think you will like what we came up with."

"Tell me what you are so proud of," said SuHa with the reptile equivalent of a smile. "The proposal sounds intriguing based on the tone of your voice."

"As we discussed yesterday, there seems to be reluctance for the United States to pick a side in the Middle-Eastern conflict we have tried so hard to start. My working assumption, unproven but plausible, is that they have some knowledge or at least a suspicion that there is a third party instigating the conflict. Therefore, they have played the peacemaker and tried to keep the other major powers from supporting a war to punish Israel for the attack on the Gaza Strip. One of the more active countries trying to get the various world powers to punish Israel is China. Their real agenda is to demonstrate to other world powers that they are a leader in world politics. They would interpret an attack by the United States at this time as a total rejection of their position in world politics. I propose we get an aircraft and a nuclear bomb and attack a vulnerable target in China and leave evidence that the United States was responsible for the attack."

"You have done well as usual," said SuHa. "If the United States will not pick a side, we will get China to make the choice for them. Now we need to work on details. Where do we get an aircraft, and where do we get the bomb?"

"We originally thought to steal an aircraft in the mammal world," said FiRu. "Presumably, it would be a US military airplane. But then I realized we have no one who knows how to pilot such a vehicle. Possibly, we could kidnap a mammal military pilot and condition him to do what we require. He could be programmed to say he was under orders from the US government to bomb the Chinese target. I think a more feasible possibility would be to steal a Gondwanian electroglider, put US military markings on it, and then somehow allow it to be captured as proof of the US involvement."

"The Gondwanian aircraft sounds more practical from an acquisition and control point of view," said SuHa. "I will check to see if our sacred scientist's time machine can handle something as large as an electroglider. Give me an estimate of the pertinent dimensions. What kind of weapons do the Gondwanians arm their airships with?"

"That is their most closely guarded secret," said FiRu. "They seem to upgrade their weapons capability every six months or so. We know they have nuclear bomb capability as a result of using nuclear power to generate their so called electricity, and we think the electrogliders that are used to protect their northern borders are always armed with nuclear bombs of some type to be ready for any attack Laurasia might launch. They use this quick response and the capability to cripple our industry in one devastating blow as the deterrent to keep us from starting a war."

"So we could satisfy our two biggest requirements for this project by stealing one of the electrogliders from a northern base," said SuHa. "Do we have any agents that have infiltrated one of those bases?"

"I have already checked, and providence is on our side for this project," said FiRu. "I found an agent who is in fact a pilot of a heavy electroglider. These types of vehicles are armed with bombs and carry only one person, although there is capacity to carry two people. They are so automated that one person can handle all of the requirements to fly and discharge the weapons. Can you imagine them trusting such an important weapon to a single person? Our Exalted Lord would never allow such a thing. They are just too trusting."

"Communicate with this agent and arrange for him to defect with his vehicle while it is fully armed," said SuHa. "This is too easy. Something serious is bound to go wrong. You know we have the top priority in case anyone in our government complains about our use of their espionage resource."

chapter 16

MISSION 4 FROM WHITE SANDS

Steven, Ellie, and Bill had accomplished the main part of their mission, getting the Gondwanians to agree to help against Laurasia. They wanted to return to the vessel so they could communicate the good news back to White Sands. However, they also thought it might be safer to keep the location of the vessel secret for a little while longer in case the Gondwanians were not as friendly as they appear.

Just as they finished discussing when to return to the vessel, WeKu came hurrying into the room, his stomach spots bright red, a condition the team members had come to associate with a high state of excitement. "We have found the specific time for the birth of WaTu and a general place and time for the invention of the time machine. Now we need to decide which way we will approach this. Should we somehow prevent the invention, or should we prevent the birth of the inventor?"

"Do you have any information on the process of the invention?" asked Ellie, Bill translating for her. "Did the government or a supervisor push WaTu to make the time machine, or did WaTu provide his own motivation?"

"Oh, I see where you are going with this," said WeKu. "The old reports of our operative in the PuRo Science Complex at the time say this invention was a complete surprise to the leadership of the science class. The preliminary work on the project was done by WaTu on his own time and in secret. Therefore, we can plan to kidnap him and all evidence of his work."

"That works for me," said Steven thoughtfully. "That way, Gondwana will gain access to time travel by fostering its invention in Gondwana. It could be used as an enticement for your government to approve our plan."

"What you say is true," said WeKu. "However, I will recommend to the Council of Mothers that we get your commitment to help us with additional operations to try to change the character of the whole country of Laurasia."

"We don't have the authority to make that promise, so at some time in the near future, we should check with our government," said Ellie. "It seems like a reasonable request to us. We will support it to our leaders. As we said, we have little experience with influencing the outcome of history. This operation to grab WaTu should give us some useful information on how it works."

The operation to kidnap WaTu before he could reveal his knowledge of how to make a time travel device was approved as expected by the Council of Mothers with the request that Team T-REX provide help with another mission to try to change the philosophy of the Laurasian leadership. The Gondwanians were busy studying the history of Laurasia to find some inflection points that could reverse the whole military dictatorship outcome of Laurasian history.

During the approval process one of the mothers on the council asked if anyone had considered the ethics of changing the lives of millions of people without their consent. The plan was finally approved because the majority of the council thought ethics did not really come into play in this situation. The natural flow of time would map out a new time line in the same way (using the free will of the participants) it always did except one variable out of millions would be changed. Also the consensus was that no one would remember that a change had been made so no one would experience loss as the result of the planned change. Lastly, the need for change was caused by the immoral actions of the Laurasian government and they were the ones that would bear the brunt of the action.

For the operation to kidnap WaTu, the team decided to send four Gondwanians and four members of Team T-REX on a raid at the PuRo Science Complex. They would be transported four per trip with two trips. One of the Gondwanians by the name of MaSo was chosen for this mission because he had spent two years as an operative in PuRo. It was standard practice that if an operative had not begun to receive promotions within the Laurasian government after he or she had spent two years there, the operative was brought home. The exact factors that determined whether or not a person would be promoted within the Laurasian government still eluded the Gondwanian spymasters. They felt that they should not waste their people's time if they were not going to be promoted to a position of usefulness within a reasonable time. MaSo picked the arrival site and the route the group would take to get to WaTu. Everything was scheduled to start the next morning.

That evening after a hearty meal of greens, nuts, and an herbal tea, the participants in the following day's operation split up. The Gondwanians went off to spend time with family or friends. Bill was engaged in a conversation with WeKu about the many and varied languages of the future world and how people dealt with the associated communication difficulties. This gave Ellie and Steven the opportunity to go for a walk through the streets of the city. The moon was almost full, and the light turned the statues and artwork of the city into a wonderland. They strolled for a long time, exchanging no words. At some point, Steven noticed they were holding hands.

"You never really told me what happened to your face back in Laurasia," said Ellie. "The last I remember was that you were already handcuffed. Why did they hit you?"

"It may have had something to do with the fact that I tried to cripple one of the confors by breaking his kneecap," said Steven.

"Then I pushed another one out the door and slammed it in his face. Finally, I offended the leader by pushing him backward over a chair. That is when the last confor decided to bash me in the face with his weapon. The offended leader also decided to put out my lights with his projectile gun when he got up. They just never should have shot that projectile into you."

"Wow," said Ellie with a laugh. "You were only one confor away from putting down their whole team. I wonder what you would have been able to do if your hands hadn't been tied behind your back."

"On a more serious note, I may have made things worse by over reacting so much," said Steven. "That situation in MeMo's and PuFo's home may have eliminated any chance we had to talk to the Laurasian leaders and resolve our differences peacefully. It just reminded me of a bad scene I lived through a little over a year ago. I promised myself not to let that happen to me again at all costs. So I just went off like a grenade when I should have used my head."

"What happened to you that made you feel like that?" asked Ellie.

"I would really rather not talk about it right now," said Steven.

Bill, Steven, and Ellie led the four Gondwanian soldiers back to the vessel. Bill and MaSo were chosen as the conduits for communication. Luckily, Ellie had insisted they permanently mark the place where they entered the road on the way to RoHo. The vegetation had completely grown over their track through the shrubs in just a few days. They missed walking directly to the site as they returned but only by a few hundred feet. Fortunately, they saw the guard tower and the perimeter fence over the shrubs and corrected their course with a minimum of fuss. The remaining five members of Team T-REX were more than ready to get back to White Sands.

"The only excitement we had was when a group of Gondwanian biologists visited and we shared lunch," said Fred.

"I learned a lot about Gondwanian technical capabilities from them. Do you know they have explored the inner part of the solar system?"

"Yeah, he insisted on engaging a potential enemy over my objections," said George. "But I guess he did pick up some pretty hot information."

"That's something I didn't hear about during our visit to RoHo," said Steven. "You can tell me all about it while we wait for the vessel to cycle to the future and come back for us."

"Ellie, would you and Bill travel home with our four guests on the first trip back to White Sands?" said Steven. "I think we can get six into the vessel so we can get back in only two trips. Based on the turbulence of previous trips, we should have two people sit on the floor and strap themselves to the ladder to pass through the transition without injury.

"It sounds like Fred has some information I should listen to. I'll come on the second trip. After you explain why we returned with four armed reptile soldiers, you can start to learn about the weapons both the Gondwanians and the Laurasians will be using. After we've seen them, I would say the weapons our new allies have are not simple stun guns."

"Okay, don't let George make you crazy," said Ellie, smiling directly at George as she spoke. Her constant teasing was based on the huge amount of respect she had for him after she had reviewed his military record.

The six remaining members of Team T-REX packed up the equipment and took down the perimeter fence so that they would be ready when the vessel returned. After the work was complete, they all settled down in a rough circle to eat their MREs. "So tell me about the conversation you had with your visitors," said Steven as he sat down next to Fred.

"Boss, we tried to keep him inside the perimeter for safety, but he wouldn't have any of it," said George. "He actually went out and ate some of their weird moon food. Then he tried to get the rest of us to eat some too."

"A group of four reptiles came to the gate, hailing to see if anyone was home," said Fred. "We were all out of sight in the tent, but we are here on a peace mission, so I decided that we should make nice with the locals. They were quite shocked when they first saw me. They really didn't know what to think. It was funny watching them try to be polite and wanting so much to ask what was wrong with me."

"So they were innocent passersby not out here hunting down stray mammals," said Steven.

"Actually they were out hunting mammals but the small local ones not the human kind. The food they were eating turned out to be a convenient new instant meal like our MREs but tailored for them," said Fred. "It was a mixture of greens and flowers compacted together in a single solid rectangle that was developed to feed the people they sent to the moon. That is what turned the conversation to interplanetary exploration."

Just as he had been told, Fred then revealed the whole story of the exploration of the moon and Mars by the Gondwanians. Steven nodded and said, "I guess we picked the right allies from a technological point of view." Then Steven told the others about the deal they had arranged with the Council of Mothers.

White Sands, New Mexico

Ellie had to start the explanations as soon as they arrived at White Sands. Before they all completely exited the vessel, Jonas came trotting up. "We are getting quite the collection of reptiles here," he said, smiling. "I certainly hope these people have agreed to help us."

"They have already begun to help us," said Ellie. "We have the time and a set of coordinates for you to send us to so that we can kidnap the inventor of the Laurasian time machine before he actually accomplishes the job. These soldiers have agreed to help us stop its invention in the hope that the Laurasians will not be able to cause trouble here. Let's get everyone into a big conference room, and as soon as Steven and the rest of the team get here, we can go over the mission strategy."

As everyone settled into seats, Ellie (through Bill) asked MaSo to describe how their weapons worked. "Our battle weapon is a dual-purpose tool that can fire a projectile about fifty yards with accuracy and soundlessly," explained MaSo. "The projectile incorporates a simple poison-dispensing system. The poison can kill a normal-sized reptile of our race within ten seconds. That is very fast, but in a battle, an opponent can do a lot of damage in ten seconds. The alternate system in the weapon is electromagnetic. It fires a pulse of energy that reverses the normal attraction between atoms in a molecule, causing the molecules within the influence of the pulse to fly apart. As the pulse leaves the focus lens of the weapon, it expands to the size of one inch in diameter at a range of two hundred yards. As a result, it puts a hole through anything solid in its path until the energy in the pulse is dissipated. It can blow a hole through a person or an inanimate object instantaneously. The weapon is soundless in this mode, but the pulse generates an explosive noise when it impacts a target. Therefore, the weapon gives us stealth if we can wait ten seconds or significant firepower if we need speed."

"That is quite a potent weapon," said Ellie. "What kind of weapons do you expect the Laurasians to have during our raid?"

"Their conformance forces are usually armed with projectile weapons that render the target unconscious within seconds," said MaSo. "The drug they use is extra powerful to put the target down quickly. They use a drug to make the target unconscious rather than a poison as we do because they use the weapons to subdue their own people most of the time. They administer an antidote to the target as soon as it is practical to reduce the effects of the drug so the target wakes up in a reasonable time. Without the antidote, the target may remain in a coma for days. We also have the same antidote chemical that we can take before we might face this weapon. With the correct dosage, it should make us resistant but not immune to the toxin in their projectiles. Unfortunately, this antidote has never been field-tested as a preventative, so we should try to avoid depending on it. If we don't do anything to alert the Laurasians that may be the only weapon we face on this mission."

"What if they sense something is wrong?" asked Ellie. "What will they use then?"

"When their confors think they will face serious opponents, they are armed with a form of laser weapon," said MaSo. "It sends out a beam of light that can burn through a target at one hundred yards. It is a very powerful weapon, and the leadership of the country does not allow it to be widely distributed. My hope is we can get into their science complex and out with WaTu before they bring in those weapons."

Steven and the other five members of Team T-REX came into the conference room at this point, and everyone started planning the raid. "We will arrive a short distance south of the city, less than a half mile," said MaSo. "Approaching the city from the south is the closest approach to the science complex. We Gondwanians will wear black medallions that you see around our necks that identify us as confor officers, and we will be carrying projectile weapons so we look like the real thing. We must try to keep you humans out of sight. We cannot use the ruse of guarding you as prisoners because at this point in time, they know nothing about your race. If we are unlucky and they do see you, we will act like we have captured unknown prisoners and are taking them to the complex for study. We will capture a tri-wheeler so that we can drive the human members of the team unseen through the city without being noticed. Once we find WaTu, we will need to get him to tell us the location of all of his working documents.

"The Laurasians have developed a mind control technology that allows them to make people do whatever they want them to do. The technology requires two steps. For the first step, they inject a liquid into the subject. This calms the person and chemically alters receptors in the brain to facilitate the second step. Next, a neurotoxin is administered that makes the subject incapable of resisting. The neurotoxin is a strange material that only exists in a gaseous state over a wide range of temperatures, which complicates the equipment required for the job. We believe they have modified the technology to work on humans, though it is not as effective. That is probably how they learned so much about your civilization in such a short time. Our scientists have duplicated this technology for use when we interrogate Laurasian prisoners. The process does not make the subject forget anything, even his loyalties. It just makes it impossible for the subject to resist doing or saying what the person who administered the neurotoxin asks.

We have brought the device along that will allow us to get the information we require from WaTu quickly. This will give us confidence that we have collected all of his working documents. Once we have WaTu programmed, he can lead us back to the vehicle. At this time in his life, he does not have the political clout that he will eventually get, but he is still a high-ranking middle-level scientist. Few people in the city will question anything he says."

"The plan sounds simple enough that it should work," said Ellie. "We need to discuss what types of weapons the human members of the team will carry. I assume it will not look convincing if we carry automatic rifles as we enter the city."

"You are correct," said MaSo. "If you are seen, you must appear to be prisoners, so having weapons will not work. From what we know, most humans are not allowed to wear clothes while in Laurasian custody because the Laurasians do not. Since this is a time before they have dealt with prisoners, I don't think that what you wear matters. So wear your standard uniforms. You should be able to hide your small handguns within those clothes."

"I think we can hide a couple of grenades in our clothes as well," said Ellie. "They could be a big help if we run into trouble."

"If there are no questions, then I suggest all of you report to the vessel in one hour ready to go," said Jonas.

chapter 17

Khaliq felt very relieved when Huda and Nadir returned and reported that the explosives had been safely hidden and the truck driver, who had been anonymously hired to bring the backpacks on the last leg of the trip from Afghanistan to Santa Monica had been silenced. He felt sure there were still no links to his working group hidden in the Los Angeles area. In two days, the actual work at the Rose Bowl would begin. Within a month, the work should be completed, and he would send everyone in the group except Masud, his electronics expert, directly to a training camp in Indonesia. They would remain there out of reach of any law enforcement organization until the early part of next year, when Khaliq and Masud would join them.

"Huda, let's get Masud to come with us, and bring his transmitter," said Khaliq. "Let's go make a final test of our electronics in the desert. We'll use the two backpacks you retrieved for our dress rehearsal."

"All is ready to go," answered Huda. "I've scouted out a place where we should be able to test undetected."

At about noon on that beautiful Sunday, they set off in the Toyota. When they reached Huda's place in the desert, they set up the test. First, they placed one of the backpacks at a secluded place. They measured off one half mile with a GPS unit and placed the second backpack there. Finally, they measured another half mile and stopped. "Okay, Huda and I will use the binoculars and watch the two backpacks while Masud activates the transmitter," said Khaliq. "If both backpacks function as expected, we know that we have plenty of range from your transmitter and that it works with the backpacks sent from Kabul." As Masud began to load batteries into the transmitter, Khaliq saw a rider in a dune buggy come over a hill near the first backpack. "Wait a minute. Someone has come into the test area," whispered Khaliq. "Let's hold a minute to see if he passes on out of our way. Oh, no, he has seen the backpack and is stopping to check it out. Activate the transmitter!"

As Masud pressed the button on the transmitter, the backpack, the person, and the dune buggy disappeared, replaced by a fifty-foot column of smoke and debris. There was also a fifty foot column a half mile closer where the second backpack had been. Each of the backpacks contained about thirty-five pounds of C-4 and a detonator receiver, all carefully encased in five layers of plastic sheeting. The outside of the plastic had been scrubbed many times to remove any trace of explosive from the outside of the parcel.

"I would say our test of the detonator system was successful," said Khaliq. "This person driving up was most unfortunate. We had better leave immediately in case he was riding with others. Do you see anyone else approaching through your binoculars?"

"No," said Huda after a careful surveillance of the area.

"Then I suggest we get out of here as quickly as possible," said Khaliq as he headed for the car.

They made it back to their safe house without further incident. Khaliq assigned a man to monitor the local news channels and newspapers to see if anyone mentioned an explosion in the desert or if anyone reported a person missing out there.

The next day, it was time to go to Pasadena to begin work

on the cosmetic renovation. The group loaded all their tools into a rented white-panel truck and the Toyota Camry and then drove to the work site. The self-propelled cherry pickers were already there waiting to begin the project. As soon as they unloaded the tools and men, Khaliq said, "Huda, take the truck and bring back as many of the backpacks as you can safely travel with. I intended to send two people on this vital part of the mission, but we are one man short, thanks to Rafiq, so you will have to go alone. Please be careful. If anything happens to your cargo, our entire plan comes to an end. We will prepare a spot here at the Rose Bowl site to hide the explosives until they are all embedded in the pillars. Make all the trips you need to transport the backpacks here by the end of tomorrow."

MISSION 5 FROM WHITE SANDS

The Gondwanians expressed their amazement that the system could move the vessel so far in time and space. They all seemed partially hypnotized by the play of colors and sound that accompanied the transition. As the first four members of the joint Gondwanian and American force climbed out of the vessel in a Laurasia twenty years earlier than they had been before, Steven looked around the new site and saw that the landscape was similar to the first site in Laurasia near SoMu. The technical staff at White Sands was apparently getting more accurate. This trip arrived at sunrise just as they had planned. It was a little cooler here, and the land was covered with a light fog. The landscape they could see was covered with the same pine needles and flowering shrubs they had seen near SoMu. While the vessel returned for the rest of the small force, the advance party made quick work of clearing a space and setting up the perimeter fence. Steven reflected on the fact that each time they visited a new place; they found no single herbaceous dinosaurs or pairs. He wondered if it was possible that dinosaurs lived in groups even more than modern birds. Only the carnivores lived and hunted alone.

Steven called Fred aside to say, "We really need you to stay here and guard the vessel while we are gone. If anything happens to the vessel, we are stuck here, and our mission fails. You are uniquely qualified because you can speak Laurasian. I'll also leave one of the Gondwanians with you for backup. Please stay away from the neurotoxin while we're gone this time."

"MaSo, let's array your three men to make it look like we are three prisoners on the off chance that anyone sees us. Let's move out," said Ellie.

As the party started walking toward the city of PuRo, the sun broke through the haze and lit up the surroundings. There was a large herd of *Maiasauras* evenly spread out over about two acres. The paleontologist in Steven realized he was seeing them nesting as a group. The nests were circular holes scooped out of the ground about three feet in diameter, and they were spaced about twenty-five feet apart to allow the mothers to move between them and attend to their nests. Based on coloring, Steven could now be sure the females attended the nest and fed the newborns. This was a behavior recently proposed by paleontologists as a result of fossil digs in Montana and Alberta, Canada. It was exciting to confirm that the work was accurate because Steven had been on most of the digs.

The shrubs and pine trees were generally the same as they had seen near SoMu and not as difficult to walk through as they had been in Gondwana. They approached a wide road after they had walked less than half a mile. Just before they reached the road, Steven saw a *Pteranodon* swoop down on an unattended *Maiasaura* nest. While it was in the process of swallowing one of the eggs whole, the *Maiasaura* returned. The *Maiasaura* gave out a shriek and stomped on the *Pteranodon* with the full force of her three-ton weight using one of her hind legs. The team heard several loud snaps, and the *Pteranodon* did not move again. The carcass was dragged out of the nesting area and left for scavengers by a male *Maiasaura*.

The road was larger than the ones they had previously seen. There were three lanes in each direction but no walkways on the sides of the road. Traffic was not heavy, but vehicles were moving past with some regularity. The Gondwanians stood by the side of the road and flagged down a tri-wheeler when they spotted one with an enclosed cargo area. They then shot the driver with a tranquilizer dart. "Without the anecdote, he will be out of it for at least two days," said MaSo. "Everyone get into the back of the vehicle, and I will drive us." Because MaSo had lived in PuRo for two years, it was easy for him to find the academy. After they stopped, he walked to the rear of the vehicle and put his head into the cargo compartment. "Everyone stay here while I find exactly where WaTu works. HiPo, sit in the driver's seat in case any confors come around."

MaSo walked into the research building of the science academy, looking for someone to direct him to WaTu. He saw a female approaching as he walked in the door. "Could you direct me to the office of Scientist WaTu?" he asked.

"Go to the third door on the left just down this hall," she replied. "If you are a student, I would warn you he really hates to be interrupted when he is working. He only allows visitors one day a week from 10:00 a.m. to 12:00 p.m. His visiting day is tomorrow."

MaSo pointed to his black medallion and said, "I am not here on student business. Thank you for your information."

MaSo tried the door the female had directed him to and found it locked. He knocked and heard someone say, "Go away. I am working and do not wish to be interrupted. Come back tomorrow."

MaSo yelled back in a cold tone of voice, "This is confor business, and you will open the door immediately, or I will send for backup."

Ten seconds later, the door opened. WaTu tentatively peeked out and said, "I am sorry. I thought it was just a student. Please come in. What can I do for you?"

"I must interview you about some of your recent research," said MaSo. "Are you here in this laboratory by yourself?"

"Is there some problem?" ask WaTu. "I have done nothing outside of my formal work outline, and there is no one else here in my office."

"Stay right here," said MaSo. "I will return immediately with my partner and some recording equipment."

MaSo returned to the tri-wheeler about twenty minutes after he had left. He was walking quickly and sporting a bright red stomach. "I found WaTu in his lab and arranged to interview him right now. I think he was afraid of me because of the medallion. I told him I needed to go out to get my partner, who would also attend the interview."

MaSo then drove the vehicle to a service entrance at the rear of the building and backed up to the ramp. It was a simple matter for Steven and Ellie to slip into the building along with MaSo and HiPo. Bill and the last Gondwanian stayed with the tri-wheeler. HiPo carried a rectangular box covered with red and orange writing in very large characters. As the team walked down a hall toward WaTu's lab, a reptile stepped out of one of the rooms and stopped frozen, staring at Steven and Ellie. He was about to say something when MaSo's tranquilizer dart hit him. Steven and HiPo caught the reptile before he hit the ground, HiPo using only one arm. They were dragging him back into the room from which he had emerged when another reptile in the same room looked up to see what was causing the commotion. MaSo's gun clicked again, and the second reptile fell across the table he had been working on.

"Let's push them under this table," said MaSo. "We need them to remain hidden until we get out of here." Back in the hall, the group made its way to WaTu's lab without further complications. As they entered, WaTu looked up, and his whole stomach and neck flashed bright red. MaSo and Steve grabbed him while Ellie helped HiPo open the box he was carrying. MaSo pulled what looked like a projectile dart from his pocket and injected it manually into WaTu's neck. Unlike the projectile darts, which put the victim down within ten seconds, this dart just calmed WaTu. As his struggles ceased, HiPo slipped a gas mask over his nose and mouth. "WaTu, you are ordered to remain calm and to cooperate with any and all orders I give you," said HiPo. "Do you understand and agree?"

"Please command me," said WaTu. "I will do as you say."

"We know you are working on a design for a time machine," said MaSo. "We require all of your notes and any hardware you have developed for this design."

"My notes are all contained in that orange binder on my desk," said WaTu. "I keep everything in one place for security purposes. The binder is kept safely locked up when I am not working with it. The prototype is in the next lab, where KiKi is making modifications to the device. She decided upon the changes just last night."

"Who is KiKi?" asked MaZu. "Are there any other people involved in working on this project?"

"KiKi is the creator of the time machine," said WaTu. "She said her father had told her a story about traveling in time when he was young. This gave her the idea. She is a mathematical genius; in fact I don't think anyone else in Laurasia could have accomplished what she has done. No one else is required. Again, this is good for security."

"Bring all of your work notes and let's go visit KiKi," said MaSo after he repeated the previous conversation more slowly to Steven and Ellie.

Ellie guided WaTu into the hall while MaSo, Steven, HiPo, and his trusty box followed. KiKi looked up as they entered her workroom and started to greet WaTu. Then she saw Ellie and froze. Before she could recover, MaSo and Steven grabbed her arms. "What are you doing?" she asked. "Who are you?"

171

"Please remain calm," said MaSo as he used another of his special darts on KiKi. HiPo applied the mask, gaining complete control over her. "Where is your time travel device?" said MaSo.

KiKi gestured to a square metal pole about three inches by three inches standing on a base in the middle of the room. It was about eight feet tall with numerous pieces of electronic equipment attached to it. Tubes connected everything together. "Are there any other pieces of hardware somewhere else?" asked MaSo.

"No, WaTu insisted that we keep our entire work secret so the device could not fall into the hands of the enemies of the Exalted Lord," said KiKi. "Only WaTu and I have ever worked on the project, and any obsolete equipment has been destroyed once it was of no further use."

After another slow repeat of the conversation for Steven and Ellie's benefit, they decided to take KiKi and the equipment along with WaTu. HiPo stayed to disconnect and pack up the equipment they found in the room. The others escorted KiKi and WaTu back to the truck. MaSo then returned to the lab with WaTu and the remaining reptile soldier to help carry the equipment to the truck.

As MaSo's group approached the exit, five reptiles with black medallions stepped through the door. "Hello," said the older one in front. He carried himself with authority, and his speech was very direct. "What are you doing here?" he asked. "I am Commander KaYo, the head of the conformance force in this city. Why are confor officers doing such demeaning manual labor?"

"My name is Corporeal MaSo, new to the PuRo Conformance Force, Commander KaYo," he replied respectfully. "Scientist WaTu here is a rising star in the scientific community and my good friend. He is taking this equipment for calibration, and I volunteered to help him put it in the truck."

"You say your name is MaSo?" said KaYo. "I have not met

you or even heard of you. You have such a strange accent. You must not be from around here. How long have you been in my regiment?"

"I am relatively new here, just four months," answered MaSo. "I transferred from the far eastern territories of Laurasia. My father is a commander of the conformance force there. I transferred because I want to make a name for myself without depending on my father's reputation."

"Actually, you sound more like a Gondwanian than someone from the east," said KaYo. "I think I will have my sergeant here call headquarters and check out your story. Sergeant, we need the communicator from our vehicle. Retrieve it and check the records on Corporal MaSo. While he is gone, you four will remain here."

The sergeant trotted off as ordered, and MaSo began to size up the four remaining reptiles. He knew he had only until the sergeant returned to get out of this situation. The commander was watching him carefully, so he probably could not raise his projectile gun and fire before the confors shot as well. Just as he was going to make his move, all four confors jerked and slid to the ground. Steven and Ellie stood in the doorway, each holding a tranquilizer gun.

"We were concerned when you didn't return to the truck in a reasonable time," said Ellie. "We almost blew our cover when that other reptile came out of the ramp and trotted off. Luckily, he didn't see us, and we could sneak up behind this group. Get the equipment in the truck. We'll drag these four out of the hall."

"Thanks," said MaSo. "I was really not interested to field-test the antidote we all took before the mission."

The trip back to the drop-off site on the road was uneventful. They even parked the truck off the road to make it look like the driver was taking a nap if anyone found it. Carrying the equipment through the shrubs was a nightmare, but they made it with only minor scratches and scrapes. Steven sent

Ellie, Fred, and HiPo along with the equipment back first since the equipment took up so much space in the vessel. Steven decided to use the waiting time to have a conversation with WaTu and KiKi, using Bill and MaSo as interpreters. Steven was beginning to pick up the basics of the language, but for this conversation, he wanted to be very sure he understood what was said. He walked up to WaTu and KiKi and offered them a drink of water.

"How close are you to a working time machine?" Steven asked, looking at WaTu.

"I believe the device you took from the academy will be capable of sending small objects through time when I finish the modifications," interjected KiKi. "It may take us a year to refine the work to transfer something as large and complex as a living being."

"Are the two of you collaborating on the work?" asked Steven.

"Not really," said KiKi. "Scientist WaTu has been kind enough to give me funds and a place to work, but he has much more important work to accomplish. By the way, who or what are you? You seem to be in charge of this group, but you look very strange. Are you taking my work for our mortal enemies, the Gondwanians, or for some other Laurasian rival of the Exalted Lord?"

"Actually, some of us are from the future," said Steven. "In a few years, the Laurasian government will promote WaTu to sacred scientist for inventing the time machine. Then the government uses the technology to try to steal energy from the future and to try to destroy the future civilization. We are here to stop these activities."

"Why would they do that?" asked KiKi, looking at WaTu intently. "How far in the future are you talking about? Are you from there?"

"Yes, I am from sixty-five million years in the future," said Steven. "Our world is populated with people like me, mammals, not reptiles. The Exalted Lord and his advisors discovered that Laurasia will run out of energy in the next twenty to twenty-five years. It does not bother them to put in motion a plan that leads to the death of billions of my people."

"We must do as the Exalted Lord commands without question," said KiKi. "That is one of the first Exulted Lord, PaKo's Four Basic Rules of Living handed down from ancient times that hold our society together. They must have a very good reason to do the horrible things you described. So WaTu becomes the sacred scientist. That is a wonderful future for him. Can you tell me what happens to me?"

MaSo spoke up and said, "I did research on the events related to the invention of the time machine before we made this trip. There is never any mention of your name. We were very surprised to learn of your existence. I believe somehow with all the secrecy WaTu required, he managed to steal the entire credit for your work.

GONDWANA, 65 MILLION YEARS BCE

The flight of four Gondwanian electrogliders took off at sunrise on a reconnaissance patrol heading north toward Laurasian territory. Although it was a routine patrol, the vessels were armed for full combat, nuclear weapons included in case they observed aggression from the Laurasians. Also, Gondwanian battle strategy called for immediate and aggressive retaliation on any antiairship weapons that were fired while Gondwanian electrogliders were in the area. The reason for this strategy was because antiairship weapons were the only Laurasian weaponry capable of inflicting damage on Gondwana's electroglider fleet. Neutralizing the antiairship weapons meant Gondwanian forces were in control of any battlefield. Nuclear bombs were used because the Laurasians spread each of their antiairship emplacements a large distance apart. They also placed a huge number of weapons within each installation, which meant the installations covered a large area. The nuclear bombs had a much wider zone of destruction, which made it possible to neutralize major portions of an installation with one bomb.

The Gondwanian Air Corp had attack electrogliders in the air twenty-four hours of every day. They took off randomly from numerous bases across the entire northern coast of Gondwana. Each flight flew two-thirds of the way from the Gondwanian coast toward Laurasia and then turned back to their home base if there was no provocation, which had been the norm for over one hundred years.

FiYo was the flight leader's wingman. He had been a pilot in the Gondwanian Air Corp for the last three years and was held in the highest regard by the squadron commander. Everyone expected him to be promoted to flight leader as soon as the new group of pilots arrived from the training academy. His life in Gondwana was very comfortable. He was even thinking of picking a mate in the near future.

All of these things were going through his mind as he cruised north in his electroglider. Last night, he had received a surprising and most disturbing communication from his Laurasian handler. His leader had activated him and told him that today he was to break away from his patrol as they were turning south to return home. He was given coordinates and instructed to fly his electroglider to a deserted stretch of road two hundred miles north of the Laurasian coastline. After landing, he could recharge the electroglider's batteries by means of a MaKe-to-electricity converter mounted on the tri-wheeler that would be waiting to meet him. Then he was to take off and fly to the confor training field in SoMu, where there was enough open space to land his craft. Here, a high-level agent in the Laurasian spy network would meet FiYo. This agent would reveal the plan for a mission of the highest priority. His handler assured FiYo that successful completion of this mission would assure him of promotion and the right to wear the Exalted Lords Golden Circle for Bravery around his black medallion. He would be famous and respected for life. This clearly meant the mission was critically dangerous. FiYo assumed the government would ask him to fly a suicide attack on some high-priority Gondwanian target and drop the nuclear bombs that were in his electroglider.

As he approached the patrol's return point, FiYo made up his mind. He had been given the honor of being sent to Gondwana to serve the Exalted Lord. He would not betray that trust simply for a comfortable life. As his patrol banked their craft to turn back, FiYo accelerated his craft to top speed and stayed on a north heading. He ignored the frantic calls from his flight leader as the rest of the flight requested instructions on how to handle this unprecedented act. FiYo had an eight-minute lead on his pursuers when they finally organized to give chase.

As FiYo approached the Laurasian coast, he reduced his altitude to only five thousand feet. This maneuver was meant to lure his pursuers lower so that they presented an easier target for the coastal antiairship weapons. He had been told that the operators of the intense concentration of antiairship weapons in the area had been given firm instructions not to shoot at his electroglider but to shoot down any craft that pursued him. After he had flown past the antiairship emplacements and regained his altitude, he began to hear conversation from his three pursuers over their communicators. Laurasian forces shot down the flight leader's craft, and they had hit and damaged one of the remaining electrogliders immediately after the squadron had come in range of the antiairship weapons. The crippled electroglider and the undamaged one were now returning to their base.

The rest of FiYo's trip to the military training field was simple; there were no electrogliders in Laurasian airspace to worry about. When he landed, he climbed down from his craft, and a tall reptile wearing cloth over his body met with him. The coat was dark gray, with an attached hood that had been thrown back to reveal his face and head. "I am SuHa, your contact. Come with me, and I will give you food and drink while I explain our mission."

Ten minutes later, FiYo and SuHa were comfortably seated in the field commander's office. SuHa dismissed the commander without explanation. SuHa laid out a world map on the desk while FiYo ate a hearty meal. SuHa told him to eat well because he was not sure where or when they would find their next meal. As FiYo looked at the map, he suddenly became very confused. It was similar to the world map as FiYo knew it, but many of the familiar land formations were broken up and separated. "What is this," asked FiYo. "It does not show a very accurate representation of the world."

"Oh, it is quite accurate," said SuHa. "It just represents the world sixty-five million years in the future. You and I will be going through a time machine along with your electroglider. I will not bore you with the political motivations for this mission, but you will be attacking a large dam called the Three Gorges Dam in a country of the future called China."

"Will we be flying through this time machine?" asked FiYo. "Is it large enough to allow such a thing?"

"No, we will not be flying through the time machine, but we will be sitting in your electroglider while we travel to the future," said SuHa. "Our time machine is large enough for that.

It is currently calibrated to deliver us to a place called Afghanistan, meaning we will arrive miles outside of China. From our arrival site, on the day of the mission, you will fly southwest across one thousand miles of what is known as the Tibetan Plateau as you see on this map. Then you will be able to make visual contact with the Yangtze River. You will fly along the river at as low of an altitude as safely possible. This low-level flying is the way you will be able to evade detection by the Chinese authorities. Flying along the river, you will arrive at a province of China called Hubei. As you can see from the map, the dam is centrally located within the country and is considered one of their most valuable assets to ensure the country's political stability and economic growth. By now, I think you understand that you will not have enough power to make a round-trip flight. My plan is for you to exit your craft in flight and allow it to crash land."

"How do you know about this place so far in the future?" asked FiYo. "What possible good can it do for Laurasia if we successfully destroy this dam?"

"I am very sorry, Agent FiYo, but I am not at liberty to answer your question," said SuHa. "There are only about nine people, including the high council, in all of Laurasia that knows the purpose of this mission. But, I can assure you there is no project more important than this one for ensuring the future of Laurasia. As for how I found out so much about the future world, I have been working in the future for several years. Our goal is to instigate a worldwide war between the future countries and destabilize their civilization. We are very close to accomplishing this goal, but we need your attack to provide the final motivation. Even as we speak, your electroglider is being repainted to look like an experimental aircraft from another country in the future called the United States."

"Do they have weapons capable of shooting down my electroglider?" asked FiYo. "What is the escape route after I have destroyed this dam and abandoned my electroglider?"

"The civilization in the future is advanced in technology about as far as our glorious country," said SuHa. "The implementation is usually different from ours but just as effective. They will not be relying on antiairship weapons. They have what they call missiles, which are capable of being launched in a target's general direction, and then the missile finds its target in one of several possible ways and will guide itself to the target to destroy it. These devices use different mechanisms to accomplish their job, so we will not be able to predict what countermeasures to use for this threat. The success of the mission will depend on your ability to fly in below the useful range of their long-range detection devices. If they do not detect you, they will not launch their missiles at you. Can you abandon your electroglider while it is in flight?"

"Yes, I can," answered FiYo. "It is not very reliable, according to some pilots I have talked to. Why does flying low protect me from detection? This is just the opposite of the airship strategies I have learned in Gondwana."

"The detectors used by the future civilization use electromagnetic waves to find their targets," said SuHa. "They send out a signal and detect returning signals that bounce off of the target. When the signal is aimed too close to the ground they receive reflections from objects on the ground that appear as so many possible targets that a real target reflection is lost in this noise."

"Are you sure about this information?" asked FiYo. "People on the ground will easily be able to see my craft."

"I am sure. This is the strategy used by all aircraft pilots of the future," said SuHa. "You will be moving too fast for people on the ground to do anything to stop you. If the evacuation mechanism is not reliable, we may need to rethink the end of my plan. We can't have you killed by a poorly engineered Gondwanian electroglider as a reward for successfully blowing up the dam. Possibly you can crash land in a deserted area and damage your craft with explosives to make it look like it would not fly anymore. As long as we preselect the coordinates of your landing, you can return to Laurasia through the time portal. Now I think it is time for us to see if your craft is ready for our trip into the future."

WASHINGTON, DC

The national security advisor sat in his office and reviewed past reports made from each agency in the government charged with protecting the nation. For the last two weeks, the reports had been getting shorter and less helpful. Jason Sanders was reviewing old reports to see if he had overlooked anything important. It was almost time to leave for the daily meeting with the president and his top advisors. Sanders decided he was tired of not making any progress toward finding the terrorists. They knew some horrendous act of terror was coming, but he couldn't get any leads about the exact nature, the time, or the target. He glanced at a month-old report with handwritten information about a border patrol guard finding the dead body of a middle-aged man carrying a backpack. The man had been shot while he was attempting to cross the Rio Grande and enter the United States illegally. Apparently, local vigilantes had killed the man. The backpack contained thirty-five pounds of C-4 explosive wired to a remote-triggering device. The whole assembly was completely wrapped in plastic. The incident had been the topic of conversation within the border patrol offices for a few days and then forgotten. *This is too suspicious not to follow up on*, Sanders thought. He immediately got on the phone and directly called the Presidio INS office that had reported the incident. The duty officer at the station did not know any further details about the murdered Mexican, but he promised to have the head agent call Mr. Sanders as soon as he arrived at work in about four or five hours. The anger Sanders expressed as he responded to the poor duty officer could have melted the insulation off the wires all the way to Presidio. The duty officer agreed to call and wake the agent in charge even though it was 4:00 a.m.

The agent in charge called back in about seven minutes. The agent sounded like he was still asleep, but he asked Sanders how he could be of service to the national security advisor. When Sanders mentioned the incident, the agent in charge told Sanders that they had not spent much time investigating it until they later found a woman lost and disoriented wandering around in the same area. She also had a backpack just like the one found on the dead person. She told investigators that each of the members of their party of illegals had been given a backpack to carry across the border. They were expected to give them to a man on the US side when they arrived. Further checking turned up the coyote that had led the group across the border, but he wasn't helpful. Apparently, he was approached by a man he did not know in Mexico at one of the staging points where illegals started their hike across the Rio Grande River. This man appeared each time the coyote had a group to take across. He would supply him with backpacks for all of his charges. After arrival in Presidio, another man would come and pay him two hundred dollars for each backpack delivered. He said that he did not know the contents of the backpacks and that he assumed they were filled with illegal drugs being smuggled into the States. He seemed genuinely surprised when they told the coyote of the contents. He said that he had delivered over two hundred backpacks before the deal was complete.

"Holy shit!" replied Sanders as he thought about what could be done with more than seven hundred pounds of C-4. "Have you been able to track down the man who received the backpacks?"

"We have questioned the coyote extensively," said the agent in charge. "Apparently, the coyote and the truck driver had many informal chats while transacting their business. We have offered the coyote immunity if he provides information that helps us track down this trucker. He only knew the guy as Antonio. Antonio was a heavyset Latino, and apparently, he lives in California, most likely the LA area. The man said he was looking forward to being able to buy his family a house in Riverside County once he completed this delivery. His rig was silver with green trim, and the words 'Dias Trucking' were written on each side. We just put this together yesterday, and we're trying to decide how to track down the truck and the driver."

"This may be the first solid lead on a potential terrorist attack on American soil," said Sanders. "Send all your information to me within the hour, and I'll make this the highest priority for every law enforcement agency in the nation until we find this truck."

"At first, we thought this was just some enterprising drug cartel going into a new business, but you're tying this to terrorism makes a lot of sense," said the agent in charge. "After we found the second backpack, we had the C-4 analyzed. The results indicate that the C-4 was manufactured in the Middle East, probably Iran."

As he left his office for the president's meeting, Sanders instructed his staff to relay the INS information all over the United States to law enforcement agencies starting in the west and working east."

About forty-five minutes into the meeting, Sanders felt his cell phone vibrate. It was his chief of staff, who knew not to interrupt him in this meeting unless it was seriously important. He decided to excuse himself to take the call. He heard his chief say he was prepared to connect Sanders to a police captain in San Bernardino County with information about the truck and the suspect.

"Hello, this is Jason Sanders. What have you got?"

"Mr. Sanders, we found the truck you are looking for on a deserted road north of Interstate 10 outside of Los Angeles County," said Captain John Edwards. "The driver was found shot, in the back of the head, in the sleeping compartment of his vehicle. According to the local crime scene investigators, the scene had been poorly manipulated to seem like a truck robbery that went out of control. The driver, named Antonio Garza, a local trucker who frequently worked between California and Texas, appeared to have been moved at least twice after he had been killed. The current theory is that he was shot at an as yet unknown primary crime scene. Then his body was dumped into the cab of his truck. This was presumably done to move the body and truck away from the primary crime scene. The truck was found with the driver dead and the doors to the trailer wide open. Some items of the trailer contents were strewed around the scene.

"In answer to what I presume to be your next question," said Captain Edwards. "There is no C-4 in the truck, but there is a concealed area in the back of the trailer that is empty and presumably could have held your seven hundred pounds of C-4. I guess this means your potential terrorist threat is headed our way."

"Captain Edwards, thank you for calling me so quickly," said Jason. "The obvious next step is to find out who killed Antonio Garza and took the C-4 out of his truck. I will recommend to the president that he order a task force with local police, the FBI, and homeland security to track down the C-4 and identify potential targets for that much explosive."

As Jason Sanders reentered the president's meeting, he had the sinking feeling that they were too far behind the terrorists to stop this attack before innocent people were killed.

chapter 18

<hr>

PASADENA, CALIFORNIA

The renovation contract with Compton Construction
Corporation, or 3C as they were called, required the sandblasting
of each of the 204 main columns around the outer edge of
the stadium. The columns are made of solid concrete, ten
feet wide by ten feet deep and sixty feet tall. Over the last
twenty-five years, the pollutants in the air of Los Angeles had
turned the outer surface of the columns to an ugly gray. After
they sandblasted off the dirty outer layer, they were supposed
to spray the concrete with several coats of sealer to protect
the exposed surface for the future. To accomplish this work,
Khaliq's men had built plywood housings to enclose the back
and sides of the elevated platform of the cherry pickers. The
front of the platform, which was against the column, was open.
This housing was built ostensibly to keep the sand coming off
the sandblasting tool from polluting the air. The real reason
was to conceal the exact nature of the work being done. As each
column was blasted from top to bottom, the work slowed down
considerably about one-third of the way down because they had
to cut a one-foot-diameter hole into the concrete column about
four feet deep. Into each hole was placed one of the backpacks
they had obtained via Mexico. The workers then filled the hole
with concrete to seal the backpack inside. They removed all
evidence of the holes by blending the new cement with the

freshly cleaned wall. Then the sandblasting continued down the remainder of the column.

By the time the crew was finished, each column of the stadium had thirty-five pounds of C-4 embedded inside. The idea was that the blasts within the individual columns would destroy each column and blast the upper deck of stadium seats up and over onto the lower-deck seats, killing the occupants of both decks. The destruction would be massive. Only persons on the actual playing field had any chance at all of survival. As many as one hundred thousand people could lose their lives. The ninety thousand spectators would die along with most of the people working at the stadium.

3C finished the job about five weeks after they began. The C-4 was virtually undetectable because it was now enclosed in five layers of plastic and four feet of concrete. The final touch was the sealer, which was specifically formulated to act as an odor barrier.

At the completion of the job, the entire crew except Khaliq and Masud were put on a plane to Indonesia. They would be cut off from outside contact until the mission was complete. Everything was in place. All Khaliq and Masud had to do was stay under the radar for three months.

White Sands, New Mexico

Steven and Ellie met with Jonas the moment they returned with WaTu, KiKi, and the prototype time machine. "It seems that your mission was a complete success as far as accomplishing the objectives we set," said Jonas. "Now we need to figure out how to measure the changes, if any, which have occurred to history. We really have no experience to help predict how our actions have affected Laurasian history or possibly even ours.

I suppose they may not be able to speak our modern languages and we should check to see if our prisoner, YaSi, is still in his cell and if he can still speak Russian. The terrorist event in the Gaza Strip has still occurred, so we didn't rewrite that part of history. We may need to send you back to Laurasia to do a little investigating. But before that, I have a new proposal for a trip.

"I don't know why I didn't think of this sooner, but now it occurs to me that we should use our system to go in the other direction," said Jonas. "We should send someone into the future to see what we can learn about the terrorist attack. We may be able to deduce the strategy of these reptiles from seeing the result. The sad truth is the law enforcement agencies have not been able to pick up a meaningful lead about the specifics of the coming attack, though we have evidence that it will occur around the LA area."

"We've already prepared the system for a trip," said Jonas. "I want you and Ellie to go on this mission, but I need to advise you that the system has not yet been evaluated going in the future direction. Theoretically the physics is different for a trip forward in time"

"For myself, I am ready to go, but what about you, Ellie?" said Steven.

"I'm in. Remember I am the volunteer that went first through the system," said Ellie. "Based on what the director of the compliance force said to us, we should only need to go ahead a year to eighteen months," said Ellie. "Is there any way to set it up so that we go meet someone who will be prepared to quickly brief us on current events of the future time?"

"What if you came to meet me?" said Jonas. "I would know that you will be coming and what you need to know from the perspective of the future and also from the perspective of today. I will also make sure you won't run into yourselves while you're there."

"While we're discussing Team T-REX missions, I request we

be scheduled to return to Gondwana," said Ellie. "We promised them we would help them execute a mission that they judge capable of changing the course of Laurasian history for the better. We aren't even sure if changes to history are possible but as a justification for the trip, it will allow us to assess the effect of kidnapping WaTu, KiKi, their equipment, and his working papers. At the time we left Gondwana, we had no detailed idea as to the effect our actions caused."

"I think from a moral and practical point of view, we should honor our commitment to the Gondwanians in case we need them again as allies sometime," said Ellie. "We should probably open up diplomatic relations with them just as we would with any other country in the present time."

"We should also return YaSi to his world as soon as it is safe to do," said Steven. "He didn't do anything so terrible as to deserve a life sentence in prison."

"I agree with both of your requests and will approve them scheduled as soon as we have addressed the terror attack situation," said Jonas. "I'll require that the whole eight members of Team T-REX go with you to Gondwana for safety sake. While you are there, you can open discussion on how we can organize to jointly study the Laurasia time machine and share the information they gain from WaTu and KiKi. As for YiSi, we can send him back to a time one hundred years before we grabbed him. That should keep him from causing any problems for our current mission."

SOUTHERN AFGHANISTAN

SuHa could not understand what was wrong with his portal to the Laurasian time machine. He had been trying for three days to return to Laurasia to talk to FiRu and his support staff. The electroglider and the pilot were safely hidden in Afghanistan, but SuHa needed to retrieve a map with a detailed approach path for the attack on the Three Gorges Dam. Also, he needed to set up a time and coordinates for a portal to be opened to retrieve the pilot after his mission was complete. FiRu was still researching to determine if there was a time that would have maximum impact to execute the attack. Now SuHa appeared to be stranded in the future with no support.

The time travel device had always been reliable in the past. SuHa had never had any trouble when he wanted to make a transition. He was confident that the Laurasian scientists would fix the problem quickly, but it was very inconvenient not to be able to contact FiRu.

Two days later, SuHa finally decided to explain the situation to FiYo. "It appears we're not presently able to contact home for further instructions," said SuHa. "Every mission seems to have at least one complication. I guess that is how we grow in our craft. The complication we must currently deal with is the fact that the time portal has been inoperable for the last five days. I expected to go back to Laurasia for an update to my instructions and an even more detailed map than the one we have to ensure you find your target. Also, I intended to bring back two technicians to go over your electroglider to make sure everything is in readiness after our trip through time. Now, my dear FiYo, I'm afraid you must check out your own electroglider while I go out to forage for some food for us to eat."

SuHa felt his mind begin to churn and worry as he walked through the barren landscape, looking for something green and edible. What if the leaders had decided to call off the project for some reason? Would they just strand him in the future with the electroglider and the pilot? Laurasian leadership was not famous for their loyalty to underlings. SuHa really did not know what had gone wrong, but this project was too important to the future of Laurasia for him to simply shut it down because of a small complication. He must continue with his mission until the time portal reopened.

San Bernardino County, California

Captain Edwards, who was in charge of investigating the murder of the Spanish truck driver, was blown away with the support he received from Jason Sanders, the national security advisor. After Edward's initial phone call, two senior-level agents from the NSA appeared on the scene to review and analyze the data already collected. The first thing they discovered was that the place where authorities had found Antonio's truck did not agree with the driver's log, the data from truck inspection stations, and the truck's odometer. The truck had traveled about 180 miles more per the odometer than one would have expected from its final placement. It appeared that the driver had backtracked at some point. After they outlined a circle with a two-hundred-mile radius centered on the place where they had discovered the truck, the NSA agents had analysts in Washington, DC, review all satellite pictures of the area looking for the truck going back over the last three weeks. This particular area always has unusually heavy satellite coverage because of the many classified military establishments in Nevada.

They found the truck on Interstate 10 going east around 9:00 p.m. eight days earlier. Using satellite images, they were able to track the truck to a rest stop about sixty miles from the final crime scene. At this rest stop, the truck driver appeared to seek out a silver Toyota Camry and then followed the car about forty miles to an abandoned farmhouse. Both truck and automobile remained at the farmhouse for about forty-five minutes, and then they drove farther north on the same farm road. Shortly after that, the car left the truck at the place where authorities eventually discovered Antonio's body. From these satellite photos, analysts were able to determine the license plate number on the silver Toyota Camry. From the license number, the police were able to determine that the car was owned by one Hashim Kader, who lived in San Jose, California. On the satellite pictures, they also saw the two men involved in killing Antonio.

The police rushed to the farmhouse where the car and truck had stopped but found that it was already empty, no C-4.

SAN JOSE, CALIFORNIA

A team of FBI agents broke down the door at Hashim Kadar's house in San Jose. Inside, they found a mild-mannered Arab man, his wife, and two daughters. The man was arrested and taken to local FBI headquarters for interrogation.

The FBI special agent in charge of the San Jose office, Frank Green, was joined in the interrogation room by Captain John Edwards. "Mr. Kader, where is your silver Toyota Camry?" asked Agent Green.

"Is that what this harassment is all about?" replied Kader. "It seems that any person of Middle-Eastern descent is constantly harassed these days."

"Please just answer the question," Green said in a menacing tone. "We don't have the time or the patience to banter niceties with you. Where is the car you purchased in May?"

"I loaned it to my brother while he is visiting me," said Kader.

"You mean the brother named Ikram Kader, the man who is in this country helping you while you recover from a brain aneurysm?"

"Yes, I'm sorry we lied, but my brother wanted to stay and

continue his sightseeing tour until the end of the year," said Kader. "He is fascinated with this country, particularly the western half with its glorious deserts. He has been driving all over as a tourist. That is why we made up the story about my brain aneurysm to get his visa extended."

"Where is he, and how can we get in touch with him?" asked Frank Green.

"Please, please— I just don't know," said Kader. "He's not traveling on a preset route, and he has not called me for over two months. I am somewhat concerned for his safety. He may have been the victim of harassment as well."

"That is the worst story I have ever heard," said Agent Green. "If you continue to cooperate in this manner, you'll win a prepaid, one-way ticket to the US prison in Guantanamo Bay."

"But it is the truth," wailed Kader.

Captain Edwards returned to Southern California, convinced that Hashim Kader did not know the location of his brother or the silver Toyota at the present time. However, he did know that the car was at the scene of the murder of Antonio Garza. There was little possibility that Hashim Kader was not part of a terrorist network. He had earned himself a trip to Cuba.

All police in the Southern California area were looking for the silver Toyota. Also, they now had a picture of the man who had met with Hashim Kader in San Jose, the man who called himself Ikram Kader, the suspected terrorist leader. Edwards was personally convinced the attack would come somewhere in the LA area, but what target could require seven hundred pounds of C-4 explosive?

chapter 19

LAURASIA, 65 MILLION YEARS BCE

In the Laurasian capital city of SoMu, the Exalted Lord YaKo was pacing in front of a meeting of the high council. "How could this happen almost before our very eyes?" asked the Exalted Lord. "My instinct is to kill everyone who had any contact with the time travel devices, but I'm sure that would not restore our time travel capability. Besides, I can always kill everyone later if I feel the urge. From all accounts, the operators of the time machines say the machines were there and fully functioning one second and gone the next. Everyone associated with the occurrence felt a strong case of vertigo for several seconds. I would think they were all crazy or traitors to the country if the story was not so consistent at every time travel site. I still wonder if WaTu is a traitor or a victim of a Gondwanian plot. Our countrywide search for him has turned up not a single lead. He seems to have disappeared just like the time machines. I guess we must choose a new sacred scientist. We'll need our very best scientist to lead us through the challenges of our uncertain future. I can only think that our mortal enemies, the Gondwanians, have invented some way to remove our time machine remotely, though I cannot think of how they would do it."

"In fact, Gondwana has dealt us a mortal blow without losing a single soldier on either side," said Chancellor FaPa.

"That sounds like a strategy their Council of Mothers would approve. I fear we have no other option, especially now that we have no access to the future's energy. We must attack Gondwana with everything we have to gain control of their energy resources. They have over 50 percent more land than we do and much of it is situated in warmer equatorial regions that promote more abundant growth of plants used as fuel. Also, they have alternative energy sources that our scientists have been unable to duplicate. Even if we cannot conquer their entire country, we should be able to gain enough technical data from a strategically placed large-scale invasion to allow us to build similar alternate energy devices. That will take the pressure off our limited energy resources until we can come up with a better plan."

"But we have discussed this many times in the past and decided we could not successfully invade Gondwana because of their superior military resources," said SaSu, the director of the confor. *With a failed invasion,* he thought, *I will become the sacrificial lamb.* "Their electrogliders will spot and attack a water-based invasion force before it gets halfway to Gondwanian shores. We have never constructed the number of seagoing vessels required to launch a massive attack like the one we would need to gain a beachhead in Gondwana. We would need to build a huge armada of vessels. This would put an impossible strain on our industrial base, and it is imperative that this move be done in secret. If the Gondwanians detected our activity and guessed our intent, we would surely fail. Finally if we should fail due to their electrogliders and nuclear bombs, we would have used up all our energy reserve to no purpose."

"I propose we invade through the most southeast province of Gondwana," said the Exalted Lord. "We have never had reports of electrogliders flying routine patrols over that part of their country. We should be able to sneak up on them in the area where they have the least military resources. Also, our far northeast province, which is opposite their southeast province, contains a secure site where we could build the invasion force in secret. If we launch this war, it will be an all-or-nothing proposition. See that SuHa and his team are assigned to define a strategy to successfully invade Gondwana in the near future."

"That is another problem," said SuSa. "SuHa was deployed in the future with a Gondwanian electroglider and a pilot to reinforce our strategy to cause a worldwide war in the future. I fear we may never see him again. However, I will appoint FiRu, currently SuHa's chief of planning, as the head of the infiltration department. I will immediately get him and his team working on developing an invasion plan of Gondwana."

"Very good," said the Exalted Lord. "I want a status report presented to me personally by FiRu one week from today, one hour before the next session of this meeting begins.

MISSION 5 FROM WHITE SANDS

Ellie and Steven climbed into the vessel again and buckled themselves into a seat, this time without the rest of their team. The computer voice in the vessel announced that they would make the transition in one minute. Steven looked at Ellie and said, "Good luck."

Ellie replied with a warm smile, "Good luck yourself." Then the sound and light show consumed their attention until the transition was complete. They both felt a little strange as they climbed out of the vessel and looked around. Everything seemed the same as it was when they had climbed in the vessel a few moments ago. The gymnasium-sized room was still filled with equipment, and the system crew was standing around and talking, but on second glance, they acted like it was just a routine maintenance day not a mission day. In fact, several of them approached, surprised to see Steven and Ellie getting out of the vessel.

The head technician walked up and asked, "What were you two doing in the vessel. Is there anything wrong in there?"

"No, no," said Ellie. "Steven thought he left his sunglasses in there after the last trip, but they weren't there."

As they walked off, Steven said, "Wow, I guess they didn't even notice when we transitioned here. To observe Jonas's policy of minimum interference with the time we are visiting, it looks like we can just walk up to his office for a visit with no one else the wiser."

When the two entered his office, Jonas gave them a measured look. "Steven, your hair is a lot longer than it was yesterday when I sent you two off on a vacation for a few days. I assume you have come from the past," Jonas said.

"Good guess," said Ellie. "So you know why we're here. Can you give us an update?"

Jonas started with a big sigh. "The disaster you need to stop is a terrorist attack on the Rose Bowl in front of a worldwide television audience," he said. The terrorists managed to smuggle C-4 explosive charges sealed in several layers of plastic into the stadium. They got access to the stadium under the guise of a renovation contract that was given to a construction firm called Compton Construction Company. No one knows where the two guys who started the company have disappeared to. Explosive charges were embedded high up on the pillars that support the upper seating deck close to the concrete structure that supports those seats. They placed the explosives in every one of the pillars.

"So the target really is in Southern California," said Steven.

"How come the explosives were not discovered during the security checks of the stadium?" asked Ellie.

"As usual, explosive-sniffing dogs and bomb squad experts with specialized equipment scoured the place for explosives when they began the security procedures a couple of days before the game. They found nothing," answered Jonas. "Investigators after the explosion found traces of what they're guessing to be plastic wrappings around the entire bomb. They've determined that the charges were sealed in the concrete of the pillars about two-thirds of the way up. They think the dogs just did not have a strong enough scent to detect the explosive. During the second quarter of the game, the explosive was detonated, and the whole concrete structure that formed the upper deck was blown over onto the concrete structure of the lower deck, killing somewhere around sixty thousand people and injuring thousands more. The television cameras in the stadium were knocked out, but the cameras in the blimp made sure this disaster was as well covered as the one on 9/11. This is clearly the worst terrorist attack to date on US soil."

"Congress and many military leaders are calling for all-out war against all of the Arab countries that have currently declared war on Israel," said Jonas. "These Arab countries all declared war because they think the biological attack on Gaza City was launched by Israel, but we know this is not true. No one seriously considers the attack on Israel since the contagion was so well contained. The problem is that if Congressional leaders were briefed on the real situation, our time machine secret would become public knowledge.

"The rationale for Congress to declare war on the Arab nations is due to the widespread assumption that one or all of those countries must have financed this large-scale terrorist attack on the Rose Bowl. If one country alone is responsible for the Rose Bowl attack, it makes no difference to the war supporters in Congress since they feel the entire Middle Eastern community passively supports the terrorists since the community makes so little effort to stop them. Recently more countries are pushing for war with Israel. The list of countries now includes Iran, Syria, Saudi Arabia, Egypt, Yemen, and Jordan. The president has been barely able to stall a war declaration by congress. Now many congressional leaders are working toward getting enough votes to declare a war and override the possibility for a presidential veto. Israel has many powerful friends in US politics that want to use this Rose Bowl attack to increase our support for Israel."

"Notwithstanding the strong push for a war declaration by congress, what position has our country taken in world politics so far?" asked Steven.

"The United States has been able to remain neutral on the topic of an Arab-Israeli war. We have tried several ways to negotiate de-escalation, but Russia and China have vetoed each resolution in the UN Security Council. They strongly support an Arab attack as a warning to Israel and any other potential aggressor nation that might think about using such heinous tactics in the future. If we did not know this problem was instigated by a third party, I'm sure that the United States would be right in the middle of the crowd calling for a strong action to punish Israel.

"After this Rose Bowl terrorist attack, public opinion in America is aligned squarely against the Arabs, who are supported by China and Russia. We have Israel and our traditional allies in our corner. The stage is set for a global war. All that is needed is a small spark like some stupid move from an Israeli extremist group against an Arab target that injures women and children, and the Laurasian's global war will be accomplished.

Israel has barely been able to finance proper defenses against so many threatened Arab attacks, Jews worldwide are donating billions of dollars to support their war effort. Several countries have used this action as an excuse to impose anti-Semitic laws, and a few have even started to imprison Jews and confiscate their property."

"This just keeps getting better and better," said Steven.

"If congress does declare war against the Arab Coalition as threatened, I feel sure that Russia and China will enter the war on the Arab side. NATO wants to remain neutral, but if the

United States declares war, they will be pulled into it as well. Once this war escalates to worldwide proportions with all the major nations participating, all that has to happen is for one of the combatants to decide to use nuclear weapons. You can bet the other side will retaliate in kind, and the reptiles will have totally achieved their goal of destroying our civilization."

"Have you come up with a strategy that will allow us to stop this disaster before it begins?" asked Ellie.

"No one has stepped up to claim responsibility for the terrorist attack on the Rose Bowl like al-Qaeda did for the twin towers. This time is also different from the 9/11 attack in that there were no suicide bombers to find in the wreckage to aid in identification of the attackers. This disaster was detonated remotely. The FBI is reasonably sure that al-Qaeda is the responsible party, but they have no proof. Our Homeland Security forces thought that they had cut off almost all of the money flowing to al-Qaeda, but this operation was incredibility well financed. That's why members of congress blame an Arab country for providing the money, but we know Laurasia somehow financed the attack. Since we now know the target and the manner in which the operation was accomplished, you should be able to stop the attack by going directly to the target and disarming the bombs."

"We'll start following up on this information as soon as we get back," said Steven. "If there is nothing else, we'll take our leave. By the way, it seems that no one in the system room was aware when we arrived here. With a little luck when we exit, you may be the only person in your time that knows about our visit."

After Steven and Ellie left his office, Jonas sat staring at his computer screen, hoping the events of the last year could be changed, and wondering what the result would be if they were. *We may be ahead of the Laurasians for the first time since we learned of the plot, but it's not over,* he thought. He decided to celebrate the small potential victory with friends at their favorite restaurant in Las Cruces, New Mexico. He hadn't been out of the facility in months.

A month after Steven and Ellie had visited from the past Jonas found a new horror as his news feed service presented an alert on his computer screen. The Three Gorges Dam in China had been hit with a nuclear bomb that destroyed the entire site and sent a wall of water rushing through the many cities that were downriver. According to CNN, the wreckage of the airplane that had delivered the bomb was found in a remote part of Mongolia, where it had crashed. No pilot was found despite an extensive search launched to find him. However, the plane, which appeared to be a highly experimental electric craft, clearly had the markings of a US military aircraft.

SANTA MONICA, CALIFORNIA

Captain Edwards's airplane from San Jose landed at Ontario Airport at about 4:00 p.m. He thought about sneaking home long enough to take a shower and reintroduce himself to his wife and ten-year-old son when his cell phone went off. "Shit," he muttered as he fished out the phone. A lady who was walking beside him as they exited the plane glared and moved away.

"Captain, we found it," shouted his aid, Sergeant Frank Fitzgerald, when Edwards finally answered the phone. "We have a verified sighting of the silver Toyota in Santa Monica. And even more fantastic is that the LAPD officers who first saw the car were able to call it in and get plainclothes backup in place without alerting the driver."

"Where is the vehicle now?" asked Edwards. "Do you have a SWAT team packed up and ready to roll? Who will be coordinating this for the LAPD?"

"LAPD has been following the Toyota for about thirty

minutes," said Frank. "At first, he just drove around aimlessly, probably making sure he wasn't followed. The guys on this detail seem really professional, so they weren't spotted. Then he stopped at a convenience store and bought some stuff. Now he's back on the move. The guy in charge of the Los Angeles SWAT operation is Sergeant Joe Foster. I filled him in on the background of this case, and he is expecting you to meet up with his team as soon as you can get there. I'll text you his phone number as soon as I hang up."

"Thanks," said Edwards. "I just got to the car, so I'm on my way now."

The LAPD plainclothes surveillance team assigned to follow the silver Toyota had just called Sargent Foster to tell him the suspect had gone to ground in a house on Melrose Avenue in Santa Monica. They posted people all around the house in case someone tried to sneak out the back, but they really did not think the suspect realized he had been followed.

As soon as Captain Edwards arrived at the scene, Sergeant Foster rapidly updated him. "When should we break in and arrest the occupant of the house?" asked Foster. "My men will be ready when you give the word."

"I'd like to wait a couple of hours to be sure no one else shows up at the house," said Edwards. "We really don't know how many people are involved in this terrorist plot. But I'm pretty sure there was more than one person to handle and place seven hundred pounds of C-4, whatever their target. There were at least two people present at the murder of Antonio Garza. We saw that from satellite photos of the crime."

"Makes good sense," said Foster. "There is only one person in the house at present. We checked it out with our infrared sensors. I'll get a few men around back to replace the plainclothes cops, and we'll wait."

Several hours later at about 9:00 p.m., Edwards decided not to wait any longer. When he gave the word, the SWAT team crashed into both the front and back doors of the little house at the same time. They chose not to use flash bangs because of the possible presence of explosives. They cleared the house in less than forty-five seconds. The suspect was restrained and taken off to the local precinct station for interrogation. Almost immediately, the forensic techs moved into the house, and information began flowing to Edwards and Foster. It was clear that the man they had apprehended was not the suspected leader; he didn't match the picture they had. It was also clear that more than one person had been living in the house but that most of the beds had not been slept in for a long time. They found many sets of fingerprints, and one set corresponded to the prints taken from Ikram Kader when he had entered the country. The other prints all belonged to men who had entered the country at about the same time as Kader. All had entered the United States through different cities. Interestingly enough, six men had entered the country on about the same date, but three of them had left during the first week of August. The most alarming thing was that there was no sign of the C-4. Someone had definitely been building electronic devices in the house, but there was no sign of any finished devices.

"Where do you think the other members of the cell have gone?" asked Foster. "I would bet a month's paycheck that we didn't alert anyone while we trailed the car or when we set up here."

"I agree with you that they were not alerted, and we know half of them have already left the country. There has to be some explanation for all this," said Edwards. "Thanks for all your good efforts. I'll make special note of it when I'm making my report to the national security advisor. Let me know immediately, day or night, if you find out anything new from the prisoner or from the forensic guys. You should push the information we have collected here up your chain of command. I suspect whatever mischief these people are up to, it will probably happen in your backyard.

SANTA MONICA, CALIFORNIA

Khaliq was going crazy with the inactivity. Every time Masud said anything, Khaliq snapped at him. Soon, he was sure they would physically fight with each other. For a man who had lived an active life, sitting around the small house was worse than being in prison. Khaliq knew he would have to do something to calm down or he might do something stupid that would harm the mission. So he used the advice he had always given his men and escaped his prison without taking the car. He found the bus routes to get him to the La Brea Tar Pits. The complete change of environment and the wonderful exhibits allowed him to relax. He pictured himself as a saber-toothed tiger prowling the terrain, looking for prey. After the museum, he treated himself to an expensive French dinner. He stood out a little because he was alone in the restaurant, but the effect of a well-deserved special meal was calming to his mind. It was late when he got off the bus on his return trip to the safe house. He felt the day had been well spent. He would be able to go back to waiting for the most glorious moment of his life, the moment when he could strike a serious blow at the infidels.

Khaliq decided he would have to let Masud do something similar next week. He knew his partner must have been suffering as much as he was. Fleetingly, he hoped Masud had not done anything stupid while he had been gone for so long.

As he strolled the final block to their little house, he sensed unusual activity on the street in front of the house. Then he saw a tall man in a suit and a shorter man dressed in SWAT equipment walk out of his safe house. "Oh, no, Masud, what have you done?" mumbled Khaliq under his breath. How had the police found them at this point in the operation? This should have been the safest time. They weren't performing any activity that would call attention to themselves. Then he noticed that their car was not parked in exactly the same place where it had been when he had left. That idiot Masud must have gone out driving the car. *What should I do now?* he thought. *First, I must find a hotel so I can get off the streets. Then I can think about what to do next.*

White Sands, New Mexico

Ellie and Steven updated Jonas on their trip to the future. They had only been at the update for ten minutes when Jonas decided they had learned enough to phone Jason Sanders, the national security advisor. After a brief recap of what they had found, Jason ordered Steven and Ellie to get on a fast military jet he made available and fly to Los Angeles. He wanted them to brief the local police currently engaged in finding and stopping the terrorists. It was Jonas' idea to tell authorities that the information was reliable and that it had been obtained from an undercover CIA agent within al-Qaeda. Steven and Ellie would be represented as NSA agents that Jason had sent to help the local police officers find the bombs so that they could be defused.

Only two hours had elapsed on their watches from the beginning of their mission into the future until the time they were seated on a Gulf Airstream jet headed for LAX. One of the two NSA agents that were already in LA to help investigate the murder of Antonio Garza would pick them up. He would drive them to the police precinct station in Pasadena, where a team was already assembling, now that the Rose Bowl was identified as the target.

When they walked into the precinct's briefing room, it was already packed with a standing-room-only crowd. First and foremost, there were five members of the LAPD bomb squad to dispose of the bombs. Sargent Joe Foster and his SWAT team were there to provide protection for the bomb squad while they worked. The FBI was present to add more SWAT team members to the protection detail. They also brought along an ultrasonic device to help find the bombs within the Rose Bowl columns. This was actually Jonas's brilliant idea. After Steven and Ellie left his office, he realized that they would need some method of finding the exact location of the bombs because they were embedded within the columns.

Steven closed the briefing telling everyone that there were over two hundred bombs placed one per support column and that they were rigged so that a person could set them off by remote detonator. "The bombs had been placed during a renovation that had occurred about six weeks prior, so they were definitely in place now. The bombs are apparently wrapped in several layers of plastic and not detectable by explosive-sniffing dogs or other conventional methods," Steven explained.

At this point, Sargent Foster spoke up and told the group that the terrorists had clearly been making some type of electronic devices in their Santa Monica house. However, they found no finished devices. The group recognized there was a very real possibility that there could be at least two more terrorists that hadn't been accounted for yet, walking around the city with a device that could detonate the explosives while the bomb squad was in the process of disarming them.

"We can place signal jammers at strategic positions around the stadium to keep anyone from setting the bombs off," said Sergeant Greg Wilson, the head of the bomb disposal team. "To do this, we need to know the exact frequency of the detonation signal. This clean-up operation could take close to a week possibly longer, depending on how difficult it is to get at the bombs. That is a long time to be exposed to the threat of explosion. We should keep in mind that the terrorists may observe the stadium periodically to be sure there is no one tampering with their work. If they see us dismantling their efforts, they will surely try to set off the bombs."

"By the way, I guess we are making the assumption that they haven't set the bombs off already because they are waiting for a football game or some other large event to achieve a maximum death count," said Sergeant Foster "I believe there is a college game scheduled in two or three weeks. That will be the next public event held in the stadium."

"We don't know the signal frequency of the transmitter and receivers. That was not part of the intelligence we received," said Ellie. "Let's find and disarm one of the bombs and learn the frequency from that."

"Great idea," said Sergeant Foster. "We get the frequency from one bomb, which can be done with a small low-profile workgroup to minimize the chances of the terrorists seeing us. After the jammers are set up, we can use a much larger work crew that would be more venerable to being seen by the terrorists. We can place SWAT officers for several blocks around the Rose Bowl with electronics to detect a remote detonation signal if the terrorists try to blow up the stadium while we're at work disarming the bombs we should be able to apprehend them."

"It's a reasonable plan. Besides, I always wanted to be the bait in a life-and-death sting operation," Wilson said sarcastically. The meeting ended with a good laugh and the determination to disarm the bombs without losing anyone.

PASADENA, CALIFORNIA

Early the next morning the bomb squad set up a scaffolding rig, the kind skyscraper window washers' use, on one of the columns of the Rose Bowl. The rig was slowly raised while two

FBI agents, versed in the use of the ultrasonic detector moved its transponder across the surface of the column. These two men were the only people visible from the ground level around the stadium. The scaffold operator and three SWAT officers in plain clothes and armed with sniper rifles were concealed on the top of the column. They were at the top of the stadium, watching the progress from a place where a person casually strolling past the stadium could not easily see them. Steven and Ellie were off-site about a half mile away, but they were patched into the police communication network in case any questions came up that they might know the answer to. As predicted, when the scaffold was about two-thirds of the way up the column, the detector went off, indicating an area of significantly different density. They marked the spot and descended to the base of the column. A second crew of two men ascended to the mark and carefully chiseled away the concrete so they could remove the explosive device.

SANTA MONICA, CALIFORNIA

Khaliq paced back and forth in his shabby motel room, wondering what he should do. He had checked in about midnight but had been totally unable to settle down enough to sleep. Somehow, the operation had been compromised, but he had no idea how. They had been so careful. He doubted that Masud would give the infidels any information, even if they tortured him. But what should he do about the mission now? The weight of the transmitter in his jacket pocket comforted him. It had not left his person since they had placed the C-4 at the stadium almost two months ago. He knew the next time the Rose Bowl would be used was still three weeks away. Blowing up the stadium at that time would not have the impact that blowing it up on

New Year's Day with millions watching on worldwide television would have. It would still be a huge victory over the Great Satan. But did he dare to wait even three weeks? That was so much time for the infidels to discover where he planned to attack. He thought about placing a call to his superior in the organization for consultation. *No, that's too risky with the many electronic ears of the Great Satan,* he thought. *I could be overheard somehow.* He decided to risk a trip to the stadium to check if the infidels had not somehow found out the location of the planned attack. He decided to leave the transmitter hidden in his motel room. If he was stopped for questioning by the police for any reason, the transmitter was the only hard evidence that linked him to the attack.

After a torturously slow bus ride to Pasadena, Khaliq walked the last several blocks to the stadium. He thought, *I should have picked a motel nearer the Rose Bowl but I wanted to get off the streets as quickly as possible.* No cars or trucks appeared parked in the stadium parking lot. However, he had limited visibility inside the column structure. He retraced his path away from the stadium and then turned left on a city street. He walked two blocks and then turned left again. This brought him to another quadrant of the stadium. That was when he saw the scaffold attached to one of the columns and two men chiseling away the concrete exactly where the backpack was hidden. There was no mistake. The infidels had somehow discovered his carefully laid plan and were beginning to disarm the bombs. It was now an easy decision. He would return to the motel to retrieve the transmitter and come back to set off the bombs. At least he would kill the police that were at the stadium, cost the infidels a huge amount of money to replace the stadium, and best of all, demonstrate the power and resolve of al-Qaeda. It was the best he could do in the situation.

PASADENA, CALIFORNIA

The two men on the scaffold had just removed the bomb from inside the concrete of the column. They were now bringing it down to Sergeant Wilson for examination. He had set up a small portable workbench, so he was ready to start disarming the bomb as soon as the work team brought it down. He placed the backpack on his workbench and examined it for booby traps that might be attached to keep anyone from opening the backpack. He saw none, so he carefully lifted the flap and looked again for any trip wires he might have missed. Once the backpack was open, he saw that it contained a package wrapped in several layers of plastic. He carefully cut away the cloth of the backpack and folded it out of his way. A drop of sweat rolled into his eye. He stepped back to wipe it away.

Lifting the plastic wrapped package he examined all sides of it. Again, there were no apparent trip wires. Very slowly, he cut away the plastic, which appeared to be thin sheets of Mylar, and finally revealed the explosive and the detonator. *I wish I could just explode the device and be done with it,* he thought. But the inescapable fact was they needed this one intact to determine how it worked and to find the signal frequency for its remote detonator. These bombs were all made the same way, according to the NSA agents. The bomb was not complicated, and it showed no sign of being rigged to explode if one tampered with it. Wilson thought, *The bomb maker must have been counting on the fact that the bomb would be encased in concrete and therefore did not need a high level of tamper resistance built into the mechanism.* After about ten minutes of study, Wilson simply cut the wire that sent the signal from the electronic receiver to the detonator. Nothing happened. After he carefully removed the C-4 and detonator and set them aside, he studied the electronic trigger receiver. The trigger receiver was a fairly simple commercial circuit that nearly anyone could build. *Now to determine the frequency the receiver works on.*

SANTA MONICA, CALIFORNIA

Khaliq could hardly sit still on the bus ride back to his motel. He didn't bother to second-guess himself about not bringing the transmitter. It was done. When he exited the bus, he nearly ran to the motel room to retrieve the transmitter. Then he walked to a nearby convenience store to get two fresh batteries. *Nothing will stop me from achieving this glorious moment.*

On the bus back to Pasadena, Khaliq entertained himself with thoughts of the torture he would subject Masud to if he could see him one more time. *It must have been Masud who told the infidels our plan was to blow up the stadium. How else could they have known? The other members of his little team had been in Indonesia for nearly two months, safe from any temptation to brag about their exploits in America. No one else really knew enough to give away the plan, not even in the highest levels of al-Qaeda.* Then a chilling thought occurred to him. *What if the hooded guy who financed this operation changed his mind? What if he informed the infidels about the target?* Well, he would just have to worry about that after he destroyed the Rose Bowl.

Khaliq had allowed himself one little indulgence for this operation. He wanted to watch the explosion and resulting destruction. He had carefully picked out a place outside the blast radius from which to watch the scene safely. It was less than a quarter mile from the stadium, so his transmitter was well within range. The place he was headed to was an eight-story apartment building with an unobstructed view of the stadium from a hall window on the top floor.

After he left the bus, he walked to the building that contained his observation post, disappointed in the outcome of his mission but looking forward to the destruction he was about to wreak on the infidels.

PASADENA, CALIFORNIA

Greg Wilson had brought along a computer-controlled variable frequency transmitter to determine the receiver frequency. *Oh, shit, there are additional bombs about fifty feet away in either direction.* He ordered one of his team members to take the variable frequency transmitter and the receiver to a precinct office five miles away to perform the testing. Twenty-five minutes later, Wilson got a call from his team member informing him of the frequency that the receiver responded to. After checking his measurements three times, his team member was confident that they had isolated the exact frequency the terrorist transmitter would be using. Wilson relayed this information on to the others involved in the operation. He had brought two slave signal-jammers to place around the circumference of the Rose Bowl along with the master signal jammer to ensure good coverage.

He jumped in his panel truck and drove to the first of three previously chosen positions. After he placed the jammer in a partially concealed spot behind a column of the stadium, he then set the device to standby. The device would activate when he turned on the master signal jammer. He quickly moved to the second position and set this jammer on standby as well. He then returned to his original work site and placed the master signal jammer on the ground by his worktable.

PASADENA, CALIFORNIA

The SWAT team members under Sergeant Foster's command set their handheld signal detectors to the frequency they had just received from Greg Wilson. Already deployed, they were all ready to catch any terrorist that tried to detonate those bombs. These dirtbags had threatened their city and their country. They wanted some payback.

PASADENA, CALIFORNIA

Khaliq arrived at the apartment building and walked to the elevator. He had chosen this building primarily because it had no special security. When he stepped into the lift, he pushed the button marked eight. After a short delay that stretched on forever in his mind, Khaliq stepped out and moved to his right. As he walked to the end of the hall, he gazed out at the subject of his total focus for the past year. Given the angle from the window, he still couldn't see the men working to dismantle his masterpiece. But he knew they were there, and he took great delight in knowing that they were breathing their last few breaths.

After he studied the view for a brief time, Khaliq took the transmitter from his pocket and put in his four digit code to release the lock on the transmitter function. He then carefully and firmly pressed the activation button.

PASADENA, CALIFORNIA

Greg Wilson activated his jammers and spoke through his communication unit to let the rest of the team know that he was finished with the first phase of their operation. He knew that Foster's SWAT team in plainclothes was spread around the general vicinity of the Rose Bowl. They covered an area about one mile in diameter centered on the stadium. Each had a signal detector set to the newly discovered frequency of the terrorist's transmitter. About fifteen seconds after Wilson turned on the jammers, Joe Foster said through their communication link, "Did anyone else see an indication that a transmit signal was just sent?"

Three additional crews of men quickly arrived from their staging area two blocks from the stadium. They all started the arduous task of removing the rest of the bombs from over two hundred columns. They immediately began to attach two additional scaffolds to adjacent pillars. They now knew the approximate placement of the bombs within the column, so they could pinpoint the location of the bombs much faster.

PASADENA, CALIFORNIA

Khaliq stood at the window, stunned. Nothing happened—no explosion, no destruction. He quickly removed the battery from the transmitter and replaced it with a new one. Still, nothing happened. He frantically removed the new battery and tried the third and last one he had. What was happening? Was he somehow too far from the stadium? He decided to go closer.

Even if he had to get within the blast radius of the bombs, he had to try to set them off. He was a dead man anyway with the failure of his entire plan. He couldn't go home now. The leadership of al-Qaeda or that hooded stranger who had supplied the money would see to that.

He hurried back to the lift. Once he was on the street, Khaliq headed in the direction of the stadium, which was about four blocks away. As he crossed each intersection and moved closer to the stadium, he pushed the transmitter button again with no result. He continued walking toward the stadium, trying the transmitter every hundred feet or so.

PASADENA, CALIFORNIA

Almost as soon as Sergeant Foster turned his signal detector on, he received a signal. He was uncertain about this reading because he had just activated the device. Maybe it was an anomaly of the device's start-up cycle. "Did anyone else see that indication that a transmitter signal was sent?" he asked. Other members of his team confirmed that the signal had indeed been present momentarily.

"Joe, do you realize you received the transmitter signal about ten seconds after I turned the jammer on?" asked Wilson. "I never want to get that close to seeing my maker again until I'm about eighty years old."

"I'll probably start shaking after this operation is over, and I have time to think about how close to disaster we came," laughed Foster. "Our luck is holding though because this means our terrorist is around here somewhere. Let's keep a sharp watch on the streets and bring this guy down." They started checking the streets in their prearranged pattern. Each man was posted at an intersection of the streets in their grid so they could see in four directions. Sergeant Foster was on the first street running in front of the stadium complex, Rose Bowl Drive, so he could coordinate everyone's efforts. As he looked up the street that intersected with Rose Bowl Drive, he saw someone walking down Westfield Avenue in his direction about two blocks away. As he watched the man approach the next cross street, he saw the subject take something out of his jacket pocket and fiddle with it. Just then, Foster's signal detector went off again.

"Gentlemen, I have eyes on our man," said Foster. "Converge on my location. The terrorist is of medium height with short black hair and a beard. He has on a tan jacket and blue jeans." As the terrorist came within one hundred feet of him, Foster drew his gun and yelled, "Get down on the ground with your hands out to the side where I can see them."

PASADENA, CALIFORNIA

As he was getting on his knees, Khaliq had a moment of clarity. Of course the infidels had jammed the detonation frequency. The bomb maker had decided there was no need for special security or protective trip wires on each bomb because of the nature of the bomb placement. The only way to the bombs would be through the wireless signals. So the only precaution the bomb maker took was a backup detonation signal at a different frequency. As Khaliq knelt on the concrete, he pushed the alternate detonation signal button and watched the stadium erupt in a cloud of smoke and dust. He had succeeded.

Now that he had accomplished his primary mission, Khaliq wanted very much to fight it out with the infidel police, to die a glorious death and receive his reward in paradise. There was one problem with that. Khaliq did not have a firearm. The two pistols the terror group had acquired were back in the Santa Monica safe house. Being shot in the back as he ran away was hardly a glorious ending. He finally gave a sigh of frustration, spread his arms, and lay on the ground. What else could he do? The converging SWAT team members quickly restrained Khaliq, searched him, and took away his transmitter, but it was too late now.

Twenty dedicated officers of the law died in the explosion that leveled the Rose Bowl. The iconic site that had seen so many glorious moments over the years was gone in the blink of an eye. Windows were broken out for three blocks around, and over a hundred people received minor injuries from various causes associated with the explosion. Luckily, no other buildings were destroyed, and the loss of life was tiny compared to the goals of the people who had instigated this stupid act.

The media's disaster coverage consumed 100 percent of network television for the next forty-eight hours. The funeral ceremony for the fallen heroes was held on the third day after the disaster. The president of the United States gave posthumous commendations to the heroes who had been at the scene for their parts in saving the lives of thousands of their fellow citizens. It was small consolation to the families and loved ones of the lost officers, but most citizens of the United States marked this incident as a small victory in the fight against the insanity represented by the pseudo-religious terrorists of the twenty-first century.

PASADENA, CALIFORNIA

A few minutes after the explosion, Steven and Ellie arrived at the scene of the arrest just as SWAT team members were putting the captured terrorist in a patrol car. "How did you find out about this location?" Khaliq yelled frantically at anyone who would listen. "Did Masud tell you, or was it that hooded man that sold us out?"

Steven's eyes met Ellie's for about five seconds, and then they both grabbed for their cell phones at the same time. Ellie got through to Jonas slightly before Steven. For privacy, they both walked away from the group of policemen as Ellie heard Jonas's voice answer on the other end of the line.

"We were just seconds too late to save the Rose Bowl," said Ellie. "The bomb squad had set up frequency jammers to be sure a remote signal couldn't set the bombs off, but somehow, the terrorists managed to detonate them. The reason we're calling is because the SWAT officers captured one of the terrorists alive near the stadium after he set off the explosion. As he was being pushed into a police car just now, Steven and I overheard him say something about a hooded man. I would recommend you get Jason Sanders to override the local police and take possession of this prisoner immediately. We should fly him to the White Sands facility before anyone gets a chance to question him. Otherwise, too many top-secret details could suddenly be at risk of exposure. I think Mr. Sanders should also get possession of that other terrorist that authorities captured in Santa Monica. We need to find out what information they have on the Laurasian spy. Since this one seems to know of him, he may have a way to track him down."

"I'll get on it at once," said Jonas. "We'll bring you two back to New Mexico on the same plane."

"I guess that means we won't be spending any tourist time in Los Angeles," said Ellie.

chapter 20

WHITE SANDS, NEW MEXICO

On the airplane ride back to White Sands, the prisoner was shackled and then bound to his seat. The police officers who escorted him aboard the plane obviously were not happy that they were losing their prisoner and apparently decided to take their frustration out on his restraints. The two NSA agents who had been helping the LA and San Bernardino police came along to perform guard duty. Steven was dying to talk to the terrorist about the hooded man, but the presence of the NSA agents meant he could not broach the topic.

After they landed, military policemen from the military side of the White Sands facility marched the prisoner off to the brig. The two NSA agents were notified that they would be returning to Washington, DC, on the same plane and that they would depart as soon as the jet was refueled.

A team of four professional military interrogators on the base would conduct most of the questioning of the terrorists. Hopefully, their prisoners could give them a lot of information about the various activities of al-Qaeda. Jonas prevailed on Jason Sanders to let Steven talk to Khaliq first to see if he could find out what the terrorist knew about the hooded man and his whereabouts.

Khaliq sat in an interrogation room, exhibiting the smug look of a man who had just accomplished the top item on his bucket list. He had spent two hours in a cell trying to figure out how he could kill himself. *I'll just have to work on that later so they can't force me to disclose any al-Qaeda secrets,* he thought.

As Steven entered the interrogation room, he saw a slightly overweight man with dark hair and a beard. His most distinguishing feature was a bright red scar that ran from the right side of his mouth to his ear. It was hard to think of him as the monster that had tried to murder one hundred thousand people and had succeeded in destroying an American landmark. "Are you the one who will torture me?" asked Khaliq sarcastically. "I don't intend to say anything to you."

"All that will come later," said Steven. "I'm only here to ask you why you would possibly work for those creatures against your own race. I thought Muslims had at least some regard for human life, even if only for members of your own religion. Do you have any idea who you have been working for?"

"I don't know what you are talking about," Khaliq hissed between clenched teeth. "I came here to deal as much death to you infidels as Allah would allow."

"You really don't even know who you are working for," gasped Steven. "Let's start this conversation over again. I heard you talking about a hooded man when you were in the police car. What do you know about him?"

"What makes you think I will tell you that or any information?" said Khaliq.

"So you know who I'm talking about," said Steven. "Very tall and wearing a long gray robe with a hood that completely covers his head. He talks in a very strange manner. I don't expect you to believe me, but he is not a human. He is a creature that is determined to start a global nuclear war to destroy civilization as we know it."

"Well you're certainly right. I don't believe you," said Khaliq. "I expected to be questioned and tortured, not entertained. I guess you want me to believe this guy is an alien or something trying to take over the world."

"I can't tell you where the hooded man is from or his agenda, but I can show you a creature that is just like him," said Steven. "He is being held in the same cell block that you're in. I could let you speak to him, but he only speaks Russian and his own native language."

"I can speak a little Russian," said Khaliq. "But what is the point of the conversation?"

"The point is I am trying to figure out why you are helping him?" asked Steven. "Since when does al-Qaeda want to annihilate the whole human race?"

"How could my attack on American infidels have such an effect?" interrupted Khaliq, his voice dripping with sarcasm.

"Don't you read the newspaper or listen to the news?" yelled Steven. "There is so much tension in the world right now, mostly between Muslims and Jews, but other countries are being pulled into the conflict for various reasons. Your attack on the Rose Bowl could very easily cause the United States to declare war on virtually the whole Middle East. Russia and China would then be forced to support the Arabs because of their recent policies. You now have at least five or six countries with nuclear arms at war with each other. What would it take to get one of them to use a nuclear weapon? I'm going to bring the creature I was talking about into this interrogation room. You can see for yourself who your ally is."

Steven had the cell block guards bring YaSi into the room for Khaliq to see. "Greetings fellow prisoner," said YaSi in highly accented Russian.

"Did that thing just greet me in Russian?" Khaliq staggered backward, almost falling, his eyes wide with shock. "What is it? Is this some kind of a trick?"

"You're welcome to come closer and examine YaSi. That's his name," said Steven. "He's actually quite friendly since we found and returned his medallion to him. Just picture him in a large gray coat. The overall look would be the same as your hooded man, correct? Why don't you come closer for a better look? This is no trick."

After a few minutes, officers led YaSi away from the room. Steven and Khaliq returned to their seats. "Where did that thing come from?" asked Khaliq. "You say those creatures want to start a war between humans?"

"I'm sorry, but I can't tell you where he's from," said Steven. "I hope you now realize you have been used by creatures that do not have the best interests of the human race at heart."

"What do you hope to accomplish by telling me all this?" asked Khaliq.

"I want you to tell me everything you know about the hooded man," replied Steven. "Do you have a way of contacting or locating him?"

"I guess it won't hurt to tell you what I know, since it isn't much," said Khaliq. "This mystery man somehow befriended a member of our organization and got him to set up a meeting in Kabul with a high-level al-Qaeda leader to discuss a donation. He offered a lot of money if we would agree to use part of it to blow up that stadium. As soon as our leaders agreed to the attack, he delivered a suitcase full of US cash. He threatened all of us if our mission failed for any reason but said he would bring another suitcase full of money if we succeeded. I just happened to be the person my organization sent to the first contact with him. Since there were no other meetings, I'm the only one who actually met him and he made sure I never saw what was under his hood. I have no way to contact him, but another person in our organization had a satellite phone number to make the initial contact. I don't know if the number still works. By the way, the hooded man's name was SuHa."

"Steven, that was a really neat strategy you used in there," said Ellie. "You just assumed he knew the Laurasian spy and started talking about him. The terrorist never bothered to deny that he knew him."

"Yes, but what do we do with this information?" asked Steven.

"I would give a lot to have that satellite phone number to try to talk to this SuHa," said Jonas. "I bet this prisoner could get it if we let him try. He should be a hero with his associates after the partial success of his mission. They would probably give him just about anything reasonable he requested."

"What have we got to lose if we tried to get that number?" commented Ellie. "His people don't know he's in custody. All we need to do is convince our terrorist friend in there to help us. He could call his colleague in Kabul on a satellite phone with some excuse why he must contact their benefactor."

"Okay," said Jonas. "Steven, you go see if you can convince our prisoner to help us on this."

In fact, Khaliq was already convinced that he and his associates had been completely duped by this inhuman monster. The organization always prided itself on its tactical thinking and planning. To have these infidels demonstrate al-Qaeda's gullibility so vividly was the height of humiliation. If only he could find a way to get payback from that hooded man or whatever he was. As Khaliq thought about his decisions, Steven returned to the interrogation room.

"I hope I've convinced you that we have an incredibly dangerous common enemy," said Steven. "We would like to enlist your help to track down this SuHa and keep him from causing any further problems."

"What can I possibly do from a jail cell?" asked Khaliq incredulously.

"We would like you to try to get the satellite phone number that SuHa gave to your organization," said Steven. "If we can call his phone and if he answers, we can track down his current position. We may be able to capture him and put a stop to his attempts to destroy our civilization. It's a long shot, but it's really the only plan we have."

Khaliq started to respond, "If I do this—"

"There can be no deals to set you free attached to this," Steven interrupted quickly. "There's no way we could ever get a judge to release you. At best you can expect to spend the rest of your life in prison."

"I'll help you anyway," said Khaliq. "I'll do it for my brothers and for my family."

NSA technicians set up a communications center in a conference room at the White Sands facility. Officers put Khaliq in a side room, off the conference room to minimize background noise. He sat with Steven, a satellite phone in front of him ready to call his colleague in Kabul. The people in the communications room could hear everything that both ends of the phone said, and they would record the call if they made contact. Jonas gave the thumbs-up sign when everything was ready.

Khaliq dialed a number from memory and waited for an answer. He wasn't sure if he trusted his captors, but striking back at the hooded man had become a matter of honor to Khaliq. He was the only al-Qaeda member who had direct contact with the monster. Khaliq was the one who had been made to look foolish.

Muhib Ali answered his satellite phone on the fifth ring. He did not recognize the caller ID, and he was tempted not to answer at all. "Hello," he answered tentatively.

"*Shalom*, Muhib, this is your old friend Khaliq. As you know, I am in the middle of a group activity of some importance. I need to consult with our sponsor, the hooded man, about the change in timing for the completion date. He was most explicit on the date, but I was forced to pull it in because of unexpected attention from the competition. Could you give me the number you used to contact him last time?"

"Are you sure this is wise?" asked Muhib. "The sponsor was quite adamant about the timing. How was the activity compromised?"

"Muhib, I would not have risked a call to you if it were not important," Khaliq said urgently. "Please do not draw out this conversation unnecessarily."

"Okay, okay, here is the number. Use it carefully and remember it may not be active anymore," grumbled Muhib. Khaliq wrote as Muhib recited the number.

"Muhib, you have no idea how much good you have just done for the world," said Khaliq. "Good-bye, my friend."

Fifteen minutes later, after the technicians in the communications center had rechecked their equipment; Steven dialed the number they had just received. Bill Thomas, the Laurasian language specialist sat next to Steven in case the conversation was in Laurasian. The phone on the other end rang about six times, and Steven started doubting there would be any answer when a voice came over the phone speaking Laurasian.

Bill said, "Is this SuHa on the phone?"

"No, he is away from our base for a short while," answered FiYo in the straightforward manner of Laurasians.

"Who are you?" asked Bill.

"I am FiYo of the confor class. Do you have a message for SuHa? He should be back soon. He will be most excited that the time travel device is working again. Why was it not working for the last six days?"

At this point, Steven and Bill heard a commotion on the other end of the line, shouting in Laurasian that was fast and sounded angry. Then someone cut the connection. Steven quickly redialed the number, but the phone continued to ring with no further answer. "We learned quite a bit from that brief contact," said Steven when he came into the communication room. "First, there is currently at least one more Laurasian in our time. Our operation in Laurasia seems to have stranded him and SuHa here. Secondly, there is a continuing mission underway in our time that we need to define. We should play that back for Bill to see if he can understand the shouting that happened at the end."

Jonas joined them and commented, "The technician couldn't get an exact location, but SuHa seems to be in Eastern Afghanistan. What could he possibly be doing there?"

SOUTHERN AFGHANISTAN

SuHa grabbed the satellite phone from FiYo and screamed, "What do you think you are doing?" Then he smashed it against a stone several times until it was only a small pile of parts.

FiYo's stomach spots turned a dark shade of orange, and he crouched slightly as if he was expecting a physical attack. "I thought you would be happy that the time portal was working again," he said. "I heard a beeping tone come from your travel pack. When I investigated what was making the tone, I found that communication device. I pushed a few buttons until I heard someone using a highly accented form of Laurasian speech. Why did you destroy your communication device?"

"That was a communication device of this world, not ours, and the time portal is still down," said SuHa. "You were talking to one of the mammals that populate this world, not to a Laurasian. There are no other Laurasians in this time. How long did you chat with the enemy?"

"I only just began," said FiYo. "The caller asked directly for you. I did not think the local inhabitants would know your name. I could not have been talking for more than twenty seconds. I am sorry, SuHa, but I do not feel fully briefed on what to do in these unusual circumstances."

"I don't know if the mammals have a way to track where we are through that device, but I think we should immediately move to a new place about thirty miles northeast of here that I prepared in case we needed it," SuHa explained. "I was supposed to receive information from Laurasia on when to make the attack. I think we really should wait a little longer to see if the portal starts working again before we launch your attack. We also need the portal to get you back to Laurasia after you crash your plane."

White Sands, New Mexico

As Steven and Ellie hurried down the corridor on their way to a meeting to review the checklist prior to their trip to Gondwana for the next morning, they were surprised to see Jonas jogging toward them, coming from the system room. "I thought you would already be in the meeting," said Ellie. "Where are you going in such a hurry?"

"I'm so glad I caught you," said Jonas as he gasped for breath. "I finally found out what it's like to go through the system. What a rush! I came back from next year to give you another warning. But I have a strong apprehension about coming face-to-face with myself while traveling through time. Anyway, I guess I've read too many science-fiction books when I was young. I remembered I would be in a meeting with you today at this time that included a teleconference with Jason Sanders. I have a message I want you two to pass along to Jason and the president."

"What is so important that it got you out of your office and into the vessel?" asked Steven.

"About a month after you two left my office during your last trip, I saw a news alert to the effect that a strange experimental electric aircraft with US military markings bombed the Three Gorges Dam in China and later crashed on the plains of Mongolia. No pilot was ever found. I waited a short time before I informed you about this to try to get more details, but the Chinese have released nothing as usual. At our time in the future, I strongly believe China and the United States will be at war within the week if we cannot find a way to stop this disaster from happening. Over two million people were killed as a result of the flooding when the dam was vaporized. This aircraft sounds like a Gondwanian airship, but I think I see the evil hand of the hooded man from Laurasia in all this."

"Unbelievable! Your timing could not have been better," said Ellie. "Just two days ago, Steven got the terrorist who blew up the Rose Bowl to help us find the hooded man we now know as SuHa. We didn't exactly find him, but we were able to determine that he is in Eastern Afghanistan with another Laurasian. We were at a dead end because we had no idea what mission they could be on. You've given us the final piece of the puzzle."

"Jonas, we'll get right on the follow-up for this," said Steven. "I guess the system has paid for itself in saved lives and saved structures in just a year."

With a gleam in his eye, Jonas answered, "You really don't want to know how much we spent to develop all this."

"Well, I'm glad you two could join us," chuckled Jonas when Steven and Ellie entered the meeting room. "Has saving the world from global war gone to your heads?"

"I'm not sure I know how to politely tell you this, sir, but we just left an impromptu meeting with you in the hall outside," said Steven while Ellie laughed at the strangeness of the whole situation.

"Jonas, it seems you need to get this Team T-REX of yours under control," said Jason Sanders from the Washington link.

"Actually, we just received some perfectly timed information from future Jonas that tells us why SuHa is still in our time on the other side of the globe," said Ellie. "And I think we will need to toss this one to you, Mr. National Security Advisor."

After he explained that SuHa's mission was to blow up the Three Gorges Dam in China, Steven asked, "How can we warn the Chinese government about this situation without giving away the existence of the system?"

"This is going to be tricky," said Sanders. "Recently, the Chinese have been very difficult to deal with in even simple matters. We need to think about how to convince them this threat is credible without revealing too much."

"I guess we can use the old tried-and-true explanation that the information came from an undercover agent planted within the senior leadership of al-Qaeda," said Jonas.

"I'll inform the president and the secretary of state about the situation," said Sanders. "I'll be dropping off the link now."

"In the meantime, we're here to plan a trip to Gondwana," said Jonas. "I see no reason to drop that agenda, so let's go through the checklist."

"Before we get to the details of the trip, could we discuss what to do with YaSi?" asked Steven. "I feel we have gotten all of the information we can from him. He has just been sitting in a jail cell for the past four months. Couldn't we just send him home?"

"Well as far as I am concerned we could, if we send him back to a slightly different time and place," said Jonas. "I know he will not be reunited with his friends and family but the Laurasians do not seem to cherish those relationships like we do. Jason what do you think about this?"

"Jonas I am willing to let you make that call," said Jason Sanders.

"Then we can send him back before your team returns to Gondwana," said Jonas. "Let's arbitrarily pick one hundred years earlier than when we captured him and a place somewhere east of SoMu. He should be able to survive that much of a displacement from his previous life fairly well and not cause us any trouble. I'll make the arrangements right after this meeting. Now let's get back to our agenda."

chapter 21

GONDWANA, 65 MILLION YEARS BCE

Team T-REX arrived in Gondwana beside the southern road into RoHo, just outside the city. They set up the perimeter around the vessel as usual, even though they considered Gondwana friendly territory. Steven, Ellie, and Bill set off to find WeKu, the national information chief. He was unbelievably easy to find, considering he was the country's spymaster. They knew roughly which building housed his office, and with Bill asking for directions from a few passersby, they found his office quickly and waited for him to return from a meeting.

When he walked in, the reunion was happy and noisy with everyone talking at the same time. WeKu had become intrigued with the human habit of shaking hands, and he greeted everyone with a limp but enthusiastic shake. After everyone settled into chairs and were given a bowl of water, WeKu started by expressing his thanks for the team's return to help Gondwana. "Laurasia has become very active in their manufacture of materials that could be used for an attack on Gondwana," he said. "Particularly the facilities they would use to make marine-based vehicles like amphibious landing craft. They would require these craft for a large-scale invasion of Gondwana. Those facilities have been active twenty-four hours a day seven days a week since we took away their time travel capability. Other potential weapon manufacturing locations also show around-the-clock activity. They have been very secretive with plans for war, but that is the way of life in Laurasia. Only a few people at the very top would know the plans and strategies. Everyone else just follows orders without question."

"If they did invade Gondwana, where would you expect the attack to occur?" asked Steven. "The borders of your country are huge. I would guess it would be very difficult to constantly monitor the entire perimeter to detect an attack in time to mount a reasonable defense."

"We monitor the northern border of our country with around-the-clock air patrols," said WeKu. "The rest of our borders are relatively inaccessible and only have widely scattered observation posts to give us notice of an attack if they discover one."

"So almost your entire defense is concentrated along the northern border," commented Ellie. "What happens if they launch an attack from your east or west flanks? It could take you days or even weeks to relocate defenses to the point of attack."

"You are so correct," said WeKu. "I fear we have grown too complacent over the many years with no real fear of attack. I have been lobbying with our national forum to extend our border defenses to cover more area, but it would require a huge expenditure of government resources, so they put off the authorization each year in favor of more citizen welfare type of expenditures."

"I suggest you could build up a quick-response force based in SoHo with an air-mobile capability," said Ellie. "From what I have seen of the Laurasians, they are strategically wise enough not to launch a frontal attack on your strongest position. If they are planning an attack on Gondwana, I would bet a lot of money they will do something sneaky like attack on the southern border of Gondwana."

"A single defense force centrally located is an interesting, cost saving idea," said WeKu. "We could staff the force with soldiers who have been specifically trained in defensive warfare tactics to slow down an invasion until we could move more substantial forces to meet the threat."

"But returning to the even more important question: Could we take some immediate action back in history that might eliminate the potential problems we currently face?"

"Ellie and I have been brainstorming this problem quite a bit," said Steven. "We want to reiterate our concerns about the potential consequences of going back in time and trying to adjust the present. There is a basis, from our working model, for expecting to be able to change the continuum of Laurasia with little change in the continuum of Gondwana. This is because the interactions between the two countries have been so limited for over a thousand years. The time threads of Laurasia and of Gondwana are relatively independent of each other, so a change in Laurasia may have zero or at least minimal effect on Gondwana. However we have no direct experience with this, so undesirable consequences are possible.

"With that disclaimer, we thought that it might be possible to go back to a time that your historians determined to be a crossroads for change in the social dynamic of Laurasians. We could pick an area and time with a predisposition toward more peaceful ways and set them up with pieces of technology that would make it probable that they would survive and gradually become the dominant force in the region. They would still have to fight to defend themselves but hopefully, their philosophy would have a stronger influence on Laurasia than it does now. They may turn out more like what occurred in Gondwana."

"Very good!" said WeKu. "That is the strategy that we have needed for the plan our historians and military strategists have been trying to develop. We have found a peace-loving group of people so we can give them the tools to better defend themselves against their more warlike and aggressive neighbors. By increasing their probability of survival, they get at least a fighting chance that their ideology will continue to exist instead of being eradicated by aggressive lords. After all, it is more comfortable and desirable for people to live in peace than to constantly be at war, Gondwana's current government is proof of that.

"As I mentioned, our historians have actually identified a pair of villages in central Laurasia near PuRo. These villages are legendary for trying to live in harmony with their neighbors. They flourished over an extended period of history; however, about one hundred thousand years ago, they were defeated by a very aggressive lord, and their peaceful philosophy completely died out over time.

"The period in which they lived is what we call the FiSo period after the philosopher who gave voice to the peace movement. During that time tools and weapons were made only of stone because metal had not been discovered as a useful material yet. If we could give these people the technology for forging weapons of metal that would give them significant advantage over their rival villages. We could also teach the villagers modern military tactics and show them to build city walls to help protect their villages from attack. We could plant the seeds for the concept of modern projectile weapons and leave it to them to develop their own specific weapons. That should give them a significant military advantage and enough of a technical lead over their enemies to ensure they come out as winners over the long passage of time. Of course they must continue to expand their technical lead in the future. We can only provide a start."

"That sounds great," said Steven. "I might suggest we add some additional commercial technology to ensure their development of nonmilitary capabilities and to keep them interested in the overall well-being of their citizens."

"I will check with our historians to be sure I know the correct timing," said WeKu. "I think that is about the time that the concept of the wheel was discovered. If I am correct, we can ensure that our chosen group of people discovers it first.

We will also check to see exactly when these peaceful cities were overrun and then decide exactly when to intervene in their affairs."

SOUTHERN AFGHANISTAN

SuHa and FiYo had been staying in a new cave for about six days after the satellite phone incident. Both of them were getting bored with sitting around and waiting. One clear and bright morning, SuHa announced that they had waited long enough. Every additional day they delayed meant a bigger chance of being discovered. "We have been cut off from Laurasia for over two weeks. Something very serious must have occurred," said SuHa. "But our country is still facing a grave crisis that we have the opportunity to fix. We have received no change to our orders so we will continue to follow them until we hear differently.

"We will be stuck in this time until the problem with the time machine is fixed or the Exalted Lord decides to bring us home. We can hide here in greater safety if we do not have to also hide an electroglider. FiYo let's get the aircraft ready. I believe you can accommodate a second passenger, so I'll fly with you. We'll fly to the target, destroy the dam, and fly back west until the airship uses the last of its power. I'll help you damage the electroglider after we land, and then we can hike back here and wait for our return to Laurasia."

"It would have been better if we had done this sooner," said FiYo. "I was planning to be picked up wherever I landed the electroglider. Now the distance we cover on the return flight is most important. We'll need to get as far away as possible from the point of attack so we aren't easily captured. I've kept the electroglider in a minimum power configuration ever since our short flight here. However, the vehicle still consumes some standby power. The batteries are only at 80 percent of the full charge. That will make a big impact on the distance we can travel on the return leg of our trip. Is there any way to get access to an electrical power source so we can recharge the batteries?"

"Maybe I can find a way," said SuHa. His chest coloration turned a bright orange. "This is the part of my job I like the most, ad-libbing my way through problems. I still have a little of the mammals' money left. I will see if I can negotiate with the local al-Qaeda people and pay them to give us access to an electrical power source."

"The electroglider requires one hundred volts of direct current power," said FiYo.

"That may be the biggest problem," said SuHa. This world seems to run on alternating current power."

MISSION 6 FROM WHITE SANDS

Team T-REX finally defined their mission to be a visit to the villages of YiWo and SaPi, two medium-sized villages whose farmland shared a common border. They were located in the area near Laurasia's current largest city, PuRo. The historians had tentatively decided that these two villages had been overrun by their aggressive neighbors 110,276 years ago. There was some confusion in the historical records about the exact date, so the team was sent back 110,281 years, five years before the villages were supposed to be overrun. *This should give them time to make use of the technologies we give them*, Steven thought. The area was famous for its stone quarries, so they could also easily build stone walls around their villages for protection.

The operational team for this mission consisted of twelve

members. Steven, Ellie, Fred, and Bill were the human members of the group. MaSo and HiPo, who had both been part of the first Gondwanian mission into Laurasia, were the Gondwanian members of the team along with six other handpicked Gondwanian soldiers. The plan was to transition to a site just one half mile outside of YiWo and a few miles from SaPi so that the team did not need to walk a long distance in possibly dangerous territory. They had decided not to use any motorized vehicles during their visit. They did not want to show the local inhabitants too much advanced technology. Also, they did not want to be perceived as gods of some kind. Each team member was equipped with projectile weapons, but they did not expect to really need them on this goodwill mission with the local inhabitants.

The first half of the team set up the barrier fence while the second half was being transported. This transfer took longer than usual because it had to be done in two steps. The White Sands system technicians had to first transit the vessel to White Sands and then send it back to old Laurasia. After they set up the defensive perimeter, Fred and a Gondwanian soldier were left to guard the vessel while the other ten team members headed for YiWo. Bill was talking to MaSo at the head of the group while Steven and Ellie brought up the rear of the little column. They were passing through a small canyon when they all heard a bloodcurdling scream. Then a stone-tipped spear flew out of the sky and hit Bill right in the middle of the chest. He fell to the ground dead while the rest of the team stood stunned. Suddenly, the little peace mission realized they were surrounded by hundreds of Laurasian savages with stone-tipped spears and stone axes. The attackers would pop up from their ambush positions and throw a spear before ducking back into hiding. A spear hit a Gondwanian soldier in the leg, and he cried out in pain. The group's emotion of surprise quickly turned to barely controlled panic.

The group began to fight back with their projectile weapons.

Steven shot two attackers and watched them drop within seconds. During the same time, Ellie put down three attackers and the other Gondwanians knocked down warriors as soon as the enemies stood to throw their spears. In the first minute of the battle, eighteen attackers lay stunned and unmoving on the ground. Unfortunately, the team was trapped in the open, completely surrounded by this new enemy. So far, the attackers had not rushed them but stayed in their hiding places in the rock and brush. An attacker jumped into the path the group from the future had used to enter the canyon blocking the group's path of retreat from the canyon. He threw his spear directly at Ellie, but MaSo pushed her out of the path just in time. The spear actually caught a part of her shirt as it passed by, tearing the sleeve. MaSo dropped this attacker as Ellie got back to her feet. "Let's try to clear the enemy out that circle of boulders on the left side of the canyon so we can use it as cover," she yelled. Everyone focused their fire on the area with the boulders and put down sixteen more attackers in the process. Unfortunately, as everyone turned to the left, two attackers popped up on the right and threw spears at the defenders' backs. They landed two direct hits in Gondwanian soldiers. The group dropped the attackers within seconds, but the damage had been done.

The defenders had not made a noticeable dent in their enemies' numbers despite their superior firepower. As soon as an attacker was shot, another one slipped into his place. A coordinated volley to the left dropped another thirteen attackers, but then the enemy killed one Gondwanian with a spear through the center of his chest. The savages were unbelievably accurate with their throws and it appeared that there was an entire army attacking them. The defending group edged slowly toward the left. The area they were moving toward seemed to provide a small defensible area within the circular grouping of rocks. They inched toward this protection, stunning attackers as they moved. HiPo was the first to reach the boulders. He stepped into what he thought was protective cover, but a Laurasian with a stone-headed axe was still hiding there and smashed him in the face with his axe. HiPo fell and curled into a ball. Ellie stunned the Laurasian who had hit HiPo but was quickly surrounded by three additional attackers as she stepped inside the rock formation. One grabbed her arms from behind while another pulled her projectile weapon out of her hands. As Steven went to her aid, someone hit him from behind, and his world went black.

chapter 22

Steven gradually regained consciousness lying on his back in what he guessed to be a cave. He felt an intermittent pain in the side of his head above his ear. He moaned and opened his eyes to find Ellie probing his head with a look of grave concern on her face. "If you're wondering, that hurts," he muttered.

"I was really worried when you went down," Ellie said. "That soldier hit you pretty hard with his stone ax. Luckily, the blow was aimed downward causing a nasty cut, but nothing seems to be broken. How do you feel?"

"Like I was stepped on by a *Maiasaura*," he groaned. When he looked around, he saw MaSo tending to HiPo's wounds. It was amazing that HiPo had survived the vicious blow to his face, but he was still unconscious.

Ellie totally surprised Steven by leaning down and kissing him. "Could you please try to be more careful?" she said. "If I thought I could get you to wear it, I would get you a combat helmet. You always seem to lead with your head."

Steven lay there, trying to clear his vision as Ellie went to help MaSo.

A short time later, a particularly tall Laurasian walked into their prison cave. Because the reptiles wore no clothing to help distinguish them, it was usually not possible for the humans to distinguish their rank or identity. The new arrival announced,

"You are claimed as slaves owned by the Lord PeTe as the spoils of war. Now you will answer our questions. Where are you from, and where did you get such powerful weapons? Why were you going into YiWo?" No one answered, and suddenly, the speaker called for a spear from one of the guards. Then instead of asking again, he walked over and ran his spear through HiPo's chest, killing him without a second thought. MaSo jumped up to attack the reptile, but the other guards raised their spears and axes in a threatening manner, so he was forced to step back.

"Why did you do such a vicious thing?" asked MaSo shaking with rage.

"Does anyone want to answer now, or does Lord PeTe lose more slaves?"

"I will kill you for that as soon as I am able," said MaSo. "We are from a distant village called MiWa, thinking now was a good time to make up a good story. "We were going to visit a relative of mine in YiWo. These are our normal hunting weapons. Why did you attack us without provocation? We offered no threat to YiWo."

"We are not from YiWo," said the Laurasian leader. "You were violating our blockade of YiWo. Lord PeTe declared two days ago that the flow of all food and any other items into YiWo should halt immediately. All of you able-bodied people will immediately go to work helping to build watchtowers as part of the blockade. Line up along the right wall so we can tie you together and march you out to work." When he pointed at Steven and Ellie, he said, "Those two sickly ones will begin burying the dead from the skirmish. You lost five from your party, including that one lying at your feet. We lost fifty-seven brave warriors because of your magic weapons." Then the reptile pointed at MaSo and said, "Later tonight, you will show me how to use those weapons."

All of the prisoners except Steven and Ellie were marched out of the cave to work on building structures that would be used to enforce the blockade of YiWo'. Steven and Ellie were taken out a little later and put to work digging graves. "I guess the ritual of feeding the bodies of the dead to mammals has not started as yet," said Steven, When they were finally reunited back at the cave at sunset, they all looked exhausted.

We gave the Gondwanian soldiers and Bill proper burials, at least according to our standards," said Ellie.

"These savages don't seem to have much regard for human life, not our lives or even their own," said MaSo when he staggered back into the cave. "But I will teach them to have a care when I get the chance. How can we get out of here?"

As all but two of their guards left, Steven said, "They don't realize those warriors aren't dead. There must be some way we can use that information to our benefit."

"Great!" said Ellie. "It will take these warriors about two more days to wake up on their own without the antidote. Our captors already think there is something weird about Steven and me. Maybe we can convince our guards that we are shamans of our village and know all about dealing with matters surrounding death. We can dig graves and just lay the unconscious warriors in the graves without covering them up. Then we pretend to perform some kind of mass burial rite that the shamans from our village say must always be performed for those who have fallen in battle. We'll tell our guards the ceremony requires the warriors to be buried with their weapons so they can defend themselves in the afterlife. Then as they start to wake up, we convince the newly awakened soldiers to go over to thank the guards for protecting them while they were unconscious and vulnerable. Seeing their dead companions coming back to life and apparently coming after them with weapons should really scare the hell out of them. We can make an escape attempt in the confusion."

"That is a pretty shaky plan but it might work," said MaSo.

"I'll be happy to listen if anyone has a better idea," responded Ellie. "But it's the best I can come up with."

The next two days were miserable for the captives. All of the slaves who were building watchtowers were beaten with straps made of dinosaur hide if they hesitated in their work for even a moment. Rickety wooden structures that were about twelve feet tall, the watchtowers sat on a six-foot-by-six-foot square base. The bases were made of tree branches that were lashed together. A soldier could climb to the top of a watchtower and become a lookout that could alert PeTe's soldiers if anyone tried to sneak in or out of the village. They built the towers lying down on the ground. When complete, they tipped the towers upright through the use of many slaves lifting the top and walking their hands down the tower. At the same time, another group of slaves pulled on ropes attached to the top of the watchtowers. The tricky part was keeping the towers from falling over in the opposite direction when the slaves finally pulled them upright. Once when a tower toppled back over, the entire team of slaves was given five lashes as punishment.

There were hundreds of slaves employed to build the watchtowers all the way around the village of YiWo. All of the slaves and guards were divided into four teams, each responsible for the watchtowers around a quarter of the circumference of the village. Lord PeTe motivated his soldiers by promising the guard team that finished its segment first promotions in his army.

PeTe's army stopped anyone coming from or going to the village. This was a strategy that PeTe had used many times before. After a month or two of this type of blockade, other villages either surrendered without a fight or put up only a token resistance when PeTe's soldiers entered their village to take control. Lord PeTe thought this battle strategy was even more likely to work with YiWo because the residents strictly followed the teachings of FiSo and would probably not launch an attack to break the blockade.

On the dawn of the third day after the ambush, most of the stunned Laurasian warriors started showing signs of waking up soon. The laborer slaves were still asleep. The graves Steven and Ellie had dug for the fifty-seven stunned warriors were only three feet deep. This seemed to satisfy their guards, so Steven and Ellie did not dig deeper. Their hands were raw and bleeding from digging in the hard, rocky soil with stone tools.

They had laid the warriors in the graves and had not covered them with dirt in preparation for the mystical ceremony Steven had told the guards about. As the guards woke up on the third morning, Steven and Ellie acted like they were performing a ceremony. The guards asked again why Steven and Ellie were doing this ceremony. "It is an important rite designed to send the dead spirits to the afterlife," said Steven. "No one is ever buried in our home village without the ceremony being performed. In fact, I am afraid we might have postponed the rite too long because we were supposed to perform it before the second sundown after a person died."

"What happens if it is too late?" asked one guard suspiciously.

"I don't know for sure," said Steven in his halting version of Laurasian. "I heard from another shaman that the dead spirits come back to their bodies and exact revenge on their comrades in arms that had not helped them into the afterlife. The old man who told me this said that he had actually seen dead soldiers whose bodies had been left on the battlefield come back to life, and attack their fellow warriors for not taking proper precautions to help their spirits find the afterlife."

"Well, hurry up and finish your ceremony," said the guard. "So we don't have any trouble with them. I've never heard of such a thing, but it's better to be safe. By the way does your shaman training cause you to look so white and sickly?"

Steven and Ellie had not found enough undamaged weapons on the battleground to put one in every grave. As they went around the graves and acted out their ceremony, they moved weapons into the graves of the ones waking up first. As PeTe's stunned soldiers began to move around and try to stand up,

Steven whispered to them, "Those guards are the ones that stood guard over your body while you were unconscious these past two days. You need to get up and formally thank them to be sure your spirit stays attached to your body."

Because the newly awakened soldiers were still groggy from the projectile neurotoxins, they did not think to question what the strange looking creature had told them. They shuffled over to thank the guards as if their lives depended on it. Their speech was not totally coherent because they had just awakened from their two-day slumber, but they overwhelmed the soldiers guarding the slaves, causing them to panic and run out of the cave. As the confusion increased, Ellie ran from slave to slave with a metal knife she had concealed in her clothes. The Laurasian savages did not seem to understand the concept of clothes since they did not wear them. As a result, Steven and Ellie had not been searched adequately. She quickly cut slaves loose to help in the skirmish. Soon, she had freed all the other slaves and Gondwanian prisoners. MaSo and his soldiers gathered at a prearranged meeting point, while Steven continued to get more of the awaking Laurasians to join in the battle.

It was time to sneak away and hurry back to the vessel to make their escape. They had no idea where their projectile weapons had been taken, so they could not retrieve them. "Jonas will not be happy about that," Ellie told Steven.

As they were leaving the area, one lone Laurasian guard who was not currently caught up in the turmoil saw them leaving the cave. "Stop where you are by the authority of Lord PeTe," the guard shouted. Because no one even glanced in his direction, he threw his spear about twenty feet, and it went all the way through the body of one of the Gondwanian soldiers, killing him instantly. Ellie picked up a loose spear from the ground and charged straight at the guard on a dead run. The spear pierced his chest, and his stomach markings immediately flared a bright orange. He made a terrible hissing, screaming sound as he fell to the ground and rolled around in pain.

The half mile back to the vessel felt to Steven like the longest distance he had ever jogged. Retracing their earlier path was made more difficult because of everyone's fatigue and the lack of food. As the diminished group entered the enclosure gate, Fred realized something had gone very wrong with the original plan.

"What happened to the rest of the team?" Fred asked.

"We were ambushed and captured by warriors from another village who were in the process of blockading YiWo," said Steven. "Because of a stroke of bad luck we ran into a disaster. We lost Bill, HiPo and six Gondwanian soldiers and we accomplished absolutely nothing while we were gone. Let's get everything dismantled and loaded into the vessel before they figure out where we went."

Gondwana, 65 Million years BCE

The vessel returned to White Sands, but because one Gondwanian soldier had suffered a leg wound, the launch team sent the vessel back to Gondwana as soon as they could cycle the system. Steven wanted to get him back for proper medical attention. As soon as Gondwanian doctors were caring for the wounded soldier, the rest of the joint force went to WeKu's office.

The surviving members of the team were all seated in WeKu's office to try to salvage the situation. "We should have been more careful in our tactics," said WeKu. "Maybe a bigger time interval before the overthrow of the village for your entry time would have been better. We also should figure out a plan for the future to effectively deal with a large-scale attack. These are warlike people. We should have realized they have armies and patrols roaming the countryside most of the time, not just before a battle big enough to be recorded in the history books. Just think of what a disaster it would be if you arrive in the middle of an enemy force prepared for battle. The whole vessel could have been captured."

"Another issue we need to address is to make sure we'll be allowed to return to Laurasia to complete the mission at all," said Steven. "Bill is the first member of our team to be killed during a mission. My superiors may put severe restrictions on further missions."

"We have a tradition of always bringing the bodies of fallen comrades back after a battle to be buried and honored by their loved ones," said Ellie. "At least we know what happened to the body of Bill, we buried it. This won't be received well in our world."

"We had a good basic plan," said WeKu. "The good that could come from it would be immense. Obviously, most of the benefit would be to our world, not yours, but if we improve the twisted morals of the current Laurasian leadership, it would ensure they do not try further aggression in your world in the future as well."

"Yes, the plan was solid, and the human members of this group are totally in favor of another mission," said Ellie. "I think we should adjust our time target a few years backward and go again."

"The Council of Mothers and all of Gondwana would be grateful to you if we could do this," said WeKu. "All signs from Laurasia indicate they are preparing for war, but nothing points to where they will launch their attack. If we cannot make some adjustment to history quickly, I fear great damage and loss of life is in store for Gondwana before such a war could be won. Also, if your original information about their energy reserves was accurate, we must assume they are burning through their future to prepare for this war. They will put up a desperate fight."

Southern Afghanistan

The contacts SuHa had within the southern Afghanistan al-Qaeda branch included a man who was university-trained as an electrical engineer. He served as their bomb maker. To help SuHa he constructed a diode bridge designed to turn the 240-volt AC power available in Afghanistan into one-hundred-volt DC power. The components where the best they could get on short notice but the power ratings of many of the elements in the bridge were not large enough to enable them to handle a large current. Therefore, the bridge charged much more slowly than they would have liked. As a result, it took three days and all of SuHa's thirty-five thousand US dollars to get the electroglider up to full power. For the charging period, the electroglider had to be relocated close to the cave the al-Qaeda members lived in. They secretly siphoned power from a nearby high-voltage distribution network for their own use. SuHa and FiYo spent most of the first day placing a camouflage net and brush over the plane to keep it from being seen by American soldiers or drone aircraft that periodically patrolled the area.

"Okay, you have the power you requested," said SuHa. "Now it is time for you to do your duty for lord and country. You have studied the maps we got locally. Do you think you can find this target and knock it out?"

"This is what I have trained for the last four years," said FiYo. "I can do it."

MISSION 7 FROM WHITE SANDS

The second attempt to visit YiWo by Team T-REX and their Gondwanian allies began much better than the previous trip. After they addressed the concerns of Jonas McCormick, the reconstituted team again transitioned to a spot about half a mile from the village. They met no resistance while they approached YiWo this time. Fred went with the main group and MaSo left two Gondwanian soldiers to guard the vessel. After Bill's death, Fred became the official translator for the team, even though both Steven and Ellie were picking up the language rapidly.

The people of YiWo were friendly, if somewhat reserved as the ten armed visitors entered their village. MaSo requested a meeting with the lord that was head of the village. A male reptile left the small group that had gathered to greet the strangers and trotted off toward the center of the village.

The village consisted of an organized array of pits dug into the ground and covered with structures made of some mottled material, probably dinosaur hide. Individuals with the coloring of females were scattered around the dwellings. They seemed to be working on various projects or preparing food for the next meal. Few men were visible.

About half an hour later, a group of eight male reptiles approached along what appeared to be the main road of the village. The man who had gone to deliver the message was walking beside a distinguished looking reptile who was wearing a necklace of brightly colored and polished stones. Steven assumed this was the lord of the village. There were three pairs of warriors carrying stone-tipped spears walking in front and three additional pairs walking behind the lord.

As they approached the group of newcomers, the warriors in front moved off to the right, and the warriors in the rear moved up to the left side of the lord. The messenger walked up to MaSo and said, "I am pleased to present our great Lord KaSo."

MaSo bowed forward in a gesture he thought he remembered reading about from history books. "Thank you, Exalted Lord, for meeting with us. We come from a distant land far to the south and would like to discuss a trade of useful ideas and technologies between your village and ours. We have many useful ideas we are prepared to show you."

"Welcome to YiWo," said KaSo in a deep, resonant voice. "You have many members in your group for a trade delegation."

"Yes, we heard reports that it could be dangerous to travel unprotected in this land," said MaSo. "We brought some warriors along as a precaution."

"I see," said KaSo. "Your warriors can go along with my honor guard. They will show your men where they can eat and rest while we talk."

MaSo, Steven, and Ellie were taken to the lord's habitat at the heart of the city, a building that had stone walls with dried shrubs piled on top of wooden poles for a roof. The inside was a single room beautifully decorated with polished stone tables and chairs. Plants grew in stone pots around the perimeter of the room, some with colorful flowers. The lord and his head scientist shared a typical reptile meal of greens with the trio. At the end of the meal, MaSo showed them an iron sword that had been polished to a mirror like surface. A wrapping of dinosaur skin covered the grip.

"We propose to show you how to make swords like this as our first trade item," said MaSo as the lord and the scientist both stared at the highly reflective surfaces with awe. "This tool is as strong as it is beautiful. It could just as easily be used to chop down a tree or an enemy. Do you have a proposal for something to offer in trade?"

"Honored guest, we are a poor, peaceful village," said KaSo.

"I doubt if we have anything worthy to trade for this miraculous object."

"Please understand our village has used this technology for many years and are looking for new technology or ideas," explained MaSo. "Our village lord feels that a sharing of ideas among the many peoples of Laurasia is a way to increase our race's body of knowledge and promote peace. We would be most interested to see any new concepts you want to share. Please feel free to make a proposal."

"Well, our village healer recently discovered a cure for weak bones, which has claimed the lives of many of our middle-aged mothers," the lord said. "This ailment seems to be caused by the depletion of resources in a women's body as she makes the shells for her eggs. The healer has saved the lives of eleven women in the last two months alone by giving them frequent doses of a powder made from a finely ground up stone found near here."

"That sounds very interesting," said MaSo. "Our village has experienced the same problem. Has your healer formalized this regimen of treatment?"

"Yes, and the treatment has been 100 percent effective so far," said KaSo.

"Well, it would appear that we have our first deal," said MaSo. "I hear this area has a bountiful supply of rock that is good for construction projects. I now propose that we teach you our strategy of using stone walls to protect our villages from enemy attack. In return we ask that you teach us the ways of your people for quarrying and finishing the stone."

And so the conversation went for the rest of the day in a friendly give-and-take. At the end of the day, KaSo invited the visitors to a celebration feast to cement their agreements. The feast was exotic with grains and nuts mixed with many types of leafy greens and colorful flowers. Everything was delivered in copious quantities by young male and female members of the village who chatted in a friendly manner with all of the guests. Steven and Ellie were introduced to a strong drink that was made with fermented barley along with eucalyptus. Soon, everyone was dancing to drums and flute music. There was hissing and singing by all the revelers. MaSo said drunkenly, "This is the best party I have ever been to. I think our ancestors know how to enjoy themselves far better than we do. Somehow, we lost this ability over the centuries. I wish I could take this spirit back with me."

"Are you having a good time?" KaSo asked, walking up to the three negotiators. "We have not had a celebration for about three months, so my people are very enthusiastic tonight."

"How is your relationship with the village of SaPi?" Steven asked in the reptile language.

"We have a formal agreement with the lord of SaPi to provide aid for each other if we are attacked by our more aggressive neighbors," said KaSo. "We also have extensive trade between our villages, and both villages enjoy living peacefully. Unfortunately, even our combined strength is barely sufficient to keep our villages from being taken over by other greedy village lords. I have good reason to fear for our future."

"It sounds like you should share the technologies we have brought to you with this neighbor," said MaSo. "With better weapons and defensive walls to repel invaders, your villages have a better chance to survive. We will leave three of our people with your village to show you how to use our technology and to learn the technology you have traded to us. They can show people from SaPi the same things. We will return for them in one month when everyone is proficient with the new ideas."

"Thank you for everything," said KaSo. "It was a historic moment when your party walked into our village."

chapter 23

The American ambassador to China was eating his breakfast when the order came in from the State Department in Washington, DC, for him to petition for a meeting with the Chinese foreign minister as soon as he could possibly arrange one. He was a very diligent and ambitious diplomat on the fast track to bigger assignments, and so he initiated contact immediately upon receiving the notice. As a result, he was able to set up the meeting by 11:00 a.m. Beijing time after he explained that the topic of discussion was newly received information that was critical to the safety of millions of Chinese citizens. He only had about three hours to be fully briefed on the situation before he went to the meeting.

The Chinese foreign minister stood formally by his desk when the American ambassador entered his office. Relations were currently very strained between China and the United States because China thought America was blocking China's plan to increase their worldwide political power through promoting a war against Israel. As a result, just the two men attended the meeting. The Chinese foreign minister started the conversation with the following remark, "I suppose you are here to make another proposal to try to ease tension between the victimized Palestinians, including their Arab allies, and the barbaric Israeli people. I cannot begin to understand why you have supported this act of terrorism." From the tone of the statement, the American ambassador knew this was going to be an extremely difficult meeting.

"Mr. Foreign Minister, my request for a meeting bears on the topic you mentioned," said the ambassador. "However, this time, I am authorized to give you some critical information about why our president has held this very unpopular position despite the feelings of many world leaders. The information I will give you now must be held in strictest confidence. You may, of course, tell the members of your ruling committee but please, no one else. We have been able, over the past eleven years, to plant an agent within the al-Qaeda organization, and we have watched him rise to the inner circle of leadership. Because of this fortunate situation, we know that neither Israel nor the Palestinians launched biological attacks on each other. A third party has been responsible for those terrorist attacks and for blowing up our stadium in California as you have probably heard. We actually knew of this plot before the attack but were unable to find and stop the actual terrorists until it was too late. This third party is trying to cause a worldwide nuclear war. We don't know why they are doing it, but they paid al-Qaeda a huge amount of money to implement the destruction of the Rose Bowl. This is how we know of their existence and how we know they are serious. The only reason they have been unsuccessful in starting their desired war to date is because we had this information and have diligently worked to counteract their activities."

"Mr. Ambassador, why have you decided to tell us this tale now?" asked the foreign minister sarcastically. "Telling us earlier would surely have helped you meet your altruistic goal of preventing war."

"The CIA jealously guards the existence of this agent," said the ambassador. "The only reason we are telling you now is so you will believe us when we pass on some information we received just a few hours ago. This third party has again approached al-Qaeda leadership with a proposal to hire al-Qaeda operatives to fly a plane into Chinese territory and use a nuclear weapon to destroy the Three Gorges Dam. In this case, al-Qaeda negotiated an even higher payment to perform the operation. They said they really had no political issues with China; however, they did agree to take the mission for the money."

"Why would anyone want to do such a thing?" growled the foreign minister. "The dam was built to protect the people living along the Yangtze River from frequent flooding by the river and to generate much-needed alternative power for those same people."

"As I said, the objective of this third party is to cause a global war," said the ambassador. "Our intel says that the plane they will use is of some strange, unknown design that does not use internal combustion engines. It runs on electricity from storage batteries and is so quiet that it can fly at very low altitude overhead and not be detected. We understand the plane has been painted by al-Qaeda with the markings of an American aircraft. With the current level of tension between our two countries, an attack like this could easily lead to a war. I have come not only to warn you but to offer any assistance to help you stop this disaster."

"We will not require your assistance to detect an aircraft flying over half the width of our country," said the foreign minister with distain.

"Don't be too quick to rebuff our assistance," said the ambassador patiently. "We have every reason to believe this aircraft is capable of unbelievable stealth. It is said to make almost no noise, and the strategy we envision for this vehicle is to fly through China's airspace at a very low altitude, well below the ability of conventional radar to detect. We have a system called TARS, which stands for 'tethered aerostat radar system." We use this system in our effort to stop drug smugglers from sneaking into the United States across our southern coast and from the Caribbean Islands. It consists of a lookdown radar system suspended from a fabric balloon filled with helium. It can carry up to a one-thousand-kilogram payload, including a Lockheed Martin L-88A radar system operating at a two-hundred-nanometer wavelength. The balloon also supports a diesel-powered generator with one hundred gallons of fuel to run the generator. This system can be suspended as high as fifteen thousand feet and can detect a flying or surface object as small as a rowboat within its operating range of 370 miles. I am authorized to make twenty of these systems available to you in order to surround the dam. Since the contact was made with al-Qaeda in Afghanistan, we expect the attack to come from the west, but our strategists recommend placing the systems in a circle completely around the dam. As is usual with this kind of information, we have good details on some aspects of the operation and nothing on other aspects. We currently have no idea when this attack will be launched, so time to set up an effective defense is of the essence. In anticipation of your favorable response, we have cargo planes flying over the Pacific right now with the TARS systems. If you decline our offer, we'll turn them around."

"We'll accept your offer," said the foreign minister reluctantly. "Your government seems to have put a lot of thought into this situation already."

Gondwana, 65 Million years BCE

The return trip from Laurasia's past was uneventful. The mixed species force was eating a celebration meal with WeKu and the mayor of RoHo, TaSu, at the intelligence unit's headquarters building. "From your reports, it would seem that the mission was a great success," said WeKu. "Unfortunately, we have not yet seen any change in the behavior of Laurasia."

"Remember, this is all unknown territory for us as well," said Steven. "When we took away the time machine technology, we had no idea that Laurasians would remember having had the capability. We have no data to allow us to predict what will happen as a result of our recent activities. We will just need to wait and monitor the situation." All interested parties agreed to wait two days and then meet again to see what was happening in Laurasia.

As they were leaving the building that housed WeKu's intelligence organization, MaSo hurried to catch the pair of humans. "Colonel Johnston, I would like to request a favor," he said. "I have just been made the head of our quick-response defense force."

"Congratulations," said Ellie. "I think they picked just the right person for the job."

"Thank you," said MaSo. His stomach turned a light red color at the complement. "But I really don't feel I know enough about the requirements. Gondwana has set up a training camp in the extreme south part of our country. I was hoping you would come to look over the facilities and make any recommendations for improvement that you see. After all, you were the person who came up with the idea. It would only require two days, and we really need the help."

"Ellie, we'll just be waiting around here to see what happens in Laurasia," said Steven. "I know you can be a big help in defining the mission and tactics of this group."

"Great, I'll do it," said Ellie with a big smile. "Steven, what will you do for these two days?"

"I think I'll see if Fred's friend ToSe at the RoHo Academy will take us in his electroglider to see some more of the dinosaur population," said Steven. "What do you think, Fred? Will he do it?"

"If he's not too busy, I'm sure he will," said Fred. "I think he really wanted to show off his new electroglider. Let's walk over to the academy now and see if he's there."

The three humans found the RoHo Academy easily and asked a male student where they could find the department of zoology. He directed them to the third building up the street on the left. Then they were to go down to the fifth level. They started off as they were told, but as they were crossing to the left side of the street, someone called out to Steven. Then KiKi stepped out of the crowd of students. They recognized her mostly because of the medallion around her neck. The Gondwanians did not wear them. She seemed very excited to see Steven and Ellie. She also seemed surprised when Fred greeted her in the Laurasian language.

"Do all of your people speak our language?" she asked in Laurasian. Then she suddenly started speaking English. Now it was the humans turn to be surprised. "I made WaTu teach me English while we were being held in detention cells. He was reluctant at first, but I told him he owed me for what he planned to do to me. It also allowed us to communicate privately while we were being examined by Gondwanian scientists about the time travel machine. During the time of our detention and interrogation, I gradually realized I don't even like WaTu. After a short time under mind control the Gondwanians were able to see that I feel no ties or loyalty to Laurasia. Just this week they released me from mind control and offered me a place to live. I asked for a habitat near the academy so I could try to make new friends. I was not sad when I found out WaTu was sent to prison for his crimes. So tell me ... why are you visiting Gondwana this time?"

"We just completed a mission to try to change the history of Laurasia to promote a more moderate form of government," said Ellie. She told KiKi the details of their last mission and said she hoped KiKi would understand that they had carried out the mission for the good of both countries. "Have you found something to do here in Gondwana?"

"Not really," said KiKi. "The people here have been so kind to me, even though we were supposed to be enemies. Seeing this has shown me that the Laurasian government lied to their people for as long as we can remember. By the way, I'm glad you are trying to improve the situation, something needed to be done, but you do realize the risks involved with trying to change the space-time continuum, don't you."

"I am not sure the Gondwanians fully grasp the potential risks, but we did try to warn them before the Council of Mothers approved the mission," said Steven. They were very determined to try anything that would end the arms race with Laurasia they have been in for as long as anyone can remember."

"I see," said KiKi. I think I will study what my model predicts for a situation like this, just for curiosity sake, since your mission has already taken place. What have you observed as a result of your activity?"

"Actually nothing so far," said Ellie. "We just decided to get back with the Gondwanian authorities in two days to review what changes we can observe."

"I would love to hear your results when you find out," said KiKi. "As to your other question, I have talked to many instructors in different fields of study here to see if I can find something new that interests me. Unfortunately, the direction of Gondwanian science and its practical uses is very different from Laurasian science. They focused more on engineering and practical development of products contributing to efficient energy, communications, and transportation. They have a very strong affinity for art in many forms. Laurasia has concentrated more on pure science and mathematics with little regard for convenience or artistic values. The Gondwanians have not spent much time at all on quantum physical pursuits, so they are not really interested in my field of study, though that may change in the future. I have been studying their flying vehicles, both electrogliders and the vehicles that can travel outside the atmosphere. The Gondwanians seem to have figured out how to neutralize gravity without understanding the basic theory. I studied this just to keep busy. Just now I was walking around the academy campus, trying to decide what to do. Suddenly, I looked up, saw you, and realized the best possible thing I could do is to work with your scientists in the future. Do you think that would be possible?"

"Why don't you walk along with us so that we can discuss this further?" said Steven. "We are on our way to find the zoologist ToSe to see if he could take Fred and me on an electroglider flight around this area."

"That would be great," said KiKi. Steven could tell she was excited, not from the color of her stomach but from the fact that she was bouncing up and down on her toes. "I can even show you where to find ToSe."

As they walked, Ellie asked, "Wouldn't you get lonesome in our world without members of your own species around?"

"I am truly disillusioned with my species and even more disappointed in the Laurasian government, which allowed me to be wiped from the history books and probably killed," said KiKi. "Besides, you may not be familiar with our social customs. If I stay here, whether in Gondwana or Laurasia, someone at whatever research facility I finally go to work in would pick a mate for me. I would have no say in the choice. From my point of view, I have seen hundreds of unhappy females under the control of a stranger called their mate. This stranger could possibly even force me to change my field of study."

"I can see how you would not like that situation with your independent mind," said Ellie. "We have only met one mated pair in Laurasia, but they seemed very happy together."

"It happens, but only about 50 percent of the time," said KiKi. "I have heard estimates that less than 30 percent of mated couples are truly happy together."

"But you would be giving up any chance to have children," said Ellie.

"I think there are many things about our race that you have

not learned yet," said KiKi. Children are born in an incubator and spend their first two weeks there. The only time the incubator is opened is to put in food. The hatchlings must fight among themselves for the food. After the first week, they are removed from the incubator, tagged with the mated couple's name, and moved to a nursery that usually has several hundred hatchlings. Statistically, 25 percent of the hatchlings never leave the incubator alive, and most do not see their parents until they are three years old. As a result, parents normally do not have a close relationship with their children. Having children is primarily a duty to our species not the source of any particular gratification for us. Customs may be slightly different in Gondwana and Laurasia but will be mostly the same. In Laurasia, some mated couples come to visit their children as they are leaving the incubator. However, most do not. At the age of three years, parents formally meet with the hatchlings and conduct a ceremony to give the young ones names and their medallions, which they will wear for life if they were born to a class. Some parents provide information on how they can be contacted if the child so desires. From then on, the hatchlings are raised and educated by organizations run by the government."

"I really enjoy my work, and so I believe I could be a useful member of your world's scientific staff," KiKi continued. "It would very nicely substitute for having members of my species around me. Could you please give me a chance to work in your world? If I do not meet your scientists' expectations, they can just send me back here."

"I will ask my boss when we get back," said Steven.

"Oh, thank you, thank you," said KiKi, happily bouncing up and down on her toes. "Here is ToSe's office."

It turned out that ToSe was very enthusiastic about taking Steven and Fred on a tour. He even invited KiKi, who had been studying electrogliders but had never ridden in one. He needed exactly three more flight hours to become eligible to apply for a higher-level pilot's license, and this trip would get him the required number of hours. They agreed to meet at sunrise the next day at the airfield.

The next morning, Steven and Ellie parted ways for the first time in many months. Ellie got on an electroglider headed to the town of KaTi on the southeastern extreme of Gondwana. As she looked out of the large window of the electroglider, she remembered the maps she had seen in a book Steven had given her before their first trip in time. The book showed estimates of the geography of the world's continents at various times during a period sixty to 250 million years in the past. At 250 million years BCE, the landmasses of the earth were all merged into a single continent called Pangaea. Some parts of this single landmass started to separate but even after 185 million years, the land was still bunched together as two continents on one side of the planet, leaving a large empty expanse of water extending from the North Pole region almost to the South Pole region. This empty area had no land, not even an island, and it covered nearly one-third of the diameter of the earth. Ellie remembered reading that the sea level during this time was much higher than the present because there was no ice at the poles yet.

The northern half of Pangaea had separated from the southern half over these 185 million years, and thus, Laurasia was created. Laurasia included the continents now called North America, Europe, and Asia. It was completely in the northern hemisphere. The movement of the southern landmass that made up Gondwana was more complicated. The areas that we now call Australia and Antarctica were connected and stretched across the southern geographic pole while South America and Africa, still connected together, jutted north from one end of Antarctica to the equator. The subcontinent of India had separated from the east coast of Africa and was slowly moving northeast. Australia was attached to the east side of Antarctica and the combined landmass of South America and Africa was attached to the northwest side of Antarctica. The geography of Gondwana was shaped roughly like an "L" with the long leg aligned east and west and made up of Antarctica and Australia. The short leg was aligned north and south and consisted of South America and Africa.

The government of Gondwana set up their new training base near a massive nuclear power plant at the far end of the landmass that would eventually become Australia. The entire first class of soldiers to be trained had already arrived at the base and had started their physical conditioning. The place for the training camp was chosen because it had some of the harshest weather in all of Gondwana. The area experienced huge thunderstorms that seemed to come out of nowhere. The temperature occasionally dropped as low as thirty degrees Fahrenheit, and snow had been observed falling there twice in the last one hundred years. It was thought this environment would prepare the soldiers to fight anywhere in Gondwana because cold weather was the harshest environment for the warm-blooded Gondwanian soldiers.

Ellie and MaSo spent twelve hours in the electroglider flying to the new base, and from high altitude, the landscape was boring. It consisted mostly of jungle that was occasionally broken by a river or lake. Ellie did see a large rift valley that she guessed would eventually become the coastline of South America and Africa. There were tall plumes of steam being released from some places along the deepest parts of the rift.

The training camp was actually still under construction, but a utilitarian headquarters, classrooms, and barracks had been dug down nine levels so far. Ellie and MaSo dropped off their traveling bags in the habitats assigned to them. Then they walked up two levels and found the conference room, where a group of seventeen reptiles sat around a polished stone table. There were two open chairs at the head of the table reserved for them.

Ellie found it interesting that the military of Gondwana had all the required elements but had never thought to organize mobile attack units. MaSo kicked off the meeting by saying, "I think it is safe to assume that the Laurasians will attack us from the ocean. They have no flying capability, and there is no land access between our two nations. Our spies tell us that they have previously built models of small boats that can hold fifty to one hundred men and their equipment. These boats have very shallow draft requirements, which mean they can be driven partially onto a beach. They currently use these boats to transport crews harvesting combustible material to their work sites, but they could easily be converted to ferry invasion troops ashore. Therefore, a basic assumption for our mobile team is that the Laurasians are capable of landing troops at random sites of their choosing that we will not be able to predict. Because of this, they will probably meet little or no initial resistance. They will have time to set up fortifications on or near the beach after they land. Our task will be to immediately mobilize a counterforce of sufficient strength to contain them within their initial fortifications until our military can mobilize the forces to drive them off of Gondwanian soil."

"I suggest you also set up a special intelligence unit to work with WeKu's spy network," said Ellie. "This group will be responsible for creating a constantly changing list of the weapons and battle tactics the Laurasians are preparing for their military at any given time. Based on the information this group collects, the training staff of this facility can prepare the correct equipment you will need and prepare tactics to use against the Laurasians. Currently, I suggest that you start practicing to defend against an army using the laser weapons MaSo told me about and those shallow-bottomed boats they would use to land an invasion force. You can use these assumptions until your intelligence force comes up with different information. You should decide what kind of fortifications you expect the Laurasians will utilize once they land on Gondwanian soil and prepare the equipment and tactics to penetrate their fortifications."

They discussed ways to set up practice drills and mock battles until about nine o'clock in the evening. After a quick dinner of greens and nuts, everyone retired for the night. They planned to document the discussion of the first meeting and quickly wrap up at about ten o'clock the next morning. Then Ellie would be put on an electroglider heading back to RoHo.

It was the winter season for the southern hemisphere. At about five o'clock the next morning, it was still dark when Ellie was awakened by sharp cracking sounds that seemed to be coming from a distance. Ellie crawled out of her blankets in the habitat where she had spent the night and ran up the ramp of the headquarters building so she could investigate the noise. At about the same time, MaSo came out of the buildings exit and handed Ellie a Gondwanian weapon. They headed in the direction of the power plant, where the noise seemed to originate.

RoHo, Gondwana, 65 Million years BCE

Steven and Fred arrived at the front of the terminal building of the RoHo Airfield at the appointed time. KiKi had stopped by to say she was not going to come along. She wanted to complete some calculations using her model of the space-time continuum.

ToSe arrived about five minutes later with a colleague from the institute, a reptile who had come to act as copilot. Gondwanian law required a backup pilot on all electrogliders, even small private ones. The only exception was military electrogliders.

ToSe was so proud of his electroglider that he walked Fred

and Steven all the way around it and pointed out all the features he thought were pertinent safety features. He mentioned that this new vehicle design had electric engines that were capable of reversing direction even while the vehicle was in flight. This feature allowed the electroglider to turn abruptly to avoid possible collision or to fly in very tight places, which the Gondwanian pilots tended to frequently encounter.

ToSe said he planned to fly over the YuKuMa highlands because it was the season for the *Anatotitan* dinosaurs to migrate there from the wet lowlands to the north. They would be making their nests and laying their eggs in the highlands. "It should be quite entertaining because thousands of the creatures were expected this year."

The *Anatotitan* was a large duck-billed dinosaur that averaged thirty-three feet long and eight feet tall at the hips. It weighed roughly five tons, which was in keeping with the "giant duck" nickname modern paleontologists had given the creature. Steven thought that it looked similar to an *Edmontosaurus* but that it was more lightly built and had longer legs. The dinosaur had short arms, a long, pointed tail, three-hoofed toes, and mitten like hands. Its flat, sloping head featured a wide, toothless beak and cheek pouches containing hundreds of closely packed teeth for grinding plant material.

Anatotitan was basically bipedal, but it could also walk on four legs to graze low-lying plants. It was a slow-moving dinosaur that's only advantage to keep it safe from predators was its keen senses of sight, hearing, and smell. ToSe said it was of medium intelligence for a dinosaur. The species had migrated to Gondwana in the last few million years. Steven thought the creature must have appeared here just before the final separation of Gondwana and Laurasia. The species had apparently originated in Laurasia but were now thriving in the Gondwanian climate. The electroglider circled above a migrating herd, and the passengers watched the herbivores tear off conifer needles, twigs, and seeds from the surrounding trees with their tough beaks and then grind up the plant material with approximately 720 teeth. ToSe said that the teeth were continually growing and that if a tooth broke off, it was soon replaced.

They spotted four large migrating herds of *Anatotitan* in transit as the electroglider flew over the northern approach to the highlands. When they reached the heart of the highland region, Steven was speechless as he saw hundreds of the dinosaurs spread out over the preserve, scooping out nests and lining the bottom with foliage. The nests covered a huge area, even though they were spaced only thirty or forty feet apart.

When they returned, Steven and Fred thanked ToSe profusely for the wonderful experience. It had been a great day.

chapter 24

CENTRAL CHINA, THREE GORGES DAM

General Lee JianGuo was a forty-year veteran of the People's Army. He was a proud man, and he was aggravated to learn the defense of the Three Gorges Dam would be entrusted to US equipment. His people were well trained and quite competent with their own equipment. However, after Kevin Adams, the US Air Force staff sergeant, had briefed him on the threat and explained the specialized mission this TARS system had been designed for, the general decided he would send a bottle of the best single-malt scotch he could find to the foreign minister for acquiring this equipment. Rumor had it that the foreign minister had been severely chastised in front of the entire ruling committee for accepting the American aid without prior approval from the party chairman. It was a very brave choice, and it did not bode well for the foreign minister's future.

The TARS systems were launched at approximately equal intervals on a one-hundred-mile-diameter circle with the dam at the center. Sergeant Adams had personally supervised the launch of the first three balloons to be sure the Chinese personnel knew the correct procedures. After that, he returned to the command center that had been set up at the dam site. He was impressed with the speed and efficiency with which the Chinese soldiers had learned how to set up and launch the systems. As he entered the communication center, he saw

General Lee overseeing the work of his troops in the command center. Lee noticed Adams enter the communication center and came over to talk to him.

"Sergeant Adams, do you feel comfortable with the performance of my troops in launching the TARS systems?"

"Just by being in this facility at the center of the terrorist's target, I'm betting my life on them," replied Adams respectfully. "Are your ground-to-air missiles deployed to your satisfaction?"

"Yes, all is in readiness," said General Lee. "We have two separate modules each armed with three ground-to-air missiles. A single missile is more than sufficient to blow the aircraft out of the sky. We also have four batteries of antimissile missiles set up in case this aircraft launches its attack before we take it out."

"I estimate all twenty TARS systems will be up and operating within three hours," said Adams. "Now comes the hard part, waiting for the attack. I would much rather be on the attacking side of a battle than on the defensive side. The attacker knows all about the timing and strategy involved. I hate waiting."

"Let's go get a cup of tea, Sergeant. It makes the waiting easier," said the general.

Gondwana, 65 Million years BCE

The morning after their visit to the nesting grounds, Steven was awakened early by a messenger from WeKu telling him that RoHo military headquarters had lost all contact with the new military training base in KaTi and the power plant located there. Something was wrong down there, and WeKu was going to see for himself. He had sent the messenger to ask Steven if he also wanted to go, and Steven quickly agreed.

As Steven was leaving his sleeping quarters to meet WeKu, he ran into KiKi, who said she really needed to talk to him, bouncing on her toes in excitement. "KiKi, I am in somewhat of a hurry. Can we talk later?" asked Steven.

"Actually, I think you will really want to hear about what I have found," said KiKi. "I will walk with you and explain. You told me that your mission to Laurasia occurred one hundred thousand years ago. Also, you mentioned that you were hoping to hear today if your mission was successful."

"Everything you just said is correct," said Steven. "What do you need to discuss?"

"Yesterday, I went back through my model of the space-time continuum and came to some startling conclusions," said KiKi proudly. "The model predicts that changes in the space-time continuum propagate in the form of a time wave at a fixed speed. The propagation delay is based on certain physical constants of our universe and is fixed at twenty-three seconds per year. That means the changes you made in ancient Laurasia will not be seen in our time for about twenty-nine and a half days. Also, just prior to the arrival of the wave, time will flow backward for ten seconds or less and then become choppy, with events moving forward and backward for a short interval. The reason we have never actually seen this phenomenon before is because no one has ever been able to go back and change history before."

When they reached the front of WeKu's office building, a member of his staff hurried them into a waiting vehicle. WeKu was already inside the vehicle, and when he heard what KiKi had been telling Steven, he asked her to come along in the electroglider to KaTi so that she could update him in detail.

During the long electroglider ride, they were periodically updated on the training center situation and what the first soldiers to arrive there were finding. Apparently, the Laurasians had attacked the power station and had been caught by surprise when their forces encountered the strong defense mounted by the power station's garrison. Soldiers from the training center also came to defend the station. A very fierce battle occurred, the Laurasians using their laser weapons, not projectile weapons, and consequently, many Gondwanians died. Those who survived were traumatized so much that the new arrivals could not yet get a coherent picture of what had actually happened. And they could not find Ellie either among the living or the dead. A soldier reported that the Laurasians had apparently stripped all equipment from the power station, leaving the nuclear reactors to spiral out of control. All of the employees at the power station were either missing or dead, so a team of experts with replacement control equipment were on their way to the site to keep the core from melting down.

WeKu concluded that the Laurasians had launched a medium-sized invasion targeted to take possession of the power plant and to gain technology. WeKu stated that Laurasia was hopelessly backward in regard to energy technologies. Apparently, they did not know about the presence of the soldiers at the training center. After they found a much stronger defense force at the power station, they must have decided to strip the power plant and leave with as much information and personnel as they could gather up quickly.

While still in transit to KaTi, WeKu dispatched two squadrons of scout electrogliders to the vicinity to look for other Laurasian troop movement in the waters to the south and west of Gondwana.

During the twelve-hour flight, KiKi was able to expand on the predictions from her model of the space-time continuum. "I characterize a change to the space-time continuum as a Fourier transform approximation of a square wave moving in the forward direction of time due to the flow of energy in the continuum, KiKi explained. No ripples survive motion in a reverse time direction because the energy flow cancels those ripples instantaneously. A wave front of change (time wave) propagating in a forward direction actually increases in amplitude as a result of the reinforcing energy from moving forward.

"Changes can be considered small when observed near their time of occurrence. Forward moving perturbations continue to gain in magnitude until they saturate within the space-time continuum in which they are moving. The saturation magnitude is again based on certain properties of the space-time continuum that hosts the wave. This square wave of change moves through the space-time continuum riding on the threads of events. Changes or ripples that are initiated with an existing thread are recorded (remembered) along that thread until the thread ends. Therefore ripples observed from a relatively short time interval within a host continuum are noticeable to observers and will be remembered. Changes that have had time to grow to saturation and have passed beyond the ends of existing threads are no longer recognizable to the observers because the observers (threads) have no frame of reference. For example, the Laurasians lose their time travel capability, and a mere twenty years later, those people who are still alive remember what they lost but can do nothing about it. However, the changes made in Laurasia over one hundred thousand years ago will be propagating on threads that did not exist when the change took place. No one in present-day Laurasia will have any awareness that there was a change because the base reference points for their threads will be initialized differently than they were before the wave passed through. Their collective minds will have assimilated any changes into an explainable, seemingly unchanged reality. To focus you on the level of problem we have here, if Ellie were to be in Laurasia while the time wave moves through, she may lose all awareness of herself as a person from the future and see herself as someone who was born and raised in Laurasia. Whether this occurs or not depends on how entwined the thread of Ellie's existence is with the threads of existence of people in Laurasia.

"What I cannot accurately predict is how close the threads

of the space-time continuum of Laurasia are coupled with the threads of Gondwana. Obviously, the two countries have been almost completely isolated from each other for a long time, but there will probably be enough random linkages for the changes in Laurasia to have some effect on Gondwanian society."

WeKu was so impressed with KiKi's analysis that he sent orders back to his headquarters to plan an information campaign for the population of Gondwana in order to inform them about what they should expect when the time wave from the past moved through their time. WeKu wanted to appoint KiKi the head of the task force to inform the Gondwanians as soon as she returned to RoHo. She took the job with the understanding that she could leave if Steven's boss approved her transfer into Team T-REX. The job would last less than thirty days anyway.

The electroglider carrying Steven, WeKu, and KiKi landed at the airport in KaTi. They saw several other electrogliders with military markings parked near the terminal building. "There were about 175 soldiers that had been sent to KaTi to investigate the attack from other nearby military bases. Unfortunately, that would not be enough to provide safety if Laurasia sent another invasion force to secure this area as a beachhead," said WeKu. "That is why scout electrogliders are in the air now, searching to the south and west. We should know the situation within the next hour. Let's go see what has happened here and find Ellie and MaSo."

"Let's go to the power station first," said Steven rather curtly. "It sounds like that was the real reason the Laurasians invaded at this particular place. Knowing MaSo and Ellie, they'll have been somewhere around the center of the action."

As they walked out of the terminal building, they were met by a messenger. "I was sent to inform you that doctors have identified Commander MaSo," said the messenger. "He was apparently found two hours ago, but he was unconscious and had severe facial wounds, so no one recognized him. This transport and driver have been assigned to your use. I can show you to the hospital so you can debrief Commander MaSo. Apparently, his wounds are serious."

"Any sign of Ellie?" Steven was starting to fidget with his hat as his concern for her grew, mostly because of the complete lack of information. The transport moved off toward the hospital.

"No information yet," answered the messenger.

When they arrived at the field hospital, which medical personnel had set up near the power station headquarters building, Steven and WeKu found MaSo sitting on a pallet that was about two feet high. It was one of fifty lined up along the front and back walls of the tent-like hospital structure. Most of the pallets were occupied by resting Gondwanians. An attendant had just finished bandaging a deep cut on MaSo's face between his ear and nose vents. His right leg was covered in a flexible green material that a doctor had wrapped multiple times around his leg until it was about one inch thick. The doctor had wrapped his leg in such a way that the lower segment of it was now immobile. When he looked up and saw Steven, all the color left his stomach region, and he looked down at the ground.

"Where is Ellie?" demanded Steven when he was still ten feet away from MaSo. He had his cap in his hands and he twisted it one way and then the other as he walked.

"I don't know for sure, but I believe she is still alive," said MaSo. He sat perfectly still, hunched over, his eyes trained on the floor. "I think she was taken captive by the Laurasians. This is entirely my fault. I will not rest until we find her and get her away from them." Steven just stood there in a daze, still twisting that hat.

"Tell us what happened," WeKu interjected. Clearly, his subordinate had bonded with the humans during their missions together and suffered great anguish now. "Tell us everything you remember about the events before you were rendered unconscious."

"We were awakened by unexplained noises at about five o'clock this morning. I ran toward the exit of the headquarters building of the training center so I could figure out what was going on. As I ran past the armory, I picked up a weapon. Then I thought that Ellie would be investigating just as I was, so I picked up a second weapon. When I reached the exit, sure enough, she was just running out as well. She is truly a dedicated warrior ready to defend her allies, even new ones. I tossed her a weapon, and we ran off toward the noise. That was my first mistake. I should have assembled a squad to support us, and I should not have allowed such an important guest to run into an unknown situation with just me for backup. Even now it is hard to believe we were actually running into just exactly the type of attack we had spent the day discussing. Who would know? The coincidence is just too great. But it is my job as commander of this quick-response unit to think of such things.

"As we approached the site of the power plant, it was just light enough to see shadows and movement. I could barely make out a large number of soldiers attacking the power plant. The guards were valiantly defending the plant from their fortified positions. It was like a vision from a nightmare. There were small fires breaking out wherever the Laurasian laser weapons hit something flammable. If they hit one of our Gondwanian weapons, the weapon exploded with a purple flash.

"They were coming from the beach in a disorganized mass, hissing and screaming like savages. Their bodies were painted with white markings. They had large white triangles painted on their backs. Also, the top halves of their heads were painted solid white almost down to their eyes. I might have expected to see something like this when we went back to ancient Laurasia but not in modern times. From the information we have on their battle strategies, I think they paint their troops like that for logistics purposes. The white head identifies their troops versus the enemy, and the triangle shows what direction they are moving even in dim light. Their troops are told that there are sharpshooters at the back of the attack force and that they'll shoot anyone not showing his triangle by attacking the enemy.

"So at this point, Ellie and I began shooting at their attack column from the flank while the power plant security guards shot from their fortified guard positions. Ellie and I took down hundreds of soldiers shooting as fast as our weapons would cycle. For a while in the confusion of battle, they didn't know we were there.

"Finally, one soldier looked to his left and saw us and started shooting in our direction. We were difficult targets lying on the ground, and it was still rather dark. An officer realized what was happening and sent a squad of ten men to take us out. I was shot in the lower leg as they approached. It was a grazing laser shot that burned off flesh but stopped at the bone. Ellie jumped up and took a defensive stance right over me and continued to shoot down the attackers coming for us.

"I heard one of them comment that she was one of those mammals from the future and they should try to capture her alive. There were four individuals left in the group still charging toward our position. One oncoming soldier yanked Ellie's weapon right out of her hands. She shot him as her finger was dragged out of the trigger guard, but then Ellie was without a weapon. I was trying to sit up to shoot the remaining soldiers attacking us, but one of them came from the side and kicked me in the face. Just before everything went black, I saw them dragging Ellie away. Steven, it just never occurred to either Ellie or me that the situation was so dangerous, that the Laurasians would be invading Gondwana so close to our new base on the very day we began to plan our defensive training."

"Do you have any idea where they would take her?" asked Steven. His eyes were blinking, and he was looking around as if he was desperately trying to think what to do next.

"We will do everything we can to find her," said WeKu. "I will alert our entire spy network to discover where they are taking her. I know she is a most important member of your team."

Actually, its way more than that, I've just realized how important she has become to me on a personal level, thought Steven.

Laurasian Transport Boat at Sea

Ellie woke up lying on the floor in a six-foot-by-six-foot cell. When she opened her eyes, it felt like someone was pushing an ice pick through her eye into her brain. After two tries, she was able to pull herself up enough to sit propped against a wall. She knew she had been shot by a stun gun, and this time felt worse than the first time it had happened. She decided they must have waited longer to give her the antidote. She also decided she was either on a boat or she was having a nasty reaction to the neurotoxin because the floor felt as if it was moving. After a long while, she drifted off to sleep, lulled by the gentle rocking of the floor. She dreamed of walking along a beautifully decorated street in RoHo, holding hands with Steven like they had before the mission to kidnap WaTu.

She jerked awake and bounced to her feet as someone opened the door to her cell. She tried to assume a defensive stance, but her head was spinning too much to even see who had entered for several seconds. As her vision cleared, she saw a Laurasian soldier with some greens and water for her.

"How long have I been here?" she asked in Laurasian.

After a brief blink of surprise, he answered, "About three days. How did you get into Gondwana?"

"Sorry, I think that qualifies as a question I can't answer," Ellie replied. "This feels like a boat. Where are we going?"

"We are traveling northwest to the Laurasian regional capital of VaRo," answered the guard.

Because she remembered how Laurasian character predisposed them to be naturally helpful when they responded to questions, Ellie continued, "Why were you in Gondwana, and why did you capture me?"

"Our Exalted Lord has declared war on Gondwana," said the guard. "We were the lead invasion force sent to create a beachhead on the southern shores of Gondwana and to capture and control that power plant. However, they were much more prepared to defend their territory than we were told. We lost so much of our force that we were unable to dig in and remain. The force commander decided to strip all the equipment and personnel from the power plant to learn as much of their technology as we could. Then you, a mammal from the future, showed up fighting on the side of Gondwana. Our commander decided to bring you along. If the Exalted Lord thinks you are valuable enough, he may not demote our commander for losing the first invasion battle."

chapter 25

SuHa was bluffing when he told the local al-Qaeda members he would pay them fifty thousand US dollars if they kept his hiding place safe. He had no more money, but he assumed he could get some when the time machine started working again. This expectation of money also gave SuHa and FiYo a much heartier send-off by the al-Qaeda members as they climbed into the Gondwanian electroglider.

The takeoff was uneventful, and they circled until the airship was lined up with their southeasterly course. For the first two hours, they flew over beautiful mountains covered in snow. SuHa had to explain to FiYo just what the white stuff on the ground was because he had never actually seen it with his own eyes before. Then the mountains began to fall away, and they began to see several river valleys roughly running east and west. SuHa told FiYo that most of the major rivers of the continent they were over had their source in the mountains and valleys below.

After they found the Yangtze River, FiYo took the electroglider down to an altitude of only seven hundred feet. "Do you think this is low enough to evade the mammal's detection devices?" FiYo asked.

"A while ago, I talked to a US Air Force pilot we kidnapped from this time," said SuHa. "He said flying below one thousand feet would cause the mammals radar to show false signals and generate too much background noise to allow for useful readings."

"According to your map, all we need to do is follow this River until we see the dam in about one thousand miles," said FiYo.

Three hours later, they were approaching the central part of China. "I have been keeping track of landmarks as we flew over them," said SuHa. "That city below us is called Chengdu. We should be only one hundred miles from our target."

"I will adjust the bomb range finder device," said FiYo. "This is a device that increases our bomb dropping accuracy. As we fly directly over the target it tells us when to release the nuclear bomb."

"You mean the bomb is not carried to the target by its own vehicle?" asked SuHa. "The mammals can shoot bombs on rockets that can hit a target very accurately, even if it is thousands of miles away."

"No, the Gondwanian battle strategy is designed for a fight against Laurasia, which has no electrogliders," said FiYo. "As long as they destroy Laurasia's antiairship weapons, nothing can hinder their attacks, so there is no need for exotic flying bombs. They use nuclear bombs to cause maximum damage when they attack Laurasian antiairship shore offenses. Their air superiority will be complete once the antiairship batteries are destroyed."

"When will you arm the bomb?" asked SuHa. "I heard that was a part of the procedure."

"Right before we drop it," said FiYo. "The arming is actually automatic as the bomb is released from the plane. SuHa, I suggest we make a loop around the target and approach from the east. That will leave us with a straight path to the west when we begin our escape even as the bomb is falling."

"Sounds reasonable," said SuHa. "I like the strategic way you think. We may survive this assignment if you keep it up.

Can you drop a little lower for this last leg of the trip? We appear to have evaded detection so far, but it would be most unfortunate if they stopped us this close to success."

"I will drop to five hundred feet," said FiYo. "Keep looking down and forward, checking for any tall mountains or other obstacles. We really would not want to run into one of them."

LAURASIAN TRANSPORT BOAT AT SEA

Ellie had no way to estimate time except to listen to the variation of the background noises on the ship. The boat continued to move at a high rate of speed for four more days. She also had no way to estimate their speed; however, the electrical motors that drove the ship remained at a constant noise level, and Ellie guessed they were nearly maxed out from the sounds she could hear. On the third day, they went through a storm, and Ellie was glad they were only feeding her greens and water. She had never been seasick before and desperately hoped she never experienced it again. During the entire trip, she neither saw nor heard anyone other than the soldier that continued to bring her food. She was not looking forward to arriving at a Laurasian city, but after so many days in the tiny cell, she was getting claustrophobic.

From the movements of the ship, Ellie could tell when they arrived in port. After an hour or so, four armed guards accompanied the jailer to her cell. They attached manacles with metal chains to her arms and feet. Only then was she led off of the boat and immediately put into a tri-wheeler along with her four guards. They drove for well over an hour away from the seaport and finally arrived at a drab city with underground buildings just like the other Laurasian cities she had seen. There were no decorations like the ones in Gondwanian cities. The tri-wheeler drove through the well-organized streets for sixteen blocks and then stopped in front of a nondescript building that was apparently the headquarters for the confors of the eastern district. Ellie was promptly taken to a cell on the sixth level down.

After several hours in her new cell, which was exactly like the cell on board the boat, two guards entered before a distinguished reptile with the erect posture of a longtime military man stepped inside.

"Do not become too comfortable," said the distinguished reptile. "You will not be with us very long. My name is HaSo, but you will address me as Commander. Some people in the capital city really want to meet you. It seems you are to be questioned about a jailbreak, murder of a prison guard, and high treason against the Exalted Lord. You have been a busy little female mammal. Do you have anything to say in your defense?"

Ellie just stood in the crowded little cell and glared at HaSo. She felt the anger and frustration of the last seven days welling up in her. She held her tongue because she did not want to make her situation any worse, but it was not enough. HaSo suddenly lashed out with his powerful right leg and kicked Ellie at the knee joint. Luckily, he was standing a little to the side of Ellie as he kicked her, so her knee buckled instead of shattering. He then hit her on the side of her face as she kneeled before him. This blow did not hurt so much because the Laurasians did not have much strength in their short arms.

"That is just a sample of the treatment you can expect if you continue to act in such a discourteous way," HaSo snarled. "I asked you a question, rat woman, and I expect a response."

Ellie said nothing as she tried to clear her head. Suddenly, one of the guards struck her with the butt of his projectile weapon and knocked her unconscious.

Ellie slowly regained consciousness only to realize that she had a headache for the record books. She was still lying in the small cell. She had bruises on numerous parts of her body, but nothing seemed to be broken. *I wonder what that was all about,* she thought. She slowly dragged herself to sit up against the wall yet again, and then she noticed that some food and water had been placed on the floor of the cell by the door. The greens were not much incentive for her to try to make it the four feet to the bowls, but her throat was parched, so she made the effort to get to the water.

Later, guards came to her cell again to put another set of manacles on her hands and feet. The one gratifying point of her captivity was the fact that the Laurasians were so afraid of her escaping. As she stumbled through the door of her cell, she found Commander HaSo waiting for her, agitated.

"Well, it seems you will not be with us even long enough for me to teach you some manners," he growled. "You are to be immediately dispatched to the capital to be interrogated by the Exalted Lord himself."

Ellie dragged herself up the ramps of the building with prodding from her guards. She was surprised to see that the sun was going down. She decided she must have been unconscious longer than she had first estimated. She must be in the eighth day of her captivity. There was a large truck-sized tri-wheeler just outside on the street with enough seating capacity for the driver and three more guards in the front and a totally enclosed prisoner area in the rear. The guards pushed Ellie into the back compartment of the vehicle, where she found a metal bench attached to the back wall. A guard then attached her leg manacles to an eyebolt in the floor of the vehicle to further ensure she could not get out of the locked compartment. She wondered why she was being treated like public enemy number one but decided this could just be standard operating procedure for the Laurasian Confors. After about twelve hours, just when Ellie thought she would scream if they hit another bump, they stopped in what was probably another town. As the guards opened the door of the compartment, Ellie was blinded by the sun just rising above the horizon on day nine of her captivity. She guessed they must be traveling due west toward the Laurasian capital of SoMu because of the position of the rising sun. They pulled her down from the back of the tri-wheeler, and she saw that one of her guards was signing a document of some kind, which undoubtedly meant she was being formally transferred to a new set of guards.

The old guards rode away in their tri-wheeler, and a new but similar vehicle pulled up to take its place. One of the new guards told Ellie, "I am sorry, but there is no time for you to rest in our headquarters building. The entire conformance force is under direct instruction from the Exalted Lord himself to get you to the capital without delay." Unlike Gondwana, Laurasia did not have flying vehicles, so the quickest means to get to SoMu was by tri-wheeler. Unfortunately, it was more than a five-thousand-mile trip across the entire expanse of Laurasia. The top speed of the prison transfer tri-wheelers was forty miles per hour with ideal road conditions. With brief transfer stops and miscellaneous short delays, the guards expected the trip to take seven to eight days.

The second group of guards was not as vicious as the first group had been. They did not attach Ellie's leg manacles to the floor of the vehicle. They also provided her with some padding to sleep on and a supply of water. The trip continued to be grueling even with these small kindnesses. The solid walls of the prisoner compartment meant no air circulation, and the temperature during the day was sweltering. The biggest health issue Ellie was concerned about was becoming dehydrated because sweat poured off of her for about twelve to fifteen hours of the day. When the sun went down, there was some respite. The roads outside of the city were bumpy, and she bounced around constantly. Approximately every twelve hours, she was transferred from one set of guards to another and given some food and time out of the prisoner compartment for personal requirements. Then she was off again in a new fully powered up tri-wheeler.

After the sixth time she had been handed off to a new set of guards, the road began to slope upward into a moderately high mountain range that was very rugged. Ellie thought it might be what she knew as the Appalachian Mountains, which meant they had probably just crossed over into the land that would become North America. They had been traveling through the mountainous area for about three hours since the last transfer when a sharp crack and a lurch of the tri-wheeler jerked Ellie into alertness and the vehicle wobbled to a stop. Soon, the door to her compartment opened, and all four of her guards were standing there with their projectile weapons pointed at her. She began to fear that the guards had stopped in this uninhabited area to kill her and dispose of her body.

"Come out of the vehicle," the head confor told her. Ellie struggled to her feet and hobbled over to the door. Every part of her body ached from the constant bouncing. Two of the guards grabbed her arms and stood her on the ground. All four of the guards continued to point their weapons at her as they marched her to the right side of the tri-wheeler. A guard removed the manacle from her left hand, threaded the chain through a metal loop on the side of the tri-wheeler, and then refastened the manacle. The loop constraining her was low enough to allow her to sit down with her arms only slightly elevated. The other three guards continued to point their projectile weapons directly at her until she was safely secured to the tri-wheeler. Ellie finally noticed the extreme tilt of the vehicle. *Maybe this unscheduled stop could provide me a chance to escape,* she thought.

"What happened to the tri-wheeler?" asked Ellie. "It looks like the wheel has come off. Can you fix it?"

"It cannot be fixed," said the head guard. "We must wait for another vehicle to be sent from the nearest town. Unfortunately, it will take two to three hours for it to get here. Eat this food and stop asking so many questions."

As Ellie looked around for some way to get away from these guards, she saw that the tri-wheeler was stopped on the left side of a road, which wound around a steep hill. The vegetation was similar to the other parts of Laurasia she had already seen. Pine shrubs and flowering shrubs covered the ground. The road followed the side of the hill around to the right, and there was a ten-foot drop-off near the left side of the road.

The guards finally settled down to lay in the shade of nearby bushes, munch on some greens, and sip their water. Three of them nodded off to sleep after they ate. Because her world was not bouncing and shaking for the first time in four or five days, Ellie dozed off as well.

She was suddenly jerked awake by the scream of one of the guards. As she tried to get to her feet, a pair of reptile legs connected by a part of a torso dropped to the ground beside her. The head of the guard and the top of his torso were gone. Ellie lurched up and turned to the direction that the guard's body had come from. She was terrified to see a medium-sized *Tyrannosaurus* in front of the tri-wheeler she was chained to. It had apparently crept up to their impromptu camp without a sound. The three remaining guards jumped to their feet and began to run in opposite directions. The huge predator turned abruptly to snap up one of the running guards near the front of the tri-wheeler. As the large dinosaur's body came around, its tail literally swept the tri-wheeler over. It rolled down the drop-off beside the road and eventually came to a stop, the top of the prisoner compartment resting on the ground. The tri-wheeler jerked Ellie's manacled arms as it rolled, and then she slammed into the ground, banging her head as the vehicle came to rest upside down. All she could hear was the trumpeting of the *Tyrannosaurus* as she slipped from consciousness.

chapter 26

CENTRAL CHINA, THREE GORGES DAM

"Could you please come back to the communication center immediately, General Lee?" queried an aid as he walked into the officers' dining room. "The technicians think they have spotted an airplane at about five hundred feet of altitude directly to the south of us."

As General Lee walked into the communications center, he called for a report from the duty officer. "The indication on the radar system appears to be a moderate-speed aircraft flying at very low altitude," the duty officer explained. "The target is south of us and moving directly to the east roughly parallel to the river. It does not appear to be coming toward the dam."

"Contact local air traffic control and see if there is a flight plan filed for a plane on that course," barked the general. "Try to make radio contact with that plane. We need to find out if this is our terrorist or if this is some kind of noise artifact. Five hundred feet is very low for an airplane to be flying, even on a covert mission. Keep your eyes on the target to see if it launches a missile. If anything appears to separate from the target on your radar screen, shoot them both down immediately."

Sergeant Adams broke in, "Sir, based on my experience, I would bet this is not a false target."

"Air traffic control sees nothing in the area of our target," reported the duty officer. "There is no response from the target to our transmissions—no communication response and no change in flight attitude."

"Keep tracking the target. If it takes any action that seems like an attack, then we will take it out," said the general. "Be prepared to launch two missiles at the target on my command and put the antimissile missiles on alert so they are ready for immediate launch."

RoHo, Gondwana 65 Million years BCE

It had been twelve days since Ellie's capture, and Steven had completely withdrawn into himself. He didn't seem to be able to snap out of his depression. He was very disappointed that WeKu's entire spy network had found no scrap of information as to her whereabouts. He spent every waking moment trying to figure out where the Laurasians would have taken her. Whenever he was in the same room with MaSo, Steven glared at him as if he wanted to attack him. It was fortunate that the Gondwanians were not familiar with the telltale signs of human body language. On two occasions Fred had asked to talk privately with Steven because he was afraid Steven was about to attack MaSo. Steven irrationally held MaSo personally responsible for Ellie's capture.

WeKu had put out a call for help to his entire intelligence network. In some cases, it took several days for spies in very sensitive positions to even receive the request. Throughout the network they passed a description of Ellie and the fact that she had been taken prisoner during Laurasia's attempt to invade Gondwana. The Gondwanian government was urgently requesting any information as to the location where she was being held. The message implied that she knew strategic secrets that Gondwana did not want in Laurasian hands, which was technically true.

They had sent out the requests eleven days ago, but there had been no word of Ellie's whereabouts. WeKu told Steven that the invasion force had a huge distance to travel by water to return to any port in Laurasia. It would probably take five or six days for them to get back to their land base. They sent electrogliders out at various points along the possible return paths of the invasion force, but they met with zero success. By the eleventh day after Ellie's capture, Steven began to fear the Laurasians had just killed her during their sea voyage or in secret when they finally arrived in port.

Steven was out walking around RoHo on the fourteenth day after Ellie's capture; trying to think of something they may have missed in their attempt to locate her. He heard someone behind him call his name, and he turned to see WeKu running to catch him. "We have our first bit of information," he yelled. "An agent on the southeast tip of Laurasia was finally able to get a message to us. He says there was a prisoner that the confors covertly took off of one of the returning invasion boats. There was much secrecy concerning the fleet's failure and unexpected return. Strangely, the Exalted Lord showed more interest in the prisoner than he did in learning about the failure. Then a couple of days later, the same agent overheard the local commander of the conformance force in their private dining room laughing because, as he said, the commander of the invasion fleet had thought he could escape punishment for his failure by coming back with a mammal prisoner. The confor commander then told his companion that the gesture had not worked and that the failed commander had been executed earlier in the day. His precious prisoner was being rushed off to SoMu, the Laurasian capital, under direct orders from the Exalted Lord himself."

Steven showed excitement for the first time since he had learned of Ellie's capture. He grabbed WeKu by the hand and started to drag him back to WeKu's office. "Come on! We need to get airplanes out looking for her," he shouted.

"What is an airplane?" asked WeKu.

"I'm sorry. I mean electrogliders," said Steven. "The time wave is coming in about fifteen days. We have to find her and get her out before it passes through this time."

"Steven, I have already organized a search, but remember Laurasia is about six thousand miles wide and about two thousand miles from south to north. That is well over ten million square miles. I fear we will need more information to narrow our search if we are to find her in time. We cannot assume they will transport Ellie by a direct route. The Laurasian leadership thinks in very devious ways. By the way, Steven, you have been acting strangely since Ellie was captured. This seems to be different from concern over a close teammate or partner."

"How long will it take for them to transport Ellie to SoMu?" asked Steven ignoring WeKu's question. "Maybe we can organize a rescue for her after she gets there if the Laurasians get her there in time."

"We can start on a plan for such a rescue mission, but traveling from the east side of Laurasia to SoMu would take them at least seven days and probably more," said WeKu. "They have no electrogliders, so they must use their tri-wheelers, which are much slower. We really need more specific information on her location to develop a successful plan to rescue her while she is still en route. The reason I hurried to tell you is because this is conformation that Ellie is still alive."

A few days later, Steven was walking near the habitat where he had been spending the night. During this stressful period Steven seldom really slept and when he did finally slip off from exhaustion, dreams tormented him with various scenarios of what might be happening to Ellie. He was startled out of his thoughts by a messenger from WeKu running to find to him.

"WeKu sent me to tell you that he received information on

the location of your partner," said the messenger. "He requests you to return to his office immediately."

Without another word, Steven raced off in the direction of WeKu's office. When he arrived, there was already four Gondwanians with military postures standing around the table, which had a large map of Laurasia spread over it.

"We have received a message from one of our agents in a smaller town called HuRi in south central Laurasia," said WeKu. "He is one of the confors in a small confor substation there. They received a call for assistance from a prison transport tri-wheeler that broke down along a road through the hills near there. They demanded the HuRi confors come with a replacement tri-wheeler as fast as they possibly could and explained that they were carrying the special mammal prisoner that the Exalted Lord wanted to interrogate personally. Apparently, they hit a rock and knocked the back wheel off their tri-wheeler while they were going to PuRo in order to transfer the prisoner to another team of guards. It seems Ellie has been on the move the entire time she has been in captivity. No wonder we have had so much trouble finding her."

"Can we rescue her from this place?" asked Steven.

"Yes, this is just the break we need," said WeKu. "We have a specifically modified, long-range rescue electroglider ready to leave. Commander FaFi and his rescue crew will leave immediately to attempt her rescue."

"I want to go along on this mission," huffed Steven. "I have felt helpless for the last two weeks knowing I was not there to protect her. For personal reasons that no one else may think are valid I need to do this."

"But you have no training with our specialized equipment," said Commander FaFi. "You could get killed and even worse you may get one of my crew killed."

"WeKu, I appeal to you on a personal level," said Steven. He was nervously twisting his hat in his hands. "I must go to try to rescue Ellie."

"Okay, go with Commander FaFi to the air terminal right now so the electroglider can take off," said WeKu. FaFi will fill you in on the rescue procedure along the way."

"There is a tri-wheeler waiting in front of the building to take us," said FaFi as he opened the door and pushed Steven through it. "Now is finally the time to hurry."

As soon as Steven and FaFi entered the electroglider, the pilots started the procedure for takeoff. "We have a long way to fly to the point where your partner was reported to be," said FaFi. "That is why we are in such a hurry. We will be able to jump out of this specially equipped electroglider when we get to the reported site and then find your partner. I hope you don't kill yourself during the jump or recovery since you have no experience with our equipment. The harness for our descent-retarding equipment (DRE) is made to fit our race. It will require some significant modifications to fit your body. These two will work on the modifications while I brief you on the general plan."

"We know which road the prison vehicle broke down on, so we will fly along the road until we spot the vehicle. If we think Ellie is there, three of us will jump to the ground to attempt a rescue. PePe will jump with us. He is an expert in this type of rescue operation. Many times, we must extract one of our spies out of Laurasian territory with little or no notice. That is why this type of electroglider was developed."

Once the Gondwanians finished their modification, the harness that was part of the DRE looked just like one Steven would expect for a parachute. They cut additional holes in the dinosaur-skin straps to allow the part that supported Steven's lower body to fit his legs and waist. The straps that went around his upper body were expanded to fit his chest, which was larger than the reptiles.

The basic premise of the DRE was that the jumper could maneuver himself down an adjustable glide path to allow the energy from the horizontal movement imparted by the electroglider as well as the jumper's kinetic energy from falling to be bled off gradually through air friction.

The DRE attached to the bodies of the jumpers like parachutes, but the comparison ended there. The main element of the device was a thin but rigid airfoil made from a light strong metal. The DRE was attached above the operator, parallel to the direction of flight, so that it cut through the air like a wing. The airfoil could rotate from this parallel position by up to ninety degrees so then it pushed against the air like a sail. This configuration allowed the operator to adjust the angle of the airfoil to provide variable lift and variable speed control simultaneously. The jumper could adjust the glide angle as well, thus descending at a safe speed, but the jumper had only a little ability to steer to the left or right.

The flight to Laurasia would take five hours, so Steven tried to get some rest once his equipment was ready. As soon as he fell asleep, he dreamed that he had found Ellie in a flat field, watching some type of herbaceous dinosaur graze. To his frustration, he could not tell what kind of dinosaur it was. When he approached Ellie and called to her, she turned and shot him with a laser gun while she screamed, "Die, mammal!" Drenched in sweat, he woke up and decided that he didn't need sleep bad enough to go through that again.

As Steven walked toward the front of the electroglider, PePe came out of the pilot's cabin to let them know they had arrived over the target road. There was an observation bubble in the nose of the electroglider that they used for searching the area below the vehicle. FaFi and Steven went to the bubble to look for the disabled tri-wheeler that was transporting Ellie.

After only twenty minutes, they spotted a tri-wheeler lying upside down beside the road in a particularly rugged area of the landscape. The trio readied their equipment while the electroglider slowed to about fifty miles per hour. The vehicle was able to fly with a slow air speed because of its large external control surfaces.

It was risky for Steven to attempt to use the DRE device without any prior practice, but he would not be denied being part of the rescue mission. Luckily, he had flown hang gliders over the mountains in Montana, and this knowledge would hopefully help him survive the jump.

They made the jump in daylight, so the view of the landscape below was spectacular. When they first exited the electroglider, Steven could see several large herds of herbaceous dinosaurs scattered around. The team planned to glide directly along the road because the rest of the landscape consisted of shrubs and small trees that would be tricky to land in. As it turned out, Steven did manage to hit the road, but he was still moving at about ten miles an hour when his feet touched down. He sprinted as fast as he could to avoid falling down, but after about a dozen paces, his harness yanked him off of his feet. He felt his ankle twist as he fell and rolled about fifteen yards. He wondered if he might have sprained the ankle, but he had landed without breaking any bones, a moral victory.

As Steven was stowing his DRE, FaFi and PePe joined him. The trio trotted back toward the site of the wrecked tri-wheeler, alert for any Laurasian guards. The first step sent pain lancing up Steven's leg. *It must be a pretty bad sprain,* Steven thought.

As they approached the vehicle, they saw no sign of Ellie or her guards. When Steven limped within thirty feet of the truck, he noticed a lump on the right side of the road, the opposite side from the truck. On further examination, he realized that the lump was actually two reptile legs and part of a torso. As FaFi studied the odd sight, he said, "This looks like the remains of a Laurasian guard who was attacked by a large carnivorous dinosaur. The only carnivore large and strong enough to wreck that tri-wheeler is an adult *Tyrannosaurus*. This is not good. Spread out and search for any sign of Ellie."

Steven slid down the grade to where the tri-wheeler was resting on its roof. He looked inside the prisoner area and found some blankets and a water bottle but no Ellie. PePe called his attention to a set of manacles. They were open but still hanging from a metal loop attached to the side of the tri-wheeler. There was blood on one of the loose ends that had undoubtedly held a prisoner's wrist. But there was no sign of Ellie or her other guards.

The trio spread out and searched the surrounding landscape for clues. After about forty-five minutes, FaFi announced that they would need to call for a pickup. If they delayed longer, the electroglider would not have enough reserve power to make the return trip. Steven objected for a while but realized they could not accomplish anything further at this place.

The pickup was unnerving because it was Steven's first time and he was too distracted worrying about Ellie to pay careful attention to the preparation. The setup was accomplished by FaFi and PePe each driving a twelve foot long metal rod into the ground about one hundred feet apart. Two additional twelve foot rods were threaded onto the tops of the initial rods creating two thirty-six foot tall metal poles with hooks on the top. They then attached one side of a strong really large loop of rope made from tough dinosaur skin to the top of the poles. The idea was for the electroglider to come in low at its slowest possible airspeed with a long metal hook protruding down. The hook snagged the part of the rope that was suspended between the poles. The three people on the ground were attached to the other side of the loop using the same harness they had used for the DREs. They were dragged up off the ground as the hook captured the loop. After the hook was set, the two ends of the loop were drawn up to the electroglider and attached to a pair of wenches. It was then a simple matter of reeling in the three people who had been on the ground.

As they were setting up the equipment, FaFi said to Steven, "I am very sorry we did not find your teammate, the confors probably put her in a different tri-wheeler and rushed her off for her interview with the Exalted Lord. At least this information greatly reduces the areas within Laurasia that we need to search to try to find her."

"Yes I guess that they will hold her in either PuRo or SoMu," said Steven.

As Steven sat huddled on the ground, waiting for the electroglider to pick them up he reflected on his time spent with Ellie. He realized that he had gradually come to love her since the first time he had met her at White Sands, and he promised himself he would tell Ellie how he felt if he ever got the chance to see her again. The rope suddenly snapped tight and jerked him and his companions into the air in a swirl of wind that battered all of their senses.

The next day, Steven and FaFi sat in WeKu's office to discuss their failed mission to rescue Ellie. Steven said, "I realize that a large predator dinosaur, probably a *Tyrannosaurus*, attacked the tri-wheeler we found and devoured at least one guard. It is possible that Ellie was killed in the attack.

"However there are facts that conflict with that scenario," said Steven. "If the creature's attack caused the initial call for help, then why was Ellie manacled to the side of the vehicle? Blood found on the manacle was the reason that we initially were concerned that Ellie was killed by the predator, but there was no reason to attach the manacle to the outside of the vehicle unless something else had disabled the tri-wheeler and the guards had bound Ellie to the outside of the vehicle while they waited for help. The body fragment we found at the scene could have been the result of some completely unrelated incident. The confors probably arrived with a replacement vehicle, and Ellie is likely still on her way to SoMu."

"The entire spy network is still on alert to report any information about Ellie's current location," said WeKu. "Will you return to your time to report to your leaders, or will you continue to wait with us?"

"Fred and I are prepared to wait until we have positive proof as to Ellie's situation," said Steven.

chapter 27

<hr>

CENTRAL CHINA, THREE GORGES DAM

"When we get ten miles behind the target, turn back on a course directly toward it," said SuHa. "As we pass over the dam, we'll release the bomb and make our escape. So far, no one seems to be aware of our presence."

As the electroglider reached the turning point, FiYo said, "Turning back now. All is ready to drop the bomb in four minutes and fifteen seconds."

"There is the dam a bit to the left of us," said SuHa. "Look at the size of the lake behind it. This should give the mammals something to be mad about."

PuRo, LAURASIA 65 MILLION YEARS BCE

When Ellie opened her eyes, she could only see blurry objects moving around her, and she hurt all over. When one of the blurs in the room saw that she was awake, it offered Ellie a sip of water and then told her to rest because she had been unconscious for almost a week. To her surprise, the figure had spoken in English.

"Where am I?" Ellie croaked.

"You are in a prison infirmary in PuRo," said the attendant. "When the confors arrived with a replacement vehicle, they found two of your guards missing and two dead from a *Tyrannosaurus* attack. You were bound to the broken vehicle with manacles. The two missing guards are as good as dead. They will be executed for abandoning you."

"Through blind luck, you survived because you were unconscious. You lay unmoving and hidden from the predator beside the tri-Wheeler. The replacement guards found you with your arm broken, apparently as a result of being dragged over the top of the tri-wheeler when the predator knocked it off the road. You were rushed to this location for medical treatment because we still have information on how to treat your race from the time when we were studying you. Now rest. You will have a big day tomorrow. The Exalted Lord himself will come here to interrogate you about all the strange things that have been happening lately in Laurasia. This is most unusual since the Exalted Lord has not left the capital city in over forty years." Ellie drifted off to sleep, thinking about Steven and wondering what he was doing.

The next day, a nurse woke Ellie early and fed her a breakfast of grain and nuts. She was given a cold drink that tasted a lot like tea, and then dressed in a bright red one-piece jumpsuit, manacles obviously adorning her wrists and ankles. Finally, a guard led her into an interrogation room that held only one older, distinguished reptile with a very large black medallion hanging from his neck. After she was chained to her chair, the reptile told her guards to leave.

"Now it is just you and me talking alone," said the Exalted Lord. "I have many tools available to me to make you tell me what I want to know. The quickest and easiest is to take over your mind. Are you familiar with the procedure?"

"That would be the gas that takes away my will and binds me to you?" asked Ellie. "I've seen its effects."

"I can have that procedure performed on you with a single

command," said YaKo. "However, I would rather talk to you in an unaltered condition if we can do that productively. It is totally up to you. My conformance force members speak of you as if you are some super mammal that should be executed immediately. They imply you are all-knowing and have the ability to read minds. According to them, you have killed Laurasians with your bare hands and have magically taken away selective capabilities like our time travel technology. We have risked our entire civilization to launch an invasion of Gondwana only to have you show up in a backwater of Gondwana and nearly single-handedly defeat our invasion force, according to my advisors. Have you really done all these things? What is the purpose of your concerted attack on Laurasia?"

"In my current position, it would seem that I should speak to you frankly because I do not want to lose my will and you do not want to lose your country," said Ellie. "Our team of humans has access to our own time machine. It was invented before we knew about Laurasia or that you could travel through time. We came here with peaceful intentions. We came to your capital city to talk and offer friendship. A mated couple of your people tried to help us and tried to get us an audience with your country's leadership. Instead, we were attacked and imprisoned. The head of your confors met with us in a room much like this but refused to hear anything we said. He claimed we were in your capital city to stop a plot to steal oil resources from our world. We had no idea about this until he told us. Then he sentenced us to death."

"How did you get access to time travel capability? Did you steal it from us somehow?" asked YaKo. "Are you telling me SaSu was the one who told you of our plan to save Laurasia from running out of energy?" Suddenly, his chest area flared bright red; he jumped to his feet and called a guard into the room.

"Call directly to Chancellor FaPa and tell him I order him to arrest and detain SaSu immediately," YaKo told the guard.

"House arrest is not acceptable. Have him taken to the SoMu city prison and isolated."

After a moment or two of pacing around the tiny room, YaKo sat down again and said, "Is this the reason you were able to halt our plans to create war within your world?"

"As you know, my partner and I escaped, and we were able to return to our time," explained Ellie. "Once we realized what you were doing, we took steps to stop a world war. Your country suffers from too much power concentrated with too few leaders. This seems to have created an irrational paranoia, which in turn causes you to make poor, badly informed decisions. We probably would have tried to help your country with its energy problem, but instead, you have put yourself on the brink of disaster by distrusting us."

"How did you take away our time travel capability?" asked YaKo. "We do not even seem to have knowledge of how to recreate it."

"That is not something I am comfortable to tell you, even considering this new spirit of cooperation," Ellie stated, staring YaKo directly in the eyes. "But I will tell you we are responsible."

"Do not provoke me. This is the most important question I have for you," yelled YaKo, his stomach again flaring with reds and oranges. "I could have a technician in this room within two minutes."

"Shit, is that all you know how to do, to threaten people?" asked Ellie. "I am trying to find a basis for our two civilizations to de-escalate hostilities, but I will not give you strategic information that could hurt my country's position. I know you can take control my mind, but I predict that will be the first step leading to the fall of Laurasia."

YaKo really did not know how to handle the situation. It had been several decades since anyone had talked to him in this way. However, he realized the words held much truth. The effort to build and equip the invasion fleet had stretched

Laurasia's energy resources to the breaking point. He still had the boats for another invasion, but replacing the equipment and personnel might be the final blow to destroy Laurasia's economy. Worse yet, the Gondwanians now knew their plans, which would make success almost impossible. YaKo finally decided that he did not become the supreme leader of Laurasia by being timid. "Guard, it is time to bring in the mind control equipment."

A few minutes later, a technician came into the room and gave Ellie an injection. He then covered her face with a gas mask and released the gas that would take away her will. The Exalted Lord waited until she said, "Please command me."

"Are you sure she is under our control?" the Exalted Lord asked the technician.

"Exalted Lord, there has never been a case where the process failed to get control immediately after administration," answered the technician. "A very strong willed human has occasionally been able to break control after a few weeks or months, so be careful with her in the future. If you so order, I can perform some testing to verify her condition."

"No! No just leave us."

Once the door to the room closed, YaKo returned his attention to Ellie. "Now you will tell me how you took away our entire time travel capability."

"Yes, Exalted Lord," said Ellie. "We went back into the Laurasian past and captured WaTu, your sacred scientist. We were surprised to find out the person who actually discovered the theory and designed the time machine was a female named KiKi. Since we took both of these two inventors out of Laurasia, the time machine could not be discovered by them in the past. Therefore, the entire capability disappeared from your present."

"Amazing story, but how do I regain my time travel capability?" asked YaKo.

After several moments of thought, Ellie said, "The quickest

way I can think of is to go to Gondwana and kidnap KiKi, the actual inventor of the technology."

"Who is this KiKi you're talking about?" pressed YaKo. "Where can she be found?"

"Before I was captured, KiKi was living in RoHo, the capital city of Gondwana," said Ellie. "I understand WaTu was put in prison."

"It is not a good idea to send you to RoHo alone," mumbled YaKo. "You might break your conditioning at any time."

"Yes, Exalted Lord."

"I know! Where is my master spy?" asked YaKo. "He disappeared at the same time as our time travel capability. He would be the perfect person to lead an incursion into Gondwana."

"If you are referring to SuHa, I believe he is stranded in my time," answered Ellie. "He was being sought in a place called Afghanistan and may be captured or dead by now."

"Very well. I will assume SuHa is not available to me," said YaKo. "You must go to RoHo and bring this KiKi here to PuRo so she can reconstruct my time machine. While you are there, you will kill the other members of your time travel team if they are still in Gondwana. Are these instructions clear?"

"Yes, Exalted Lord, it is my honor to serve you," said Ellie.

"Good, then you will be taken to the local confor training facility. There you will be briefed on how you are to accomplish your mission," said YaKo. "You will be given equipment to help you accomplish your task and more appropriate clothes. Guards, take this mammal out of here. Watch her carefully to be sure her mind remains under my control."

During the next two days, Ellie was put through intensive testing to be sure she was truly under mind control. She was given a laser hand gun that was very compact and spent several hours learning how to use it. They also taught her some reptile techniques of hand-to-hand combat. These techniques focused specifically on using the legs and feet because those were the strong points of Laurasians and Gondwanians. She also discovered that the reptiles were very susceptible to punches to the head once she slipped inside their personal defenses.

YaKo's plan was simple. Ellie would be taken by fast naval cruiser to be dropped off with a fishing boat as close to the northern coast of Gondwana as possible. She would use the fishing boat to land in the Gondwanian port of MiPi. Once she arrived ashore, she would claim that she had escaped from the Laurasians and stolen a boat to get back to Gondwana. When she was taken to RoHo for a reunion with her team, she was tasked to kill them using the newly developed but very powerful laser pistol provided by the Exalted Lord. Then she was supposed to kidnap KiKi at gunpoint and bring her back to MiPi for pickup. Another fast Laurasian boat disguised as a Gondwanian pleasure craft would be waiting to pick them up at the same location where Ellie initially landed. YaKo knew that many things could go wrong along the course of the plan, but it really did not matter if Ellie was discovered and killed during her mission. She had to die when she got back to Laurasia anyway, so there was no downside and lots of potential upside.

The ocean crossing, directly south from SoMu in a fast naval cruiser, took four days to deliver Ellie to the point where she would begin the solo leg of the trip in her smaller craft. It took the majority of another day to reach the northern coast of Gondwana in the small fishing boat she was provided.

Ellie reached the coast at a major port city of MiPi. The port workers that first found Ellie did not know what to think about the poor, deformed creature getting out of the fishing boat, which was clearly of Laurasian design. After a couple of hectic hours, someone finally called WeKu as Ellie had been requesting all along. As soon as he heard that she was back in Gondwana, he ordered the local law enforcement personnel to escort her to the nearest airport for a private flight to RoHo. He quietly requested that she be guarded at all times in case she was under Laurasian mind control.

RoHo, Gondwana 65 Million years BCE

Steven was beginning to doubt that they would find Ellie in time. He felt very confident that she was alive, but after the failed rescue attempt, they didn't learn any more information about her whereabouts. The Gondwanians took this to mean Ellie had been killed by the *Tyrannosaurus* when it attacked the prison vehicle. They didn't say it but Steven knew that was what they were thinking. Steven took the lack of information to mean that the Laurasians had tightened up their security so no more news could leak out. The predicted arrival for the time wave was down to twenty-four hours. Soon, even if Ellie was alive, it would make no difference. If they hadn't rescued her before the time wave passed through Laurasia, she would be transformed to fit some scenario that explained her presence in Laurasia. She would be lost to Team T-REX and Steven.

RoHo, Gondwana 65 Million years BCE

When Ellie finally arrived at WeKu's office, she was given the royal treatment. She was offered time to rest, but she wanted to know what had happened since her capture.

"We need to get some details about your imprisonment first," said WeKu courteously. "Tell us what happened."

When she suddenly realized that the purpose of WeKu's question was to determine if she could be trusted or if she was under mind control, Ellie decided to at least appear as if she was cooperating and described the events exactly as they had occurred up to her waking up in the PuRo hospital bed. She then told WeKu a revised version of her interrogation. After she regained consciousness, the Exalted Lord had questioned her about her and Steven's activities in Laurasia. "I told him how we learned of Laurasia's plot to create world war in the future from the director of his compliance force, SaSu," said Ellie. "He became livid and told someone to call the capital to put SaSu under arrest immediately. I also told him how we took steps to stop the conflict they wanted so badly in the future.

"When he asked how we stole their time travel capability right from under their noses, I refused to answer. Again, he got angry, but he seemed reluctant to turn me into an unthinking robot with their mind control gas. He appeared to be creatively looking for a way out of their disastrous energy situation. I got the impression that their economy is in even worse trouble than we had thought due to the cost of building that invasion force. At this point, they put me in a cell while YaKo consulted with his chancellor. When a guard came to put food in my cell, I overpowered him and escaped. I made my way to the Bear Paw Sea on foot and stole a speedboat that was tied up to a dock in a secluded area. I knew I flew Southeast with MaSo to the training center, then traveled north to the east side of Laurasia as a captive in a boat. I then rode back to the west by tri-wheeler and I knew that PuRo is about three quarters of the way back across Laurasia. My conclusion, just head south, thinking that I would run into Gondwana sooner or later, I just didn't know what city. I followed the coastline to the southern tip of Laurasia. Then I snuck ashore in the dark to recharge the batteries of my boat before heading for Gondwana."

"It sounds like you had a very difficult time," said WeKu. "Are you sure you are all right?"

"I'm fine. Where are Steven and Fred?" asked Ellie. "I hoped they might be waiting for me."

"Steven has been most upset since your capture," said WeKu.

"He participated in a rescue mission to try to free you when your tri-wheeler turned over. When they arrived, all they found was a set of bloodstained manacles on the vehicle. Everyone except Steven gave you up for dead. Steven was still convinced you were alive, but as time dragged on with no further information about you, I think even he was beginning to believe you had been killed by that *Tyrannosaurus*. An hour ago, Steven, Fred, and KiKi went to get lunch. They will return soon. Just stay here in my office with me until they return. I am sure they will be most excited to see you here and in good condition. By the way they do not know that you have been found yet."

Later after they had returned from KiKi's habitat, where they had eaten lunch, Steven, Fred, and KiKi went to the conference room at WeKu's request. As Steven stepped into the room, he felt like he had been zapped by a Taser. There with WeKu and MaSo, looking as if the last month had not happened, stood Ellie. When Steven saw her, he wanted to run to her and hug her he was so relieved to see her. However, something in her demeanor made him hold back.

"Hello, Steven," she said. She gave him a smile that was not quite reflected in her eyes.

"Ellie, how did you get here?" Steven babbled. "Are you all right? We have been so worried about you since you were captured. Please tell us what happened to you." Fred and KiKi greeted Ellie warmly, and everyone looked at Ellie expecting her to tell them about her captivity.

"We can catch up later," said Ellie. "I have something to tell the team confidentially that could change the outcome of our mission." The atmosphere suddenly became very tense.

"You are among friends here Ellie," said WeKu. "You can speak freely."

"No I can't," snapped Ellie. "I have something I must tell my team in private and it won't wait."

"Ellie are you sure you are okay?" asked WeKu sounding concerned but looking directly at Steven. "Remember you were captured and under the control of the Laurasians for a month. Let us have a doctor check you, please."

"I am fine," said Ellie slowly with no emotion. "But I need to talk to the team right now."

chapter 28

"General Lee, this is a real target on your radar screen, and if it does not respond when you call the pilot, it must be our terrorist," shouted Sergeant Adams. "You need to shoot it down before it gets any closer to the dam."

"But we can get no confirmation that the image on the radar screen is real," argued the duty officer. "Air traffic control cannot see it, and no one in the area has reported a low-flying aircraft. It must be a false blip. If it was an enemy warplane, it would have launched missiles at us by now. It is only twenty-five miles from the dam."

"General, these are all the reasons why we provided the TARS systems," explained the sergeant. "Our covert information predicted everything you are currently seeing—a very low flight path and not enough noise to alert people on the ground, even though it is flying so low. Please launch your strike before it is too late."

"Okay, Sergeant, we shall see," said General Lee. "Launch two antiaircraft missiles at the target and hold the antimissile ordinance at this time. Do it now."

About ten seconds after the two missiles where in the air, they appeared on the radar screen speeding toward the target. When the missiles were within one mile of the target, it made a drastic maneuver. It turned abruptly left and climbed three hundred feet much faster than any known military aircraft could. The first missile streaked by the aircraft about one hundred feet below it and missed. The second missile trailed slightly behind the first, and therefore, it was able to correct its flight path, but not enough. It also missed the right side of the plane by less than thirty feet.

"Are you convinced now that we have acquired the target?" asked Sergeant Adams.

"How could that plane make such an abrupt maneuver?" gasped General Lee. "Are we dealing with some kind of spaceship with rocket propulsion?"

"We really don't know specifics on the plane's design other than the fact that it is propelled by electric motors," replied Adams. "I would love to see it up close to find out more about it, but we must shoot it down before it destroys the dam."

The general barked to the duty officer to launch two more missiles at the aircraft and then launch two antimissile missiles thirty seconds later. "That should blow the plane out of the air and give us a good chance to take down a missile if they launch one toward the dam before we destroy them," said General Lee.

As before, the missiles appeared on the radar screen and raced toward the target. Again, as the first missile approached within five hundred feet, the craft jogged right and down. The first missile missed, flying above the plane, and the second missile behaved as if it never locked on the target. It flew in a flat trajectory until the controllers destroyed it to ensure it caused no collateral damage to anything on the ground.

"Launch the remaining two missiles," shouted the general. "This time, launch the second missile about thirty seconds after the first. Maybe we can catch them after they finish their evasive maneuver."

"These are the last two missiles we have," said the duty officer as he quickly executed the order. He called out that the plane was only five miles from the dam.

"General, are the two antimissile missiles still flying?" asked Sergeant Adams. "I suggest you direct them toward the target from behind it. The pilot may not see them coming, and I would guess they are lighter and more agile than the ground-to-air missile. They may be able to follow the pilot's evasive maneuvers."

"Duty Officer, do as he says," yelled General Lee. "Turn them around and do not allow them to self-destruct. Sergeant Adams, I don't think the antimissile missiles are powerful enough to down the plane unless we get lucky and hit a vulnerable spot. Maybe they will keep the pilot busy so we can hit him with a ground-to-air missile."

RoHo, Gondwana 65 Million years BCE

As Team T-REX walked out of WeKu's office, Ellie insisted that they meet in the habitat she was using before her capture.

"Wouldn't you rather go to White Sands so a doctor can check you over?" asked Steven. "We can talk after we find out that you are in good shape."

"No," snapped Ellie. "I feel perfectly fine except for a few bumps and bruises. I have something very important to tell you in private."

"Okay, we'll go with you if it's really that important," said Steven. "Show us the way."

Ellie seemed nervous as she led the way back to her temporary habitat. *I must find a way to transport KiKi to MiPi for pickup by the Exalted Lord's men after I kill Steven and Fred*, she thought. *That was the Exalted Lord's specific instructions. But wait! What if Laurasia was changed because of our mission and the Exalted Lord does not exist anymore? Must I still carry out his commands, which may have no useful purpose anymore?* As she stepped out of WeKu's building on the way to her habitat next door, she noticed the sun was going down. *I so enjoyed my walks with Steven, taking in the sights of this exotic capital city together at sundown.* She thought of the nights in the prison cells or prison tri-wheelers when sleep only came to her exhausted body after she had thought of those peaceful walks with Steven. But whenever she even thought of not following the Exalted Lords orders, she got a crippling headache.

Every cell in my brain is telling me to listen to my personal thoughts and ignore the Exalted Lord. But my body does not respond when I try to act against his instructions. YaKo is the wise, all-powerful leader of Laurasia. But what if he is no longer a part of the new Laurasian government? After I get KiKi to the seaport, there will probably be no one there to take us to Laurasia. What will I do then?

"Turn in the next door on the right," said Ellie. "We can talk in private in there."

"Now tell us what is so secret and important to risk alienating our friends and allies by excluding them," said Fred. "We could have been home in White Sands by now."

"This," said Ellie as she pulled out her pocket laser pistol. "I am under direct orders from the Exalted Lord to kill you and Steven."

Saying his name triggered a whirlwind of emotion in Ellie. *I can't kill him. He could be the person I was meant to be with, but I can't disobey the Exalted Lord. What can I do?* "Fred, there are some plastic handcuffs in the outer pocket of my backpack on the bed," said Ellie. "Get them out and tie Steven's hands behind his back."

"Ellie, why are you doing this?" asked Fred. "I am not going to help you with this insanity."

"I know you are under YaKo's mind control but try to resist it," pleaded Steven. "Just hand me your gun, and we can help you."

"Fred if you don't restrain Steven, I will just have to kill you both right now," growled Ellie as she cycled up the power on her laser pistol.

"Okay, Ellie, you win," agreed Fred as he took out the plastic restraints and tightened them onto Steven's wrists.

"Now, KiKi, use another set to tie Fred's hands," said Ellie.

"Please don't do this," said KiKi. "These are your friends."

"I can shoot you just as easily as Steven and Fred if you don't cooperate," said Ellie. *I hope she doesn't realize that I can't shoot her. I must get her back to Laurasia alive.*

"Restrain Fred's hands now. I'll do the same for you, KiKi," said Ellie "And don't any of you try anything while I restrain her."

After she checked the security of each tie, Ellie marched them all out of the building and onto the street. There was a tri-wheeler idling at the side of the street. *A deliveryman must be making a quick stop at a customer's store.*

"Calmly walk down to that idling tri-wheeler and get in," rasped Ellie. "We're going to take a little trip north."

"Ellie, you can overcome this mind control. Stop this now," said Steven.

"Shut up! I really don't need to hear from you right now," yelled Ellie.

I should have shot them in my room. I'm just making trouble for myself, and my head's killing me. I'll just drive outside the city, and then I can kill them. It will give me a better head start to get to MiPi if their bodies are not found for a while. But after she left RoHo behind by two hundred miles, she still did not stop to accomplish her onerous task. The further she drove, the more her head hurt.

"I am going to need to switch tri-wheelers at the next town. We are running low on power," Ellie told her prisoners. *I'll shoot Steven and Fred during the stop.* That helped her headache a little.

"Ellie, I know what you are going through," said KiKi.

"Remember, I've been under mind control myself. You have to fight the control. At some level of your resistance, the control will just break, and the pain in your head will instantly stop."

"You shut up too," screamed Ellie. "I have got to follow the Exalted Lord's instructions and take you to Laurasia. I've got to kill the rest of my team if they are still in Gondwana."

"Ellie, you should know that I am not going back to Laurasia with you," said KiKi very calmly but with determination. "I will not go back to that life, so you need to kill me as well. You do realize that if he still exists, the Exalted Lord will kill you whether or not you follow his instructions."

"It does not matter," snapped Ellie. "I must follow my orders."

"Ellie, fight this," pleaded Steven. "You can beat it. You're strong, and I know you can do it. I love you." It just popped out of his mouth with no advance warning. Fred already knew it, and KiKi did not understand, so his handcuffed companions had no reaction.

Suddenly, Ellie slammed on the brakes of the tri-wheeler. KiKi was thrown forward and nearly hit her head on the windshield. Ellie jumped out of the tri-wheeler and pointed her laser pistol at Steven. Her hand was shaking so badly that Fred was afraid she would shoot Steven by accident.

"Don't tell me what I can and cannot do," she screamed. She glared at Steven and stepped closer, moving the laser pistol to an inch from his nose. She was shaking as if in a rage, sweat pouring off her. She took a deep breath and screamed at the top of her voice. Then she threw the pistol into the shrubs at the side of the road and collapsed, unconscious.

Steven was stunned by the violence of her actions and sat in his seat, staring at the place where Ellie had been standing just seconds ago. Finally, he struggled out of the tri-wheeler and used a piece of rough metal by the wheel well of the vehicle to slowly saw through the plastic restraint. He knelt by Ellie and took her into his arms. She was barely breathing, and he could not rouse her. At last, he helped KiKi and Fred cut through their ties. Fred turned the tri-wheeler around and headed to RoHo while Steven held Ellie in the backseat.

They decided getting Ellie to a human doctor at White Sands far outweighed any advantage a Gondwanian doctor would have, even if he were an expert in mind control technology. They drove directly to WeKu's building, and while Fred and KiKi carried Ellie into the vessel on the roof, Steven went to tell WeKu what had happened and that they would need to leave at once to get Ellie medical care.

"I wish you good luck with the time wave passing," said Steven. "We probably should have learned more about the results of outside intervention in the time continuum before attempting to meddle with it."

"What's done is done," said WeKu. "Let's hope what we did results in an improvement."

Steven shook hands with WeKu and headed back to the vessel. He had just exited the building and turned left when he ran head-on into a Gondwanian. It was KiKi. She was also running toward the vessel, a small package in her hands. "Steven, I am so glad I got back before you left," gasped KiKi. "I realized that I would be in a much better position to evaluate what happened if I am not affected by the changes of the passing. I request that you take me with you to your time."

"I guess its okay," said Steven as if he were in a daze. "You can meet Jonas and interview for a position on Team T-REX."

"Thank you, Steven," said KiKi. "I ran back to my habitat after Fred and I put Ellie into the vessel. I got some clothing that's similar to what humans wear so I would fit in if you allowed me to go with you. I did not want to delay you at all."

"Welcome aboard the vessel," Steven said as he gestured for KiKi to climb up the outside ladder.

The three travelers hurried to settle in along with their unconscious companion for the voyage of sixty-five million years. They strapped into the seats, and Steven pushed the release command button. When the light and sound show began, KiKi's mouth dropped open and her feet started twitching. Steven knew these were signs of KiKi's intense excitement. She was silent and spellbound for most of the buildup to the jump but hissed loudly when everything went black. Shortly thereafter, light reappeared, and Steven began climbing out of the vessel. KiKi took the opportunity to put on the set of gray coveralls that she had brought.

Jonas and some medics had been alerted to the vessel's pending arrival by Fred while he waited in the vessel. Steven and Fred carefully carried Ellie out and put her on a gurney for transfer to the infirmary. She had not made a single voluntary movement.

As KiKi's head cleared the hatch of the vessel, she stopped at the top of the ladder and stared. Again, her mouth dropped open, and she began to bounce up and down on her toes. After a full minute, with encouragement from Steven, she finally descended the outside ladder, still looking around in awe.

"I see you brought home another guest. I'm Jonas McCormick the head of this project."

"This is KiKi, the inventor of the Laurasian time machine," said Steven. "She is the person who would like to join our team as I have already mentioned to you. At the last moment before we returned, she realized she would be better able to evaluate the effect of our little trip to ancient Laurasia if she was not there when the time wave passed through. It is her calculations that allowed us to predict when the wave will pass through. We all think it is of the utmost importance that we use this opportunity to understand the potential threats from our time voyages."

"I'm most honored to meet you at last, KiKi," said Jonas. "I've heard many good things about your work and look forward to discussing it with you. I suppose we should find some place for you to rest and whatever else you may require. I'm sure we can handle food for you, and you may be surprised at the variety of things we can offer."

"Thank you, Mr. McCormack," said KiKi, extending her arm for a handshake as she had seen Steven and WeKu do on several occasions. "But I do not think I could possibly rest or eat before I get a chance to see all of this marvelous equipment. Does it take all of this to propel your vessel through time?"

"I'll leave you two alone to talk while I go to the infirmary to see about Ellie," said Steven. "We need to return to Gondwana in the near future to see what happened. I am hoping Ellie wakes up in time to go with us."

WHITE SANDS, NEW MEXICO

Steven sat in the dimly lit room, watching Ellie breathe and listening to her vital signs monitor. The doctors had no idea why she was still unconscious, so they could not even begin to predict when she would wake up. There appeared to be nothing wrong with her. Steven had only slept in a bed once in the four days since they had returned from Gondwana, and that was only when Jonas had come in and given him a direct order. Even then, he was back in five hours. He had no idea what Ellie had gone through while she had been held captive in Laurasia. Worse yet, he had not been there to help her get through it. He had witnessed the titanic battle she had fought within herself to keep from following the orders the Exalted Lord had given her. The only thing he could do now was be here when she woke up.

At one point in time, KiKi appeared at the door of the room. "Steven, I came to visit you," she said.

"Don't you mean you came to visit Ellie?" Steven asked.

"No, she is asleep and will not know that I was here," KiKi

replied. "I have decided I will never fully understand what you are feeling now. I think my race does not have the capacity for such a thing. I came to offer to sit with her so you can get a little rest. I can call you immediately if she starts to wake up with this new cell phone Jonas gave me yesterday. I already have your ID programmed into my phone."

"Thank you, KiKi," said Steven. "I would like to go talk to Jonas for a few minutes. I won't be long."

Jonas's office was only a ten-minute walk from the infirmary. He was alone, so Steven popped in. "I think I may have to resign from my job," Steven blurted out.

"Why is that?" Jonas asked. "I thought you were enjoying this saving-the-world stuff."

"I really am," said Steven. "The problem is I hope to create a conflict of interest when Ellie wakes up. Having a relationship with her is even more important to me than doing this job. She is a career officer in the army. I would not want to get in the way of that. You should probably put her in charge of Team T-REX after I leave. She will do a wonderful job."

"Actually, I really liked the synergy of the two of you together running the team," said Jonas. "Do you realize how well the two of you have worked together during this crisis? Due to the extreme secrecy with which we cover this operation, I think a decision on how it should be run is totally up to me. My boss, Jason, has bigger things to worry about on a day-to-day basis. Also, this is not really a military project. I do not think their code of conduct applies here. What I am trying to say is let's just keep our organization the way it is right now. Everyone who has seen you two together knows there's more there than meets the eye. If conflicts arise in the future, we can discuss what measures we should take at that time. So I suggest you go back to your vigil and stop trying to fix something that's not broken. While you're here, I need to discuss something with you about KiKi."

"Are you going to let her be on our team?" asked Steven. "She is really smart and possibly knows as much about the space time continuum as you do. I think she would be a good addition for the type of activities we expect for our future work."

"Oh! That is a foregone conclusion," said Jonas. "I plan to tell her before Team T-Rex goes back to Gondwana. The reason I want to talk to you now is that something most interesting came out when I was asking her about her past. It seems that the reason she began working on time travel is because of some discussions she had with her father. Apparently she contacted him when she was about 20 years old and was trying to choose a direction for her life."

"Kiki told me that for a long while she thought possibly her father was a little crazy. He seemed to do very well in his profession of confor, the problem was that he told anyone that would listen that he had been to the far future and talked to mammals that were the dominant race. He said he was kept in a jail cell for a long time but the future people finally let him go back to Laurasia. However they sent him back to a different time than when he had originally lived. Her father said he saw their time machine once, when he was being sent back to Laurasia and he described to KiKi in good detail. She told me that is why she was stunned when she climbed out of the vessel and saw our equipment."

"As you might guess I was beginning to have a really weird feeling about this. I asked her what her father's name was."

"YaSi," said Steven. "So it was not a coincidence that the Laurasians developed time travel just when they needed it. That invention was the result of our sending YaSi back."

Just then, Steven's cell rang. It was KiKi. "I don't know if she is waking up for sure; however, she just made a noise, and her face muscles twitched," she said.

"Thank you, KiKi. I will be there right away," said Steven, already rising from his seat.

"I would love to go with you to see how she is," said Jonas. "But I guess you may want to be alone for a little bit when she wakes up. Call me when I can bring the rest of the people who are worrying about her."

Steven entered the hospital room on a dead run. KiKi was standing by the bed, bouncing up and down on her toes. "She just made that noise again," she said. "Maybe she really will wake up soon. I have never seen or heard of someone going into a coma as a result of breaking mind control. But I have never heard of anyone breaking the control so soon after it was administered. Usually, it fades away after six months to a year. After being under mind control, I spent a while researching it. I was worried if I would have any lingering aftereffects. But Gondwanian studies show that once the control is broken, the mind goes back to its normal patterns. I think the control depends on the chemicals injected in the subject to start the process. They usually need to have been eliminated from the person's system before they can break the control themselves. I have no idea how Ellie could disobey the Exalted Lords commands while the chemicals were still at full force in her body. This may have something to do with the structure of the human brain. I hope this means she is free of the mind control when she awakes. I will leave you now, but please let me know when she wakes up. Do you know my new cell phone ID?"

"Yes, KiKi," said Steven, smiling for the first time in over a month. "When you called me, my phone captured your number."

KiKi left, and Steven settled down into his watchful position, leaned over the bed, and watched Ellie breathe. She made a small moan, and her eyes opened a crack. "Steven is this still a dream?" she whispered.

"Oh, I really hope not," said Steven with a hitch in his voice. "You've been unconscious for four days. It's good to have you back."

"We have just been walking around in RoHo in my dreams," she whispered. "It was pleasant, but I have this strange recollection of being in the middle of combat that has been troubling me. There was noise and pain all around. I wondered if I had been injured. Then you appeared in the middle of the commotion and told me you loved me. All the noise and pain just stopped. Was that a dream too?"

"No, Ellie, that was not a dream," whispered Steven.

chapter 29

CENTRAL CHINA, THREE GORGES DAM

"Look out! We have been detected," said SuHa. "There are two objects launched from near the dam coming at us at a very high speed."

FiYo did not even look for the objects SuHa was talking about. He just yanked the steering mechanism to the left and up, causing the plane to turn and climb at a very steep angle. The electric turbines were an integral part of the electroglider's steering. The turbine on the left side actually reversed direction when an emergency turn to the left was required. The other turbine also sped up. This design provided an amazing emergency-turning capability. The powerful turbines along with large control surfaces allowed the plane to climb or dive at rates a human pilot could not remain conscious through. Because of their different physiology, that was not a problem for the reptiles.

Both missiles missed, the second one by less than twenty-five feet. As FiYo put the electroglider back on course toward the dam, he saw two more flames sprout up from the same place near the dam and realized the enemy had launched additional weapons. Having gained experience from watching the first two missiles, he waited for the weapon to fly somewhat closer; he yanked the steering mechanism to the right and downward. The plane again responded immediately and avoided the missiles.

They were only five-miles from the dam when FiYo saw two additional flashes. He decided to wait until the missiles were closer to make it easier to outmaneuver them when he heard an explosion and felt the electroglider shutter. The sound was followed by another louder noise and shudder on the opposite side of the plane.

"We have been hit by something," said FiYo. "Luckily, it does not seem to have done too much damage to the electroglider."

"Look out! We have more of those weapons coming our way," shouted SuHa. His chest flashed a bright orange in excitement. "Get ready to evade them once again." But as FiYo yanked the steering mechanism to the left and tried to climb, the electroglider did not respond as rapidly as it had before. He looked over at SuHa and saw him expectantly waiting for the evasive maneuver. "Our luck just ran out," said FiYo, and then the world exploded around them.

chapter 30

Mission 8 from White Sands

Steven, Ellie, Fred, and KiKi returned to Gondwana the second day after Ellie woke up. Ellie's doctors thought she should rest more before she returned to duty, but Ellie was not going to miss the finish of the most important mission she had ever been on.

They almost had to tie KiKi to her seat she was so excited during the trip. Just before they left White Sands, Jonas told her that she would be welcomed as a member of Team T-REX. Also, KiKi's thread must have had enough time to untangle from the mass of Laurasian threads or else her moving sixty-five million years into the future caused her to create a new thread. She felt no ill effects when they returned to Gondwana.

The vessel arrived in an empty space on top of the building that housed WeKu's office. This place was now designated as their official arrival site in RoHo. It took only a short time to walk down to WeKu's conference room.

RoHo, Gondwana 65 Million years BCE

"Sorting out this situation has been very confusing," stated

WeKu. "The lives and destinies of many people in Laurasia are not as we knew them before the passing. Apparently people experienced great change or little change depending upon the entanglements of their time threads. Some of our agents in Laurasia disappeared and other people we had never heard of began checking in and submitting reports as agents. We have had to be more or less flexible in many cases and trust whatever we were being told. Also, we probably don't recognize some of the changes, based on the predictions of KiKi's space-time continuum model.

"In general, Gondwana is the same as it was with only minor changes. I guess our separation from the daily events in Laurasia shielded us. Some of our technological capabilities seem to be slightly different, maybe these are capabilities we learned indirectly from Laurasia. Nothing is drastically changed.

"Laurasia, on the other hand seems to be vastly different. We find that we have been communicating at a moderate level with the Laurasian government. This is positive. There is also some commerce between the two countries, though Laurasia has erected trade barriers to protect their domestic manufacturing. They are apparently afraid they cannot compete with us.

"Similarly, Gondwana has enacted laws restricting the sale of advanced technology products and military information to Laurasia since we are concerned that they might attack Gondwana if they achieve equal military capabilities. By the way, they have developed airship capabilities, which meant major changes to our battle strategies. Laurasia severely restricts the travel of its citizens to Gondwana, and they restrict Gondwanian citizens travel to Laurasia."

"Did their political environment improve?" asked Steven.

"Laurasia itself is so significantly changed that even their form of government is radically different," WeKu stated. "I guess you could call it improved. They are nominally ruled by two monarchs with the authority of these monarchs limited by a Codex for Rulers that was signed into law about nine hundred years ago. It appears the monarchy has been passed down for one hundred thousand years through the descendants of the original two lords of YiWo and SaPi, the villages we visited. There has been some form of popularly elected body to govern alongside the dual monarchs in existence since the time we intervened. This body has had varying amounts of actual power, depending on the personalities involved at any given time in history. The Codex for Rulers was created because the monarchs of that time started usurping more and more control. There was a civil war in which one of the rulers was killed and the other imprisoned until he agreed to the terms of the Codex for Rulers. An elected assembly called 'the Diet' was established under the Codex for Rulers, with two houses. One house is comprised of the lords of each canton, a geographical territory of which there is currently eighteen. This house has one member per canton. The other house is made up of representatives who are elected by popular vote within each canton of the country. There are 180 members, ten per Canton. These two houses of the Diet nominally create the laws to rule the country.

"The dual monarchs have the power to veto any law created by the Diet. They also have the complete freedom to choose a prime minister and the subordinate ministers who actually run the government. At this time, we do not know how the two monarchs settle disagreements, should they arise between the two of them, but over most of Laurasian history, they have worked well together."

"Have these changes reduced the Laurasian threat to Gondwana and to our world?" asked Ellie.

"The result of your intervention and of this new government is that the citizens of Laurasia seem to have better lives and some protection under the law. The government of Laurasia has not demonstrated the aggressive behavior we were familiar with before. Now the monarch's highest priority seems to be remaining in power. Their people are subjected to twice-per-day propaganda broadcasts about how great their living conditions are. Therefore, they try to keep their people isolated from Gondwanian ideas of personal freedom rather than educating their population to constantly think of us as their mortal enemy, that's progress.

"The reduction we see in the aggression and the top-down control from their government has been reflected in the daily activities of their citizens. For example, their scientists have been much more creative in the types of technologies they developed to meet their citizen's needs. Instead of the old brute-force approach of just making functional products larger and more powerful, they began to creatively design products from the ground up, using improved technologies. Their old approach is what got them into their energy crisis along with the other problems they had. They have now developed nuclear power generators and an innovative new energy source from wind to reduce their dependence on plant fuel. This means over the past few centuries, they did not need to harvest their trees to extinction, and their current energy situation is much improved."

"At this time, I think we can consider your mission to ancient Laurasia a reasonable success. The only cloud we see on the horizon is the rise of a small but powerful group of industrialists who have been quietly grabbing power over the last twenty to thirty years.

"We did not change Laurasian civilization into a utopia or even a copy of Gondwanian civilization, but they seem to be much easier to deal with now and represent much less of a military threat to Gondwana."

"I guess we can all be happy nothing terrible happened," said KiKi. "But I strongly recommend that we more carefully consider the effects of our time travel on the space-time continuum when we are planning future voyages. I intend to work on perfecting my model of the continuum based on the actual data we have gathered from this experiment."

The mayor of RoHo, TaSu, along with KoSo, the eldest member of the Council of Mothers, accompanied WeKu to formally send off Team T-REX. A crowd had gathered around to watch the departure. TaSu thanked the team for their efforts in trying to make it possible to improve relations with Laurasia. As any good politician, he could not pass up the chance to speak to the crowd at length. KoSo gave all four members of Team T-REX full citizenship in Gondwana and gave them each a golden medallion to hang around their necks to mark the occasion. "We thank you for your sacrifices and for trying to make our world a better place," she said. "I would also like to formally invite you back in two months to begin to draft a Declaration of Peace and Alliance between our two governments and to explore the opportunities for commerce between our worlds."

Privately, Steven and Fred thanked WeKu for all he had done to rescue Ellie while the Laurasians had held her captive.

Team T-REX returned home after WeKu's update on conditions in Gondwana and Laurasia. They told Jonas about the improvements in conditions for the people of Laurasia. Jonas informed them of the results of the battle over the Three Gorges Dam.

"With the Laurasian crisis averted, we can go back to some simple exploration for Team T-REX," said Jonas. "Take a week off for some rest and recreation, and then we can all discuss plans for the future."

SoMu, Laurasia 65 Million years BCE

The sun was just setting on a warm summer day in SoMu when the guild master was summoned before Monarch FaKa. It was not unusual for the monarch to summon him, but the tone of this request sounded different this time, possibly more urgent. The habitat that Monarch FaKa called home had been built on a grand scale, twenty-five levels deep, and it housed only the monarch and his retinue.

The guild master was one of only seven reptiles who controlled 85 percent of the manufacturing capacity of Laurasia. Each of the seven reptiles was the head of vast business entities called combines that had highly diversified holdings manufacturing everything from arms to tri-wheelers, from boats to plastic incubator inserts. The combine that the guild master owned was the second largest one, the Three-Moon Combine.

As the attendant showed the guild master into the presence of the monarch, he realized he was on the twenty-fifth level, the very lowest and most secure level. Neither he nor any one he knew had ever been on this level before. The monarch greeted the guild master in a warm, courteous manner.

"We have worked together on many projects over the last fifteen years," said Monarch FaKa. "I have come to trust you completely. Now I am ready to share my deepest secret with you. May I count on your complete discretion?"

"Of course, my monarch," said the guild master. "How may I serve you?"

"You have been given increasingly large contracts to provide weapons and equipment for the Laurasian Military," said FaKa. "Now I wish to test our mutual trust to its limit. I want you to build a secret force of one hundred thousand elite troops that you will train and equip at your own expense. I wish to have an extra dagger up my sleeve in my dealing with Monarch HuPi. If I finance this project with government funds, it will not be a secret project for long."

"I am not sure I fully understand your request," said the guild master. "You would not be paying my combine for the creation of this force?"

"Not in the usual sense," said FaKa. "I intend to use these troops to take over sole control of the Laurasian government. That means a coup to eliminate Monarch HuPi and his cronies from the government. Their thinking is far too conservative. They insist Laurasia work in partnership with Gondwana, even though the Gondwanians refuse to sell us advanced products that would make our industry and our military stronger. Our spies tell us Gondwana has developed the capability for time travel, but they refuse to share the technology with us at any reasonable price.

"Once I take over the government, I will staff the top posts with those who have helped me along the way. I propose to repay you for your elite force by making you the prime minister of the country. This office has a lot of perks associated with it, which I am sure will profit a person as motivated as you."

"My monarch, I am proud and anxious to help you in this way," said the guild master. "When would you anticipate this coup would take place?"

"I want to be ready by next spring," answered FaKa. "We will then be able to negotiate from a much stronger position in the talks on commerce between Laurasia and Gondwana next summer. If they are still not flexible enough after the talks, we will need to be more forceful."

"Thank you for the opportunity," said the guild master. "I will begin preparations before the day is over."

"Excellent," said the monarch. "I knew I could count on your support, Guild Master YaKo."

appendix

PaKo's 4 Basic Rules for Living

1. Do not ever question a superior
2. Never eat another's eggs
3. Learn all you possibly can during life
4. Teach your fellow man at every opportunity

Laurasian Syllabary

Fa	▼	Fe	◀	Fi	◆	Fo	▶	Fu	▲
Ha	▽	He	◁	Hi	☐	Ho	▷	Hu	△
Ka	✔	Ke	◀◀	Ki	■	Ko	▶▶	Ku	●
Ma	↧	Me	⊢←	Mi	⇆	Mo	→⊣	Mu	⊤̄
Pa	↓↓	Pe	⇇	Pi	⇄	Po	⇉	Pu	↑↑
Ra	↙	Re	←	Ri	↔	Ro	→	Ru	↗
Sa	⋒	Se	↺	Si	↗	So	↳	Su	↻
Ta	⌠	Te	↵	Ti	↓↑	To	↪	Tu	⌡
Wa	∧	We	♎	Wi	⌁	Wo	✕	Wu	⊠
Ya	⊘	Ye	↻	Yi	⊙	Yo	☾	Yu	⊖